CW01653555

Also by Pauline Barclay
www.paulinebarclay.co.uk

Magnolia House
Satchfield Hall
Sometimes It Happens…
Storm Clouds Gathering
In The Cold Light of Day
The Wendy House
The Birthday Card
Serendipity
Past Secrets & Lies
Tormentors

Dare

Pauline Barclay

www.paulinebarclay.co.uk

Dare

Copyright © Pauline Barclay 2024

Cover design by Pauline Barclay
Copyright © Pauline Barclay 2024

The characters in this novel and their actions are imaginary.
Their names and experiences have no relation to those of actual people, living or dead, except by coincidence.

All rights reserved. No part of this publication may be reproduced, stored in a retrieval system, or transmitted in any form or by any means, electronic, mechanical, photocopy, recording or otherwise, without prior written permission of the copyright owner. Nor can it be circulated in any form of binding or cover other than that in which it is published and without similar condition including this condition being imposed on a subsequent purchaser.

Dedication and Special Thank You....

This is one of the most important pages in my book. By the time I am at this page, the many months of hard work in writing, *Dare*, has come to an end. There is always a feeling of loss when my characters are released out there into the big wide world sharing their story with you. The journey to this stage could only have been achieved with the help of many wonderful people.

More than anything, I want to thank my very best friend, my husband, for all his support in writing this third book in my cosy mystery series. We spent many hours mulling over my characters and the situations I put them in. Thank you so much, for your endless patience. Loves you.

My appreciations would not be complete without mentioning my wonderful dear friend and editor, Julie Dexter, who makes me smile and my books shine beautifully. Thank you for your first-class editing skills, your keen eye to detail and honesty makes a huge difference – any mistakes still there are mine!

With regard to the skating part of the story, a big thank you to Barry Bridger. Barry is a real person and he does have a skating club in Reigate, Surrey, UK. www.rrarsc.co.uk He is also a fantastic skater.

Equally important, is a thank you to you lovely reader for reading my books and encouraging me to continue writing. I hope you have enjoyed reading *Dare* as much as have had writing it.

And finally, a mention to Barney, our real-life dog.

Chapter ONE

'Morning, Boss,' Roo called in a cheerful voice as she breezed into the office. A warm draft of summer air followed her through the open door.

Yapping with excitement, Barney raced towards her.

'Hello, Barney,' Roo cooed, as the honey-coloured cocker-poo sat squarely in front of her. His tail thumped a beat on the wooden floor in anticipation of a treat.

Pulling out a small biscuit from her pocket, Roo bent down and offered it to him. 'You are just so spoilt,' she said as Barney took the treat.

'Morning, Roo,' Craig called over the noise of Barney's greeting. At the same time, he stared down and pointed at his young assistant's feet. 'Please tell me you haven't come on those!'

A wide grin filled Roo's face. 'Of course, I have,' she chuckled and dropped down onto her chair. 'I've got to get in as much practice as possible for the marathon. This year I want to make sure I'm up there with the first to cross the finish line.' As she spoke, she bent down and unclipped her roller blades before pulling them off. Wiggling her toes from the confines of the hard boots, she slipped her feet into a pair of white trainers. As she laced them up, she added, 'It's all for charity and I'll be asking for sponsorship.'

Craig ran his fingers through his mop of copper hair and frowned. He was more than aware of his young assistant's passion for skating. Roo was an amazing skater and as accomplished as she was, he regularly found himself shuddering at the breathtaking moves she performed with wheels strapped to her feet. Despite this, he was immensely proud of her.

'Now as you turn your attention from the disguise of Jane Torvill to Roo the sleuth, we have the vicar calling in ten minutes to have a chat.'

'Confessions do you think?' she sniggered as she spoke.

'Ha ha! No, something to do with things happening and disappearing.'

'With all those bodies in the graveyard, maybe ghosts!' she said.

'Very funny,' Craig said with a smirk.

'Interesting to know what is *disappearing* and *happening*,' Roo said and at the same time tucking her roller blades under her desk. 'Shall I wait for the vicar before I make our coffee?'

Before Craig could answer, the office door swung open sending Barney into full volume security guard mode as he let out an ear-piercing bark.

'Goodness, you are a good guard dog,' cried the vicar with one foot in the office and the other on the threshold. Reaching down he offered Barney the back of his hand to sniff. Cautiously, Barney nuzzled the vicar's hand and at the same time wagged his tail. 'I can see we are friends already,' the vicar said and rubbed the top of Barney's head.

Craig strode over to his visitor. 'He's a pussycat really. Please, come on in.' As Craig spoke, he shooed Barney to one side.

'Thank you for seeing me. I'm Nicholas Howard, vicar at St Julian's church in Cavendish Road.' He held out his hand to Craig, 'Though everyone calls me Nick.'

Craig shook Nick's hand. It was soft, but with a firm grip. No doubt a reassuring hold which his parishioners appreciated. Craig released his grasp, 'Let's sit down,' he said and pointed to an area with two sofas and a low table.

'Thank you,' Nick said affably, but made no attempt to move, simply gazed around the office. 'I do believe this was once an artist's studio.'

'That's right and before that it was a pigsty,' Craig responded, delighted the vicar was aware of the building's history.

'Now you mention it, one of my parishioners did tell me that. In fact, it was the same parishioner who suggested I speak with you – Peggy Hill. She lives in Grange Road with her friend Molly Wells. They've not been in the neighbourhood long, but two very kind ladies, and have absorbed themselves nicely into the community. They both help with the church and are wonderfully supportive with our other activities.'

Craig nodded. He knew the ladies and remembered only too well the terrible problems they'd had to deal with when they'd first moved into their bungalow. It turned out to be a nasty business and the catalyst to solving a thirty-year-old mystery.

'Yes, we know the ladies and agree they are both charming,' he replied, not wanting to let his mind go down that murky road. Before he could think further, Roo appeared at his side. 'This is my assistant, Roo Chattaway.'

'Pleased to meet you,' Nick said and offered out his hand.

Roo shook it. 'Nice to meet you. Would you like a coffee, vicar?'

'That would be very welcome – black and no sugar – and please call me Nick. We don't get called vicar very much these days, especially by the younger generation. Times have changed since I took the cloth.'

Craig guessed Nick was in his early sixties; he could see laughter lines that crinkled around his eyes. His hair showed streaks of grey, but despite this he had a youthful shock of hair, which he guessed would have been dark brown in his younger years. 'Tell me about it. Like you I've seen and experienced too many changes, some for the better but far too many not always for the good.' As he spoke, Craig indicated they move to the sitting area.

Roo headed to the kitchen.

'How can we help?' Craig asked as he sat on the sofa opposite Nick.

Leaning forward, Nick rested his elbows on his knees and looked straight at Craig. 'I'm not sure if it is something you would deal with, but the police appear not to be too interested. Unfortunately, there have been a few unpleasant things that have been happening. It is rather disturbing and I'd like to try and find out who or what is behind it.'

'Money going missing from the collection box?' Craig ventured.

Nick rested his chin on his hands and regarded Craig. 'Not these days; there is little that goes in there. Those who do support the church pay monthly contributions. The days of dropping coins in a box appear to be behind us. Certainly, in my church.'

How things have changed, Craig thought, and remembered, how as a boy, he'd mithered his parents for a handful of coins when he'd had to attend church as a cub and later when he'd been in the scouts.

'The problem is we have minor vandalism in the church yard along with a few incidents inside the church. A few bibles have been stolen along with kneeler cushions. Flowers have been pulled out of their vases and trampled on. In the church yard, like the indoor flowers, flowers from graves have been stamped on and flung across the church yard. In the great scheme of things, it appears to be all small items, but nonetheless it is distressing. I appreciate this may come across as trivial by comparison to some of the crimes reported in the news, but our budgets are like everyone else's: they get smaller every year leaving little to purchase these losses and put right any damage. And, notwithstanding these issues, it appears there is someone entering church property with intent to be mischievous.'

As he listened, Craig understood why the

local police weren't overly interested. They had bigger things to worry about and like the church, their budget didn't get raised enough to meet the ever-increasing demands. Even as he thought this, he wasn't sure what the police could do.

'I take it you keep the church doors locked?' Craig asked.

Nick shook his head. 'Not all the time. The church is there for people to visit, to pray and feel it's a place of peace for reflection.' He sat up straight. 'It's normally opened around eight o'clock and locked by five o'clock. It varies depending on what is happening that day.'

Craig couldn't imagine why anyone would want to steal bibles and kneeling cushions. Surely it would be cheaper to lock the doors than ask for their help. 'What about CCTV cameras?'

Nick gave out a chortle. 'No! Goodness, it has never crossed my mind.'

'Maybe it might be more prudent to install a couple of cameras rather than …' He stopped himself before saying, hire a private investigator. Instead, he said, 'These days CCTV are relatively inexpensive.'

Knitting his eyebrows together, Nick looked at Craig. 'Sorry, I've taken up your time.' As he spoke, he got to his feet.

'Please sit and have a coffee. I understand your frustration. I was in the police for over thirty years and as much as we would have wanted to deal with these sorts of issues, we were kept busy with, well, let's say, the darker side of life most of the time.'

Nick sat back down. He crossed his legs. 'I

imagine you saw the other side of humanity.'

'At times, yes.'

'Here we are,' Roo said, stalling conversation. 'One black coffee, no sugar.' She placed a mug on the low table in front of Nick.

'A milky weak one for you.' Roo raised her eyebrows as she placed Craig's mug down.

'Perfect,' Craig said, not missing Roo's look of disdain at his penchant for dish water looking coffee.

'Thank you,' Nick said, leaning forward to pick up his mug. 'Mmm! That smells good.' He took a sip, 'and tastes good too.'

Roo returned with her coffee and settled next to Craig. Barney padded over and laid down at Roo's feet.

'Apart from bibles being stolen tell me more about the vandalism,' Craig said as they drank their coffee.

After taking a mouthful of his drink, Nick placed his mug down on the table. 'As I mentioned, it's nothing major, just annoying and needless. A few gravestones have been pushed over and a couple broken. Flowers and plants have been trodden on and uprooted. It is petty and mindless, but very upsetting for those who have loved ones buried in the church yard.'

It was mindless, Craig thought and sadly this kind of anti-social behaviour was on the increase. It was the bane of the police force and society. 'Have you managed to witness any of this?'

Nick shook he head, 'No. The odd thing is, I never see anyone lurking around when I'm at the church, yet these incidents continue to happen.'

'Maybe considering a couple of CCTV cameras could deter would-be vandals and it would also give you an opportunity to see who's hanging around and when,' Roo suggested.

Nick frowned, 'As I mentioned to Mr Gardner, I know nothing about these things and besides, I believe those gadgets are rather expensive.'

'Things are changing and you can get very inexpensive ones,' Roo added. 'Let me have a look on the internet and find out what could be available. I think you might be pleasantly surprised.' Roo smiled.

'I'm not sure,' Nick said, his face clearly betraying his scepticism. As if to hide disappointment, he picked up his coffee mug. 'Surely it would be easier to keep a watchful eye on the place. Maybe you could swing by from time to time and wander around the grounds – it might help.'

Craig almost choked on his coffee, but before he could comment, Roo jumped in.

'Mr Gardner has a full schedule at the moment. May I suggest that I look up the possibility of a couple of cameras and the next time I am close to your church, Barney and I will have a wander through the churchyard.'

Craig saw the vicar was not impressed. 'I think Roo's suggestion about investigating the possibility of cameras would help. From experience, cameras do offer a deterrent especially if it is local youths messing around. In the meantime, let me take a few details and then we can ask around to see if anyone has seen or heard anything.' He picked up a note pad and pen from the low table and as he turned to a clean page, he didn't miss the look of relief on Nick's face at his suggestion.

'Thank you,' Nick said.

'When did these incidents start happening?'

'Now let me think. I would say about three weeks ago, maybe four.'

Craig jotted down the specifics before asking for contact details and Nick's home address. 'That should be enough for now. I can't promise, but we'll keep our eyes and ears open.' Craig placed his pad and pen down on the table. He had kept his tone professional but couldn't help wondering what the general public thought private investigators did. Clearly not *real* crime!

'Thank you,' Nick said and finished off his coffee. 'If I'm honest I thought it was a long shot coming here, but the ladies were quite enthusiastic about you. At least I can report back that we've had a chat.' He stood.

'We will do what we can to help,' Roo said, getting to her feet. 'I'll look at CCTV cameras and let you know.'

Not missing the look of doubt on Nick's face, Craig said in attempt to offer a positive note, 'I can see you are not sold on the idea, but if anyone can find something suitable and cost effective, Roo can.'

'Again, thank you both. I appreciate your time.'

Barney also stood up and leaned over to sniff at the vicar.

'You're a lovely one,' Nick said, reaching down and stroking Barney's back. 'I lost my girl a couple of months ago. She was a rescue, a mix with a lot of terrier. She was part of our lives for ten years. She was small and fearless. Thinking about it, it seems much of the vandalism has escalated since Poppy no longer does her patrol.'

Craig and Roo looked on in silence.

Nick removed his hand from Barney's head and smiled. 'Maybe I need to get another dog.' As he spoke Barney nudged his knee.

'I understand,' Craig said, wondering how they would cope when the time came to have to say goodbye to Barney. He shook himself mentally; it was years away. He smiled at the vicar. 'As I've said, we will see what we can come up with. In the meantime, when we are in the vicinity of the church, we'll have a stroll around the grounds and see what we can find.'

'Thank you again for your time. I can't ask for more.' Nick stepped back and navigated around Barney. 'Thank you also for the coffee.' After shaking hands with Craig and Roo, he headed to the door.

'We'll be in touch,' Craig said, following Nick.

'Talk again soon,' Roo called as Craig and the vicar headed out of the office. Roo picked up the mugs and made her way to the kitchen. Barney trotted over to the window as if to keep an eye on Craig.

A couple of minutes later, Craig returned to the office. No sooner had he stepped inside when his phone rang out. He strode over to his desk and looked down at his phone. It was DI Andrews. He swiped the screen and answered. 'Hello Pete. What can I do for you?' Pete and he went back over three decades. They had both joined the force around the same time, but unlike Pete, Craig had taken early retirement after thirty years. He listened to Pete's response and a smile crossed his face. 'OK. I'll see you in ten minutes.'

Chapter TWO

Entering the Butterfly Café, Craig made his way to the table next to the window. He pulled out a chair and sat opposite Pete.

'Thanks for coming,' Pete said and placed his phone on the table.

Craig didn't miss a couple of day's stubble on Pete's chin. A man who used to pride himself on a clean shave and a smart appearance at the start of his shift had succumbed to the pressure of long hours.

'I guess you want to get something off your chest or, more likely, you want something from me.' Despite keeping his voice light, Craig realised he sounded cynical, but he knew they both needed each other. There were times when he couldn't have resolved some of his cases had it not been for Pete and his old colleagues at the station.

'I shouldn't answer that, but you're right.'

'Morning, gentlemen.' A cheerful voice filled the air as Steve, the café owner, strode over to their table, a wide smile filling his face.

'I take it it's your usual?' he asked, his pen poised over a small note pad.

'Morning, Steve. Two coffees and – what's the cake today?' Pete asked.

Steve turned and pointed to a glass dome sitting on the counter housing a large, decorated cake. ‘Karen’s specialty today is, *Taste the rainbow*.’

Pete and Craig looked at each other. ‘Rainbow you say?’ Pete queried, his eyebrows meeting in the middle as he studied the masterpiece that sat proudly on display.

Stepping towards the counter, Steve lifted the cake dome. ‘As you can see, it is filled with coloured speckles, hence, taste the rainbow.’

‘We really shouldn’t,’ Craig said, then ordered two slices.

‘Right, coming up, two coffees – one with one shot, the other normal and milky – plus two slices of cake.’ He wrote down the order. ‘Be with you in a moment.’

Craig and Pete watched as the cheerful owner headed back to the kitchen area.

‘So, what’s the favour you need that has you meeting up for coffee?’ Craig asked. As he spoke, he noted Pete looked drained. It was nothing new these days, he thought.

‘The other day we had a model submarine brought into the station.’ Pete rolled his eyes as he spoke.

Craig sucked in his lips to prevent himself from laughing out loud but could not stop the amusement travelling to his eyes. ‘If that’s all there is to worry about, model submarines, we’re on safe ground.’

‘You might smirk, but we do have a very strange submarine at the station. The person who brought it in told us they had found it in the river. Not far from the wooden footbridge along Riverside.’ Pete took a deep breath then continued. 'Apparently, it was caught up in a clump of weed and semi-submerged. As you know the river isn't that deep and despite it being well stuck in the water, it was visible enough for someone to clock it. It was pulled out and brought to the station.'

Craig tried not to see the funny side, but it had come to something when his old colleague invited him for coffee to discuss model boats caught up in weed in the river.

'That was admirable of them. These days people who find generally keep.'

'You are such a cynic,' Pete said, shaking his head.

Before conversation could continue, Steve appeared at their table. 'Two coffees,' he announced, placing two large mugs on the table. Turning, he picked up two plates from the counter, 'And two slices of cake,' he added, placing a plate in front of each man along with a small fork.

Craig looked down at the creamy, colourful slice and wondered if he would ever lose weight, then concluded, it was unlikely. He sighed at his lack of self-control.

'Enjoy,' Steve said before walking away.

Both men remained silent as they tucked into the cake.

Pete was the first to speak as he wiped crumbs from his mouth with the back of his hand. 'That was far too nice. Now, what was I saying before we were hijacked by Karen's cake?'

'Submarines,' Craig said scathingly as he

placed his fork down on the empty plate. He gazed at Pete and wondered what he was going to come out with next.

'That's right, but it's not just an ordinary sub.'

Craig raised an eyebrow, 'Really! What's not an ordinary sub?'

'You might ask that, but it turns out one of the uniforms is an enthusiastic model boat builder. His eyes lit up when he saw the model and said it's worth a few hundred and before we could take it all in, he explained that it was a steam punk sub.'

'A what! What on earth is a steampunk sub?'

'You might well ask. We were as taken aback as you are. However, it appears it's a model that is not meant to represent any particular historical or modern design.'

'Really!' This was getting better, Craig thought and wondered if Pete was heading for a breakdown. 'So, what in the world does it look like?' Craig couldn't believe there was such a thing as steampunk and wondered what else he was about to learn.

'A whale!'

Craig let out a loud guffaw.

'Sounds like fun on your table,' Steve called over as Craig's voice resounded around the small café.

'You couldn't make it up,' Craig called back to Steve.

'Oh right,' Steve muttered, flipping over several rashes of bacon on the hot plate.

‘I wish he wouldn’t do that,’ Craig said, turning back to Pete, ‘and that is fry bacon when we are in here.’

Pete inhaled, ‘It’s a killer, but let’s be honest, the full English breakfast and the cakes keep us coming back. My waist will never reduce as long as Steve owns this place. Anyway, let’s get back to the steampunk.’ He picked up his phone, ‘I have a couple of photos.’ As he spoke, he swiped his forefinger over the screen. ‘Here it is.’ He handed the phone to Craig.

Craig studied the photo briefly before enlarging the image. His face reflected surprise at what he saw. ‘That is a serious piece of work,’ he said, taking in the intricate details of the model. He could see that it had been constructed in the shape of a whale and guessed it was likely made of metal. He studied the second photo. He was impressed.

Handing the phone back, he added, ‘It must be about three foot long. How on earth did the owner lose it? It’s not as if they are lying around every corner.’

‘It is and heavy too. And it’s a metre long, so said one of our young officers. Don’t think they understand feet and inches,’ Pete chuckled.

‘So, if it’s been stolen and I think it’s safe to assume this, why abandon it? And why hasn’t it been reported missing? It’s not something that’s easily concealed?’

‘Agree! But so far, we’ve not had any reports that a model has been stolen.’

‘Why?’ Craig asked but knew Pete didn’t have the answer or he wouldn’t be sitting drinking coffee with him. 'The question is, why did it end up in weed under the footbridge?'

'That's where you and your young assistant come in. You both have the ear with the locals who live near the river, especially those residing on the boats. Maybe you can find out if anyone saw it or someone with it. It's remote control so they would have been standing on the side holding the control unit.'

'I take it you've had a few uniforms out.'

Pete shook his head, 'No. It's not been reported missing so in theory it's not a crime incident, though I suspect there is more to it than just being dumped, but we haven't the resources. I'm not asking you to give up time on it, just ask the locals whenever you are walking that mutt of yours.'

'Barney is a good asset to the team I'd like you to know.'

'I'm sure. As I say, could you ask around when out with him? I can't put my finger on it, but there is something that doesn't quite add up about this.' He shrugged and added, 'Though, trying to explain to the hierarchy that I have a gut feeling won't get me any resources to find out.'

'Will do. I'll see what we can find out to help ease that gut feeling.'

'Thanks.'

'I would imagine it's worth a bob or two, which has me wondering why someone would leave it in the water,' Craig said.

'I know and that's why I can't understand it's not been reported stolen. The young officer reckoned it would be worth a few hundred, maybe as much as a thousand pound or more.'

Craig let out a low whistle, 'We'll have a sniff around and maybe someone will have seen something. Looking at the photos it's not something you could easily miss.'

'Indeed.'

'Send me the pic.' As he spoke, Craig didn't miss the tiredness in Pete's face. He needed to change his lifestyle, he thought, but knew any words would fall on deaf ears. Instead, he asked, 'Do you fancy another?'

Pete looked at his watch, 'Why not and you can tell me what's keeping you busy.'

'We have a few cases on – the usual. We even had the vicar from St Julian's pop into the office. Seems they are having problems with petty crime. Roo's going to look into CCTV cameras for them.'

'It's a rum do when the local church is looking at electronic spies,' Pete said as Steve placed two fresh mugs of coffee on the table.

'Spies!' Steve said in mock surprise, looking from Pete to Craig.

'You'd be surprised what we get involved in,' Pete said and winked at the café owner.

'If you say so.' Chuckling, Steve headed back to the kitchen area.

'I'd better get back to the station, but not before finishing this cup of coffee.' Pete picked up his fresh mug. 'Let me know if you find out anything. I need to still my strange feeling about this.'

Chapter THREE

Having scrolled through several pages on the internet for CCTV cameras, Roo finally noted something that she felt might help the vicar. As far as she knew there was no internet at the church. This thought was reinforced at how the vicar appeared to be bewildered at the mention of cameras and the internet. Roo guessed he didn't understand this new world.

Now, as she read the information, she smiled because this could be the one. It was inexpensive, battery operated and recorded to a SD card. The SD card could be removed and the vicar review the footage on a computer. She wondered how the vicar would view the recordings, and decided to cross that bridge later. She copied the link and took several screen shots. With the details sent to her phone and also printed off to paper, Roo pushed back her chair and stretched her legs. She hoped the vicar would be impressed.

Lost in her thoughts of CCTV cameras she almost leapt out of her skin as Barney let out a heart stopping bark. Jumping to her feet, she swung round and watched as the office door opened.

'Quiet, Barney,' she cried, as a smartly dressed middle-aged woman walked in.

Rumbling, Barney ambled over to the visitor

and sniffed the air in front of her.

'He won't hurt you,' Roo said, as the visitor took in Barney.

'He looks like a teddy bear and I bet he can smell my dogs,' the visitor said. Then looking at Roo, added, 'I'm sorry to call and not phone to make an appointment, but I felt I would change my mind and then end up cancelling.' As she spoke, she pushed the door closed. 'My name is Katie Everett and, if possible, I would like to talk to Mr Gardner.'

Roo didn't miss how Katie Everett fiddled with the buttons on her white blouse and wondered what was worrying her. 'I'm afraid Mr Gardner is out on an appointment…'

'Oh goodness!' Katie blurted out. 'I should have thought of that before I came. What must you think of me?' Still twisting at her blouse buttons, Katie turned to leave.

'Please! Don't leave,' Roo called. 'Come and sit down and let me take a few details on how we might be able to help. I guess that is why you are here?' As she spoke, she pointed to the sofa area.

Katie hesitated, 'Are you sure?'

'Of course and as soon as Mr Gardner is back, I can let him know you called,' Roo added, moving towards the seating area.

'I really should have phoned first, but if you are sure?'

'Yes, no problem.' Roo ushered Katie to the sofas and watched as she sat on the edge of one.

'Would you like a cup of tea or coffee?'

Looking up at Roo, Katie smiled for the first time since entering the office. 'A white coffee with one sugar would be lovely.'

'Coming up. In the meantime, I will leave you with Barney. He loves nothing more than being fussed.'

Roo headed to the kitchen and after switching on the coffee machine, she took a peek over to the sofas and smiled. Katie was stroking Barney who had one of his front paws on her knee. If anyone could calm someone, Barney could.

A few moments later, Roo placed a mug of coffee on the low table in front of Katie. 'I hope this is OK. I'll just get my phone and then I can take your contact details.'

Katie reached over Barney and picked up her mug. She took a sip. 'Thank you. It's perfect,' she said as Roo sat down opposite.

Roo noticed Katie's fresh complexion and high cheek bones. She smiled at how Katie's blonde curls bobbed when she spoke, though she didn't miss the anxiety in her blue eyes.

'Mrs Katie Everett,' Roo said as she entered their, possibly new, client's name on her phone in the note section. 'May I have your address and phone number, please.'

'Don't you young ones ever use pen and paper?' Katie asked, her focus on Roo's phone and appeared mesmerized at the speed in which Roo tapped at the screen.

Roo glanced over and smiled. 'Sometimes, but it is easier to have everything here and of course I can send it to Craig, Mr Gardner, and my laptop if I need to.'

'Goodness. My daughter uses her phone for everything too. I often wonder how everything worked without them.' She gave a short laugh. 'Oh yes, my address. It is 22 Bishy Barnabee Close. It's on the new development, Rosehill Gardens on the edge of Castleton Green.'

'Really?' Roo laughed.

Katie nodded, 'Yes. It always has people reacting in a similar way to yours. Our house was built just over five years ago and nothing prepared us for the name. As you probably know, it is a local word for ladybird. Goodness knows where it came from, but we love it.'

'I love it too,' Roo said, her face lighting up as she entered the details. Surreptitiously, she glanced over at Katie and saw she appeared more relaxed as if talking about the street name had eased her tension, though she felt it was more likely down to Barney: Katie had been petting Barney with one hand while holding her mug of coffee with the other.

'I'll give you my mobile number because at the moment I don't want my husband to know I've been here.' A shadow crossed Katie's face as she rattled off her number.

Roo didn't miss the sudden change in Katie's features and as tempted as she was to ask why, she thought it would be best for Craig to deal with this. Instead, she said, 'Would you like to tell me a little about why you might need our help?'

Katie shuffled to the edge of the sofa as if deciding whether to flee or stay. She remained.

With her mug placed on the low table, Katie placed both of her hands in her lap. 'It's rather complicated so if you don't mind, I'll wait to talk to Mr Gardner.'

Roo smiled. 'Of course, no problem. As soon as he arrives back, I'll ask him to call you.'

'Thank you for your time and understanding.' Katie rose. Barney was on his feet instantly.

'Please finish your coffee before you leave,' Roo said and hoped whatever was troubling Katie they would be able to help.

Katie looked down at her mug, 'There's only a drop left. It was lovely, but I won't take any more of your time. Thank you again.' She strode with purpose to the door. Barney followed.

As she opened the door, Katie looked at Roo. 'Just talking to you has made it already seem easier.' She smiled, then reached down and patted Barney's head. 'You are gorgeous,' she added before leaving the office.

Roo watched as Katie crossed the parking area and noted there was no car. Maybe she had parked down the road and at the same time wondered what was troubling her that she needed to talk to a Private Investigator. Whatever it was had her a bag of nerves. The sound of her phone ringing broke her thoughts.

'Hello PI Roo,' a familiar voice said. Instantly, her features broke into a picture of happiness at the sound of Taylor's voice.

Chapter FOUR

After leaving the café, Craig headed back to the office. With each step his mind travelled over the conversation he'd had with his old colleague. Why would an expensive model be left in the river and why would no one report it missing? It was odd. Lost in his thoughts he almost missed the cheery greeting that rang out. Turning, he came face to face with Harry Morgan.

'Mornin',' Harry said, as Craig came to a standstill in front of him. 'Looks like you've a lot on your mind.'

'Morning, Harry. As you know there is always something. How are you?'

Harry leaned on his walking stick as he took in Craig. 'Not so dusty and these old bones are feeling much better for the warm weather.'

'I think we all feel better for the warm sun rays. It even makes some people smile.' Craig grinned as he spoke.

'Most, but there's always the exception,' Harry pulled a face.

'I take it you're referring to Jacobs.'

'Is it that obvious?'

Jacobs was well known in the area for being a busy body. 'What's he been up to now?'

Harry looked around as if to check there was no one in ear shot. 'I've no idea, I just keep out of his way, though I did see him writing down a couple of car registration numbers earlier this morning. No doubt he thinks he's the car police along with everything else.' Harry sniffed with contempt.

Craig understood how Harry felt; he too had no time for Jacobs. In his book he was a nasty piece of work and dangerous too. He'd not forgotten what the old, interfering, nosey parker had done last year. Just thinking about it made his hackles rise. Feeling his annoyance building, he needed to change the subject. 'I believe you like to have a little wander along the river path.'

'I do, though the path is in a shocking state. Even your Barney must stumble from time to time with all the potholes and unevenness.'

Craig was aware of the poor conditions of the footpath, but didn't want to waste time with the topic – it would take all day! Right now, he had other things to occupy his mind.

'I don't suppose, during your meanders, you've noticed a submarine by any chance?'

Harry laughed out loud, then a gasping cough stole his mirth.

'Are you OK?' Putting out his hand, Craig stepped closer to the old man.

Harry thumped his chest with his left fist. 'Phlegm, son, nothing to worry about. Though it sticks to my chest like a dog grips a bone. Now what were you saying about a submarine?' Despite the discomfort of coughing, Harry shook his head in amusement. 'What have they been putting in your coffee?' he turned and, with a gnarled finger, pointed in the direction of the Butterfly Café. 'Submarines,' he repeated and rolled his eyes.

'Good to know my question amuses you, but one was found under the wooden footbridge. It's a submarine that looks like a whale.'

Harry glared at Craig as he pulled out a white linen handkerchief from his cardigan pocket. He wiped it over his face, then pushed it back into his pocket. 'What size do you reckon this whale sub was?'

Craig didn't miss Harry biting down on his bottom lip as if to stop himself from chuckling again. 'I know what you are thinking, but before you think I've gone ga ga, it's a model.' He explained what he knew whilst trying to describe how it looked from the photograph.

Harry, resting on his walking stick, placed his other hand on Craig's arm. 'Well, that makes more sense. I just couldn't imagine a full-size sub – or whale – getting down our river!' He winked at Craig.

Nor could Craig, but before he could say anything, Harry continued.

'You might not believe this, but many moons ago, I built a couple of models. Well, to be fair it was only one and that was a tug. The other was a duck.' He smiled and removed his hand from Craig's arm before pushing it in his pocket.

'A duck?' Craig exclaimed. He raised an eyebrow and thought Harry was making fun at him.

'That's right.' There was a sparkle of amusement in Harry's eyes. 'It was a mallard and I'd made it for my June. I thought it would be fun. From the ship chandlers – we used to have them in my days – I bought a life size, realistic looking, plastic duck. I fiddled around with it and made it into a remote-controlled model. I even had it making a quacking noise. My June loved it. Though she was a renegade at the park pond and was almost banned from going.' He smiled mischievously.

Craig listened and wondered what he had missed out on. The best he could come up with was his office was once an old pig sty!

'You'd be surprised what you can make as a model,' Harry said, a glazed look filling his rummy eyes. 'Good to know there are still people out there making models, but a whale sub? Now that's something different.' He shook his head. 'On that note, I'd best be on my way. I'll catch you later and don't forget to let me know if you learn anything more.' He laughed as he slowly walked away.

'Nice to know I've made your day,' Craig called, glad Harry had seen the funny side. 'You take care and I'll let you know if I hear anything.' He had no idea why he'd said that, though he was heartened that it had brought a sparkle to Harry's eyes. What he would really like to know is why it was left abandoned in the river weed. As his mind contemplated this, he watched Harry amble down the road. Being old wasn't much fun.

Chapter FIVE

With another coffee sitting at his elbow, Craig listened as Roo told him about their latest visitor. 'She seemed a little tense, though a mug of coffee and Barney sitting at her feet helped her relax. Unfortunately, she wouldn't tell me why she came to the office and insisted she needed to talk to you. I have her address and number.' As she spoke, she tapped on the screen of her phone and brought up the notes she'd made earlier. 'Her name is Katie Everett, and she lives just a few miles down the road.' Roo gave the address.

'Now that's a local word, "bishy barnabee,"' Craig said, smiling and at the same time writing down the details on his note pad. 'I never thought it would end up the name of a street.'

'It's a great name,' Roo said, then continued. 'She mentioned she had a daughter, but one thing she was clear about and that was she doesn't want her husband to know she's been here. Do you think he's having an affair?'

'Who knows, but I'll find out when I call her. Anything else?'

'Not on Mrs Everett, but I think I might have found a suitable CCTV camera for the vicar. If you don't mind, I could call and arrange to talk to him about it.'

Craig knew if anyone could scour the

internet and find what they were looking for, it would be Roo. He admired her tenacity to root things out until she had a result. 'No problem and thanks for looking for something. Let's hope he will be encouraged to have one because it will help.'

'I'll do my best to persuade him,' Roo said and grinned.

Craig didn't think for one minute she wouldn't.

'How did your chat go with DI Andrews?' Roo asked, changing the subject in a heartbeat. 'Are we going to be asked to help out in a murder case or a drugs raid?'

Craig grinned. His young assistant would make a good detective; she had all the qualities needed to seek answers, leaving no stone unturned, but he also knew she would never cope with the discipline. Roo was a one off and would go far. He hoped so. She was not just his assistant, but also Ella's niece and he was very fond of her. 'We are private investigators not Scotland Yard, but I do have something that will interest you, and that is… a submarine.'

'You are kidding me?' Roo's face lit up.

'No. Though it is not a full-size one. Apparently, it's a steampunk sub and looks like a whale. It was found in the river under the wooden footbridge.' Even as he spoke, he couldn't quite believe what Pete had told him.

Roo, wide eyed, asked, 'What does a punk submarine look like?' Not waiting for a response, she turned to her laptop and tapped with speed on the keyboard.

'Got one!' She cried with excitement. 'Wow! These are seriously cool. My grandad used to make model boats, but nothing like these. If he had I'd have been there at the park pond with him.'

Craig chuckled. He had no idea there were so many people who enjoyed model boat building.

'Just how did we end up with a whale sub in our river?'

'That's what we need to find out.'

'A mystery then! I can't believe we have something so exciting found in our river. It's normally bikes, rubbish, but never a punk sub.' She continued tapping on her keyboard as she spoke. 'My grandad is going to be so interested in this when I tell him.'

Craig rolled his eyes at Roo's exuberance. Oh, to be young again and full of energy and optimism, he thought.

A pinging sound alerted Craig to a new message on his phone. Glad of the distraction, he checked his messages and saw it was from Pete.

I meant to send this. Hope it helps to find out more. Craig looked at the photo and without hesitation forwarded it to Roo. 'I've sent you a photo of the sub. Now you can see what has been found.'

Roo picked up her phone. 'Wow! Now, that is a serious looking model,' she cooed as she enlarged the image to take in the detail. 'I know from my grandad that a lot of work would have gone into making something so amazing. So why would someone leave it abandoned?' Flashing a look at Craig, added, 'I suspect it's been stolen.' Returning her focus back to the photo, she frowned.

'That is the strange thing; no one has reported it missing.'

'No way! But if it hasn't been stolen, how did it end up in our river?'

'That's the question on DI Andrews' lips along with others at the station.'

'I am going to try and solve this,' Roo declared, grinning at Craig.

'Well before you do, please speak to the vicar about the CCTV camera. Then afterwards take a walk along the river path and see if you can have a word with those living on the boats. Hopefully someone may have seen something.'

'Leave it all to me, boss – I'm on the case.'

Craig didn't miss the sparkle in Roo's eye at the prospect of trying to find any information on the strange sub. 'Good you are happy about this. Whilst you are out, I'm going to call Katie Everett and see what brought her to our office.'

'Right, boss.' Roo picked up her phone and called the vicar. Two minutes later she ended the call. 'He's happy to hear what I've found.' She pushed back her chair and called over to Barney. 'Come on boy, we have work to do.'

Thrilled at the prospect of an outing, Barney padded over to Roo and waited for his harness and lead to be fitted. 'The vicar can't believe in less than a few hours I have found something.'

Craig would have been surprised if she hadn't but remained silent.

'Once I've done my spiel, Barney and I will head to riverside and the boats.' With Barney ready to go Roo headed to the door. 'See you laters,' she cried. Not waiting for a response, the two headed out into the warm sunshine.

'Laters,' Craig repeated and wondered how the English language had changed and not for the better. He picked up his phone and called Katie Everett.

Chapter SIX

Twenty minutes later, Craig greeted Katie as she entered his office. 'Thank you for seeing me so soon. It means a lot,' she said, as she shook Craig's hand.

Craig didn't miss the anxious look that filled her face. He remembered Roo saying she was not at ease during her earlier visit and wondered what was causing her distress.

'Let's take a seat over here,' he said, pointing to the sitting area. 'Can I get you a drink?'

Katie shook her head. 'I'm fine. Thank you. Your young assistant made me a coffee earlier.'

With note pad and pen at his side, Craig made himself comfortable opposite Katie. 'Now what can we do for you?'

Katie fiddled with the buttons on her blouse. Then, as if aware of what she was doing, she clasped her hands together and placed them on her knees. She turned her attention to Craig. 'You'll probably think I'm crazy.'

Craig grinned. 'We are all crazy at times, but I'm here to listen and, if possible, help.'

'Thank you.' Katie unclasped her hands and then re clasped them, all the while keeping her focus on Craig. 'Forgive me if I ramble, but it has taken a lot of courage to come and see you and talk about ...' she hesitated, a few seconds passed before she continued. 'I need to go back many, many years to when I was in my mid-teens, sixteen to be precise.' She paused as if thinking about what to say next.

'I found myself pregnant. In those days, as modern as times had become, for my parents, it wasn't accepted even though I had a steady boyfriend. My parents had met him a few times. They didn't like him. They said we were far too young to be getting serious with each other and far worse what we had been up to. On top of everything, they kept saying there was something about him that didn't add up. They didn't trust him. I couldn't see it then and looking back, I still can't see what they saw.

'When Chris, my boyfriend, learnt I was pregnant he was brilliant and there was no question of him not standing by me especially when we found out we were having twins. He was so caring, but my parents would have none of it.

'Our babies were born prematurely and our little boy died within hours. Our little girl survived. We were grieving and ecstatic in equal measure. We named her Megan.'

Katie looked down at her hands. She wrung them as if all she was suffering would come out of every pore. She looked up with watery eyes then ploughed on.

'Whilst I was trying to come to terms with all that I had gone through, my parents, unbeknown to us, had organised the baby's adoption. My mental state had me signing forms which I later learnt would take my little girl away forever.'

Craig sat up straight. He had not been prepared for such an outpouring and he could see Katie needed to get everything out. Sensing her anguish, he remained silent.

'It was the end of Chris and me, my mother made certain of that.' Katie said matter of fact. 'My mental health was precarious after that, but I was determined to get away from my parents and build my own life. Eventually, I managed to get a job in an account's office. In those days it was a small office, but after being taken over by a large company, it grew. Of course, you don't want to know all this.

'A few years later I met Drew. He had charm, wit and good looks and as it turned out he was everything my parents had said Chris was and more. Needless to say, they didn't take to him. At the time I didn't care. He made me laugh and he made me feel special and I also saw it as a way to get away from home. Within a year of going out with each other, we rented a little terraced house and it wasn't long before I found myself pregnant.

'By now my parents had washed their hands of me. Would you believe it, we had twins – two little girls. And as much as I love my girls, I never stopped thinking about my first babies. Not a day goes by without me thinking of Megan and I wonder where she might be. She would be fifty-nine now.'

She stopped and took a deep breath then looked into the middle distance as if the past was playing out before her. 'Despite having to give her up, I had hoped that one day she might look for me, but she never has. I understand, I think.' She made a weak smile. 'Sorry, but do you think I could have a glass of water?'

'Of course.' Jumping to his feet Craig headed to the kitchen area, he didn't want to make assumptions, but had a feeling he knew where all this was leading.

Returning, he placed a glass of water in front of her and sat down. 'Is there anything else I can get you?'

'No, thank you.' Leaning forward she took hold of the glass and took several large gulps, then placed it back down.

'Mrs Everett, it is a tragic story. I am sorry you've had to suffer all these years. I am assuming you are looking for our help?'

Katie nodded.

'How do you think we can help you?'

Despite Katie's emotional story, her voice was clear. 'I need you to look out for a woman who, I believe, lives on or close to our development.'

Surprised at the direct response, Craig opened his mouth to speak at the same time Katie continued. 'At first, I thought I was imagining things, but there is a woman who looks very much like my Holly.'

'Holly?' Craig interrupted.

'One of my daughters. The twins are not identical, but this woman, I have seen a few times and could almost be my Holly's twin.'

'I see,' Craig murmured whilst trying to piece together all the details he had heard.

'The resemblance is so striking, the curls,

the high cheek bones that I found myself calling out, *Megan*.' Katie stopped and stared at Craig, 'but the woman didn't stop, she just carried on walking away from me. I called out again, but she didn't turn round. Of course, why would she – her name is probably not Megan. I followed her for a short distance but lost her as she hurried across a busy road. The heavy traffic prevented me keeping up.' Katie's voice trailed off and she took a deep breath, then continued. 'I have seen her a couple of times since that day though it was always at a distance. I have walked miles around the area in the hope I would see her again, but she's never there.' She reached forward, picked up her glass and finished off the water.

'I constantly think about that moment I saw her. Of course, there are times I believe I have imagined it, but then I convince myself I haven't. Then I argue maybe I wanted this woman to be my Megan.' She placed the empty glass down on the table and resumed wringing her hands tightly.

'I'm a silly old woman who sees her lost baby everywhere. I think that is normal.' She made a face that conveyed resignation. 'I am sure there is some simple explanation. I've worked at making myself strong, capable and able to cope, despite those earlier years of suffering with depression. I've had to, but for reasons I can't explain, seeing that woman has tormented me. She visits me in my dreams. I simply can't get her out of my head. I'm sorry to burden you with my past, but it all just tumbled out. I knew if I stopped, I wouldn't finish.'

Craig understood; it was as if someone had removed the stopper from the bottle that held it all in and once Katie had started talking, the stopper flew out. Over the years he had heard many sad and distressing stories and no matter how many times he'd had to listen, he still felt a surge of pity and sorrow for what these people had gone through and all because of prejudice.

'What does your husband say?'

Katie shrugged her shoulders and made a soft mewl noise. 'I've not told him.'

Tempted as he was to ask, he refrained from doing so, instead kept to the details he needed.

'How old is this woman you saw?'

'Thinking if it was my Megan, she would be fifty-eight. My Megan will be fifty-nine on the third of October. I just wished I had been able to speak to her when I first saw her.'

'Do you have a photo I could have?'

'Of the woman?'

'Your daughter, Holly.'

A nervous giggle escaped Katies's lips, 'Of course. A photo of my Megan wouldn't help as she was a tiny baby when we were parted. But I do have one of Holly.' Katie reached down and picked up her handbag. She rooted through its contents as if half her home was in there before pulling out a photo. 'Here, this is Holly. It was taken a couple of months ago on her birthday.'

Reaching over, Craig took the photo. A smiling middle-aged woman stood in front of a large birthday cake, knife in hand, poised to cut into it. She stared back at the camera. He could see there was a striking resemblance to Katie. 'She looks like you.'

Katie's eyes sparkled at Craig's observation. 'Thank you. Everyone says that.'

Taking another look at the photo, he asked, 'And you believe the woman you saw looks similar to your daughter?'

Katie nodded, 'Yes, I do.' She hesitated, 'I think so.'

For the briefest of moments, a fleeting, shadow of doubt crossed Katie's face. Maybe the opening of the flood gates with everything pouring out had unnerved or confused her, Craig thought. 'Let me make a few more notes and then let's see what we can do?'

As if a weight had been lifted, Katie's shoulders visibly relaxed. 'Does this mean that you will try and help me find out who this woman is?'

Craig smiled, 'Let's see what we can do.' Despite his positive tone, he wasn't sure how they would find something akin to a needle in a haystack, but they would try.

For the first time since Katie had entered the office, she beamed a broad smile that lit up her face. 'Tell me what you need to know and I will do my best to provide you the answers.'

'Let's begin with names. Your name at the time you had Megan and what was registered on Megan's birth certificate.' Craig wrote down the answers before asking several more questions. Satisfied he had enough information for now, he placed his pen down on his notebook. 'I think that is it for now. I can phone you if we need anything else.'

'Please don't hesitate. I can't thank you enough.' As if animated by the positive outcome of her visit, Katie gushed out. 'We moved to our house to be nearer our daughter, Holly. My other daughter, Suzie, lives in Australia. We do get to see her and her family, though not that often; it's such a long way.'

'The other side of the world. But an adventure, I'm sure.'

'It is and though it is hard leaving them all behind, I belong here and more so as I still hold out hope that Megan might one day look for me. The clock is ticking and although I'm not a religious person, I pray I will be here for many more years so one day we can be reunited.'

He could see how desperate his new client was to find her lost baby. He just hoped it was possible, though he didn't believe in miracles.

'By the way, what is Holly's surname and where does she live?'

'Oh, please, no. You mustn't contact her.' As she spoke, her hands flew to her buttons on her blouse and like on her arrival, she fidgeted with them. 'She doesn't need to know about this.' She placed her hands in her lap then looked straight at Craig.

Craig saw tears pooling in Katie's eyes.

'She doesn't know anything about Megan. It's my secret. My shameful secret.' Dabbing her eyes with the back of her hand, Katie continued. 'For now, I just want you to find out who this woman is. I so want it to be my Megan, but I know I might have to accept it isn't.' Katie looked with pleading eyes at Craig.

He was a hardened ex police detective and throughout his years in the force he'd had to deal with some of the most terrible crimes committed. Crimes that had broken people physically and mentally, some beyond repair. He'd had to learn to sit back and not get emotional. It had never been easy and he probably had never totally managed it. Yet, despite all this, he felt the pain of this woman and the injustice of attitudes.

'We will do our best. We will not be contacting your daughter, however, knowing her surname might help us. Roo, my assistant is a whizz kid on social media and makes surprising finds and leads from there.'

'I know nothing about all of that. It's another world for me.'

'Me too,' he confessed.

'Her married name is Westwood, Holly Westwood, but please do not contact her.'

'You have my word.' As he replied he hoped that would be the case.

'Thank you. Secrets are terrible things.'

Craig nodded. He certainly knew about that. The case they had been involved in at the end of last year had been riddled with them. No one could have predicted the outcome. 'They are,' he said. 'In the meantime, let's see if we can find the woman you saw.' He looked down at the photo Katie had given him, then at his notes. 'We will do our best. Any information we gather we will keep you updated.'

Katie nodded. For a moment her eyes

glazed over. 'I just want to throw my arms around her.' She smiled at Craig. 'I know, I'm getting ahead of myself.'

Again, Craig was mindful of the pain Katie was wrestling with. 'We can hope. Have you any questions?'

Katie shook her head. 'I don't think so, Mr Gardner, you have asked so much. I can't thank you enough for taking your time to see me and listening to my story.'

'My pleasure. Thank you for sharing. As I said, we will do our best to try and locate this woman. Now, please let me see you to your car.' He stood.

Standing on the gravel parking area he watched Katie Everett drive away. He had no idea how he was going to find the woman she believed was her long-lost daughter, but they would certainly have a go.

Chapter SEVEN

With her head filled with Taylor's call and punk model submarines, Roo was buzzing. There was no doubt in her mind that she had a fantastic job and the best boyfriend on the planet. With these happy thoughts and Barney at her side, she headed down Chestnut Lane. With a spring in her step, Roo took in the pretty cottages and gardens filled with fragrant, colourful blooms and realised she would have missed all of this had she driven to the vicar's house. Instead, Zippy, her little white Fiat 500 with its red decal of a zip down the side, sat at home on the drive.

Skating to work had been fun and she smiled at how she had breezed along the pavements and road. Her passion for skating was equalled by Taylor who loved skating as much as she did. They were both fearless; nothing daunted either of them; jumping, spinning and racing, it was all an exhilarating thrill. Just thinking about what a perfect match they were had the butterflies fluttering in her tummy. He had been part of her life for just over a year, yet it seemed she had known him forever.

Lost in her daydreaming, a sudden tug on her arm brought her happy thoughts to a rapid close. Stopping dead in her tracks, the lead on full stretch, she glared at Barney who had his nose in a large flowering shrub and was in no hurry to move.

'Barney,' she called, as her thoughts of skating faded and replaced by the need to get to the vicar's house. Gently she tugged on his lead. 'Come on, boy,' she encouraged, aware new smells were overwhelming his senses; the area was new to him. 'We will never find the vicar's house at this rate,' she said, trying to work out which property was Apple Tree Cottage. At last, Barney trotted over.

After no more than half a dozen steps, Roo spied Apple Tree Cottage nestled between Plum Tree Cottage and Ivy Cottage. All had thick thatched roofs and white picket fences. 'Here we are,' she said and realised the lead had gone tight again as Barney found another new sniff. Standing outside the gate, she paused and waited for him to catch up. At last, at her side, she pushed the gate open and together they walked down a narrow paved path that snaked to the front door.

As she stood facing it, Roo was surprised at how impressive it was – a grand, ornately carved, dark wooden door that wouldn't look out of place at the church. She pushed the doorbell button and a heard a faint *ding dong* ring out from inside.

Within seconds, the door opened and a casually dressed woman in pastel shades, with a beaming smile, spoke affably. 'Hello! I believe it is Roo,' she said and at the same time took in Barney. 'He looks like a teddy bear,' she added. Barney dutifully wagged his tail at the attention.

'I'm Heather.'

'Hello, Heather, pleased to meet you, and yes, I'm Roo and this is Barney.' She held Barney on a tight lead as he tried to nudge forward to lick Heather's legs. 'Earlier today, the vicar visited our office and I offered to look up the possibility of a CCTV camera for the church. I think I've found something that should be perfect. I did phone earlier so I can explain about what I've found.'

'Yes, of course. Nick told me you would be calling, however, I'm afraid he's been called out. Maybe I can help.'

Roo tried to hide her disappointment with a thin smile. 'That's a shame, but I could leave the details with you and when he returns maybe he could call me and then I can go over what I've found.'

Heather took in Roo's expression. 'Why not come inside and you can explain what you have found to me. To be honest, I'm more likely to understand than Nick. He's not the most tech savvy.' Heather chuckled.

'That would be great. I am sure what I've found will be very useful,' she said enthusiastically, then looked down at Barney.

'I'm already interested,' Heather responded with a genuine smile, 'and, as for Barney, no worries, he's more than welcome. Do come on in.' Heather stood to one side offering space for Roo and Barney to enter. Roo decided she already liked Heather.

Once inside, Heather ushered them through to the kitchen. 'Tea, coffee or a cool drink?' she asked, as Roo took in the large country style kitchen. French doors opened onto a long garden filled with colour.

'It's like the Tardis, you don't expect all this from outside,' Roo admired.

'It is a little like that. That's what makes it so charming. We love it.'

Roo could see why.

'So, hot or cold?' Heather asked.

'A cool drink would be great, thank you,' Roo replied with Barney sitting at her heals and looking perfect and cute.

'And water for you too?' Heather offered, holding a large pottery bowl under a running tap. 'Here you are, little cutie,' she said, while placing the bowl on the floor. Barney instantly lowered his head and slurped loudly, water splashing everywhere. 'I think you were ready for that,' Heather said, ignoring the mess Barney was making.

'Come on, Roo, let's go and sit out on the patio. It is such a beautiful day, let's not waste it indoors.' Holding two large glasses of juice, Heather led the way.

Roo settled on a comfortable chair. Heather sat next to her. Barney laid down under the table in the shade.

'Now tell me about what you have found as it all sounds rather James Bond to me,' Heather laughed.

Roo laughed too. 'I think I have found something that will suit the church and help you keep an eye on what is going on there. The details are on my phone, but I have also printed them off.' She took a sip of her juice, then reaching into her bag pulled out A4 sheets. She beamed with enthusiasm as she handed the papers over. As Heather scanned the sheets, Roo pulled out her phone from her pocket and brought up the details on her screen.

'The good thing about this model is that it has its own chip which will talk to your mobile phone. This means there is no need for internet in the church. It really is a smart camera for places that need an electronic eye kept open. Here is a short video that shows how it works.' Roo handed her phone to Heather.

Heather watched the video. 'This looks very interesting,' she said, handing Roo's phone back. 'I admit I'm not that great with all the technology out there, but watching this makes it not only suitable, but easy enough to understand.' She smiled at Roo. 'Thank you for taking the time to search out something that might be suitable. It is very kind of you and I for one appreciate this. You really are a whizz kid on the internet.'

Roo blushed. 'I love searching the internet to find things out. You'd be surprised what you can uncover on there.'

'In your line of business, it must be very useful,' Heather smiled at Roo. 'It must be interesting what you do, though I am sure there is a dark side to some of the things you end up being involved in.'

'Sometimes, but overall, it really is a great job. I feel very lucky doing something I love. As for the internet, I don't know how anyone found things out before.'

'It does seem to be a font of information and I admit to wondering too.' Heather looked again at the pages. 'I'm glad you showed these to me. As much as Nick would have sat and watched the video, he wouldn't have understood the finer details. To be honest, he's hopeless at all of this. He's fine with his mobile phone to make calls and receive them, but that's about it. Our son, Matthew, would understand about these things,' she nodded to Roo's mobile phone, 'but he's so wrapped up with his studies he hardly has time to talk to us these days.' Heather rolled her eyes as if to say, *what are students like*? 'At least that's what he tells us! He's away at university in his final year.' Tapping the sheets. 'Can I keep these?'

'Of course. I printed them off so you could take time to check the details. And I'll be more than happy to go over it all again once the vicar is available. Cameras do deter people and if undesirables are hanging around the church, the camera will pick them up and let you know.' She felt it was sad that a church needed to consider such technology. The area wasn't one that had high crime, yet despite this, they still had mindless vandalism.

'From what I've seen, it sounds just what we need. Thank you again. Unfortunately, what goes on there worries Nick. Thankfully, so far, it hasn't been anything serious, just petty, mindless behaviour. It's as if people have nothing better to do than spoil things.' Heather looked at Roo and frowned. 'I am assuming it is youths, of course I could be wrong. Whoever they are, they are thoughtless of the distress they cause others.'

Roo nodded, 'I agree. It really is awful.' Pointing to the information she'd given Heather, she added, 'If you both think you would like this, I can order it for you. It is an on-line company and I could also help set it up.' Roo saw Heather's face change to one of uncertainty. Keen to reassure, she added, 'It is a well-known company with a good reputation.'

'Thank you, I'm not doubting you and I am sure Nick will be keen once he sees the details and I explain the benefits.'

'I can always come back,' Roo offered. Then reaching out she picked up her glass of juice and finished it. 'Thank you, that was delicious.' With her empty glass on the table, she pushed back her chair and stood. 'I have taken up enough of your time and now we had better head back.' At Roo's movement, Barney jumped to his feet letting out a silly squeaky bark.

'I am the one that needs to say thank you. You've given your time to help and I more than appreciate this.'

'No problem, let's just hope we can stop the vandalism or at least see who are responsible.'

'I hope so. Nonetheless, thank you so much.'

As Heather spoke, she watched Barney jumping with excitement. 'He's eager to leave.'

'He just loves going out on walks,' Roo said, clipping on his lead.

'Then I'd better let you go.' Heather headed

through the cottage to the front door. Barney, tugging on his lead, kept pace with her.

Standing outside with Barney, 'Please let me know what the vicar thinks,' Roo said before heading down the path.

'I will and of course Nick or I will be in touch as soon as he gets home,' Heather said and watched as her visitors walked through the open gate.

Clicking the gate closed, Roo waved back before heading down Chestnut Lane. Her step had an extra spring in it as she recalled the positive response. All being well she would be back very soon to help them order the camera – hopefully sooner than later. She wondered if Nick's absence was down to another incident at the church. If so, they definitely needed a CCTV camera. And as tempted as she was to swing by St Julian's, she thought it would be wiser to head back to the office. Checking out the riverside path she would do later. Tugging gently on Barney's lead she quickened her step.

Chapter EIGHT

Craig paced back and forth across the office as he absorbed the details from Katie Everett. It was a distressing story and unfortunately not untypical of those times. He crossed back to his desk, sat down and picked up the photograph of Holly Westwood. She'd smiled at the camera. He could see there was a clear resemblance to her mother – the blonde hair, high cheek bones and blue eyes. There was little doubt that she was Katie Everett's daughter. He studied the photo to see if there was anything distinguishing that would make Holly Westwood stand out. There wasn't! Yet it appeared this woman had a double according to Katie Everett.

He wondered how they would be able to help and, more to the point, how they were going to find the other woman. They only had a photo of someone who, according to Katie Everett, looked like the person they were asked to find. He ran his fingers through his mop of copper hair as his mind took him down rabbit holes and cul-de-sacs as he pondered how to find a baby from fifty-nine years ago.

Even though his thoughts raced, he knew once Roo was onboard, she would pounce onto social media and trawl through it until she found something that might connect Katie Everett and Holly Westwood with a missing baby of over half a century ago. If anything could be found, Roo would ferret it out. Despite these thoughts, he wasn't convinced. Fifty-nine years and a photo of a daughter who appeared to have a double wasn't much to go on. He sighed.

The silence of the office was suddenly shattered as Craig's phone rang out, jolting him out of his thoughts. He slapped his hand on his chest as the sudden din made his heart give an extra beat. Reaching over he noted Pete's name flash on the screen. 'Now what does he want?' he muttered, having seen him early that morning. He tapped the answer button and was about to speak when Pete's voice rang out.

'I thought you'd like to know we've just received a call. A body's been found in St Julian's church.'

'What! St Julian's!' Craig cried. 'I was only talking to the vicar this morning and right now, Roo's at the vicar's house talking to him.' As he spoke, Roo and Barney walked into the office. 'Having said this, she's back.'

'OK. I'm heading over to the church right now,' continued Pete. 'And I'd be grateful if you could let me know what Roo might have learnt.' Before Craig could utter a word, the call ended.

'That turned out to be better than I had expected,' Roo said, sounding pleased as she unclipped Barney's lead from his harness. 'Heather, that's the vicar's wife, is really a cool person and was so interested in the details of the CCTV. I am confident they will order one.' With positive steps she made her way to her desk. 'I think we might have a result there,' she added unaware of Craig's alarmed expression.

'Does that mean you didn't see Nick?'

Sitting down, Roo rested her elbows on her desk. 'No, he'd been called out, but it didn't matter it all worked out well.'

'Where to?' Craig asked, a sharpness to his voice.

'What?' Roo cried, looking at Craig mystified.

'The vicar, where had he gone?'

Roo shrugged. 'No idea. Heather never said. Is it important?'

'It could be. I've just had DI Andrews on the phone and a body has been found in the church.'

'No way!'

'I'm afraid so and I'll guess that is where Nick was called out to. Odd that, only this morning, he should come here asking for help with petty theft and vandalism and now a dead body has been found in the church. What has been going on there?'

He grabbed his phone and got to his feet. 'I'm going to head over there, see if I can find out anything. DI Andrews is on his way there.' He picked up his car keys from his desk. 'It's unlikely I'll find anyone that will talk to me, but I need to see for myself. Nick didn't suggest anything serious enough to result in a dead body.'

Craig sighed. In a matter of a few hours, he'd learnt about a submarine that had been found, a daughter who appeared to have a double and petty vandalism which had turned into a dead body in a local church. If this was a

TV series, no one would believe it. Trying to shake these events into some semblance of reality, Roo's voice sliced through his thoughts.

'If only the vicar had come to see us sooner, we could have had the camera up and working and maybe what has happened could have been avoided.'

'I hear what you say, but we can't think like that Roo. Life is full of ifs. My old grandma used to say, "if ifs and ands were pots and pans what would we do for tinkers."'

'Really! What's a tinker?'

Craig rolled his eyes, 'Never mind. Put it like this, we can always see the benefits of doing this or that with hindsight.'

'I guess, but…'

'I know. Roo, what we need to find out is when Nick was last in his church and how long the body has been there. I've no idea if going over there will yield us the answers just yet, but nonetheless, I'm going. When I get back, I need to talk to you about Katie Everett.'

'Something interesting?'

'We have been asked to try and find someone, but I'll explain when I get back. In the meantime, have you been able to speak to any of the residents on the boats about the submarine?'

Roo's eyes lit up. 'We've been asked to try and find someone?' she cried. 'Now that sounds interesting. Can you tell me anything now?'

'No, we'll go through the details later. For now, let's find out anything we can about the sub whilst I see what I can learn at the church.'

Disappointment etched on her features, Roo answered, 'OK, boss.'

Craig didn't miss the look on his asstistant's face. He could almost hear the cogs in her head whirring and imagined her thoughts about looking for someone was far more exciting than asking questions about a missing model submarine. She was right!

'I'm on to it,' she said, her voice not betraying Craig's thoughts.

'Great. I'll see you later and let's hope we both come back with information.' He smiled at her as he closed the office door.

Chapter NINE

Ten minutes later Craig pulled up at the bottom of Cavendish Road. He locked his car and with measured steps walked the short distance to where several emergency vehicles blocked the road. Incident tape flapped in the warm breeze where officers had cordoned off several sections of the area.

Before he had time to take in the scene further, he heard his name called. Turning, he came face to face with his old colleague.

'What's under that bonnet of yours?' Pete queried, pointing down the road to Craig's car, 'You didn't waste any time getting here. Tell me, what did young Roo have to say?'

'As it turns out, nothing! Nick wasn't there. He'd been called out and now we know why. I doubt his wife knew as she never mentioned anything to Roo. Odd that the vicar came to our office about a few minor incidents and now this.' He looked towards the police tape, then turned his attention back to Pete.

'Also, there was nothing in Nick's demeanour that indicated he was worried about anything other than petty anti-social behaviour.' He ran his hand over his chin. 'I know it's very early stages, any details yet?'

Pete shook his head. 'All I can tell you is – it's a hanging – from the rafters. The white suits are in there. Once they've finished, I'll see what I can find out. In the meantime, anything you learn, share with me and, where possible, I'll do the same.' Pete laid a hand on Craig's shoulder. 'I'd better go.' Not waiting for a response, the DI turned, ducked under the police tape and headed back towards the church.

Craig watched his old colleague, shoulders hunched, stride down the short gravel path, now flanked by uniforms. Sadly, for now, there was no chance of him getting any closer to the scene. He was about to head back to his car when he caught sight of the vicar heading in his direction.

'Mr Gardner, one moment, please,' Nick called in a tense voice, his breath coming in short bursts.

Craig barely hid his shock at the change in the man in just a few hours. He opened his mouth to speak, but Nick didn't give him an opportunity, as the distraught vicar gushed out, 'I was going to call you as soon as I could get away. We've had the most terrible incident in the church. I am beyond shocked.' As he spoke, he made a cross over his chest. His voice quivered with emotion and as if to still his hands from shaking, he pushed them into his trouser pockets. 'I hadn't long left your office when I received a call from Mr Boxhall.'

'Mr Boxhall?' Craig found himself repeating.

'We don't have the luxury of a verger; we are far too small. However, Bill Boxhall is as good as one. Amongst his duties, as a volunteer, I might add, he unlocks the church and it is also him who has reported much of the damage and vandalism,' he rambled as if there was a need to go into detail. Then pulling his hand from his pocket and clasping a white handkerchief he raised it to mop his brow. Beads of perspiration had formed and now trickled down his face.

'Today when he unlocked, Mr Boxhall, that is, he noticed soil and grass clippings on the floor. He had no idea how they had got there as the church was locked. Annoyed he marched to the back of the church to see what else might have happened. It was then that he saw …' The vicar closed his eyes as if to remove any image that might be there. Taking a deep breath he looked straight at Craig. 'A body. It was hanging from one of the rafters.'

Nick's face paled further and Craig wondered if the man was about to pass out. 'Do you need to sit down?'

Nick shook his head. 'Thank you. I'm fine. It is just such a shock.' He ran his hand over his face which did nothing to improve his pallor. 'The police are talking to Bill. Though he told me he couldn't see who it was. The body was facing in the opposite direction to where he was standing. He thought about stepping round the pool of water to look up, but he said he was afraid he would vomit.'

'Pool of water?' Craig queried.

'It's likely the person had urinated.'

Craig nodded. He'd seen enough bodies to understand what happens in death.

'Thankfully Bill has a mobile phone,' Nick carried on. 'It has only three numbers in the contacts list and one of them is mine. Of course, he'd called the police first. Poor chap was in a terrible state.' As if to steady himself, Nick leant against the railings that boarded the church yard and the public pavement. He ran his hand across an imaginary stubble.

'I'm not unversed at seeing dead bodies, but I've never seen one hanging in my church.' As he spoke, he looked up heavenward and Craig wondered if he was offering up a silent prayer.

'The police have taken over and hopefully they will quickly find out what has caused this dreadful accident.' Craig didn't miss the word accident and wondered what made Nick think it was an accident. Tempted as he was to ask, he decided to wait until he had spoken further with Pete. It was clear, the vicar was in shock.

'Goodness knows how we have ended up with such a terrible tragedy,' Nick eventually said. His eyes darted around as if the answer lay around them.

'Mr Howard, please could you come with me,' a young, uniformed officer called out as he strode towards the two men. 'Please, sir, we have a few more questions.'

Nick gazed at the constable: the officer's uniform appeared a size too large for the young man's frame along with a helmet that fell almost over his eyes. He gave a weary smile. 'I thought I'd answered all your questions.'

'I'm sorry, sir, but there are a few more the inspector would like you to answer,' the officer politely said.

‘Of course,’ Nick said. He turned to Craig, ‘I’d better go. I’ll call you as soon as possible.’ He then followed the officer.

Watching the two men walk away, Craig pondered on what had really been going on at the church because things had morphed from the vicar talking about petty crime to a dead body. As keen as he was to know what was going on, he had to accept that, for now, he’d have to wait. Resigned to this fact, he turned and headed back to his car.

Chapter TEN

Unclipped from his lead, Barney ran off along the river path, his nose close to the ground. He sniffed wildly before scampering to a large clump of vegetation that clearly gave off an enticing scent. Roo watched the dog sniff his way through the foliage all the while her mind going over what had been discovered at St Julian's. What on earth could have happened? With no answers to the endless questions racing around in her head, she just wished the vicar had come to see them sooner. Had he done so, they may have had a CCTV camera fitted and could have seen who was going into the church. Totally lost in her ruminations, Roo didn't see the person approaching her.

'You look miles away, no doubt trying to solve another local mystery,' a voice rang out bringing Roo to a sudden halt. Startled, she looked up and saw Joe Burton standing in front of her.

'Hello, Mr Burton,' she said, as he stepped to one side. She often encountered the cheerful man on her walks, but no matter what the temperature was, freezing or a heat wave, he always sported a colourful neckerchief tied loosely around his neck. His attire was like a uniform with a corduroy waistcoat, which varied in colour, worn over a t-shirt. Dark coloured trainers poked out under his denim jeans. His greying hair was tied back in a band at the nape of his neck. He was what her nana would call a *local character* because of his appearance.

Mr Burton lived on one of the boats that was permanently moored along this stretch of the river. And, like him, it was rather colourful with different splatters of paint as if he'd been trying to decide what colour his boat should be.

'So, what's keeping you busy today?' he asked, his voice friendly, as he leaned on a hiking pole.

She didn't think it wise to talk about the goings on at the church. 'Would you believe a submarine,' she replied with a ring of humour.

'Oh, right,' he said in a tone that conveyed disbelieve. He chuckled. 'It's the sort of thing you see lurking around here in our murky river.' He pointed to the dark brown water and at the same time winked at her.

'I can see you're making fun of me,' Roo said good naturedly, 'but one has been found.'

'Of course, it has. Let's me see,' he said, tapping the finger of his right hand to his lips as if to concentrate on an answer. 'Was it one of those Russian spy subs or a nuclear one?' He chuckled again then ran his fingers over his thinning grey hair.

'Ha ha,' Roo laughed. 'And no to both. As it happens, I am being serious, but I'm not talking about a real one…'

'Of course not,' Joe cut in with an expression that conveyed mirth.

'You can laugh, but the one found is a

model and near the wooden footbridge. In fact, it's a steampunk model and looks like a whale. Let me show you.' Before Joe could comment further, Roo pulled her phone from her pocket and flicked to the photo. 'Here, this is the baby.'

With her phone held in front of Joe, she watched as he stared at the image. He shook his head. 'Goodness. What is that? A sub you say?'

Roo nodded. 'I know it takes some believing, but it is a sub of sorts. My grandad used to make model boats, though none like this. And if built well they can be worth a lot of money.'

Joe looked suitably impressed. 'Who would have thought it. Something as ugly as that worth a bob or two.' He continued to stare at the photo. 'It's not something I've ever thought of doing – too busy trying to keep Lady Jane afloat and watertight. Though I might have made a few coins doing something like this than constantly repairing my old tub.' He nodded to further down the river where his small houseboat was moored.

Roo slipped her phone back into her pocket. 'From your surprise, I take it you've not seen it in or out of the water?'

Joe shook his head. 'It's not something that you'd forget if you had. Though, it begs the question, how on earth did it end up here?'

'That's what we're trying to find out. I'm going to ask the others who live on the boats to see if they've seen anything or anyone out of place.'

'I haven't seen anyone handling anything

like that. It would stick in your mind if you did.' He rubbed at the short stubble on his chin. 'Of course,' he pointed towards the footbridge. 'Often there's a group of youngsters hanging about there. They lark about a bit, but to my knowledge they've not caused any trouble. I've never had any reason to complain about them, though lord knows what they get up to.'

Roo was aware of the group and though they sometimes called out to her when she was walking with Barney, she never felt threatened; it was only banter. Occasionally, one of them would give Barney a stroke. It wasn't often she saw them and thinking about it, she hadn't seen them of late. Maybe they had found somewhere else to hang out.

'If I hear of anyone who might know anything about the sub, whale or whatever it is, I'll let you know,' Joe said, breaking into Roo's thoughts. 'Good luck with your search and if you find anything, let me know. In the meantime, I'll keep my ear to the ground.'

Barney strolled over from a clump of bushes he'd been sniffing and turned his attention to Joe.

'Hello, boy,' Joe said, reaching down to pat Barney's head. 'Thanks for letting me know about the sub. You learn something new every day.' He chuckled as he stood up. 'I'd best get off. I need to pop to the Post Office to post a birthday card. I'd like to think I'd be going to collect my pension, but I've another six months before that privilege.' He chuckled again, patted Barney, then set off along the pathway, his hiking pole swinging in step with his gait.

Well, that was one question answered, Roo thought with amusement. Now she knew how old Mr Burton was, though she didn't think he looked anywhere near being a pensioner. Noting Barney had wandered over to a large tree, she called, 'Come on, Barney.' At the sound of his name, he turned and ran towards her, his tail wagging happily. Together, they headed towards where the house boats were moored. Roo hoped she would find out more than she had with Mr Burton.

Chapter ELEVEN

Disappointed, Roo ambled back under the footbridge. She had found out nothing about the punk sub. In fact, she was of the opinion the people she'd managed to speak to hadn't believed her despite showing them the photograph. Yet, all were starkly aware of the boys who gathered under the bridge.

Thinking what she might need to do next, she looked round for Barney. 'Where are you?' she muttered, scanning the grass edges and bushes when she saw a flash of light. Perhaps the sun had reflected on something shiny. Curious, she moved towards the area where the light had flashed. Gently she swept her right foot over the grassy clump. To her surprise it revealed a silvery object peeping out from under a stone. Reaching down, she pushed the stone over and there it was – a chunky silver chain necklace. She cleared the area further before picking it up.

As she held it between her thumb and forefinger, she saw it was grubby. With her other hand she rubbed her fingers along its length and removed a thin layer of dust and a few grains of light soil. With the grime removed the chain looked in pristine condition. Further inspection revealed a crystal in the shape of a heart which, when held up, sparkled.

Rolling her find over in the palm of her hand, she could see it was not only attractive, it was also heavy. Someone must be feeling pretty upset at losing this, she thought.

It was then she noticed the clasp was broken. No doubt that was how it had been lost: having come undone and falling from its owner's neck. Despite this, Roo smiled at the find and carefully slipped it into her pocket. Looking around, she spied Barney ambling over to her.

'Come on boy, let's head back to the office.' As if the prospect of going back was more inviting than all the weeds and shrubs, Barney ran ahead.

~~~

At the same time as Roo and Barney walked along the riverside path, Craig drove back to the office from St Julian's. Knowing he would have to wait to hear back

from Pete, he turned his attention to the meeting with Katie Everett. The more he thought about her request, the more he realised he had no idea where to begin. One thing he did know and that was, you couldn't go and stand on street corners in the hope of seeing someone you'd never met. If nothing else, there would be some kindly passer-by thinking he or Roo was up to no good and call the police. He would need to think of a plan that would help Katie. All they had to go on was the area Katie had seen a woman who, she believed, resembled the daughter she'd had to give up fifty-nine years
~~~

ago along with a photograph of a younger daughter – a needle in a haystack might be easier to find.

Slowing down, he approached the roundabout and indicated to turn left. The traffic was light and he quickly slipped round and onto the road that would take him to the office. The empty roads allowed his mind to wander and as much as he tried to concentrate on a plan for Katie Everett, his attention returned to the incident at the church. What had really happened there and how had anyone entered the church? It was supposed to be locked! And yet a body was found hanging there! How? What has really been going on? Suddenly, he was snapped back to his driving, as the car in front stopped without warning. He stamped on his brakes and came to a shuddering halt. Checking his rearview mirror, he was thankful no one was behind him. He saw the deer run into the wooded area, as the car in front of him started moving again.

Craig gave out an audible sigh knowing how dangerous this road could be with the wildlife.

He was less than a mile from the office, but to his dismay, a car pulling a caravan pulled out in front of him. Whilst there was little traffic on the roads, what there was, was frustrating. He could never understand why someone would want to drag a smaller version of their home around the country. Resigned at having to stay behind the double length vehicle, he wondered how Roo had got on with the steampunk. He just hoped she'd had more luck than he was having.

Eventually, Craig took a turning to his right. Thankful to leave the caravan and its driver to pootle along to wherever it was heading.

He wondered if Roo was there as he pulled into his parking space. On entering the office, he was almost bowled over as Barney charged to greet him.

'Goodness boy, I've only been out a short while.' As he spoke, he leaned down and rubbed his hand across the dog's head.

'Come on boy.' And with Barney close at his heals, he headed to his desk, acutely aware what Barney was after - an *entry* treat. Innocently they had created a reward routine which meant if Roo or he returned to the office, they had to give Barney a treat. Knowing there was no escape he pulled open the top drawer and took out a bone shaped biscuit.

'Sit,' he said. Barney was ahead of him and already sat waiting, 'Good boy. Here you are.' Barney gingerly took the treat and stood as swiftly as he had sat and headed straight to his bed.

'That dog is spoilt. Rod and back come to mind,' Craig said with a resigned smile and sat down in his chair. Placing his elbows on his desk he rested his chin in the cup of his hands and glared at Roo. 'Before you ask, my morning hasn't been all that great. Many questions and no answers. I'm hopeful you have answers to questions.' He raised an eyebrow as he spoke. He took in Roo's face but couldn't read her expression.

'How did you get on with the boat people?'

'I'd like to report it was worth my time, but I can't,' she pulled a face. 'Nobody seems to have seen anything.' She threw her hands in the air, 'How could anyone miss seeing that sub? It's pretty big and unusual and if I may say, ugly.' She looked at Craig.

'I'm not sure they believe me! Let's be honest, it is a bit farfetched and science fiction when you talk to people about it. Though, I did have a chat with Mr Burton. He was quite chatty. I think he's a bit lonely at times. Unfortunately, like everyone else he hadn't seen anything either.'

She paused for a moment as if to think. 'Are you sure DI Andrews said it had been found under the wooden bridge?' She didn't wait for a response. 'What I can't get my head around is how it managed to end up there and no one saw it. No one! What is going on?' A baffled look filled her face. 'I take it from your earlier comment you've not come back with much either.' Frowning, 'Are you listening?'

Craig shrugged. 'Yes, no and yes! Yes, I am listening and no nothing specific about the body except…' he looked straight at her, 'it's a hanging.'

'What?' Roo almost leapt out of her chair. 'Hanging from what?

'From a rope, around the neck – dangling from the rafters.'

'You mean a suicide … in a church? Oh my goodness, that is so creepy.'

'That's the "nothing specific" part. The verger, Bill Boxhall, didn't see the face; it was hanging facing the other way. As expected, I couldn't get anywhere near the scene. It was all cordoned off and surrounded by uniforms. Despite the number of officers there, I did manage to speak with DI Andrews but he didn't have any further information. He'd only just arrived himself, though, he has promised to keep me informed. The second yes is that no sooner had DI Andrews headed towards the church when Nick called out to me.' He grimaced. 'The poor chap looked terrible. Within the last few hours, he appears to have aged years.'

'Poor vicar. Did he have any idea what had happened?'

Craig shook his head. 'At this stage all we know is that a body has been found hanging in the church. As you can guess, that is why he wasn't at home earlier. For now, we have to wait for more information. Forensics are there and there will be a post-mortem at some point. And I'm sure Nick will talk to us as soon as he knows anything.'

The expression on Roo's face warned Craig her mind was racing. He didn't have to wait long before she burst out.

'There must be some information. It's not possible to know nothing! The basics must be known. Is it male or female? Roughly what age?'

He stared at Roo. 'I don't know yet, but we will in time, don't worry.'

Rolling her eyes and in an exasperated tone, she added, 'This is sad, but at the same time exciting to be able to find out what happened and why. I love my job. Right now, I'm getting straight on to the internet; you never know what's been added already on the local news or social media.' Without hesitation her fingers raced across the keyboard, her eyes glued to the details appearing on the screen.

Craig loved Roo's zeal and not for the first time thought she would enjoy working in serious crime. There was no doubt in his mind that she would make a first-class detective.

'Great!' Roo said sarcastically. 'Lots of details on nothing of interest, but *nada* about what's happened at the church.'

Craig was relieved to hear that. It was important to know what had happened before people started speculating on the internet. He tried to keep an open mind about the World Wide Web, but there were times, too many times, that he thought it was a dangerous place. Despite his reservations, Roo certainly appeared to cope with it all. He put it down to youth and having known nothing else. There was no doubt about it, he was turning into a dinosaur!

'I'm sure we will find out as soon as DI Andrews knows something.'

'I guess,' she said, shrugging her shoulders. Then, as if remembering something, she pushed back her chair and dug her hand into her pocket. 'I meant to tell you about this earlier. Look what I found along the river path.' As she spoke, she pulled out the necklace – a heavy silver chain – found in the undergrowth and dangled it in front of her. 'Would you believe, this was peeping out from under a stone.' She reached over and carefully placed the chain on Craig's desk. It clunked heavily on the surface.

'What's this?' he asked. Picking it up, he dropped it into the palm of his hand before studying it. 'I'm no expert on these things, but this doesn't look cheap.'

'It's heavy and I wouldn't have seen it had the sun not reflected off the crystal heart. It flashed like a torch light which caught my attention.' She reached over and pointed at the crystal heart. 'Someone must be feeling very upset at losing it,' she added, watching Craig inspect it. 'The question is, how did it find its way under a stone?'

'It doesn't look like it's been there long as it looks almost new.' He placed the chain down on his desk. If he was honest, at this moment in time, he wasn't overly interested; right now there were more pressing issues on his mind. 'Next time I call into the station, I'll pop it in. You never know, someone might have reported it missing.'

'Hopefully. Though if it had been mine, I would be upset to have lost it. Fingers crossed it can be reunited with its owner. I'll take a pic of it before you take it to the station. You never know, a pic could be useful if I get to talk to any of the people living on the boats. They might be the one who's lost it.' Picking the chain up, Roo placed it around her neck. 'It's beautiful,' she said, holding her phone up with her other hand to see the effect in the screen. Smiling, she gently placed it on her desk and took a couple of photos. Satisfied they were acceptable she handed the chain back to Craig.

'What a strange day it's been so far. I think

we need a coffee and then you can tell me what Katie Everett needs help with.’

Chapter TWELVE

The coffee machine gurgled, its aromatic aroma permeating the office. The distraction of the body in the church had meant they'd not had an opportunity to discuss Katie Everett's visit. She was always excited and curious when a new client came to the office. Now as Roo waited for the coffee to pour, she could feel her adrenaline rise at the prospect of another new case.

With two mugs of fresh coffee, she headed back to her desk.

'Here you are.' She placed a mug in front of Craig. 'Now please tell me how it went with Katie Everett,' her voice trilling with anticipation as she settled down at her desk.

Craig sniffed at his coffee before taking a mouthful. 'With all that has happened this morning it already seems days ago since she came into the office not just a few hours.' He took another mouthful of coffee then continued. 'It's not that straight forward as she would like us to look for her lost daughter.'

'Lost daughter! Did she just leave home and not come back? You know like Mr Cooper did?'

Craig shook his head. 'No, nothing like Mark Cooper and what he'd been up to. Katie Everett's story is very different and rather sad.' He placed his coffee mug, now half empty, down on his desk. 'When she was in her mid-teens,

Katie Everett had a baby. Pressure from her mother saw that the baby was adopted. That baby would be fifty-nine now.'

Roo listened in silence.

'The last time she saw her baby was when the baby was just a few weeks old as she was handed over for adoption.' He lifted his coffee mug and drank the last drops. 'Despite it being nearly six decades ago, Katie is convinced she has seen someone near to where she lives, who she believes is her long-lost baby.'

Frowning at how unlikely that could be, Roo felt she would be hard pressed to recognise herself as a baby and how she looked now. 'How could you recognise someone that you haven't seen since she was a tiny baby?' Roo crossed her arms. 'It's not possible.'

'I agree. However, Katie Everett has a daughter that is four years younger than the baby who was adopted. The woman she has seen appears to resemble this daughter.' Craig went on to further explain all Katie had told him.

'Sometimes we all see doubles of someone we know, but that doesn't make them a relation.' Roo lifted her mug and drank down the entire contents. 'Goodness, that would be one coincidence if it was,' she said, wiping the back of her hand over her mouth as she placed her mug down on her desk.

Craig watched amused. 'Indeed! Katie as asked if we would try and find the woman she saw.'

Roo raised her eyebrows.

'I know this isn't going to be easy, but that is

why people come to us. We take it seriously and do our very best to get a result. When did Poirot ever say it was easy?'

Roo chuckled at Craig mentioning her hero. 'Right. I assume we have a photo of this woman?'

'Yes and no.' He picked up a photo from his desk and handed it over.

'Yes and no again!'

Craig chuckled. 'The photo you are looking at is of Katie's daughter, Holly Westwood. Katie is adamant that the woman she saw looks very much like Holly. So much so she is convinced the woman must be her long-lost daughter.'

'Oh, my goodness. What happens if we do find this woman and it turns out it's nothing to do with her long-lost baby?'

'I'm glad you've thought of that. It's a sensitive case and we must tread carefully. Our work is to try and locate this person and find out where she lives or at least where she can be found. Depending on what we find, we then report back to Katie. For now, we need to work out how to do this. It's not going to be easy.'

Roo studied the photo; her face crinkled in concentration. 'There's nothing obvious that makes her stand out, though I can see there is a resemblance to her mother.' She lifted her head and looked over at Craig. 'Where did she see the woman?'

'Rosehill Gardens which is on the edge of Castleton Green, close to where she lives.'

Placing the photo down, Roo turned to her

laptop. Her fingers raced across the keys before a Google map appeared on her screen. 'Rosehill Gardens is a large development and Castleton Green is even bigger.' She picked up the photo again. 'Let's see what we can find on Holly Westwood; it might help as we have so little to go on.'

'You never fail to impress at how you flick through the internet as if it were pages in a book.' Craig looked on, shaking his head, then added, 'Not everyone is on social media, Roo.'

'Yes, they are, with the exception of you.' She grinned as she looked over the top of her laptop at Craig.

Knowing he was not going to win on that argument, he turned his attention to his own laptop. No sooner had he nudged his mouse, bringing his screen to life, when Barney raced to the door, his tail wagging frantically from side to side. Instead of barking, he made a silly squeaking yap.

Pushing back his chair and with purpose, Craig strode towards Barney. Reaching round the excited dog, he opened the door. At the same time Barney pushed against his legs and dashed out.

'Barney!' Craig called when Barney came to an abrupt halt in front of Harry Morgan.

Standing on the gravel area, Harry leaned on his walking stick. In his other hand he clutched a thick rope; a small black and white fluffy dog was tethered to the other end.

Chapter THIRTEEN

Standing in front of the visitors, Barney yapped and wagged his tail manically as if unsure who to fuss first.

'Thank goodness you're in,' Harry puffed, his cheeks a rosy pink as beads of perspiration trickling down his face.

Craig stared, firstly down at the dog, then up at Harry. 'What are you doing with a dog?' As he spoke, he took hold of the rope from Harry. Instantly, the little dog nuzzled his legs. 'Hello,' he said and bending down, Craig untied the rope letting it fall from the dog's neck. He picked the dog up. 'What's going on Harry?'

Barney sniffed around Harry.

'I wish I knew. It's not mine, if that's what you're thinking.' A look of relief flooding his face as Craig held the dog in his arms. 'I found it about half a mile down the riverside path. At first, I thought he was with someone, but I didn't see anyone. I waited a few minutes thinking he would be called back. Nothing! I set off walking, but he kept following me. I did try to shoo him away in the hope it would return to its owner, but he's just kept with me.' He pulled a handkerchief from his pocket and wiped at his eyes. 'Even in the summer my old peepers still water!' He groaned and stuffed the handkerchief back in his pocket.

'Come on inside and sit down and then you can tell me what's going on.' Craig clutched the dog under his arm and at the same time helped Harry into the office. It was clear both needed a drink. Not to be forgotten, Barney kept pace with them both.

Once everyone was inside, Craig closed the door and placed the little dog down on the floor. Instantly, Barney sniffed him. After walking round him a couple of times, he decided Harry Morgan was more interesting.

'Sit yourself down on one of the sofas,' Craig said, assisting Harry to the one next to him.

'What's going on?' Roo asked, taking in Mr Morgan, who looked flustered and the little dog who sniffed around the office.

'Mr Morgan will explain in a minute. First, we need to get this little one a small bowl of water and, get Harry a cold drink.' Craig headed to the kitchen and the little dog followed.

'Would you like a nice cold drink?' Roo asked Harry.

'Would you mind if I had one of your hot chocolates, please?'

'Not a cold drink?'

'If you don't mind, a chocolate would be champion,' Harry replied, wiping his handkerchief over his eyes and face.

'Coming up,' Roo said and joined Craig in the kitchen. 'What's Mr Morgan doing with a dog?'

'He said he found it running about along the riverside path.' As Craig spoke, he bent down and placed a bowl of water in front of the dog who greedily slurped up the water, droplets spraying everywhere.

'Perhaps he got out and the owner is busy looking for him,' Roo suggested, whilst she switched on the kettle to make a hot chocolate for Harry.

'It's a possibility. While you sort out Mr Morgan's drink, I'll see how he ended up with a dog on a rope.'

'Crikey! The word of the day – rope!' Roo exclaimed.

Craig shot her a look, then rolled his eyes.

Now, perching on the edge of the sofa opposite Harry, Craig took in Harry's face. He looked tired. He hoped it was nothing more than the heat. The little dog following him no doubt hadn't helped. 'Are you OK?' he asked as Harry laid his walking stick down on the floor next to where Barney had settled himself.

'I'll be fine. The heat doesn't agree with me these days,' Harry replied and settled back in the sofa. His gaze focused towards the kitchen area where the dog was drinking water loudly.

'As I was saying, I was unsure what to do. I tried to bend down and give it a stroke or two,' he wheezed loudly. 'I tell you old age is a bugger! Anyway, I managed to get down enough so I could have a look at the dog more closely, but I couldn't see a collar. Not sure what to do, I carried on down the path in the hope I would see someone who owned it. Not a soul! And the little mite just kept following me.

'As I passed the house boats, one of the

residents was out mopping their deck. I called over to him. The bottom line was they knew nothing about the dog and hadn't seen it before. I told him I didn't know what to do with it. He just said he was sorry but couldn't help. I couldn't just let the little fella roam around. With no obvious alternative, I thought it best I take it home with me. Even as I thought this, I wasn't too keen. As good as my Oscar is with your Barney, he wouldn't be overly happy at a dog living with us.'

He stopped talking and took several breaths. Once his breathing was under control, he carried on.

'I was wondering what I should do, when old Fred, who lives on the yellow boat, spied me and came over. Once he understood the pickle I was in he offered me a length of rope to make a collar and lead. It was a bit of a struggle, but we got him tethered up. Fred suggested I have a word with you. He thought you might be able to help.' Harry shook his head in dismay. 'What's the world coming to, eh?'

Craig was tempted to say, *it's gone to the dogs*, but decided it was best not to.

'I'm sorry to trouble you, I know you are a busy man, but without a collar and name tag, I didn't know what to do. I can't have him not only because of Oscar, but I'd never be able to look after him.' Harry sniffed. 'I couldn't just leave him, could I?'

'Of course not.' Craig knew Harry wouldn't hurt a fly yet as good as his intentions would be, the old boy struggled to look after himself.

'He might have a chip,' Roo called from the kitchen area.

Harry looked puzzled. 'Chip?'

'A microchip.' Craig explained how some cats and dogs have them inserted under their skin by a vet. 'The chip gives details of the animal and its owners. If he has one, we'll be able to find out where he lives.'

'Really! Whatever next?' Harry looked suitably taken aback. His gaze strayed to the kitchen and watched the dog sit bolt upright as Roo handed him a bone shaped biscuit.

'I bet his owner must be worried sick. He looks like a terrier type of dog. Good thing I was walking along that stretch of the path. Who knows what might have happened to him.'

Craig smiled. He knew it couldn't have been easy for Harry to keep the dog under control. Harry was not that steady on his pins these days. 'He's a lucky one to be found by someone like you. We'll get him to the vet so they can scan him, see if he has a chip.'

Harry chuckled. 'I'm out of touch with the world. In my days, a collar and tag would be good enough.'

With the little dog at her side, Roo returned with a mug of chocolate. 'Here you are Mr Morgan. I know how much you like our chocolate drink.'

Harry grasped the mug in both hands. A wide grin filled his face. 'You'll make a man very happy one of these days.' He winked at her then sipped at the frothy drink. 'Mmmm delicious.'

Roo looked on as Harry's eyes sparkled.

'Whilst you enjoy your drink, I'll call the local vet, see if they'll scan him and hopefully, find his owner.'

Leaving Harry chatting with Craig, Roo strode over to her desk, the little dog following. Barney watched, then stood and ran over. He bounced down on his front paws, an indication he wanted to play. For a few minutes the two dogs chased each other around the small office.

'He would make a good play mate for Barney,' Harry said, looking over his mug as the dogs raced around the furniture.

A look of horror passed over Craig's face. 'I don't think so, Harry, one dog is enough.' Before anything else could be said, Roo called over.

'Good news. I can take him to the vets for a scan.'

'Let's hope they can find his owner,' Harry said, as a chocolate moustache glistened over his top lip.

'Fingers crossed for some good news.' Roo gathered up the little dog into her arms and slipped-on one of Barney's harnesses. She adjusted the fit, attached the lead, and headed for the door. 'Come on,' she said and with a gentle tug, the little dog followed. Barney ran round in excited circles yapping.

'You're staying here with us,' Craig called out to Barney. The dog stopped in his tracks and at seeing a treat appear from Craig's pocket, he hurried to his side.

'See you all laters,' she called and headed out of the office.

Chapter FOURTEEN

Less than an hour later, Roo returned to the office. For the first time that day, she felt a sense of achievement. It had been a day with no results, but thankfully, she was about to end on a high. Sashaying across the room, she cried out. 'Good news about the dog. His owners have been found. At last, we have a result from a busy but negative day.'

Craig stared at Roo. 'It's not been that bad and Rome wasn't built in a day.'

'Maybe not, but it is always a warm feeling when you solve a mystery, even if we didn't know we had one at the time.' She laughed.

Craig frowned and ran his fingers through his mop of copper hair and realised this was becoming a habit.

Barney didn't waste time greeting Roo. His tail wagged excitedly as he hurried to her.

'Cupboard love, Barney, cupboard love,' Roo pulled out a biscuit from her top drawer and handed it over to him. 'And spoilt, too.'

Back at her desk she turned her attention back to Craig. 'The lovely little dog is called Toby and the owners are on their way to the vets to collect him. Thankfully he had a chip which made it simple to trace his owners. It's a pity because I would have loved to have kept him.' Roo sighed.

Craig rolled his eyes. 'What would you do with a dog? On the other hand, don't answer because the poor little mite would end up wearing roller skates. I am just glad that the dog and owner will soon be reunited. Anyway, you have a share in Barney.'

'Ha ha! Maybe I should get a couple of pairs for Barney.'

Hearing his name, Barney trotted over and pressed his muzzle on her leg. 'You've had your entry treat,' she reminded him. As if ignoring her words, Barney sat down and placed a front paw on her knee then looked up at her with doleful eyes. 'You are a cunning little monkey.' She opened her top draw and once again pulled out a small biscuit. 'Here you are, Mr Spoilt.'

Barney took the treat and headed back to his bed.

'Did you find out where the dog owners live?' Craig asked.

'It seems they live on the other side of Robinson Glen.' Roo knew Robinson Glen would always stick in her mind after what they had found there eighteen months ago. She didn't want to dwell on that nasty episode.

'They live in Birch Close. Though it's strange he should be wandering around the riverside walk. It must be at least a couple of miles away from Birch Close.'

'Dogs can travel miles if they get out.'

'I guess so. I am just happy he's going home.' Roo reached over to her laptop and although still thinking about Toby, she wanted to try find anything on Holly Westwood. It may not help in their search, but she needed to have a go.

Craig checked his watch and wondered where the day had gone. It had been a crazy day with far too much happening. Yet, Roo was right in one respect, they appeared to have achieved very little despite the workload. He watched as Roo clicked endlessly on her mouse. Her command of the internet amazed him. He wished he could master it, but realised he had no interest.

Roo, with her eyes glued to her screen, scrolled through page after page of information. 'I would never have thought that it would be such a popular name. Do we know how it is spelt?'

'Spelt?'

'Holly. Is it with a y or an ie?'

'I've no idea. What do you hope to achieve by looking Holly up?'

Glancing up at Craig, she said, 'I don't really know to be honest, but I want to have a look. If I could find photos of her, different angles, that would help to recognise the other woman.' Her brow creased as she flicked through the list of names that appeared on the screen. 'It seems there is no one in this area with that name.' She groaned and leaning back she placed her hands behind her head. 'Looking for hen's teeth comes to mind.'

Craig's phone rang out.

'Gardner PI,' he answered and listened. 'No problem, you will find us at the old pigsty on the … I see you know of it. OK.' The call ended.

'More visitors?'

'It's the owners of Toby – Trudi and Michael Wells. It seems they want to come along and say thank you.'

Roo's face lit up. 'That's nice of them, but the thank you should really be to Mr Morgan. He found the dog and brought him to us.'

Craig nodded. 'I agree. For now, let's see how we get on with them and then we can tell them about Mr Morgan.'

Ten minutes later, a red mini pulled up outside the office and an elderly couple with Toby in their arms climbed out of the car.

Barney ran to the door barking excitedly.

Roo sprinted over and taking hold of Barney, opened the door. At the same time, Toby jumped out of his owner's arms and ran towards them.

Barney and Toby touched noses before racing past Roo's legs and chasing each other around the office.

'Goodness, me,' cried Trudi Wells. 'He's never done anything like that before. I am so sorry.'

'Don't worry. He likes our Barney,' Roo said with a broad smile as she ushered Toby's owners into the office.

'Hello,' greeted Craig as the owners approached him.

'Hello and a thank you,' Trudi said, taking in the office. 'It looks a lovely room,' she added, her gaze taking in the modern furnishing. 'Nothing like we expected.'

Trudi's husband cleared his throat. 'Yes, very nice,' he said as he placed a hand on is wife's arm. 'We felt it important to come and see you to say thank you for finding our little man.'

'Come and sit down,' Craig steered Michael and Trudi towards the sofas. The two dogs played tug of war with Barney's blanket.

'Can we offer you a drink?'

'No, thank you. We just wanted to say a very big thank you for getting our little man reunited with us.' As Michael spoke, he squeezed his wife's hand. 'He's very special.'

Craig could see Trudi had been crying and tears were pooling again in her eyes. As if seeing him studying her, she said. 'Forgive me, it was such a shock him going missing like he did. We thought we might never see him again.'

'Did he jump the fence or did someone leave the gate open?' Roo ventured, standing at the side of the sofa.

Michael shook his head. 'No. We believe he was stolen.'

'Stolen!' Craig repeated.

'He was in the garden yesterday evening and when we went to call him in, he wasn't there.'

'Maybe he saw another dog and managed to get out,' Roo said.

'We thought that at first, but there is no way he could have gotten out. It's not like him to even try to get out,' added Trudi, dabbing at her eyes.

'We called him, but to no avail,' Michael said. 'I went out to look for him, though where he could be we had no idea. I trudged round the area calling out his name, nothing!

'I spoke to a few neighbours who were in

their gardens, but no one had seen him.

'Needless to say, we were worried sick thinking the worst that he might have got onto the road and been killed. It was getting dark and with a heavy heart I went home. Trudi was in bits.' He turned to his wife. 'Weren't you love?' He squeezed her hand.

'Heartbroken, we didn't know what to do. In the end we called the police, but there was nothing much they could do in particular, as by now it was dark. They were kind and said they understood our concern and told us they would keep an eye out for him.' He stopped for a moment and sniffed as if to hide his own emotions.

'We didn't sleep a wink and at first light I was back out again.'

He shook his head. 'Thankfully we have him back.' His eyes filled with tears as he looked over to where both dogs were still playing with Barney's blanket.

'Mr Gardner,' Trudi said, 'we can't thank you enough for bringing him back to us.'

'To be honest, Roo took him to the vets to see if he had a chip, but it had been Mr Morgan who found him wandering along the riverside walk.'

Trudi and Michael looked at each other. 'Thank goodness we had the chip put in when he was a puppy. It probably saved his life,' Michael said.

A silence hung in the air for several seconds. Roo eventually broke the peace. 'If you would like to meet Mr Morgan, I could take you to his home?'

'Oh, my goodness, so many good people,' Trudi burst out. 'Yes please.' As she spoke, she rose to her feet. 'That is, if it isn't no trouble.'

'No trouble at all,' Roo said. 'Mr Morgan, I know will be more than pleased to see you.'

Chapter FIFTEEN

Craig arrived early in the office. He had a headache and the thought of the peace at being alone before Roo arrived, would help him to take stock of the events of yesterday. He couldn't remember when a day had been so chaotic. It seemed to be one thing after another: a dog brought in by Harry Morgan that appeared to be lost; a weird looking model that was purported to be a submarine had been found in the river under the wooden footbridge; a middle-aged woman, who had been adopted nearly six decades ago, had allegedly been seen in the area according to the woman who had given birth to her. On top of all this there was the petty vandalism going on at the church.

With all of these shenanigans, it was hard to believe they lived in a low crime part of the country. Yet all that had paled with the shocking discovery of a body hanging from the rafters in St Julian's church. He sighed and gently rubbed his temples; he needed a coffee.

As Craig switched on the coffee machine, he was consciously aware his headache was self-inflicted. If only he could muster the will power to say no to Juan and Louis's *complimentary* after-dinner brandy, he knew he wouldn't be suffering. At what had now become a weekly event, he and Ella had dined at the Spanish restaurant the previous evening. The owners insisted on the brandy; it was offered to special customers. Despite telling himself every week he must say 'No', he always weakened and ended up downing a large brandy. These days it didn't sit well with him. He sighed and vowed he must try harder at saying no!

Picking up his mug, he breathed in the aroma of the rich coffee and as welcoming as it was, he was unsure it would be enough to reduce the pain he suffered. With the need to get his head thinking straight, he reached up to a narrow cupboard and pulled out a packet of paracetamol. Pushing two from the foil packaging he popped them into his mouth and swallowed hard. He just hoped they worked and quick. With the painkillers back in the cupboard and his mug in his hand, he headed to his desk. Believing he had at least thirty minutes to gather himself before Roo arrived, his peace was shattered by the ringing out of his phone.

'Go away,' he mumbled and at the same time hit the answer button.

'Good morning, Copper,' Pete's chirpy voice trilled through the tiny speaker which sounded akin to a loud hailer to Craig's ears.

'Morning Pete,' he managed in a flat voice.

'Don't tell me, you didn't say no again!' Pete sniggered down the line. 'When are you going to learn?'

He didn't need snide remarks at this time of the morning, but couldn't help a sharp retort,

'Probably the same time as you retire.'

'Very funny.'

'So, what has you disturbing the peace at this time of the day?'

'As you well know, we police officers don't sleep, especially when we have a dead body on our doorstep.'

Craig heard Pete chuckle. Whatever his old colleague was taking, he'd have some of it this morning.

'I don't want to ask what's got you all chirpy this morning, but whatever it is enjoy it.'

'And you're the one telling me to retire and have a life like yours,' Pete batted back.

'OK you win. What can I do for you as I guess that is why you are ringing?'

'You cynic. For a change, I'm talking to you so to impart a little information about the body found hanging in the church, but if you are feeling too delicate, I can leave it for later.'

Craig heard Pete laugh. It was clear he'd forgotten the times he was hungover from nights out with so called informants. Not wanting to prolong the agony, 'I'm all ears,' he finally said.

'I can tell you it wasn't suicide.'

Craig sat up, suddenly alert and wished he hadn't as the throbbing in his head protested. 'What makes you believe that?'

'A number of things, but importantly the rope marks. We are looking at a suspicious death.'

'Murder?'

'At this stage we can't say. It's early days, but why would someone choose a church for a hanging?'

Craig thought about the question and couldn't help wonder if the vandalism of late had something to do with it. Was it connected or a coincidence?

'Are you able to tell me anything about the body?'

'It's a white male, likely late teens. What is odd though, there was no phone on him or anything that might help ID him. Assuming the age we think he is, I thought millenniums had their phone surgically inserted into their hands!'

Craig chuckled, his sense of humour slowly returning. 'I've yet to see one who isn't glued to a phone and knowing how Roo uses hers it's like it is the only source of life outside her body.'

'Uniforms have scoured the church and the church yard along with the streets that are close by – nothing found.'

'Mmmm. I'm assuming you've not been able to identify him?'

'No and no one has come forward saying they've a member of their family missing. Hopefully the local news bulletin that was put out and social media will help.'

Craig nodded to himself. Although he didn't use social media, he knew the power it could evoke.

'Maybe he's not local?' Craig said, wondering how a young person could be found dead and not missed. He didn't share this thought. 'As you know there's been petty vandalism at the church and its grounds, hence why the vicar came to see us yesterday.' Was it only yesterday? He thought. Then added, 'But petty behaviour is not about someone being strung up from the church rafters.'

'I agree. We've spoken to the vicar and he told us more or less what he told you about what's been going on there. He's in shock. It's not the sort of thing that normally happens in a church, well at least not around here. Of course, death is part of church life with funerals, but finding a body, and hanging no less, is a trauma for most people.

'We've also had a word with Mr Boxhall,' Pete continued. 'Sadly, he's told us nothing more than what we know.' There was a brief pause before Pete carried on. 'Maybe in a few days either or both will remember something.' Another pause. 'It's good the vicar talked to you; it tells me you've gained his trust.'

Craig rolled his eyes and guessed what was to follow. He knew his old colleague like the back of his hand.

'Could you and Roo talk to the vicar again as he just might remember something and is more likely to open up with you?'

Craig quietly snorted. By dangling a nugget of information, Pete knew he would hook him. It had! Though he wasn't too sure he'd get any more information from the vicar than Pete and his team had. None the less, Roo had a knack of gaining information from the most unlikely. There were times he wondered if his young assistant would get blood from a stone!

Instead of admitting he'd been taken in, he said, 'You know how to buy us. Yes, we'll see what we can do, but don't hold your breath.'

'I knew you'd help. Thanks, Copper, I appreciate it. I owe you.'

'As I've said before, the debt is now so big, but coffee at the Butterfly will be on you next time.'

'It's a deal. In the meantime, let me know if you find out anything. So far nothing has been found that might help at this stage. Disappointing to say the least.'

Craig didn't miss the sigh of resignation that echoed down the line. The earlier liveliness in Pete's voice had faded. 'That's not good. Leave it with us.' The call ended and Craig wondered why no phone had been found. If it had been stolen, was it stolen before he was hung or taken after?

Chapter SIXTEEN

With keys dangling from her fingers, Roo stared at Zippy then down at the pair of roller blades held in her other hand. She smiled broadly. The memory of the previous evening flooded back and, for the moment, her dilemma of whether to skate to the office or go in Zippy was forgotten. She'd had a great skate home, though no sooner had she arrived and taken off her skates, then Taylor bounded down the front path.

'Surprise,' he'd called as she pulled open the front door. Before she could utter a word, he took hold of her hands and gently pulled her towards him. He dropped a tender kiss on her lips.

Not letting go of her hands, he'd said in an excited voice, 'Mr Beddingfield said we can use the racing track for an hour before the skating club arrives so I'm dragging you off for more skating.' Before she could protest, he'd ushered her out of the house and into his car.

Two miles out of town was Westleton, originally an airfield used in the Second World by the RAF. Today, a well-known racetrack for motor car and motor bike racing. Last year it held its first cycle race. To Roo's knowledge it had never been used for roller skating, but Taylor's dad knew the owners, the Beddingfield Brothers, Kevin and Stuart, and had persuaded them to allow Barry's skating club to have their annual charity marathon there. And if that hadn't been a triumph, the brothers had offered the club's circuit, depending on what activities they had on, for practise. Barry had been over the moon having tried for several years to be able to use the track.

For an hour before the club members arrived and full of excitement and energy, they had raced each other and despite her own speed, Taylor had managed to pip her at the post every time. Taylor's years at the skate parks had given him confidence and style to be an amazing speed skater. After their second circuit, he had taken her hand.

'Come on PI Roo, we can do this together.'

With the warmth of his hand in hers and ignoring the ever-present butterflies in her tummy, when in the company of Taylor, she had almost flown round the circuit. Gasping and out of breath, they came to a halt and he'd hugged her tight.

'You are amazing,' he'd said as much out of breath as herself. She loved him so much that not a day passed by without her wondering how she had ever lived without him. She was sure they would still have been in their embrace had Barry and several club members not turned up.

So lost in her thoughts, she almost missed her phone ping as a message came through. Still glowing from the memory, and with her hands full, she couldn't pull her phone out of her pocket. 'OK, you win,' she giggled and stepped over to Zippy. Skating to the office yesterday was great fun, but not the most convenient for her work. She unlocked the driver's door, leaned in and dropped her skates into the passenger's footwell. After shuffling into the driver's seat, she pulled out her phone. It was Taylor; her smile widened as she read his message. With nimble fingers she quickly sent one back adding several heart emojis. She sighed with happiness; life was so good.

Needing to get to work, she turned the ignition key and instantly Zippy sprang into life. With her heart filled with love and the thought of another interesting day solving mysteries, Roo reversed Zippy out of the drive. She was about to drive forward when Mrs Palmer, with her little dog, stopped and waved at her.

'Good morning, young Roo. You look happy. It must be that lovely young man I've seen you with.'

'Hello Mrs Palmer, I think so,' she replied. 'Nice to see you, but I'd better get going or I'll be late. Have a fab day,' she called and nudged Zippy forward. In her rear mirror she saw Mrs Palmer watching her drive away. For as long as she could remember, Mrs Palmer always smiled. Her old, wrinkled face lit up for everyone. Maybe she had much to be happy about and maybe Mr Palmer was once like her Taylor and that's what kept her smiling. She hoped she would still be smiling when she was old.

Chapter SEVENTEEN

'Good morning, Roo,' Craig called, getting to his feet. 'Don't sit down, we are going out.' Then wished he hadn't got up so quickly as it jarred the pain in his head.

'Morning, boss,' Roo said, stopping in her tracks. 'What's happened?'

'Nothing other than we are off to have a chat with the vicar and his wife. I've had a good chat with DI Andrews this morning and…'

'Do they know who the body belongs to and was it murder?' Roo burst out.

'Hold your horses. And no to your first question and, as far as murder, it seems at this stage it is indeed a suspicious death.'

'Oh, my words, we have a suspicious death on our patch. You don't think the vicar did it, do you?'

Craig rolled his eyes. 'You have a vivid imagination, Roo Chattaway, but no. Come let's get Barney hooked up and then I'll explain what DI Andrews had to say.'

Within moments, the three headed towards Chestnut Lane and as Barney sniffed at everything in his reach, Craig relayed what Pete had told him. 'He believes the vicar and his wife will open up more to us, even more so as you seem to have got on well with Mrs Howard. Of course, there is a chance he won't know anything more than he's told the police, but it's worth trying.' He looked at Roo and smiled. 'They are expecting us.'

'Good morning,' Heather Howard said as she opened the door to Craig and Roo. 'How lovely you have brought Barney.' She bent down to stroke him. 'I think it will help to keep the atmosphere calm.' Turning her attention back to her visitors, added, 'Please come on through.'

Craig and Roo with Barney close at heel followed Heather out onto the patio. As they stepped into the sunny garden, they found themselves gazing onto a large round wrought iron table laden with four mugs, sugar bowl and milk jug along with a large, creamy Victorian sponge that filled a round plate. Added to this was a pile of biscuits on a separate plate. Craig stifled a deep sigh. It was the last thing he needed to be staring at after last night. They were here to talk about a suspicious death not to enjoy a tea party, though, maybe for the vicar and his wife, food was a comfort in times of stress.

'Thank you so much for coming,' Nick jumped to his feet and reached out his hand to Craig then Roo.'

'Please sit down and do help yourself to tea and cut yourself a slice of the cake, homemade of course. Heather loves to make everyone feel welcome,' Nick said, as if he needed to talk and fill in any gaps in conversation. He remained standing until Craig and Roo were seated. Reaching down, Roo unclipped Barney from his lead. Instantly he headed for the bowl of water that had been placed near the French doors.

Clasping a large teapot, Heather strode over to the table and placed the China pot, decorated with pretty pink flowers, in the middle of the table. Turning to her husband, she laid a hand on his shoulder. Her face a picture of deep concern.

'It's been such a shock and Nick is very troubled at what has happened. As the vicar of the church, he feels responsible.'

Nick looked up at his wife. 'Thank you,' he said, dark circles evident under his eyes that had not been there when he'd visited their office. Heather sat next to him.

Craig didn't miss the strain on Nick's face. 'You can hardly blame yourself.'

'If only I had noticed what was happening earlier, things might not have escalated to a death.'

'But you had no suspicion that petty vandalism would lead to such tragic circumstance.'

Nick's face remained strained.

'Do you have any idea who the young man might be?' Craig asked, trying to ignore Heather slicing into the cake.

Nick shook his head. 'The police asked the same question yesterday. As I told you, it was Mr Boxhall who found the body and he told me he didn't see the face. He said the same to the police.'

With a mug of tea in front of him, Craig stared into the milky liquid and wondered why

Pete thought he would find out more than he had.

Barney muzzled Heather's leg. She turned and stroked him. 'Can I give him a biscuit?'

Craig smiled, 'Only one. He's spoilt enough.'

Whilst Barney snaffled the biscuit from Heather, Roo suddenly burst out, 'It was a strange day yesterday.'

For a moment there was a hush, then Nick piped up. 'I'll second that.' He rubbed a hand over his tired face and before more could be said, Roo continued.

'Did you know a model whale submarine was found in the river and a dog that had gone missing was found and, I found a beautiful chain. It seemed it was a day for things going missing.'

Craig glared at Roo. His face creased in a frown and wondered what had got into her, but before he could utter his thoughts, Nick turned to Roo, an animated expression lightening his strained features. 'What kind of chain?'

'The kind you wear around your neck.' As she spoke, she pulled her phone out of her pocket and flicked to the photo album. 'You can see it here.' She handed over her phone. 'I am sure someone must be missing it.'

Craig looked on bewildered.

'Goodness,' Nick gasped, his eyes taking in the details. He took a deep breath and handed the phone back to Roo. 'Remarkable. I didn't see the body, but I did see the left arm hanging out of the covering. On the wrist was a chain not dissimilar to the one in the photo.' He pointed to

Roo's phone as he spoke.

Craig stared at Roo than at Nick, rousing himself, he asked, 'Are you sure?'

Nick nodded. 'There was definitely a chain on the wrist. Of course, I can't be absolutely certain it is the same style as the one Roo found, but from memory, it looks very similar.'

'I have the chain at the office,' Craig said, 'perhaps you would take a look.'

As if animated by this sudden find, Nick added, 'I'd very much like to see it. I can walk back with you. It would save time especially if there is a chance of a connection. The walk would do me good too.'

'Yes, of course. Anything that might give us a clue to the identity of the body,' Craig said and felt a surge of energy at this unexpected development. Roo's sudden ramblings had been very useful and he wondered what else Nick might remember.

'Is there anything else you can recall that has happened over the last few weeks which springs to mind?' He realised it was a long shot.

Steepling his fingers, Nick held the tips against his chin as if to concentrate on the question. He shook his head. 'No. I'm sorry, I can't think of anything. Yet there must be something.' He placed his hands back on the table. 'I'm sorry.'

'Never mind, darling,' Heather said in a low voice and placed her hand over her husband's. 'It is just a pity we didn't know about the CCTV camera before as I'm sure it would have helped.' Nick and Heather looked at each other.

‘I know,’ Nick said.

‘We can still look at a camera when you feel up to it,’ Roo added. ‘I have all the details when you are ready.’

‘Thank you. I think it will be useful,’ Nick said. ‘You have both been very kind. For now, let me join you back to your office and I can take a look at the chain.’

Chapter EIGHTEEN

Nick confirmed the chain found by Roo was close to the one he had seen on the body.

'I can't be one hundred percent certain, but there is a similarity; the links look very similar in size and there is a sheen to it like the one on the body's wrist.'

Craig thanked Nick and as soon as he'd left the office, he was on the phone to Pete.

'I think we might have something that might be of interest. The vicar has remembered something.'

'He has?'

'He recalls seeing a chain on the wrist of the body. What makes this particularly interesting is that earlier Roo found a chain in the undergrowth along riverside walk. Now having shown it to the vicar, he seems to think it is not unlike the one he saw on the body.' Craig didn't miss an intake of breath from his ex-colleague. He smiled that they might have uncovered something useful.

'Sounds intriguing,' Pete said, a hint of excitement in his voice. 'Let's meet at the Butterfly and you can bring the chain Roo found.'

Craig sighed. If they carried on drinking coffee at Steve's, they would soon be taking up residence at the café. Yet despite this thinking, he was aware, Pete liked to keep their meetings away from the station. The station's politics added another layer of stress and wherever possible Craig went out of his way to avoid getting caught up in them. His days were over in being embroiled in all of that carry on.

~~~

Craig sat opposite Pete, a mug of coffee at his elbow and explained further on the revelation from the vicar. 'It was Roo who mentioned the chain she had found. And Roo being Roo, she had a photo of her find. The vicar was transfixed as he took in the image.' Craig pushed his hand into his pocket and pulled out the chain.

'This is it.' He dangled the chain in front of Pete before placing it on the table.

'I was going to drop it into the station the next time I was passing, but in light of what the vicar noticed, it's good you have it.'

'Thanks, appreciated,' Pete said. Then carefully picked up the chain. 'Forensics will have bagged anything found on the body along with the clothes.'

Craig watched as his old colleague examined Roo's find, turning it over several times. Leaving the DI to inspect the spoils, Craig looked around the little café. To his surprise it was quiet. Unusual, he thought, he'd never known it anything but busy. It must be a fickle business and probably not unlike his own work, famine or feast, he pondered.

'Looks expensive,' Pete's words sliced into Craig's thoughts bringing him back to the reason why they were sitting in the café.
~~~

'A few days ago, we had a couple from Elderfarm Brooks report a burglary. There were a few pieces of jewellery taken and from the photos we were given I would hazard a guess that this could be one of them. I'll check to see what else was taken.'

'Elderfarm Brooks,' Craig repeated. 'I believe that's mainly bungalows and quite expensive ones.' He remembered the development being built. Although it had never been advertised for the elderly, it had attracted many there. It was a desirable area to live.

'That's the place. It's not an area that comes up on our radar often. A nice part of the town.'

'Hopefully no one was hurt?' Craig said, knowing how mean burglars could be.

Pete shook his head, 'Thankfully not. The odd thing is the place wasn't trashed and there was little damage. The thief had got in through a bathroom window. That in itself is strange because they are not that large. At the time, the couple had been out grocery shopping at Marks and Spencer.'

'So how did an expensive chain end up in the undergrowth on the riverside path?' Craig said.

'And equally as important, how did another chain, similar, end up on a body hanging from the church rafters?' Pete added.

Both men looked at each other as if the answer could be found in the other's face. As if breaking the spell, Pete looked down at his coffee mug. It was empty. 'Another one?'

Craig shook his head. 'As much as I want to say yes, I need to cut down. All this caffeine gets the old ticker going.'

'Tell me about it,' Pete smirked and at the same time popped the chain into a small plastic bag before slipping it into his pocket. 'In the meantime, I'll get someone to contact the couple and ask them to have a look at it.'

'If it is, it's a bittersweet find if the one on the dead body is connected to this robbery.'

Pete agreed. 'The big question is, who is the poor soul found hanging and is he the thief or someone wearing stolen goods?'

Craig nodded as he took in what Pete suggested.

'Everything alright here, gentlemen,' Steve asked, appearing at the table. 'Refill?'

Craig was about to say no when Pete piped up, 'Go on then.'

'Right, coming up.' Steve smiled and nodded over at Karen, 'Two more for these gents.' Turning back to Craig and Pete, 'I'd best leave you to solve more crimes, though I don't know why you don't move your HQ here, it's far more pleasant.' Steve grinned.

'I'd be the size of a barn door if we did with those *death by chocolate* cakes Karen makes and your big breakfasts.' The three chuckled. From the other side of the counter, Karen smiled at them.

With the second coffees drank, Pete headed to the door. 'I'd better get back. Let me know if you come up with anything else and I'll do the same,' he said as Craig followed him. As

Pete opened the door, both men turned and called out, 'Thanks and we'll seen you soon.'

A cheery goodbye was called from Steve and Karen.

Standing outside, Pete looked to Craig. 'Thanks again for finding out about the chain. I knew if you and Roo went along to talk to the vicar, he would likely remember something.' He tapped his pocket. 'I'll contact you once I know if it's related to the robbery.'

'Great. That will be good, and despite how we both work, we still sing from the same hymn sheet,' Craig said, knowing how at times he missed working with Pete, though he didn't miss being a DI. He slapped his old colleague on the shoulder, 'Talk soon.'

Chapter NINETEEN

Roo sat at her desk and, with Barney curled up at her feet she mulled over the conversations they'd had with the vicar and his wife. All thoughts of Taylor and their skating at the race circuit were temporarily forgotten. Right now, all she could think about was what an amazing coincidence that the chain she had found was similar to the one on the dead body. How could that be and was there a connection? If so, what was it? Had both chains belonged to the same person? Her head reeled with questions.

Getting to her feet, Barney jumped up instantly. 'Sorry little man, I didn't mean to disturb you.' Undaunted, Barney stood staring at Roo and wagging his tail. Negotiating around him, Roo headed to the kitchen; she needed a drink. Barney followed.

She stared at the coffee machine and frowned; she really didn't fancy a coffee. It was a hot day and the office was stuffy.

With a glass of water in her hand, and Barney closer than her shadow, she walked back to her desk. As she sat down, Barney placed his paw on her leg. 'What do you want?' she asked as if Barney would burst into conversation and explain.

'OK, I get it,' she opened her drawer and pulled out a doggy treat.

Instantly, Barney sat bolt upright. 'So, this is what you want.' She offered the treat to him and with gentleness he took it. With his treat safely between his jaws, he settled down. Roo listened to the crunching.

Watching a contented Barney, the scene reminded her of the little dog, Toby. Mr Morgan's face had lit up like a beacon when Toby and his owners had visited him. As soon as Mr Morgan had sat down in his armchair, Toby had leapt onto his knee and nestled himself there as if he belonged with the old man. Poor Oscar had made a hasty retreat into the kitchen and out through his cat flap. Mrs Wells had wept with joy as she thanked Mr Morgan for finding her dog. It was an emotional moment and a happy end to what had been a crazy day.

Bringing her mind back to the chain, she hoped Craig would come back with more information from DI Andrews. Unable to go any further with the chain mystery, she turned her attention to their new client, Mrs Everett and her missing daughter.

Roo reread Craig's notes and frowned. There wasn't a great deal to work with, just a photograph and a sad story. She couldn't imagine what it must be like to have a baby and then have to give it away. She just hoped Mrs Everett was right in what she had seen and that the look-alike stranger was her lost daughter.

With the photograph at her side, Roo decided to try social media again. She signed into Facebook and entered Holly Westwood into the search box. Within seconds a list appeared.

She scrolled down the list, checking the photo against the ones on screen. Nothing! She tried again with a different spelling. Still nothing that resembled the woman on the photo. Leaving Facebook, she looked on Twitter. Nothing resembled the Holly Westwood they were looking for no matter how she spelt the name. She checked a couple of other sites and still drew a blank. Finally, she signed into Instagram, another blank.

Sitting back in her chair, she let out a long, exasperated breath and admitted defeat in assuming she would find Holly Westwood on social media. Maybe it was a harebrained idea after all.

As a distraction, she signed back into Facebook and went through the latest updates from her friends. There were several photos on the Skating Club's page from the previous night's practice. Amongst the collection was one of her and Taylor. Roo smiled at how gorgeous he looked. Feeling the now familiar butterflies flutter in her tummy, she downloaded a copy to her phone. It was then she had a light bulb moment.

Moving her mouse across the screen, she clicked on the search button and keyed in Rosehill Gardens. To her surprise there was a page for Rosehill Gardens Community. Several photos of local gardens and one of a street party had been added to the page. She clicked on members, but it wouldn't let her see the list. That was disappointing, she thought, then made a new search.

This time, Castleton Green and found a running club with that name. Again, there were many photos of various age groups running and was surprised to read that they had their own 10k race each summer. The list of friends was many and this time she was able to see who had friended the group.

Despite scrolling through the list twice, there was no Holly Westwood, but there was a Ben Westwood. His photo showed a man who could be early sixties; whatever his age, he looked fit. Was he Holly's husband? She scrolled through more of the pictures that had been added in the hope to see him. There were none. Disappointed, she realised it was a gamble, but acknowledged that was how they often found things out. She signed out of Facebook and went into Instagram on her phone. This time she searched for Castle Green Runners.

'Yes!' she cried out, seeing the same group. Once again, she scanned several photos; a number included Ben Westwood. She looked to see if Ben had his own account and he did. Roo punched the air. She checked who followed him. To her dismay no one stood out that could be the long-lost daughter of Mrs Everett or even Holly Westwood. She threw her arms in the air. 'I give in,' she said.

Looking over at Barney, she decided even if he didn't need a walk she did.

'Come on little man,' she called, pushing her chair back. Plucking his harness and lead from the coat rack she slipped it on.

Chapter TWENTY

Leaving Barney to rummage amongst the foliage, Roo tried to marshal her thoughts. Not for the first time in the last couple of days she thought how bizarre things were at the moment. She kicked a small stone into the river, then looking ahead, her heart sank.

As if things weren't crazy enough, walking towards her was Mr Jacobs from Grange Road. She grimaced as his tall frame strode towards her. There was something very unpleasant about him and she was convinced he enjoyed being mean. His eyes had a piercing glow that appeared to bore through you. Despite it being a warm sunny day, she could see he was dressed as if it was still winter with his flat cap, dark corduroy trousers and a black padded jacket. He looked sinister. And, like the other times she'd had the misfortune to cross paths, he always made her feel uncomfortable. Resigned that there was no way she could avoid him, Roo took a deep breath and reminded herself to remain calm.

'Come on Barney,' she called and behind her back crossed her fingers in the hope Jacobs would walk past without a comment.

'I hope you are doing something useful,' Jacobs snapped as he approached Roo. 'There is little doubt the area is turning into a den of iniquity. The boys in blue ignore my calls about the riff raff that collect along here and particularly under the bridge.' He sneered and pointed towards the wooden footbridge. After glaring at it for several seconds, he turned back to Roo.

She wondered what she had done to deserve such an onslaught of the local area's issues as if, single handed, she was supposed to sort them. She thought of her hero, Poirot and could imagine him walking past Jacobs with a haughty glare, his walking cane flicking just close enough to miss him. She smiled at the imaginary scene.

'Nice that you can find something to smile about,' Jacobs commented, taking in her happy countenance.

'Hello, Mr Jacobs,' she finally said, keeping her voice even and a pleasant smile on her face. She knew this was the best way to deal with the miserable old goat.

Ignoring Roo's greeting, Jacobs continued, 'From time to time, I come along and give them boys a piece of my mind, but all I get is foul language hurled at me. The place is going to the dogs, but rest assured I will continue to make a nuisance of myself in order to get things done. Those louts will be sorry.'

Roo stared at Jacobs and wondered what he meant by that. She knew he could be a nasty piece of work. Last year there had been an incident that had ended in a man being found dead in Robinson Glen. Whilst nothing could be proven that Jacobs had anything to do with what happened, everyone believed he had far more to do with it than he told the police. Roo wondered to what lengths he would go to sort out what he called, *riff raff*.

Not wanting to linger longer than necessary, she simply said, 'I'm walking Barney, he needs his regular exercise.'

Jacobs looked round for the dog and saw him sniffing intently at a large shrub. 'No doubt you've heard about the body hanging in the church?'

Taken aback at his words, Roo stared up at him.

He sniggered. 'It's no good looking surprised; it's the talk of the neighbourhood. But I bet you don't know who was dangling there?'

'Do you?' Roo found herself saying before she could bite back the words.

'You're the one that's supposed to have your finger on the pulse on what's going on around here, young lady. So, in my book, you should be telling me.'

'We are dealing with several cases and the police are dealing with the incident at the church,' she said, feeling pleased she had remained calm and not let Jacobs intimidate her.

'Incident,' he scoffed. 'You call swinging from a rope an incident?'

Roo felt her face flush and was annoyed with herself for reacting so obviously. 'Barney, come here,' she called in an attempt to disguise her annoyance. She was starkly aware that Jacobs was playing a game in order to gain information by bluffing about who the victim was.

'As I said, the police are dealing with it.' Roo

clipped Barney's lead on to his harness and turned to walk away.

'Before you walk away, another thing. What about that idiotic fish thing those young layabouts where messing with the other day?'

Roo stopped and turned, what was he up to now? 'You mean the punk submarine?'

'So, you do know what's going on,' he laughed, but it was a sardonic sound.

'What do you know about it?' she asked.

'Well, I can tell you this and that one of those hooligans messing around with that fish or whatever it is, was with the one swinging from the rafters in the church.'

Roo drew in a sharp breath.

'How do you know this?'

Smirking, he said, 'Let's say, I keep my ear to the ground. Someone has to around here.'

'Yes, but....'

'When I say it was one of the hooligans, I am making an assumption. They had a coil of rope that they dragged that fish thingy about with.'

Assumption, Roo thought and was tempted to scoff loudly. She realised Jacobs was playing one of his nasty games or worse that he had something to do with the incident. She needed to get away and call Craig but before that she needed to hear just how much he really knew.

'Do you know his name?'

Jacobs appeared to think about it and after several seconds spoke. 'No, but I do know that at least two of the thugs live in Cavendish Road.'

That was not the answer to her question,

but it had helped as they had no idea where any of the boys lived.

'Do you know which of them live in Cavendish Road?'

Jacobs appeared to ponder over the question. Then with a haughty manner replied. 'Difficult to say, it is something I thought I'd heard.'

Although Jacobs didn't seem to know as much as he purported to, this snippet of information could be useful. She mentally filed it away and asked another question.

'How many are there in the group?'

Jacobs sucked in his cheeks and glared at her. 'It depends on what they are up to. Sometimes four other times as many as seven.' He smirked. 'I can do better than that.' He pushed his hands into his pocket and pulled out a mobile phone. 'I've taken a few snaps of them a couple of days ago. Of course, they didn't know I was doing it. I took them for insurance purposes. You never know when you might need to recall something.' He handed the phone to Roo.

Surprised Jacobs had passed his phone to her, she took it carefully and flicked through the photos. They were a total of four, though not all that clear, but enough to give an idea. 'Can you point out who if any of these live in Cavendish Road?'

'Not really,' he said and put out his hand for his phone to be returned.

'Please can I have a copy of these?'

Jacobs took hold of the phone and for the

first time since she had come across him over eighteen months ago, he looked sheepish. 'How do I do that?'

Roo explained what needed to be done.

'If you say so, but I'm none the wiser.'

'Would you like me to do it for you?'

Jacobs considered this. 'As long as it doesn't infringe my privacy?' He handed the phone back to Roo.

To ensure she did not share her mobile phone number with Jacobs she sent the photos to the office email address. As she tapped away, she showed Jacobs what she was doing. He looked suitably perplexed.

Handing the phone back, 'Thank you, Mr Jacobs, this could be very useful.'

He smiled as he took the phone and slipped it into his pocket.

Roo had never seen him smile and wondered why he was being so helpful. Tempted as she was to say something, she decided it was best to remain silent. 'Thanks again, Mr Jacobs. I will let you know if anything comes of the information you have given.'

'You'll learn young lady, that life isn't all about smiles and being kind, it's about making sure the riff raff doesn't take over.' He nodded his head before adding, 'I'll bid you a good day,' and before Roo could open her mouth to speak, he set off at a brisk pace leaving Roo and Barney standing.

As soon as Roo was out of ear shot of Jacobs, she called Craig and told him everything she'd learnt.

Chapter TWENTY-ONE

Craig was mulling over the conversation he'd had with Pete when his phone rang. It was Roo. He slowed his pace as he listened; a frown creased his face. 'Thanks, Roo, that is useful.' He ended the call. 'What was Jacobs up to now?' he muttered with annoyance. He didn't like the man and couldn't think of anyone he'd come into contact with who did. There was no doubt in his mind that the man was a nasty piece of work, yet when anything happened in the area, he had the knack of being around and always with something scathing to say. He scoffed derisively. If he wanted to play games, he would play too. He tapped Pete's number and was relieved when he answered after two rings.

'What have you lost, Copper?' Pete teased.

'Marbles!' he replied without humour, though of late he was beginning to think he might well have. Despite this, he smiled at the use of his old nickname. 'Seriously, our nemesis in the name of Jacobs, just implied to Roo he knows who the young man found hanging in the church is likely to be.'

'What!' he shouted. 'Hell's teeth! I'll get the boys round and we'll have him down here at the nick to find out just what he *really* does knows.'

Craig pictured the smile that would be on Pete's face at the thought of having Jacobs brought in.

'I'm sure he knows nothing, but for once let's give him a little of what he gives us… the runaround!'

Pete remained silent then burst out. 'No, no. Change of plan. Meet me at the end of Grange Road and we'll go together to see *Mr* Jacobs. Let's see what he has to say to *us*.'

'It will be a pleasure to see the look on the nosey sod's face when he opens the door and is confronted with the two of us,' Craig said, then heard a snort of derision from Pete before ending the call.

Twenty minutes later, DI Andrews with Craig stood on the doorstep at number five, Grange Road. Pete pressed his finger on the doorbell.

Both men waited.

No response.

Pete turned to Craig, 'He's either ignoring us or he's out.' This time he held his index finger on the button for several seconds and at the same time, with his other hand, knocked heavily on the door.

Still no response.

Pete raised his eyebrow, disappointment etched on his face as he removed his finger from the doorbell.

'We'll return,' he said.

With a shrug, both men turned and walked down the short path. No sooner had Craig placed his hand on the gate when they came face to face with Jacobs.

With full carrier bags hanging from each

arm, Jacobs blocked their path. His face a picture of thunder. 'Pity you don't appear when I call you lot about the antics that go on around here, yet when I'm minding my own business, you turn up, uninvited!'

'Mr Jacobs,' DI Andrews addressed him politely and at the same time looked him straight in the eye. 'We believe you have information that might be of assistance in our enquiries regarding the body found in the church.'

Jacobs glared at Andrews and then at Craig; a muscle twitched in his right cheek. 'That girl has a vivid imagination,' he spat. 'What's she been saying now?'

'Please may we go inside so we can talk and ask a few questions?'

Jacobs stepped forward and, without a word, pushed his way between Craig and Andrews. 'I've nothing to say, but it would help maintain my equilibrium if you kept a close eye on the oiks that gather under the footbridge. Don't forget, we taxpayers pay your wages.' The corner of his top lip curled with smugness.

Craig didn't miss Pete grind his teeth, a sign that he was well agitated.

'OK, Mr Jacobs if you feel you can't help, then you leave me no alternative. I will now call the station and have a couple of uniformed officers escort you to Markham Road police station where we can officially ask you questions.'

About to slip his key into the door lock, Jacobs swung round. The earlier look of smugness had turned his curled lip into a snarl.

'You think you've the upper hand because you have a warrant card. An intimidation card more like, but we will see! I have done nothing wrong yet here you are on my doorstep harassing me.' He looked from one to the other. 'You can rest assured, Inspector, I will be making an official complaint in the strongest of terms to your superiors.'

Tapping his index finger over his lips, DI Andrews ignored the outburst, then moving his hand to his side, calmly said, 'We have a suspicious death of a young man and we believe you have information that could help identify him and even offer help into what might have happened.'

Jacobs put down his two carrier bags, then placed one hand on the door handle. He remained silent as he glared at the detective and private investigator. Anger flashed in his eyes that could have cut the two men in half had it been a laser beam. Remaining silent, he then pushed his door open and grabbed his bags.

Pete nodded to Craig, both men turned and with heavy footsteps headed back down the path.

'I'll have him down the nick before he can put his shopping on the table,' Pete hissed. He pulled out his phone and called the station.

A loud bang told the two men, Jacobs had slammed his door shut.

Chapter TWENTY-TWO

Unsettled at the outcome with Jacobs, Craig left Pete and headed back to his office. Whether any information would be gleaned from Jacobs he was unsure and as to why Jacobs wanted to wind everyone up, he had no idea and like previous occasions, he always seemed to be around when there was a serious incident in the area. He sighed heavily. He should be resigned to having to deal with people like Jacobs, and of course, he was, but it just never got any easier. Despite Jacobs being an irritant, he hoped, though he wouldn't hold his breath, that there might be a nugget of information they could use from him. Pete had promised he would get in touch if there were any developments. It was a sorry affair when you had a death in the area especially when it was a young person. What baffled him was why in a church?

With his mind trying to analyse the events of late and his foot fall brisk, he didn't hear his name being called.

'Mr Gardner,' a gentle voice called.

The caller called out again, this time louder.

Hearing his name, Craig slowed and at the same time felt a soft tap on his arm.

'Mr Gardner.'

Startled, Craig swung round and came face to face with an elderly woman with silver grey hair cut into a bob. A broad smile greeted him.

'My apologies, I didn't intend to alarm you. I did call out, but you didn't appear to hear me.'

Craig returned a smile. 'Sorry, I was miles away.'

'I'm not surprised with what's happened. It's all rather disturbing and sad, and in a church of all places.'

It seemed the death at the church was top news in the area. 'What can I do for you?' he asked, hoping not to sound snappy.

'Mr Gardner, my name is Mrs Gilly Peach. I know you are a private investigator,' she beamed as she spoke the last two words. 'We all know how marvellous you and your young assistant were at dealing with Peggy and Molly's dreadful situation. You are their heroes!' Her smiled broadened further at this statement. 'So, knowing how you help with our local problems, I assume you are involved with the terrible happening at the church.'

'Well, yes, but…'

'Of course, you are. I simply can't believe who it is.' She shook her head to convey her shock.

'You know who it is?' Craig tried to keep the surprise out of his voice but was sure it had risen an octave. What was it with everyone suggesting they know who it is, yet no one has come forward with information. How could she know and the police didn't?

This time Gilly Peach nodded. 'I do believe it could be Flyn Ford's grandson. The boy lives with him. Though of late he appears to have gone off the rails. His poor grandfather is far from well and has a touch of dementia and has no control over him. He's a little wild, Charlie that is. What an awful tragedy.'

'How do you know it's Flyn Ford's grandson?'

Gilly Peach looked him in the eye. 'It's obvious. Him and those boys he hangs around with. If they are not under the wooden footbridge, they are often in the church yard behaving badly. The poor vicar and Mr Boxhall are beside themselves with the petty vandalism.'

Craig took a deep breath. If everyone speculated about who it was or might be, half the residents in the area would be named. Though in fairness, he thought, Gilly Peach had confirmed the issues both Nick and Jacobs had mentioned. Even so, it didn't mean one of them was the person found hanging.

'Mrs Peach, where does Flyn Ford live?' With this information he could go and have a chat with the grandfather and see what he could find out before alarming Pete with a possible name that might prove to be false.

'Poor old boy,' she said, then turned and pointed towards Grange Road. 'Flyn lives in Grove Close. Number fourteen. It's the road on the right just before you get to Grange Road.'

'Have you told the police what you know?'

Gilly Peach shook her head. 'No. I heard there was enough of them at the church. They will know.'

'Of course,' Craig responded. He found it fascinating that she believed the police knew just because they had been at the scene.

'I just had to say something when I saw you, you being a PI and a responsible person looking after our neighbourhood. What a business this all is.'

Tempted as he was to suggest she speak to the police, he realised it would be a waste of breath, instead he said. 'Indeed, it is. And if you hear anything else that might be of use, please don't hesitate to call me or tell the police.' He fished into his pocket and pulled out one of his cards. 'Please take this. It has my number.'

She took the card and read the details. 'Thank you, Mr Gardner. I know we are in good hands.'

'Thank you, Mrs Peach.'

'Don't forget the police too.'

Mrs Peach smiled but remained silent.

'Before you go, please tell me where you live.'

'I live next door to Flyn Ford, number sixteen. That's how I know how young Charlie has caused his grandfather so much upset.'

'Thank you.' He mentally made a note of both addresses.

'You are welcome. Now I'd better not keep you as I know you are a very busy man.' Mrs Peach placed her hand on Craig's arm. 'Thank you again.'

Craig stood and waited as Gilly Peach ambled down the path, he considered her words. He was only a few steps away from Grove Close and decided he would go and try to have a word with Flyn Ford, but before he did, he realised that it would be wise to let Pete know what he had heard. After all, it was a police matter and he needed to tread carefully. Seeing a bench ahead of him, he strode towards it, sat down and called Pete. With no response, he left a message then rang Roo.

He explained about Gilly Peach and who she thought the body was. He heard Roo draw breath at the mention of Charlie. ‘I’m heading to Grove Close now. Hopefully I can have a chat with Flyn about his grandson. I’ll be in touch as soon as I can.’ He didn’t like leaving Roo on her own for so long, but events kept getting in the way.

Chapter TWENTY-THREE

Keen to look more closely at the photos from Jacobs, Roo opened the files on her laptop. The four photos popped up. She could see they weren't brilliant. No doubt Jacobs had snapped the boys in a hurry to ensure his covert activity was not detected, hence the poor quality. Nonetheless she zoomed in on each one in an attempt to see more detail and was certain they were the boys she'd seen from time to time under the footbridge.

Jacobs said he'd taken them two days ago. She clicked on the details which confirmed he was telling the truth. Could it be possible that Charlie was the body found in the church?

Unable to pull her gaze away from the screen, it was then she saw it. She took a deep breath and enlarged the photo. Was she imagining it or was it there? The more she stared the more she was certain. Her mind raced and knew there was one person who might be able to help. She jumped up, reached over to Craig's desk and picked up the notes on the vicar. Flicking through she couldn't see a number for Mr Boxhall, but she knew who would have it. Without delay she punched in the number and listened as it rang out.

'Hello!' Roo said, expecting the vicar to answer.

'Is that you, Roo?'

'Yes. I was hoping to talk to Mr Howard.'

'I'm sorry, but he's not around at the moment and he's left his phone at home, hence why I'm answering,' said Heather Howard. 'Perhaps I can help?'

'Yes, of course. Please could you give me Mr Boxhall's number? I have a few photos I'd like to talk to him about.'

'Is it something I could help with?'

'Thank you. I think Mr Boxhall is who I need to talk to at the moment.'

'If you are sure, Roo, then let me get his number for you.'

Roo could hear the rustle of paper as if Heather was flicking through a book and wondered why Heather didn't just look at the phone's contacts. She was about to call out and suggest this when Heather picked up the phone.

'Sorry about that. Here it is.' She rattled off the number, then added, 'Don't be alarmed if he doesn't answer straight away. Apparently, he's one for leaving his phone lying around.'

He wasn't the only one, Roo thought as she added the number to her phone.

'Any problems, please call back. I'm here to help if I can,' Heather trilled.

'Thank you. I will. Thank you again.'

After pleasant goodbyes, Roo called Mr Boxhall. It only rang twice when her call was answered.

'Hello Mr Boxhall, my name is Roo Chattaway and I work for Craig Gardner.'

'Hello Miss Chattaway, I've heard all about

your office and I understand you're involved with the tragic goings on at the church. What's the world coming too, eh?'

She had no answer to his question, but confirmed they were involved.

'We are helping the police where possible.'

'It's a sad business. So, what can I be doing for you?'

'I have a few photos and I would like you to see them. I am hoping you might recognise the boys on them.' She didn't mention what she had noticed. She needed to see if he noticed it too.

'I don't see why not. I'm not home right now, but I can pop into your office later if that would suit?'

'Are you sure, because I can drive over to your home when you are back there.'

'No need, maid, I'd be happy to come to you. Keeping busy is the best to keep my mind from going doolally with it all.'

'If you are sure, then it would be good to see you. Let me tell you where we are…'

'No need, maid, I knows exactly where you are. I'll be there shortly.' This said, the call ended.

At the prospect of new information, excitement ran through her veins. It was then she recalled what Craig had told her and wondered if it was Charlie, Flyn's grandson. Suddenly it didn't seem exciting at all, just tragic and sad. With this came an unsettled feeling. She stood and was about to get herself a drink, but decided to work on another problem while she waited. After all she loved finding answers.

She sat back down and turned her attention to the weird punk sub.

Apart from Jacobs mentioning it, she'd drawn a blank on finding anything about it. She took another look at the photo of the model. How could it not have been seen? Then like a light that had suddenly been switched on, it occurred to her that there was one person who might be able to help and wondered why she hadn't thought about this earlier.

She tapped the button from her contacts and listened as the phone connected. It rang and rang. 'Mmmm…' she muttered, already feeling deflated that her light bulb moment wasn't going to go any further. She was about to end the call when it was answered.

'Hello!' The greeting rang out with caution.

'Hello Nana. It's Roo. How are you?'

'Hello, my lovely,' Sarah Pearson cried, caution having been replaced with a suspicious tone. 'Now there must be something you need, or you wouldn't be calling our number during the day, and a workday at that.'

'Oh! Nana, that is not true, but you are right I do need something and I'm sure Grandad will be able to help.'

'No doubt you are trying to solve some wicked crime. I just hope it's not anything dangerous.'

Despite her nana's words, Roo knew she was always pleased when she phoned about her work. She rolled her eyes, 'No, Nana, it is nothing dangerous at all. It's about a missing submarine.' She tried not to giggle as she imagined the look on her nana's face at her words, then added. 'It's a model not a real one!'

'Goodness! And there's me thinking the Russians had lost one in our area. How disappointing.'

Roo heard laughter filter down the phone and loved how her nana always found something to laugh at. She was the bubbliest person she knew and had made her smile all her life.

'But, before I call him and you start talking detective stuff, how is that nice young man of yours?'

The mention of Taylor's name had butterflies flutter in Roo's tummy. To her delight her grandparents had taken to him straight away. 'He's just fine and we are busy practicing for the summer skate marathon. Did I tell you it is taking place at Westleton racetrack. Can you believe it?'

'You did, lovely. Just thinking about it has my heart missing a beat. Yet despite this your grandad and I will be there to watch you go faster than those cars that normally race there.'

'We're not that fast!'

'If you say so. Nonetheless, we are very proud of you and, if all you haven't achieved so far wasn't enough, you've found a nice young man.'

Roo was more than aware how much her grandparents loved her. She was more than lucky having such a wonderful family.

'Thanks, Nana. He really is special.'

'I'm glad. Now before we forget why you phoned, let me go find your grandad. The last time I saw him he was skulking off to his garage. He seems to think I don't know what he's up to, but I do. No doubt he'll be sorting himself out to make another brew of his beer.' Sarah tutted, then continued. 'Between him and the neighbours they drink enough to keep a pub open. Garage beer I call it!'

Roo knew all about her grandad's brew; it was well loved in the neighbourhood, particularly as it was free. Even Taylor had tried it and approved.

'I'll go get him before he starts whatever he intends to do.' Roo winced as the phone clunked down on the hall shelf omitting a loud crackle sound. In the distance she heard her grandad's name being called.

A few minutes later, the tip tap of footsteps could be heard on the laminate flooring before the phone was picked up.

'Hello, Rhyleigh, my favourite granddaughter,' Mike Pearson said, jovially.

Roo smiled; she was the only granddaughter! 'It's Roo, Grandad, nobody calls me Rhyleigh.'

'I would if you let me, such a lovely name. Never mind, your nana tells me you've lost a submarine and in need of some help.'

Roo heard him chuckle. 'No, Grandad! A submarine has been found and we are trying to find out who owns it. It's a model.'

'Well, I didn't think for one minute it was a real one.' This time there was a loud guffaw. 'I used to know a chap who made them, Robert Southbank, he made several, though HMS

Pandora, a British Parthian-class submarine, was his favourite. He was a man of detail. Do you have any idea what the model is?'

'Oh yes... it's a whale!' She grinned to herself as she imagined her grandad's face.

'Whoa! I thought you said it was a submarine. Are you having me on?'

'No. Honestly it is a sub, a steampunk in the guise of a large whale.'

Laughter rippled down the phone. 'How big is this thing?'

'It looks pretty big. I haven't yet seen it, but I have a photo on my phone. The thing is do you know anyone who would make such a model?'

There was a pause. 'Oddly enough, I used to, though not seen him for some time. Let me see the photo you have.'

'OK. I'll text it to your mobile.'

Roo heard a sigh at the other end.

'Go on then, but you know how useless I am, but I'd like to see it. The phone is sitting here.'

Her grandad was a lot better at using his phone than he liked her to think, but it didn't stop him from sounding helpless. Roo sent the photo.

'It's on its way,' she said, hitting the send button.

Roo could hear several heavy sighs before her grandad spoke.

'I've got it. Goodness, it's a beauty.'

'Do you know anyone who would have made it?'

'I'm not sure but leave it with me and I'll make a few calls. This is a serious looking model and someone must be hurting to have lost it.'

'Thanks, Grandad, your help is really appreciated.'

Roo ended the call with the knowledge her grandad would do all he could to help; he liked a mystery as much as she did. No sooner had she thanked her grandad when Barney raced to the door, barking.

'Whoa, Barney,' she cried and hurried behind him.

Chapter TWENTY-FOUR

Opening the door, Roo saw a wiry elderly man dismount a bicycle that looked as ancient as its rider. His flat cap shaded his eyes as he bent down and snapped off bicycle clips from around the ankles of his dark corduroy trousers. He stuffed them into a pocket. From the same pocket he pulled out an off-white handkerchief, shook it out then mopped his brow. He looked over to where Roo stood with Barney.

'Miss Chattaway, I take it,' he puffed.

'Hello Mr Boxhall,' she replied, pleased he had arrived. She headed over to him.

'Phew! It's hot again today,' he gasped. 'Though the goings on at the church have my blood running cold.' He took a deep breath that wheezed down into his lungs. 'You wants me to squint at a few snaps?' He puffed, then added, 'Not sure I'll be of much use, but anything to help with what's happened.' He pushed his bicycle towards her and at the same time offered his right hand.

'Thank you for coming, though I would have come to you,' Roo said, taking hold of the proffered hand and shook it.

Pulling his hand back, Bill wiped his palm down the leg of his trousers.

Roo looked on amused and as tempted as she was to do the same on her three-quarter shorts, she refrained. It was hot and sticky, but she didn't want to appear rude.

'No need. I told you that I'd come on by. I goes everywhere on my bike.'

'I really appreciate you taking the time to come in this heat. Finding the body must have been a terrible shock.'

Suddenly the colour drained from Bill's face.

'Are you OK?' concern making Roo's voice rise. She wasn't sure if it was the heat, the exertion of cycling or the mention of the dead body that had caused his face to pale. Probably all three, she thought and reached out her hand.

'I'm fine,' he said, while waving her hand away. 'It just takes some taking in.'

'Come on, let's go in and get you a cool drink and we can talk all about it.'

Mindful of her hand being brushed away moments ago, she restrained from offering support again. Instead, she took hold of the bicycle and leant it against the railings near the entrance. She didn't miss the look of concern from Bill. 'It will be fine there and anyone near will set Barney off!'

Bill smiled and as the colour returned to his weathered features, Roo gently ushered him into the office.

No sooner had they set foot inside when Barney was there, his tail wagging at the excitement of a visitor.

'So, this must be the famous Barney I've heard about,' Bill said, slowly stooping to stroke Barney. 'Nick and Heather have mentioned him as does my old friend, Harry Morgan.' After several pats and with a look of discomfort on his face, he stood up.

'Let's take the weight off your feet,' Roo said pointing towards the seating area. 'While you take a seat, I'll get us both a drink.'

'A glass of duck's wine would be perfect.'

Roo laughed. Her nana always called tap water, duck's wine.

As Bill settled on one of the sofas, Roo returned with two glasses of water and handed one to Bill.

'Here you are,' she said and sat down opposite him.

Bill took his and emptied its contents in one go.

'Would you like another?' Roo asked, surprised at the speed the water went.

Shaking his head, 'No that hit the spot perfectly. Thank you. As I said, it just takes some taking in. It might be a church yard where I helps out, but normally the dead are in the ground. I can tell you it was a heart stopping moment seeing that body dangling there.' He took a deep breath and continued.

'I called 999 and before you knew it the place was crawling with police. I told them all I could.'

Roo nodded her understanding and picked up her phone. 'I have the photos here. The ones I spoke to you about.'

As if not hearing her, Bill cried out, 'I've just placed your boss. I knew the name was familiar and now I knows why. He was once a young bobby in uniform. Just thinking about it, takes me back.' His expression took on a dreamy appearance.

'If I recall rightly, he were involved in that nasty business to do with the missing young woman and the owner of Clayton House.' As he spoke, he rubbed a hand across his forehead. 'Thinking about it, it must have been over thirty years ago. It caused quite a stir round here.'

Roo listened with interest. 'You have a good memory. Craig told me how he had spent many hours standing at the gates of that big house freezing to death when he was a young constable.' She thought about the events that had Craig talking about those days and shuddered. Last year they had been involved in a case about that old house. The secrets and shenanigans of Clayton House had taken over thirty years before they were revealed and nobody could have predicted the outcome.

Bill smiled at Roo. 'It was such a long time ago.'

Long before I was born, she thought as she handed her phone to him. 'Here are the photos.'

Bill took the phone. 'It's like all those years ago – no good going on in our area.' He shook his head as if to convey his dismay.

Roo hoped it wasn't anything like what had happened at Clayton House, though a dead body in a church was close.

'I am afraid they aren't that brilliant, but I think good enough to make out their faces. I could print them out for you, but I think it is easier to see them on the phone as you can enlarge them.'

Bill gazed down at the photo in front of him. To Roo's surprise, he enlarged the image and moved his finger over the screen for more details. His face gave nothing away. Then crossing his legs, he turned his weathered face to her.

'The photos are poor but thank you for asking me to take a look.' A sheepish grin crossed his face. 'To be honest, I'd rather be here helping you than having to talk at the station. It don't seem so formal being here.'

Roo felt a surge of pride that they offered a friendly atmosphere for people to come and talk. 'Thank you and our door is always open and of course, we work closely with the local police too.' Roo added, 'Craig is in daily contact with DI Andrews.'

'I guess you must do these days,' Bill nodded and turned his attention back to the phone. 'Do I recognise any of them, you wants to know?'

She, nodded.

'Right then.' Bill continued to stare down at the image on the screen, then back at Roo. 'These days my eyesight is not what it used to be. I'll be honest, it's hard to say. I can just about make out a couple of them that I've seen messing around in the church yard. Despite there being a few issues in the church, I've never seen them in there.' He pointed out the two to Roo.

This was progress, she thought, feeling her adrenaline rise. 'Do you have any idea who they are?'

'I don't know their names, though I believe one of them might live in Cavendish Road.'

'Did you say Cavendish Road?'

'I did, but I can't be sure. It's just that they were calling to each other as they ran out of the church yard and one of them said, something about meeting at one of their homes in Cavendish Road. I didn't catch much else, sorry!'

Interesting, Roo thought. Jacobs said something too about Cavendish Road. Then recalling the names Craig had mentioned earlier, she asked. 'By any chance do you know Flyn Ford and his grandson?'

Bill's face creased. 'Not really, though I knew Flyn's grandson lives with him.' He frowned. 'That was a rum business. The mother just upped and left. Went off with a man ten years older than her. Charlie was about twelve at the time. Flyn took him in. I heard the boy's gone off the rails. Sad as Flyn's not so good these days.'

'Hm… Do you know what he looks like? Would you recognise him?'

'I think I would, although it's been some time since I last saw 'im.'

'So, you don't think he's been in the churchyard?'

Bill shook his head. 'Nope. Having said this, it's not to say he's not been with them. As I said, I don't always see anyone. On one of the occasions I did, I was pebbled-dashed with the "f-word" as they ran off.' Bill shook his head in dismay.

'It seems the word of choice these days,'

Roo said and realised she was beginning to sound like Craig!

'I take it none of the faces in the photos belonged to the body?' And as tempted as she was to say more, she remained silent.

Shaking his head, 'Sorry. As I told the police, I never looked up at the face. He had his back to me when I walked in. My eyesight might not be up to much, but I'll never forget that sight.' He ran a hand over his face as if to erase the image.

'Are you OK?'

He nodded.

'I really appreciate you taking time to look at the photos. Thank you. And thank you too for mentioning Cavendish Road. I'm sure that is going to be very useful.'

'Let's hope so. Those young devils need to be caught and dealt with. I'm just glad I could be of use.'

'You certainly have, but if you think of anything else, please let us know.'

Roo was about to take back her phone when Bill took another look at the screen. She watched him flick through all four photos. Then he stopped, squinted and tapped the screen. 'Look at this,' he said, his voice had a tremble.

Roo tried not to hold her breath as she got up from the sofa and sat next to Bill. She leaned forward and gazed down at where Bill was pointing. She looked from the screen up to Bill.

'You knew that was there didn't you?' he smirked. 'That's why you wanted me to take a gander at them?'

Roo nodded. 'I needed you to confirm what I saw.'

'It's difficult to make out, but there is definitely something on that wrist,' Bill confirmed.

'Thank you so much. I am sure this is going to help. Hopefully the police can enhance the photo.'

'They do all that on the telly. So can't see why not. Well, if that's all, then I'll be on my way.' As he spoke, he rose slowly, alarming Barney who jumped up. 'You alright my man?' he said and gently patted Barney's head. Turning to Roo, 'This carry on ain't what we expect around here.' He tutted and with short steps he headed to the door. Roo ushered Barney to his bed and followed Bill.

'Thank you again, Mr Boxhall,' she said, walking with him to his bicycle.

'Glad to be of service. Hopefully the boys in blue can do something to help with that photo.'

'Let's hope so.'

With a smile he snapped on his bicycle clips, ruffling the bottom of his trousers. Then taking hold of his bicycle, he hoisted himself up onto the saddle. Wobbling precariously, he waved and set off down the road. Holding her breath, Roo waved back. She was charged by what she had learnt from Bill's visit and punched the air with glee. She rushed back inside to call Craig.

Chapter TWENTY-FIVE

Unable to get hold of his old colleague, Craig had left a voice message with a brief outline of what he'd learnt from Gilly Peach, adding that he would go and have a word with Flyn Ford. Ending his message, he'd spoken to Roo, then he'd made his way to Grove Close. It was important to find out about Flyn's grandson and what he'd been up to of late. Gilly Peach seemed to think he'd been up to no good, but what did no good really mean? And why did she think he was the body found at the church?

He mentally organised a few questions to ask the old boy. Comfortable with his mission, Craig strode down the short path to the front door of number fourteen and couldn't help noticing the pocket handkerchief-size garden was unkept. Weeds filled the narrow border and the grass was in need of a cut. He was about to place his finger on the bell when he noticed the front door ajar. Stepping forward, he pushed it open further. 'Mr Ford,' he called out.

Remaining on the doorstep, he waited and called out again. No response. This time he pushed the door fully open and entered the property. The small hallway was poorly lit, yet despite the dim light he didn't miss several pairs of trainers and other footwear cluttering up the narrow passage. Gingerly, he stepped around them to reach the door opposite. He tapped on the door, then opened it. It led into the kitchen.

'Mr Ford.' This time he raised his voice to almost a shout. He stopped and listened. Silence. Not even the sound of a ticking clock. He entered the small room and was instantly assailed with the fetid odour of stale food. Taking in the small kitchen, he cringed at what he saw: a pile of dirty dishes were stacked in the sink; crumbs and pieces of food peppered the surface top along with empty crisp packets; the linoleum floor was grubby and looked like it hadn't seen a mop in weeks.

He reached out and felt the kettle. It was cold. No hot drinks had been made for some time, he thought. Trying to avoid contact with the pile of dirty dishes, he leant over the sink and squinted through the grubby window that overlooked a small garden – it too was unkept. Weeds were knee high and an old shed at the bottom looked dilapidated. He tried the handle on the glazed back door. To his surprise it opened. He peered out and again called out for Flyn Ford.

With no sight or sound of the occupant, Craig closed the door. His thoughts returned to the front door and wondered why it had been left open? Despite the place being unkept, he could see no evidence of a break in. He headed back into the hall. The door to his right was closed. He opened it and peered in.

It took a moment for his eyes to adjust to the dimness of the room. The curtains were still drawn and a table lamp that sat on a small table, was switched on. The bulb was so weak that a candle in a jam jar would provide more light. Next to the table was a winged back chair, its back to him. He moved towards it and was taken aback at the sight of Flyn Ford. His head rested on one of the wings. His arms crossed over his chest. Flyn's eyes were closed. He was wearing pyjamas that were stained and buttons missing from the jacket. Craig stooped down and noticed Flyn's eyelids flutter.

'Hello, Mr Ford, can you hear me?' Craig touched Flyn's hand and was startled at how cold it felt. Flyn opened his mouth to speak, but only a gurgle sound came out, followed by a drop of saliva trickling down his chin. Flyn made an attempt to raise his right hand, but no sooner had it barely moved when it fell back onto his chest.

Craig checked Flyn's pulse; it wasn't strong.

Pulling his phone out of his pocket Craig called for an ambulance.

'Hang on in there, Flyn, I'm getting you some help.'

Craig wasn't sure if the old man had understood him, but there was a little movement behind his eyelids.

With an ambulance on its way, Craig looked around the messy room for something to wrap over Flyn. He could see nothing that would be of use. He swept into the hall and plucked a fleece jacket from one of the hooks.

'Hang on in there, Flyn,' he repeated as he draped the jacket over the old boy. 'Help is on its way.'

Holding one of Flyn's hands, Craig continued a one-way conversation as he waited. The sound of a siren had him striding to the front door.

The ambulance pulled up outside the house. Instantly, two paramedics jumped out and headed down the short path towards him. In silence, he showed them into the lounge. 'I was calling to see him when I noticed the door open. Alarmed as he has dementia, I called out. Nothing, and then I found him like this. I tried talking to him but there was no response.'

'What's his name?' asked one of the paramedics.

'Flyn Ford,' Craig replied looking over at the frail man who appeared oblivious to all that was happening around him.

'Hello, Flyn,' said the paramedic who leaned over the patient. 'Can you hear me?' As he spoke, he examined Flyn. 'Right, I think it's best we get you to hospital where we can have a proper look at you.' Flyn's eyelids flickered but didn't open. The paramedic turned and nodded to his colleague who left the room returning a few moments later with a wheelchair.

Flyn was carefully lifted into the wheelchair, an oxygen mask placed over his face and a warm blanket draped over his body and around his shoulders. He looked weak and frail.

Once Flyn was settled in the ambulance, one of the paramedics stayed with him. The other jumped down and turned to Craig. 'Thanks for calling us. The hospital is the best place for him right now.' As he spoke, he closed the rear doors. 'Are you a relative?'

'No, but his grandson lives with him, though there was no sign of him when I arrived. But leave that with me.' As he spoke, he hoped Gilly Peach had got it wrong and the body found in the church did not belong to Flyn's grandson. Otherwise, he had no idea who to contact.

'That's great. Please get them to call the hospital so they can get an update on Mr Ford's condition.

Craig nodded, 'I'll also call the hospital later to see how he's doing.'

'Great.' The paramedic climbed into the driver's seat.

Craig watched as the ambulance turned round and sped off down the road, its blue lights flashing and siren wailing. He hoped Flyn would be fine and despite the disturbing information from Gilly Peach, he was grateful she had stopped him. Had she not, he would never have gone to number fourteen Grove Close. He could only hope that by entering Flyn's home he might have made a difference to the outcome for one member of that family at least.

Craig turned and walked back up the path; he needed to secure the house. As he entered, his thoughts returned to the young man found hanging in the church. Was it Charlie? And, if so, was there a link between his death and Flyn Ford slumped and unresponsive in his chair? The questions raced through his head and with no answers he knew he needed to speak to Pete, but before that he would use the opportunity to have a look around. Finding a photo of Charlie would help with ruling him out. He hoped that would be the case because Flyn needed his grandson.

He didn't have to search far. Sitting on an old-fashion sideboard that took up the best part of one wall in the lounge was a dark wooden photo frame with the glass missing. He picked it up and looked down at two smiling faces. One he could see was Flyn. He guessed it had been taken a while ago as Flyn looked fuller in the face. The other in the photograph was a young man, mid-teens, he guessed. Was this Charlie? he wondered. He placed the frame back down, took a photo with his phone and looked around for more. But it was the only photo to be seen.

Satisfied there was nothing else he could do without disturbing anything more, he picked up a set of keys that lay on the cluttered coffee table. After a few tries, he found one that worked for the front door and the back door already had its key in the lock. He let himself out, engaged the lock, slammed the door shut and placed the keys in his pocket. His phone rang and he saw it was Roo.

'I think we might have something from the photos of Jacobs,' she gushed. 'I saw it and Mr Boxhall saw it too. We're sure one of the boys appears to be wearing a chain around his wrist.'

'Whoa!' Craig cried as Roo's voice sang down the phone.

'The photos aren't brilliant, but to be certain maybe the station can do something with them because there is a strong possibility that whoever is wearing the chain in the photo is the same person found in the church.'

Craig whistled through his teeth. Roo appeared to have found a link.

'Well done, Roo. Send the pics to me and I'll get them to the DI and see what can be done.' Only Roo would question a photo, even one of herself, if it didn't look right. Having four photos from Jacobs would be too much for her to ignore and the need to check them out would be a necessity. 'Well done, Roo,' he said again. Then went on to explain about Flyn and the photo he took.

'Send me the pic,' Roo said. 'I often see the boys under the footbridge and although I don't know Charlie, I might recognise the face.'

Craig sent the photo and waited for Roo's response.

Within seconds, Roo confirmed he was one of the boys she'd seen under the bridge. 'But I don't think he's on the photos Jacobs took. It's difficult to be certain as they are poor quality.'

Craig shook his head with pride. Roo never ceased to amaze him. 'Excellent! I'll be in touch once I have more information and hopefully back to the office soon,' he added before ending the call. He smiled at Roo's tenacity to check everything out and gazed down at the photo of Flyn and Charlie. The smile slipped from his face, 'Do you wear a chain on your wrist, son?'

~~~

Craig was leaving Grove Close and about to call Pete with an update when his phone rang out
~~~

and he saw it was his old colleague.

'Sorry, I didn't pick up earlier, but I take it you've uncovered something,' Pete said, his voice suggesting he was in a hurry but had noted his missed call.

'It's been a very interesting half hour! After leaving you…' Craig explained about meeting Mrs Peach, Flyn Ford and Roo's observation, though didn't miss the silence at the other end. 'Is everything OK?' he asked as he got the impression the DI wasn't listening.

'It's fine, just everything needing attention at once, nothing new. You know what it's like. Carry on.'

'What is disturbing is that Gilly Peach is of the opinion that the body found in the church is Flyn Ford's grandson.'

'Really! What with Jacobs and now this,' Pete said, exasperation evident. 'Pity they don't contact us too!' An audible sigh echoed down the line. 'In that case we need to talk to both of them, this Flyn and Gilly Peach.'

Craig was more convinced his old colleague wasn't really listening.

'Flyn Ford is in hospital.'

'I see. Did you get the details of this Mrs Peach?'

'I did, but more importantly, I have a photograph of Flyn with a young man whom I'm guessing is his grandson. I'll send you the photo so you can find out if it resembles the body found.' As he spoke, he forwarded the photo. 'Also, I am sending four photos Jacobs took. Is there any chance one of the techie boys can sharpen them up. We need to see the face of the one wearing a chain around his wrist.'

He was about to add that it could be the body found, then decided to wait and see what the force came up with for now. It was evident Pete was distracted.

'Thanks, Copper. As I keep saying, you should be back with us. But I know I'm wasting my breath. Do you think the grandson had anything to do with his grandad being found unresponsive?'

'Difficult to say. From what I've seen it doesn't appear intruder motivated. It seems the old man hasn't been up to much and from what I've seen the boy appears not to have bothered either.' He didn't wait for any response and ploughed on. 'By the way I have a set of keys. I was worried if it is the grandson and the old boy being in hospital than who else, if anyone, has a set. I can hand them over to you.'

'What's the address?'

Suddenly, Pete seemed animated and he had his attention. Craig smiled and rattled off Flyn's details.

There was a brief silence before Pete spoke. 'Any chance you can hang around and I'll gather up a couple of uniforms and we'll head out. I think we need to have a look at the place.' He stopped talking and Craig guessed he was opening the photos he had sent.

'Got them,' Pete called out. 'Thanks! I'll get someone to check them all and get back to you. God knows, we need to find out who this lad is.'

Craig was still baffled that no one had come

forward reporting a missing person. 'By the way, the grandson's name is Charlie.'

'Thanks again, we'll be with you shortly.'

Chapter TWENTY-SIX

After letting Craig know about what she and Mr Boxhall had seen, Roo hoped the police would be able to enhance the photos. Maybe she should look for software that does that; it could be useful in their line of work. About to delve into a search on the internet, when her phone rang.

'Grandad,' she answered, pleased to hear from him yet, at the moment, she had her mind on software.

'Rhyleigh, my love, how did you know it was me?'

Roo rolled her eyes and was about to correct him on her name, but decided it wasn't worth it. 'I recognised your number,' she said instead.

'That's my little detective.' He chuckled. 'I've been doing a bit of detective work myself and you'll be pleased to know, I have a name for you. John Williams. He used to be a member of our model club. Can't say I remember him. And you're right, it is a punk submarine. You learn something new every day.' Mike chuckled again. 'Never heard of one until you told me about it.'

'That's great, Grandad, thank you, but why hasn't he reported it missing?'

'Well, my love, it's not!'

'I take it then he's been to the police station and collected it?'

'Ah! You see he built it and then sold it.'

'Who did he sell it to?' Roo's interest back in full flow.

'I thought you might ask that, so I asked and it was to a lady called Bridget Chadd. She bought it as a gift for her husband. That was about eighteen months ago.'

'Grandad, you are amazing. Do you know where she lives? Or do you have a phone number?'

'No idea where she lives, but I have a phone number.' He rattled it off. Instantly, Roo added it to her phone. 'It looks like a local number,' she said. 'You are one in a million. Thank you so much.'

'You're welcome, my love. Now don't forget to keep me posted on the outcome and if you need anything else, just call Inspector Clueless.' Mike chuckled.

'Don't worry, I promise to let you know. Love you Grandad.'

'Love you too, Rhyle… Roo! I'll leave you to carry on playing Poirot.' He laughed out loud before ending the call.

A wide smile filled Roo's face at the mention of Poirot. Her family knew she idolised Poirot. He was her hero and she wanted to be as good as him in solving mysteries. Now she had a dilemma – did she call Mrs Chadd or continue her software search? Wanting to do both, she decided the police, no doubt, had what was needed and talking to Mrs Chadd might solve the mystery of the found sub. Accepting this, she hit the number for Mrs Chadd. After several rings, the call went to voice mail. Not wanting to leave a message, she decided to try again later.

Disappointed, she placed her elbows on the desk and rested her chin in her hands. Her phone pinged and she glanced at the screen. Her face lit up as she read the text.

Can't wait to see you tonight, Taylor had written followed by several hearts and kiss emojis. Just reading Taylor's message had her heart beating faster. She responded instantly with a string of emojis. There was no question in her mind, that meeting Taylor was the best thing that had ever happened to her. She never thought she could love someone so much and hoped she would always feel full of love with him.

Her mind drifted to later that day. They were going to practise in the park for the skating marathon and she couldn't wait. Lost in her thoughts she was brought out of her daydreaming when Barney nudged at her knee.

'Hello, boy,' she said, reaching down to pat his head. To her surprise he laid down next to her chair. With her thoughts on skating melting away, Roo turned her attention back to work and the name her grandad had given her. She would try calling Mrs Chadd again. She punched the recall button, and to her surprise it was answered straight away.

'Hello,' a pleasant female voice answered.

'Hello, Mrs Chadd?'

'Yes. Who am I speaking to?'

'My name is Roo Chattaway. I'm sorry to trouble you, but I am trying to find the owner of a punk submarine that has recently been found.'

A brief pause followed before Bridget Chadd spoke. 'Goodness me that was swift!' Her voice was filled with surprise. 'I take it you've found the model?'

'Well yes and no,' Roo replied confused. 'We have been trying to find the owner and it was only down to my grandad that I eventually found you.'

'Forgive me, but what do you mean yes and no and what has your grandad to do with the police? I am assuming I am talking to the police.'

Roo grimaced; this was not how she expected the phone call to go. 'Mrs Chadd, I think we are at cross purposes. Please let me explain.'

Silence from the other end which Roo took as agreement to continue. 'A punk submarine has been found in the river near the wooden footbridge at Riverside. It has been taken to the police station, but no one has reported it missing. My boss is an ex-police officer, now a Private Investigator, and the police asked for our help as we know the area and a number of the locals who live near where the model was found.'

Crikey, she thought she was making a meal out of this yet felt the need to continue. 'My grandad knows a few people from the model boating club and that's how he gave me your name.' She frowned at her long-winded explanation and hoped Mrs Chadd hadn't drifted off to sleep. 'Sorry about all of that, but I wanted you to know.'

Laughter tinkled down the phone. 'Oh, my goodness! What a story. Sorry to laugh, but you couldn't make that up.'

Roo smiled with relief.

'Please forgive my confusion,' continued Mrs Chadd, 'but it was barely moments ago that I'd phoned the police station to report it missing. They said they would get back to me and so I assumed it was them.' She laughed lightly.

Roo listened and wondered why it had taken Mrs Chadd so long to report the model missing? Before she could voice this, Mrs Chadd continued.

'The model is my husband's. I bought it for him as an early present for his seventieth birthday. And that is why we haven't reported it missing until now.'

Confused, Roo was about to speak, when Mrs Chadd carried on.

'You see, we have spent the last six weeks at our daughter's in Australia. We only got back last night and we've only just got round to checking Brian's workshop. It was then we found it had been broken into and the punk model gone. I contacted the police as soon as we saw what had happened. Not the best home welcome from our wonderful time away.'

'No,' Roo said, imagining the shock. 'Was anything else missing?'

'That's the odd thing, no! Which is strange as there are other much smaller models in there. Also, there is no damage to the workshop, only the punk sub missing.'

'That's a relief,' Roo said and wondered

why only the punk sub was taken. Very odd! 'Thankfully your model is in safe hands and if you contact the police again, they should be able to help you.' As an afterthought, she added. 'I am assuming you live local.'

'We live on Cavendish Road.'

There it was again – Cavendish Road. Jacobs had mentioned it when talking about the *oiks* and also Mr Boxhall. What was the connection?

'A lovely place to live,' Roo said, keeping her thoughts of a connection to herself. She knew it was an opulent tree lined road with a number of large, detached properties.

'It is, though we live in a modest bungalow.'

Roo could image Mrs Chadd smiling as she said the word, *modest*. Maybe their home was modest, but the model stollen was anything but. 'I am glad I've been able to talk to you and the mystery of the punk sub's owner is solved.'

'It's you I need to thank. I can't believe the model has been found and is safely at the police station,' Mrs Chadd said. 'Thank you again. Goodness so unexpected. I will now contact the police station again. What a relief.'

As the call ended, Roo was certain she heard a cry of glee from Mrs Chadd. Though why the station hadn't called her back to say they had the model, she had no idea. Not letting this concern her, Roo punched the air with a high five and couldn't believe she had found the owner. She punched the air again. What a day she'd had so far. Her excitement over-spilled and, unable to wait for Craig's return, she grabbed her phone; she just had to share her latest results.

Chapter TWENTY-SEVEN

Two uniformed officers along with DI Andrews had turned up at Grove Close. After spending no more than fifteen minutes in the house, the uniforms had left.

'As you say, the place is a tip,' Pete said, wrinkling his nose as he pulled shut the front door. A loud click followed as the Yale lock engaged. On hearing the resounding click, Pete slipped the keys into his pocket. 'It's clear the grandson has no sense of tidiness and basic hygiene. If the old boy has a touch of dementia, he needs help.' He shook his head as if to convey the dismay of the situation.

Craig didn't miss Pete's use of the present when talking about Charlie and wondered if he knew more than he was saying. He followed him down the path and agreed the place was in a sorry state. He would try and talk to someone in Social Services to see if there was any help for Flyn, but before that he would find out how the old boy was doing. A visit to the hospital was on his mental list of things to do. The list was growing. He sighed at how one thing could snowball. Right now, it would be useful to know if the body belonged to Charlie. Looking for an answer, he turned to Pete.

'Any idea when you'll hear if the body belongs to Flyn's grandson?'

A strained look creased Pete's pale face. 'I'd have thought we'd have heard by now.' Pete looked at his watch as if that would help speed the answer. As he did, his phone rang out. He checked the screen. 'This could be the answer we are waiting for.'

Pete turned his back on Craig and answered the call.

Craig strained to listen, but his concentration was halted as his own phone rang out. It was Roo again. *What had she unearthed this time*? he thought and at the same time felt a twinge of guilt at having been away from the office for so long.

'Hello, Roo,' he said, 'what have you found now?' his interest in Pete's call evaporating. He took a few steps down the road to distance himself from his old colleague as he listened to Roo.

'Oh! How do you know I've found out anything else?'

'A wild guess,' Craig replied with a grin. Roo would only call if it was urgent, or she had found something she was too excited to wait for his return.

'Well, you are just not going to believe this, but I've found the owner of the punk sub!'

Craig took a deep breath, 'Sounds like you're running the office single handed,' he laughed and continued to listen as Roo, once again, filled with excitement, explained how she had solved the mystery.

'Poirot would be proud of me,' Roo concluded.

'Never mind Poirot being proud of you, I am and that is great news. That was a great move asking your grandad.' There was a brief pause, then he added, 'I'm sorry I've not been there much today, but you have been brilliant and I'm pleased to say things are unfolding here too. After speaking with DI Andrews, I am now going to the hospital to see Flyn, assuming he's conscious.'

'Don't worry about here, everything is under control. Barney and I are holding the fort,' Roo said in a voice that conveyed animation. 'See you soon,' she added.

Craig smiled at Roo's cheerful and optimistic outlook on everything. When did it all change for him? Age? Life's ups and downs? Dealing with humanity that, at times, ground you down? He didn't have an answer. He hoped Roo would always have her happy, self-assured countenance no matter how life worked out. It was times like this that he felt old and too cynical, yet at the same time, privileged to be working with someone young, full of eagerness and positivity. She kept him on his toes and that he needed. Seeing Pete striding towards him, his brow furrowed, he called out. 'Any news?'

As if the troubles of the world sat on his shoulders, Pete replied, 'It seems the body isn't that of Charlie. The photo you sent of Flyn and his grandson was a great help, but it appears it's not of the body.'

A sense of relief settled over Craig that it wasn't the wayward young man. As things looked, his grandad would be needing him. 'Any idea who it is?'

Pete shook his head. 'Not at the moment.'

'What about the other photos? Any joy on them?'

'One of the young graduates has his nose in his laptop. We can only hope when he pulls it out, he'll have some results.' Pete snorted.

Craig was aware Pete had little time for new recruits. As far as the DI was concerned, they were molly coddled; unlike when they had joined the force, they had been thrown to the lions. Despite the changes in training, he just hoped the young officer would be able to do something to enlarge and sharpen the photos.

Chapter TWENTY-EIGHT

As Pete headed back to the station, Craig made his way to the hospital. Now as he entered the ward, he was taken aback to see Flyn sitting up in bed, drinking a mug of tea and munching on a biscuit. A sense of relief flooded through him and a smile creased his face as he strode to Flyn's side.

'Mr Ford, it's good to see you looking a lot better than the last time we met.'

With a biscuit held close to his mouth, Flyn surveyed Craig suspiciously.

Craig didn't miss the wary stare and was quick to reassure he had come to see that he was OK. 'Mr Ford, I'm Craig Gardner, I found you in your lounge.'

Flyn took a bite of his biscuit. He remained silent as if assessing what he should say. Then swallowing down a chunk, he asked, in a none too friendly tone, 'Why would you be in my house. I don't know you?'

Seeing a green plastic chair positioned between Flyn and the next patient's bed, Craig pulled it close and sat down. 'I called at your house hoping to have a word with your grandson, Charlie, but when I arrived your front door was open.'

'Open you say?' Flyn looked perplexed. 'I always lock it, always.'

He probably did, thought Craig. 'I'm sure you do, but perhaps your grandson hadn't closed it properly when he went out.' He watched Flyn's face crease as if trying to understand Craig's explanation. Flyn finished off his biscuit, crumbs sprinkling on his hospital gown and the covers.

'I always lock it,' Flyn repeated and took a loud slurp of his tea, drops trickling down his chin.

'I'm sure you do,' Craig said, noting the look of concern on Flyn's face. 'Though it was just as well it wasn't locked this time or else I wouldn't have found you.'

Flyn continued to stare at Craig. 'I was just having a little nap,' he said and wiped the back of his hand over his chin.

'You were slumped in your chair and I couldn't wake you. That's why I called for an ambulance.'

Craig watched as Flyn tried to digest his words. 'Do you know what happened?'

Not taking his gaze off Craig, Flyn shook his head. 'I don't think anything happened. I remember Charlie saying something about going out. He's in and out all the time. I can't keep up with him. I sat in my chair.' He looked down at his mug of tea. 'I spend a lot of time in there these days.' He looked up at Craig, 'I remember feeling tired.' He shrugged his shoulders; the tea sloshed in its mug, but didn't spill out. 'I must have dozed off.'

Craig felt sympathy for Flyn. It couldn't be much of a life having a come-and-go teenager living with you. 'Do you have any idea what time that would have been when Charlie went out?'

Flyn grinned; a couple of his front teeth were missing. 'I don't know. He's in and out all the time. I get confused sometimes because I'm not sure whether it's night or day.' He drained the last drops of his tea, then offered the empty mug to Craig.

Taking it, Craig placed it on the bedside cabinet.

'He sounds a bit of a lad, your Charlie.'

Flyn huffed. 'He's a good boy, but I'm not sure who his friends are. Young uns. Not like it was when I was a lad.'

Craig nodded in agreement. 'Flyn, it would be helpful if you had any idea where he goes. I ask as I need to let him know you are here. He'll be worried if he goes home and you're not there.'

With vacant eyes, Flyn stared at Craig as if thinking of an answer. 'He's in and out like a yo-yo. Sometimes he brings them back home. They all call out hello, but I don't understand what they're on about most of the time. They whisper a lot.' Flyn put a finger to his lips as he spoke and surreptitiously looked round the ward.

'Is everything all right?'

'Just checking, no one's listening,' he mumbled, then returning his attention back to Craig, added, 'It seems we're OK.'

'Everything is fine,' Craig comforted, unsure what Flyn was looking out for and then realised he was expecting a lot from Flyn. It was tough to expect answers to all the questions, but he needed to find his grandson. 'Do you know if

Charlie's friends live close by?'

Flyn rubbed at the grey stubble on his chin. 'I don't think so.' He faced Craig, 'but they might do.'

Craig placed his hand on Flyn's and gently squeezed it. 'Sorry to keep asking so much. I just need to find your grandson.'

Flyn nodded.

Craig wasn't sure if he understood, but he would try one more time. 'Has Charlie ever mentioned their names?'

Flyn's face suddenly broke into a broad smile and he proudly announced, 'Fenton.'

'Fenton? Is that one of the names?'

'What a name. I've never heard anyone called that before, but I think it is. I've heard it a few times when he brings them back. Fenton Fellows. I remember because there's a garage called Fellows. I bought a car there once. Can't remember what it was but I think it was a new one.' Flyn smiled as if recalling the memory; his eyes took on a faraway look. 'It was red.'

'You must have been very proud of it.'

'I think I was,' he said, the smile brightening his sallow face.

It suddenly occurred to Craig that there was a car showroom in Upper Giles Street. He was sure it was called Fellows. He would look them up or at least get Roo to do it – she loved that kind of work.

'Did you hear any other names mentioned?'

Flyn shook his head. 'Can't say I did.'

'Grandad!' A voice cried out and a young man in jogging bottoms and a zipped-up hoodie appeared at the bottom of Flyn's bed.

Craig swung round and recognised the visitor from the photo on the sideboard in Flyn's home.

'Charlie,' Flyn cried out, his arms outstretched as if he'd not seen the young man in a long time. 'Where've you been? I've been waiting days for you to come home.' Tears slipped down Flyn's pale cheeks.

Craig didn't miss the startled look on Charlie's face or the grubby clothes he wore. The dark hoodie top and track bottoms were stained. His trainers had their laces missing. Charlie's eyes darted from his grandad to Craig and then back to his grandad. Craig watched as Charlie took hold of his grandad's hands, pulled him to his chest and hugged him. 'It's all right grandad.'

Releasing his hold on his grandad and settling Flyn back on his pillows, Charlie turned to Craig. 'Mrs Peach told me about the ambulance and grandad being taken away.'

Good on the neighbour, Craig thought and couldn't help noticing the young man's breathing was a little fast as if he'd been running. Holding onto his grandad's hands, Charlie plonked himself onto the side of the bed. It sagged – almost toppling Flyn over.

Craig looked on at the tender scene. The state of the house and the fact that Flyn was still in dirty, unwashed pyjamas when he'd found him didn't quite match the care in which Charlie was embracing his grandad. Before he could respond Flyn, cried out.

‘You left me,’ he said, his bottom lip quivering as he pulled his hand free of Charlie’s grasp and swiped at his tears.

‘I didn’t. I haven’t been out long.’ Charlie turned to Craig.

Craig was sure he saw worry in the young man’s eyes and it appeared he’d also been crying. He was puzzled. If the boy cared so much for his grandad, why was the house looking like a tip and where was he when his grandad needed him?

‘You didn’t come home last night,’ Flyn suddenly said.

‘What! I did, but you were in bed. I brought you a mug of coco. Don’t you remember?’ As he spoke, he gazed back at Craig. ‘Grandad gets very forgetful these days, don’t you?’

Flyn didn’t respond. He just stared at Charlie with sad, watery eyes.

‘I’m glad you’re here. Your grandad needs you,’ Craig said. As tempted as he was to confront Charlie to find out where he had been, he knew he needed to tread carefully. Flyn was not only upset, but far from good health. The last thing needed was for Charlie to create a scene or worse, run off. Even though he had decided not to question him now, it didn’t mean he was going to be ignored; he would visit Grove Close later. He’d very much like to know what young Charlie gets up to and who with. Also, where he’d been during the last twenty-four hours. Though, on a positive, the fact that he was here, meant he most certainly wasn’t the body found in the church, but did Charlie know who it was?

With this on his mind he got to his feet and smoothed down his jacket. Charlie watched him closely with a nervous gaze. Craig hadn't missed the young man's shiftiness and inability to sit still; that boy knew something and he was determined to find out what it was.

Resting a hand on the side of the bed, Craig leaned over and smiled down at Flyn. 'I'll leave you to catch up with your grandson. You take care and I'll try to visit again soon to see how you are doing.' Taking a step back, he stood up straight and looked pointedly at Charlie. 'Make sure you look after him.'

Charlie simply stared at him through eyes that conveyed something close to panic.

Oblivious of the tension between his grandson and Craig, Flyn gazed up at Craig, 'Thank you.' He held out his hand. Craig took hold and gently squeezed it. 'You take care.' Placing Flyn's hand down on the covers, he walked towards the end of the bed, then turning he looked pointedly at Charlie, 'By the way, have you seen Fenton Fellows lately?'

Charlie's face turned ashen. His hesitation lasted for no more than a couple of heartbeats before replying. 'No,' he said, a tremble in his voice betraying the unexpected question.

'I see.'

Charlie was lying, Craig was certain. He turned on his heel and left the ward. What was Charlie hiding? he wondered as he walked to the car park: leaving his grandad in a house that resembled a tip or knowing Fenton Fellows? Maybe both, but he would find out – of that, he was certain.

Chapter TWENTY-NINE

As Craig made his way back to the office, his head filled with the day's events. He needed to find out if Fenton Fellows was a relation of the owners of Fellows Garage. He called Roo and asked her to look up the garage adding he would be back in a matter of minutes. Despite the short distance to the office, he knew she would have an answer before he even tapped a key. He smiled at how she called him a luddite!

Entering the office, Barney raced up to Craig as if he'd not seen him for years. 'Hello, boy,' he said and pulled a treat out of his pocket and offered it to him. It was devoured in a nano second.

'How did your visit to the hospital go?' Roo called, looking up from the web page on her screen.

Craig moved over to his desk. Sitting down, he placed his elbows on his desk and clasped his hands together. In a serious voice he spoke. 'To my surprise, Flyn was sitting up eating a biscuit and drinking a mug of tea.'

'That's good, isn't it?'

'I guess so, but to be honest Flyn's a little confused.

'Was he able to talk to you about Charlie?'

'Better than that, Charlie turned up. The look of shock on his face spoke volumes, though whether that was because his grandad was in hospital, or he had a visitor or something else!'

'Really! Well, that definitely rules him out as the body in the church, thank goodness,' Roo said, looking at Craig.

'It does, but we still don't know who the body belongs to. However, all is not lost as interestingly before Charlie arrived, Flyn told me that Charlie often had friends around the house and that he's in and out like a yoyo. Flyn has no idea where he goes off to or anything about the lads he hangs around with.'

'Not even a name?'

'That's where it became interesting, because Flyn mentioned the name Fenton, Fenton Fellows. He remembered the name because, it seemed years ago, he'd bought a car from a garage in town called Fellows.

'Fellows,' Roo repeated. 'That's why you asked me to look up Fellow's Garage, see if there is any connection?'

Craig nodded. 'I'm hoping it might yield some information, though what at this stage, I'm not sure.' As he spoke, he unclasped his hands and ran one over his face. 'Clutching at straws comes to mind,' he sighed. 'Another thing, when Charlie turned up, I mentioned the name to him and he looked decidedly uncomfortable. It was clear he was not expecting that, but the question is why?'

'Interesting,' Roo said as she read the details displayed on her screen, 'Look at this. There's a Fellows Garage in Upper Giles Street.' She made a quick scan of the site. 'There's not much here. It's mainly details of new cars and quality used cars. There's an endorsement statement of the first-class service they give along with several five-star reviews from satisfied clients.' Moving her mouse along the screen, 'What's this?' As she spoke, she clicked on a page with photos of staff and their job title. She took in their faces and details; most were middle aged with long service records and all appeared to have worked in the motor trade for years. At the bottom of the page, two boys in their late teens, sporting modern hair styles wearing light green overalls had smiled for the camera. Against each photo was the title, Apprentice. Unlike the other photos there were no names. Roo stared at the two images, then turned to Craig.

'Take a look at these.' She swivelled her laptop round to face Craig. As Craig took in the details on the screen, Roo flicked through her phone to the photos from Jacobs. 'I'm not too sure, but I think one of them could be this one.' She enlarged the photo and handed her phone over to Craig. 'The one on the left looks a little like one of the apprentices.'

Craig squinted at the one she suggested, then turned his gaze from her phone to the laptop. He pursed his lips, 'There's a possibility, though difficult to be certain due to the photo quality.'

Roo pulled a face. 'Let's hope they are working on these at the police station. It could be important.'

'I agree. Those photos could provide some

vital information, including a clearer picture of the face of the person wearing the wrist chain.'

'How long do you think it will be before we hear?'

'Who knows.' Craig got to his feet. 'I'm going over to Grove Close; I need to have a word with Charlie. I have a feeling he wouldn't have stayed long at the hospital with his grandad after I left. Something is bothering him and I want to find out what that is.' He handed the phone back to Roo and checked his watch.

'It's been a long, busy day and thanks to you the owner has been found for that odd model and we have Jacobs' photos being looked at.' Roo's face brightened.

'And, more importantly, we have a few more details about what might have been going on at the church. All in all, you've done a great job juggling so much in my absence – Thank you.'

Roo blushed.

'Right, you get off home. I'm going to try and see Charlie.'

Shutting the lid on her laptop, Roo stood, 'I'll come with you. It might help.' She looked at Craig, 'At least I'm closer to Charlie's age.'

Craig grinned. 'I thought you had a skating practice tonight for the marathon?'

'We do, but I can still get there in plenty of time. It starts at seven and I'm sure we won't be that long. Please!'

Craig couldn't ignore the pleading glint in Roo's eyes and knew she deserved to go with him after all she had achieved. 'Go on then. We will go in our own cars just in case time runs away and then you can get off to your skating. I'll take Barney as he has a knack of softening up people. That's the deal. OK?'

Chapter THIRTY

Craig and Roo parked around the corner from Flyn's house. With Barney on a short lead, they set off to number fourteen. As they approached, both noticed lights were on in the lounge and hall despite the sunny late afternoon.

'We could be in luck,' Craig said and led the way down the short path towards the front door. They didn't need to ring the bell as the door flew open at the same time as Craig reached out to press the button.

With a look of fear in his eyes and in bare feet, Charlie stood in front of them. 'I don't know anything,' he cried and began to push the door closed.

'That's odd as we've not asked you any questions,' Craig said and didn't fail to notice Charlie had changed from the clothes he wore at the hospital. He now appeared in a clean white t-shirt with an unknown motif stitched in red on the left breast and a pair of green shorts that hung to the top of his knees. He looked clean and fresh as if he'd taken a shower, yet he still sported a designer stubble.

'I take it you were expecting someone, or you were on your way out as the door was open?' Craig said.

'I was on my way out,' Charlie mumbled in a low tone, different from his greeting that was more of a screech. 'I'm going back to the hospital to see grandad.' He looked down at the dog and stepped back. Barney wagged his tail in a friendly gesture. 'Maybe you should come back later.'

Gazing down at Charlie's bare feet, Craig added. 'I think you've forgotten to put on your shoes.'

Charlie shuffled his feet and made an audible sob.

'Maybe we should come in and you can talk to us. It might help and if you still want to go to the hospital, I could drop you off there,' Craig said. Then nodding down at Barney, 'He won't hurt you, though having said this, he might lick you to death!'

Without uttering a word and not taking his eyes off Barney, Charlie acquiesced and stood back. Craig and Roo, with Barney, entered number fourteen. Roo closed the door.

Ushering Barney through to the lounge, Craig noticed the place looked much tidier than it had when he had been there earlier. He could only assume Charlie had left the hospital more or less after he had to have had time to tidy the place and clean himself up.

'You're not the police,' Charlie said, a statement not a question. With his hands plunged deep into the pockets of his shorts he stood in the middle of the lounge as if unsure what to do next. 'I know she's not,' Charlie glared at Roo. Then pulling his hands out of his pockets he folded them over his chest.

'You know we are *not* the police. We are

here because I found your grandad unconscious in that chair.' Craig indicated the chair where Flyn had been slumped. 'I called an ambulance. Thankfully he is sitting up in bed and looking a lot better than earlier.'

Charlie mumbled something that Craig guessed could be a thank you.

'Having seen you at the hospital I thought it would be good to pop round to see how you are doing. It must be very stressful looking after an elderly person who is not that well.'

The relief on Charlie's face was measurable. 'It can be,' he said and a hint of a smile flicked across his face.

'Can we sit down for a minute?'

Charlie looked Craig over, shrugged and, unfolding his arms, indicated at any one of the seats.

Craig and Roo perched on the two-seater sofa. Barney sat on Craig's feet. Charlie flopped in the winged back chair that had seen better days. He placed his elbows on the threadbare arms.

Craig leaned forward and rested his elbows on his knees. 'How do you know Fenton Fellows?'

Startled, Charlie looked from Craig to Roo. 'I don't.'

'Are you sure?' Craig queried, not missing the panic that, once again, filled Charlie's face at the mention of Fenton Fellows, not dissimilar to the look he had received at the hospital.

Charlie looked down at his hands and started picking round his fingernails.

'Charlie, I've often seen you with a group of boys under the footbridge and we would like to know their names. If I show you a few pics can you help us?' Roo asked, her voice friendly yet cajoling.

Checking out Craig, 'I thought you were here about my grandad?'

Craig didn't miss how Charlie side-stepped Roo's question. 'We are, but we also would like to know who your friends are. Your grandad told me you have friends often in the house.'

'Grandad doesn't mind them coming.'

'That's good, but if you could help with the photos.' Without waiting for an answer, Roo flashed her phone, with one of the photos on the screen, in front of Charlie.

Charlie glanced at the images but shook his head.

'Does that mean you don't know who they are?' Craig asked.

Charlie shrugged his shoulders.

'What about the one with the chain around his wrist?'

Charlie shot up from the chair and ran through to the hall. His feet thundering on the stair treads as he raced to the top. A door slammed shut and a few minutes later Craig and Roo heard the flushing of the toilet. The sound of steps echoed as Charlie slowly came down the stairs and back into the lounge. He dropped back into his chair. His face pale and his eyes watering.

A faint odour of vomit filled the air.

'Who or what's upset you?' Roo asked,

leaning forward. Reaching out she placed a hand on the chair arm.

Charlie sniffed loudly. 'None of it has anything to do with me.'

'What's got nothing to do with you?' Roo's voice was soft.

Barney nudged up against Charlie's legs.

'Even Barney sees you are upset.'

Charlie looked down at Barney who stared back up at him with soulful eyes. 'I never agreed with any of it. That's the truth.' Charlie kept his head down as if trying to work out the best way to pick at his fingernails.

'Clearly there is something going on. Whatever it is has made you sick. Have you been to the church of late?' Craig asked.

With no eye contact, Charlie spoke. 'My grandad needs me and I've not looked after him as much as I should.' He looked around the room as he spoke. 'I need to do more. He's old.'

'I understand,' Craig said, 'but you said, it's got nothing to do with you. What is this nothing?'

Charlie bit on his bottom lip and tears formed in his eyes.

'Who are you afraid of?' Craig asked and watched as Charlie wiped his arm across his face.

Craig almost spit when his phone pinged alerting him of a message. He pulled it out of his pocket and saw Pete had asked him to call. He wasn't happy, but decided there must be some new information. 'I need to make a call. Roo will talk to you.'

A few minutes later, Craig walked back in

the room. He looked from Roo to Charlie. 'Charlie, do you know Jack Beamish?'

What colour he had drained from Charlie's face as he answered. His words came out like a sob, 'I don't think so.'

Craig knew he was lying. He would try again. 'Jack Beamish, known by his mates as Jack Frost. Are you friends with him?'

'I wouldn't call us friends, but, I guess, I know of him,' Charlie said, his words broken, catching in his throat.

'So, you do know him.'

Craig waited.

Charlie let out a choking sob but remained silent.

'OK, it's up to you. You can either talk to me or I can take you down to the police station. You choose.' What he didn't reveal was that Pete was on his way.

Chapter THIRTY-ONE

Despite the threat of taking Charlie to the police station, he remained sniffling and repeating it had nothing to do with him. In the end he had told Charlie that DI Andrews was on his way. Now as he sat opposite Charlie, he waited for Pete to arrive. Knowing it could be another thirty minutes, he had suggested Roo get off home.

'You'll be far happier strapping your skates on, racing like a lunatic round the park, than sitting here.'

'Skates!' Charlie suddenly cried.

'Yes, I roller skate,' Roo said.

'I used to go to the skate park but haven't been for ages.'

'Why?' Roo asked.

'Things happen.'

'What things?' Craig asked.

Charlie lowered his head as if thinking whether to answer. 'Are the police really coming? I haven't done anything,' Charlie suddenly exploded.

Taken aback at the outburst, Craig looked over at a frightened young man who was now shaking. He nodded. 'DI Andrews is going to come along and talk to you about what's been happening, especially about the bit where you said it had nothing to do with you.'

Charlie swallowed hard and glared at Roo.

'I wish I could come skating with you.'

'I'm not going anywhere for now, but maybe another day.'

Ignoring Charlie's remark to Roo, Craig continued. 'Charlie, we need to understand what things have happened.'

Charlie stared at Craig, the outburst of earlier evaporating as quickly as it had appeared.

'Whilst we wait for DI Andrews, why don't you tell me about the group. Who are the members?'

Charlie looked down at his fingers where beads of blood bubbled from the picking they'd received. He shook his head.

'Fine. Just let me remind you that there has been a death at the church. Murder has not been ruled out.' Craig wasn't too sure about that, but he noted the shock register on Charlie's face.

As if unable to cope with the tension in the room, Charlie's shoulders slumped. Not taking his eyes off of his bloody fingers, he spoke.

'There are five in the group: Fenton, Jack, Clayton and Dylan, but I don't know them that well.' There was no eye contact. Charlie leaned back in his chair and folded his legs underneath him, then wrapped his arms over his chest as if to protect himself from all that was happening.

Craig raised an eyebrow. He was surprised how quickly Charlie had acquiesced to his question. 'I take it that you are the fifth member?'

Charlie didn't respond.

Craig decided to ignore the lack of response and carried on. 'You've just said you don't know them that well, yet you still hung around with them and brought them here.'

Charlie bit on his bottom lip. 'It's not that easy. You have no idea.'

Craig knew how local youth gangs could behave; sadly he'd plenty of idea. 'If that is the case, why didn't you keep out of their way?'

Charlie snorted loudly and kept his arms wrapped tightly around his body. 'As I said, you've no idea.' He stole a glance at Roo.

'So you keep saying, so tell me.' He knew it would be a waste of breath letting Charlie know he did understand.

As if thinking about his response, Charlie loosened his arms from around his body and returned to picking his fingers. All the while he kept his gaze on the bloody mess he was creating. 'Fenton is the ringleader. He sees himself as someone important. Nobody questions him.'

Craig lent forward. Resting his elbows on his knees he steepled his fingers and stared at Charlie. 'You don't look like the kind of young man who lets others intimidate you.'

Charlie shrugged and stared down at his hands. 'It's not that simple.'

'Then tell me so I can begin to understand.'

'He's always been like that, but of late he's got worse. What happened at the church is how he's got out of hand.'

Tempted as he was to say so you were there, he knew he needed to get Charlie to open up on everything, 'Tell me.'

Charlie rubbed his hands over his face.

Craig could see he was struggling and without taking his eyes from him, he waited.

As if trying to put the words together, trying to formulate his words, Charlie clasped his hand together. With tears, once again, pooling in his eyes, he looked up. Tears rolled down his cheeks.

Roo sat motionless as she listened.

'We all went to the church. We all knew why and I wasn't keen. It was all getting stupid. I said I was leaving, but they circled me. Fenton told me in a menacing tone, I was going nowhere. Fenton carries a knife and although I've never seen him use it, it doesn't stop him from flashing it and threatening people.'

Craig whistled through his teeth. Carrying a knife was against the law if intended to use as a weapon. He'd seen enough victims from knife crime and it made him sick to the stomach at what damage a blade could do.

'Did he threaten you with the knife?'

Charlie shook his head. 'No. Fenton punched me on the shoulder and walked away. The others followed.'

'Now, you are saying the others were up for whatever was going to happen?'

Charlie shrugged but continued. 'They all went inside the church. I wanted to go in if only to stop this latest prank, but I just walked away.'

'They didn't come back and drag you in?' Roo asked.

'No. Fenton said he would deal with me and it would be worse, much worse.'

Craig found it hard to believe Charlie could

be pushed over that easily. The lad was well built and guessed he was around five foot ten inches. He carried no fat, which these days was rare in the younger generation.

'Yet despite this you knew what they were intending to do?'

Charlie took a deep gulp as if trying to swallow something, 'It's not what you think.'

Craig remained silent but didn't move his steely gaze from Charlie.

Charlie continued. 'I didn't think they would go ahead with it. After all, it was only a dare.' He started to cry. 'I can't believe from something that started as a simple dare, ended up with…' Charlie sobbed into his hands.

'Why didn't you go to the police and tell them what had happened?'

Charlie looked up at him with horror and through his tears cried. 'Are you for real?'

Craig ignored the outburst and the gushing of tears. 'Have there been other dares?' He checked his watch and wondered what was keeping Pete.

Waiting for the sobs to subside, Charlie, with red eyes and streaming tears, nodded. 'Fenton said we all had to do a dare to stay in the group. I wasn't keen, but crossing Fenton wasn't something you did lightly. Jack wasn't keen either, but we decided to go along. It was meant to be a laugh – at least that's how it started.'

Craig sighed at the idea. 'At your age didn't you think it was childish?'

Charlie shrugged his shoulders. 'As I said, it

all started as a laugh.'

'A laugh!' Craig shouted out and jumped to his feet startling Roo and Barney who gave out a loud woof.

Craig sat down and Barney settled at his feet.

'As I said, that's how it started. The freaky sub was the start of it. That was my dare. It was easy enough. We'd seen the weird model on the park pond. It didn't take much to find out who it belonged to. Even better the owners lived in the same road as Fenton…'

'Cavendish Road,' Roo cried out interrupting.

Charlie glared at her and nodded. 'Fenton had found out they were going away. Once they'd gone, I went in and grabbed the model.'

This young man might be sitting here sobbing and feeling sorry for himself, but he wasn't the innocent he wanted us to believe, Craig thought, anger rising. 'What was the idea behind all of this?' he found himself snapping.

'Like I said, we had to prove we were… you know.'

'No, I don't.' Suddenly things began to slot into place. Craig glanced at Roo then back to Charlie.

'Tell me what do you know about a missing dog and an expensive chain? Because I am guessing you know about these incidents too.' His voice had risen.

A derisive smirk, flicked across Charlie's face. 'They too were dares. Everything was a dare.' Charlie said matter of fact.

'I'm glad you find this amusing all of a sudden. Now, tell me about *the dare* in the church.'

The smirk of moments ago vanished, replaced by a look of horror and tears of earlier filled Charlie's eyes. He took a deep breath then spoke.

'Fenton had insisted Jack pop his head in the noose that had been made earlier. It was the same rope used to pull the punk sub along in the river. The dare was for Jack to climb up one of the columns and onto the rafters and tie the rope up there. He was supposed to hang onto it with his head in the noose while the others counted to ten. Then slip it off and climb back down. He was strong enough to do it, but the rope was still wet and slippery, and his hands slipped.' Charlie sobbed loudly, burying his head in his hands.

A heavy banging on the door halted the conversation. Craig jumped to his feet. Barney ran through to the hall barking loudly. Striding around the dog and commanding him to shut up, Craig opened the door. He didn't miss the police car at the kerb side with a uniform officer in the driving seat. Pete had brought a backup; he should have guessed.

Craig nodded. 'Come on in, I think we have the full story.' He gave a brief resume of what Charlie had told them. 'Of course, the church was a convenient place to hang out as you know it too is in Cavendish Road.' Both men looked at each other, for a moment a silence hung between the two of them.

'Well done,' Pete finally said and tapped

Craig on the shoulder.

Aware of the enormity of what had taken place over the last few days, Craig remained silent as he ushered Pete into the lounge.

Charlie bounced to his feet.

'Sit down lad,' Pete said, his voice gentler than the look on his face. He rubbed the palm of his hand over his nose.

Roo didn't miss the disdain on the DI's face at the odour in the room.

Remaining standing, Pete continued. 'I'm DI Andrews.' Pete flashed his warrant card at the pathetic young lad in front of him. 'I hear you've told Mr Gardner what's been going on. As you must know by now, it is all very serious.' And in a commanding voice, he continued. 'I am now taking you down to the station to be formally questioned, but before we go I have one question: what happened to Jack's phone?'

Charlie shrugged, 'Fenton took it.'

Pete looked at Craig, neither spoke.

'Right, lad let's be on our way.'

'What about grandad?' Charlie cried.

'I doubt he'll be home for a few days yet.'

Pity he hadn't thought about his grandad sooner, Craig thought, he might not have got himself into so much trouble.

Charlie didn't move, just stared up at Pete as if all the fight had gone out of him. Barely above a whisper, he added, 'It was never meant to get to this. It started as a crazy dare and got out of hand. I wanted to stop it.'

'Right,' Pete said and stepped forward. 'There's an officer outside in the car, so let's be having you and you can explain all of that down at the station.'

With his head bowed, Charlie got to his feet and with Pete's hand on his shoulder, he allowed the DI to usher him out into the hall where he slipped on a pair of trainers before being taken to the police car.

After placing Charlie in the back seat, Pete joined his uniformed officer in the front. Craig and Roo, with Barney watched the police car drive away.

'All because of a dare and a young life has been lost,' Craig said, turning to Roo.

Chapter THIRTY-TWO

With her rollerblades and her protection pads on, Roo skated over to the green bench where the others from the club were assembled. The bench was a significant landmark in the park having been placed there in memory of Sam Fitzgerald who had designed the gardens. She looked around for Taylor and was disappointed not to see him. *Where was he?* she wondered. He had messaged her earlier to say he was on his way.

'Helloooo PI.'

Roo turned so quickly she almost lost her balance. Her heart skipped several beats as Taylor skated towards her. Standing at her side, he draped his arms around her. 'Sorry I'm late, traffic!'

He wasn't late. She just needed to see his infectious smile and feel his arms around her. Thoughts of Charlie and what he had told them had played heavily on her mind, and now, having Taylor holding her, helped the thoughts ease.

'Are you OK? You look distracted.'

'I'm fine. It's been a busy day.'

'Sure?' Taylor asked, placing a hand under her chin and dropping a kiss on her lips. 'What's happened to make you look as if you are somewhere else?'

She smiled up at his gorgeous face. There would be plenty of time to tell him; now was not that time. 'A good skate around the park will shake all the cobwebs away.' She took hold of his hand and clasped it tight and felt so lucky.

'Right, are we all ready?' Barry called out loudly.

A loud, *Yes* filled the air.

'That's great,' Barry called back, then blew on a whistle. His face lit up at the excited screams from the youngsters. 'Remember there is to be no pushing or jostling.' He looked down at the skaters with a proud grin, then added, 'There is plenty of space for everyone. And don't forget, it's meant to be fun not a competition.' Barry took in the eager faces.

'OK, ready steady, go!' he bellowed and waved a large white handkerchief that served as a flag. Stepping to one side the youngest skaters slowly set off, their squeals and shrieks filling the air. Several of the skate teachers slowly skated with them and like Roo and Taylor they were there to keep an eye on the little ones.

Thirty minutes later the younger skaters were ushered back to where they had started: Parents patiently waiting to take them home.

With the young skaters heading home, the older skaters were given free reign. Roo and Taylor stopped and faced each other.

'I'll race you,' Taylor said. A mischievous grin filled his face making his eyes sparkle with the challenge.

'You're on!' Roo let out a yell and pushing off she left Taylor standing.

'You devil,' he cried. Swinging his arms to gain more momentum, he set off to catch up with her.

With shrieks of delight, Roo kept pace with Taylor. The day's issues and revelations temporarily forgotten.

After three circuits, breathless, Roo and Taylor flopped down on the dry grass next to the green wooden seat and exhaled loudly. Neither had allowed the other to race ahead. They had matched each other perfectly, the same as if they were performing in the shows.

'Phew!' Taylor groaned, as he lay down on his back. His arms stretched above his head, he turned and grinned at Roo. 'I'm going to have to stay fit to keep up with you.' Bringing his arms down, he rolled over and wrapped them around her. He kissed her gently. 'I so love you, my very own PI.'

'Hello!'

Startled, Roo and Taylor sat up. Two fluffy dogs on leads sniffed at them. 'Sorry, they are just so friendly,' explained an attractive, slim, middle-aged woman, wearing denim shorts, a vest style t-shirt and trainers. She smiled down at them.

'I didn't realise that you roller skated,' the woman said with surprise. At the same time, she slackened the leads allowing the dogs to move further forward and lick Taylor.

'We are members of the skating club,' Taylor answered as he made to stand. 'Tonight, we've been practising for the marathon which is taking place at Westleton.' Taylor held out his hand and pulled Roo up. 'This is my gorgeous girlfriend, Roo.'

‘Hello Roo, I’m Paula. Pleased to meet you and these two,’ she nodded towards the dogs whose tails wagged maniacally, ‘are Finlay and Olie.’

Without taking her eyes off Paula, Roo reached down and ruffled the curly coats of the dogs. ‘Nice to meet you all.’

‘Nice to meet you also.’ Paula tugged on the leads to bring the dogs back to her. ‘I’d best be going and let you two enjoy your skating. See you tomorrow, Taylor,’ Paula called and set off down the path, both dogs out in front.

Roo looked puzzled.

‘That’s Mrs Graystone. Dad and I are painting the outside of her house.’

Roo remembered Taylor mentioning something about their latest decorating project. Something about it being a large house, but nothing much else. This time of year, they were always very busy with outside decorating. ‘They are cutie dogs,’ she said as she watched Paula Graystone walk briskly behind her two hounds. Her mind tried to place her as she was sure she had met her before.

Chapter THIRTY-THREE

The vision of Paula Graystone had nagged her all night and Roo now needed to look at what had kept her from getting a good sleep. Picking up the file from Craig's desk, she flicked it open. Staring up at her was the photo of Holly Westwood. She studied it despite having seen it many times. She frowned. She had been so certain. She rubbed at her eyes, as if to improve the clarity, then took another look. 'I don't know,' she said out loud and walked away. Maybe coming back in a few minutes to take another look would help, she mused and headed to the kitchen.

With a cool fruit drink in her hand, Roo returned to the file. Her mind was unsettled as it went over and over the brief moments when Paula Graystone, with her dogs, had stopped to say hello to Taylor. It had woken her in the night as she realised where she had seen Paula Graystone, or at least, she thought she had. Leaving her drink to one side and with her phone, she took a pic of the photo.

Once again, she studied the image. Maybe she was looking for something that wasn't there. Maybe she'd become confused, hardly surprising, she thought, with so much going on over the last week. Then it came to her, there was only one person who would be able to help.

Animated at finding a solution to her nagging thoughts, she messaged Taylor. *Please look at this pic and tell me if you think it looks like Paula Graystone?* Crossing her fingers she pressed the send button. Needing to quell her impatience for a swift response, she picked up her glass and sipped at the cool drink.

'Good morning, Roo, you're in early,' Craig called, closing the door as Barney raced towards her.

Startled, Roo swung round and was almost knocked out of her chair as Barney, excited at seeing her, jumped up and licked her hand. Keeping her balance, she cried. 'I know just what you want,' and gently pushing him down, she pulled open her desk draw and plucked out a packet of doggy treats.

'Here you are,' she handed over a chunky treat that vanished in an instant. Satisfied, Barney spun round and headed to his water bowl.

'Are you OK?', Craig asked, his eyebrows knitted together in concern, as he settled down at his desk. 'Yesterday was pretty heavy with a tragic outcome.'

Roo nodded, although the events of yesterday had dulled after the brief encounter with Paula Graystone.

Oblivious of Roo's mental turmoil, Craig continued. 'You couldn't imagine the outcome. Carrying out dares to show how brave or stupid a person was and then it all ending in tragedy.'

Roo suddenly realised Craig was talking about yesterday. A stab of guilt engulfed her; a young man was dead and here she was trying to match two people who she was unsure had anything in common. 'Sorry, my mind was miles away. I take it DI Andrews has arrested all of them?'

'Yes. They have all been taken to the station where they will be charged on various offences.'

For a moment they both fell silent as if reflecting on the last few days. The beeping of Roo's phone broke the frigid peace.

A message from Taylor. Roo grabbed her phone, her face unreadable as she read his message. A photo followed. *I thought it best to take this for you. I hope it helps.* She wanted to jump down the phone and hug him. She hadn't asked for a photo, just for him to look at the one she had sent. Once again, excitement engulfed her.

She handed her phone over to Craig.

Craig looked startled as he stared down at the photo. 'Where did you get this from?'

'Taylor. During our skating practise, a woman with two dogs stopped and spoke to him. It turned out he and his dad are repainting the outside of Paula Graystone's house. That's her name. Don't you think she resembles Holly Westwood?'

Craig rubbed a hand over his chin and before he could speak, Roo plucked the photo of Holly Westwood from the file. 'Now what do you think?' she asked, thrusting the photo into his hand.

Craig studied the two photos. 'There is a

possibility,' then looking over at Roo, added, 'maybe a little more than that.'

Roo sat up straight, a positive sparkle returning to her eyes, 'You can't believe how I was taken aback when I saw her in the park. I had to keep blinking to make sure I wasn't seeing things. Then I checked the photo we have on file of Holly Westwood, but doubt crept in. I guess I wanted it to be Mrs Everett's long-lost daughter, so I asked Taylor if he could see a resemblance of Holly Westwood to Mrs Graystone. He did one better and took a photo of Mrs Graystone.'

She waited for Craig's reaction. There was none. 'I know it was a little wild, but I wanted to see what Taylor thought.'

Deadpan, Craig asked, 'I'm assuming she wanted to know why Taylor wanted to photograph her?'

A little deflated, Roo answered. 'She was surprised at the request and yes, she did ask. Taylor didn't have an answer. Rather than make something up he suggested she call our office. He gave your number after explaining you were a private investigator. She was curious and said she would call you, but she did allow him to take the photo. And you will never guess where Mrs Graystone lives.'

Craig raised his eyebrows, 'Surprise me!'

'Rosehill Gardens. How coincidental is that?'

Craig looked at Roo, but before he could make a comment, his phone rang out. He answered and listened.

'I understand, but...' Craig said unable to get a word in. 'Of course, yes, thank you. No problem that would be perfect. And I can…' The call ended. Craig stared down at his phone as if it would suddenly burst into conversation. He looked over at Roo. 'That was Mrs Graystone. Sadly, she wouldn't let me get a word in edge ways.' He rolled his eyes.

'However, she's coming to the office straight away as she has something to tell us.'

Chapter THIRTY-FOUR

Thirty minutes later, Paula Graystone settled on the edge of the sofa opposite Craig. Her fingers clasped the photo so tight her knuckles had turned white. Her eyes feasted on the image of Holly Westwood. A look of disbelief creased her face and barely above a whisper, she spoke, 'This is beyond belief. In fact, it is utterly bizarre.' Her blonde curls bounced as if in time to her words. 'I am trying to get my head around all of this,' she nodded at the photo, 'and all because my young decorator asked if he could take a photo of me.' A thin smile curved her lips as she looked over at Craig.

Craig opened his mouth to speak, but Paula continued, 'Are you able to tell me anything about the woman who is in the photo?'

Craig steepled his fingers and brought them up to his chin. 'The photo is of the daughter of a lady who came to our office.' He couldn't bring himself to say, client – it seemed too cold in light of the situation.

'She came into our office a few days ago and asked for help to try and find a person who she had seen.' He thought about his next words before continuing.

'She was convinced the person she saw resembled her daughter.' He pointed at the photo. At the same time, he wondered how much more to say about Katie Everett.

From the moment they'd been asked to try and find the woman Katie had seen, he was aware that if they did find anyone, it would be a sensitive situation to deal with. He wasn't a counsellor, just a humble investigator and he needed to tread with care. Knowing this, he still continued.

'The person asked us for help…' Craig went on to explain how she'd had a child when she was very young and the baby had been adopted. And whilst it was many years ago, the shock of seeing a woman who resembled the daughter she'd had later was too much. So much that she wanted this woman to be found and with this need she had come to us to try and help trace this person.

'The photo you have in your hand is the woman,' Craig finally added.

Paula listened. Her face gave nothing away as she placed the photo on her knees. 'Where did she see this person?' Paula asked, her voice flat.

As she listened, Roo couldn't take her eyes off Paula Graystone. The more she scrutinised, the more she saw resemblances to Katie Everett: the high cheek bones and curly hair. She didn't miss Paula reach for the three buttons that decorated the side of her denims and fiddle with them. What was even more striking was the likeness to Holly Westwood. Was it pure coincidence or something more?

Several moments passed before anyone spoke. Craig broke the silence.

‘It was around Castleton Green,’ he replied in the knowledge it was close to where Paula lived – Taylor had given the details to Roo. He braced himself for further reactions.

Paula’s face paled. ‘Goodness, I live near that area. In fact, I live at Rosehill Gardens as you probably know from Taylor.’ She turned to Roo as she spoke.

Craig could see Roo was thinking the same thoughts as his; this was far more than a coincidence.

In a voice, barely above a whisper, Paula carried on. ‘I never thought it would be like this. You think about how it would be or could happen. I never set out to find her, though it was always on my to-do list.’ Paula lifted her gaze to Craig as if eye contact explained her words.

‘I was adopted as a baby. I’ve always known.’ Returning her attention to the photo of Holly Westwood, she continued.

‘I guess I was afraid of what I might find. Who would have thought a walk through the park would find me sitting in your office hours later looking at a photo that disturbs me.’ Surreptitiously Paula wiped at her cheek, then took a deep breath and looked from Roo to Craig.

‘Please could you give me the details of this woman so I can contact her.’

‘I can ask her to contact you if you give me permission to give her your details,’ Craig suggested knowing he couldn’t give Katie’s details without her permission.

Paula nodded. ‘Of course, please share

them. This is hard to take in. I've lived in the area for most of my life. I only left to go to university and that was a very long time ago.' She paused as if thinking about her next words, her fingers reaching out to play with the buttons on her denims.

'Never in my wildest dreams did I think someone locally had recognised me enough to talk to you. It's the sort of thing you'd watch on TV programmes.' Once again she took in the photo. 'There is some resemblance isn't there?' She looked to Craig for confirmation.

Craig nodded. 'A little uncanny. Would you like me to call her?'

'Yes please, let's do it before I overthink everything and run away.' Paula's eyes were a mixture of fear of the unknown and excitement of what was happening. 'I would love to meet her.'

Craig nodded. 'Please sit with Roo and I'll make the call to give her an update.'

Leaving Roo and Paula to make small conversation, Craig strode over to his desk. As he sat down, about to call Katie Everett, his phone rang. He looked at the screen and drew in his breath. *What was it with coincidences at the moment?*

'Hello,' Craig answered, not wanting to use Katie's name. He didn't think his conversation could be heard over at the sofas, but nonetheless, he applied caution.

'I was about to call you as we have some developments.' He heard a sharp intake of breath. 'We believe we have traced the woman you saw around Castleton Green.'

An audible sharp intake of breath resounded down the phone.

'Good heavens. Have you really? Have you spoken to her?' Katie's voice was soft and Craig strained to hear.

'Yes. In fact, we have met her and shown her the photo of your daughter.'

'Oh, my goodness. I was hoping but not expecting this. Does she look like Holly?'

He found himself smiling as he answered, 'Yes. There is a strong resemblance.'

Again, there was an audible intake of breath. 'What was her reaction?'

Once again, Craig thought carefully before he replied. Paula Graystone was keen to meet Katie Everett and he decided to go for it.

'She would like to meet you. Would you like to see for yourself the resemblance?'

Silence.

'Are you OK?'

'Yes, thank you, I am fine. Just trying to digest what you have said. It's been such a long time. What if it is not her? What do we do then?'

'One thing I can tell you is that the person we have found told us she had been adopted as a baby.'

Craig heard an intake of breath followed by a sob.

'I need to meet her!' Katie's words came out in a rush and Craig could visualise his client nervously fiddling with her buttons.

'Of course,' he said, before deciding to add that the woman they had been asked to look for was sitting in the office talking to Roo. 'As mentioned, we believe we have found the person you saw, and … actually, at this moment … she is sitting in the office.' He stopped to allow this information to register with Katie, then added, 'You are welcome to come here or for me to arrange a meeting.'

Without hesitation, Katie responded. 'I will come to you. If I don't act now, I will overthink everything and find myself not coming just in case it leads to disappointment.' Katie hesitated, then added, 'I am on my way.'

Craig found himself smiling at the words, *overthink everything*, the very same words spoken by Paula. 'That is…' Craig realised the call had ended. Events had happened at an alarming speed. He sat for a moment to digest it all, then rose and strode over to the sitting area. Paula looked up, an anxious expression clouding her features.

'Will she see me?'

Craig nodded. 'Yes, she is eager to meet you. So much so that she is on her way to the office.' He caught the look of shock and surprise in Paula's eyes at his words. 'However, if this is too early for you, I can stop her from coming in.'

Ringing her hands in her lap, Paula almost jumped up from the sofa. 'No, this is the perfect moment. It's been a lifetime for her and for me too.'

A silence hung in the air. Roo turned to Paula, 'I still can't believe that whilst we've been trying to find someone who resembled Holly Westwood, Taylor was decorating your house.'

Paula looked at Roo and bit her lower lip,

her eyes welling up. 'Yes!' It was as if that was all she could say.

Fifteen minutes later, Barney ran to the door. Paula leapt to her feet. Craig followed closely behind Barney.

'I'm sorry, I really couldn't wait a moment longer. I'm sure I broke the speed limit,' a soft voice said as Craig greeted Katie Everett. 'Is it OK to be here?' Katie said, short of breath as she asked.

Craig nodded. 'Of course, as long as you are happy too?'

'Thank you,' she whispered, while placing her hand on Craig's arm. The expression on her face spoke volumes.

'Let's go and meet the person we have found.' He indicated the sofas.

As soon as Katie walked towards the sofas, Paula was on her feet. The two ladies locked eyes and both moved forward. They hesitated for no more than a heartbeat, then wrapped their arms around each other.

'I've found you,' sobbed Katie Everett, tears streaming down her face. She folded her long-lost daughter into her arms. Katie and Paula hugged each other as if they had spent a lifetime waiting for this moment. 'I feel whole again,' wept Katie.

Pulling apart, they looked at each other, 'Where do we begin?' Katie said, letting her tears fall unchecked. Pulling Paula back into her arms, she hugged her tight. 'I can't believe I am hugging my baby after all these years.'

Chapter THIRTY-FIVE

Placing new plasters over her knees, Roo grimaced as she eyed the mess. Thankfully her cuts were nothing more than surface wounds, though they looked much worse and were sore. The previous evening Taylor and Roo had had another skating practice around the park. After all that had happened over the past week, she had found it exhilarating. The park had appeared quiet – how wrong she had been. Moving at a fast pace she had been floored when a football had caught her on the back of the shoulder. Down on the ground, her knees and palms had worked as brakes! Taylor had been at her side immediately along with the boys whose football had caused the accident. Thankfully, there were no bones broken.

'Don't tell me,' Craig said as he glared at Roo's raw knees, 'you've had another tumble on your wheels.'

Roo flashed him a withering look. 'Nothing serious,' she said and at the same time pulled down the legs of her three-quarter length shorts. 'Only thing bruised is my ego as whilst I was sprawled out on the ground, I was surrounded by half a dozen young boys who'd been playing football and their ball had ended up glancing off my shoulder.'

Craig rolled his eyes. 'I've told you it's a

dangerous sport,' he shook his head. 'Now remind me what time the marathon starts?'

'Sunday at nine-thirty.'

'Promise me you'll ...' he stopped mid-sentence. 'It's pointless me saying anything, but you can be sure we'll be there cheering you on along with Barney,' he smiled as he spoke. 'I know you'll go crazy,' he chuckled, 'and I know all you do is for a good cause.'

'I might get you on skates one day,' she said in mock seriousness.

'Dead body and over,' Craig retorted. 'By the way, Katie Everett will be popping into the office shortly.'

'I am really looking forward to hearing how they got on after they left,' Roo said excitedly. Then with a dreamy look added, "I still can't believe that while we'd been busy trying to find someone who resembled Holly Westwood, Taylor was decorating a house close to Mrs Everett's.'

'Sometimes chances and coincidences change the course of events. In this case it was a skate in the park, a stranger walking her dogs and a decorator. That weird combination brought a mother and daughter together after fifty-nine years.'

Now as Katie Everett sat opposite Craig and Roo, a broad smile made her eyes twinkle. 'You have no idea what the last twenty-four hours have been like.' Her words tumbled out.

'Paula is indeed my daughter. She's lived in the area most of her life. In the few years we have lived here, I never could have imagined she was so close to me. On the occasions I saw her, I could only dream it might be her, but of course, you never dare believe it could be true.' Tears slipped down Katie's cheeks. She didn't attempt to wipe them away.

'There are so many coincidences in both our lives that it is beyond me.' She took a deep breath. 'You know, she had thought of looking for me. Can you believe that?'

Craig and Roo listened in silence. Craig was the first to speak. 'This is wonderful news. I am delighted you came to talk to us because without the photo of your Holly, Roo would never have made the connection when she saw Paula in the park.'

'I can't thank both of you enough.' She turned to Roo. 'It was your sharp attention to detail that brought my baby back to me. Thank you from the bottom of my heart.' Wiping her hand over her wet cheeks, Katie rose and stepped towards Roo who instantly stood and met her halfway. Katie thrust out her arms and pulled Roo into them. Wrapping her arms around her, she hugged Roo tightly.

'I can never thank you enough.'

Chapter THIRTY-SIX

A warm sun in a sapphire blue sky beamed down on a large crowd that had gathered at Westleton Racetrack for the yearly charity skating marathon organised by Barry's skating club. Wearing a bright pink vest and denim shorts, Roo sat on the grass and strapped the safety pads around her knees and elbows, the Velcro crackling as she adjusted the straps. She stared in awe as she took in the large crowd of people meandering around. Barry had organised a special spread in the local newspaper and had posted many updates on their Facebook page to promote the event. There were over fifty skaters taking part and with this large number it was certain they would exceed the two thousand pounds Barry hoped to raise for the special school in Saldown.

Pushing her feet into her roller blades, Roo locked the straps then placed her bright pink helmet over her bouncy hair. She giggled how it matched her sassy vest top. She was about to adjust the straps when Taylor leaned forward to help.

'You look delicious, like a marshmallow,' he chuckled and dropped a gentle kiss onto her soft lips, letting his linger for a few seconds. 'I love you, PI Roo, or is it I love you *pink* PI Roo.' He laughed and popped a kiss on the tip of her nose.

The familiar feeling of fluttering butterflies surfaced in Roo's tummy. 'I love you too,' she said, her voice just above a whisper. Her heart pounded madly in her chest. It always did when she was with Taylor.

Not taking his eyes off Roo, Taylor took hold of her hands and pulled her up. Then wrapping an arm around her shoulder, he cried, 'Smile, it's selfie time.' Instantly he produced his phone and held it high enough to frame their faces. Two smiling faces appeared on the screen. 'One more,' he called and this time, he kissed her while snapping the photo. 'Perfect,' he said after checking the two photos.

'Perfect,' repeated Roo, remembering the first time they had made a selfie. What a moment that had been and the start of their wonderful relationship.

'Right, are we all ready?' cried Barry, standing on a small podium, giving him advantage over the gathering crowd. To bring everyone to attention he blew on a whistle that filled the air with a shrill.

'Yes!' Loud cries filled the air.

'Wow! That is fantastic. Now can I have all the skaters over there, please,' Barry shouted above the excitement. He pointed to an area of the track where a young woman, wearing a high-glow vest and a huge smile, stood holding a chequered flag.

'The young ones at the rear and the older ones at the front,' Barry continued, his voice already straining as he tried to be heard over the noise.

A rush of skaters pushed forward to the area Barry had indicated; laughter and screams of excitement added to the animated atmosphere. Holding hands and with wide smiles, Roo and Taylor joined the throng.

'Ready, PI?'

'You bet,' answered Roo. 'This is one of the best events in the club calendar.'

Five minutes later, the whistle shrilled out again. 'Ready. Steady. Go!' screamed Barry. With an exaggerated swish and a flourish of flapping material, the chequered flag was lowered. A crescendo of clapping and cheers erupted. The annual skating marathon had begun.

Craig and Ella clapped enthusiastically. Then to Ella's horror, Craig stuck his fingers between his lips and whistled loudly until the last of the skaters had rolled past.

'What an amazing site,' he eventually said, slightly out of breath, as he took hold of Ella's hand. Ella rolled her eyes at Craig's over exuberant behaviour. 'You're supposed to be a respected pillar of society,' she said with a cheeky grin.

'I'm off duty today,' he smirked.

Still smirking, he turned and came face to face with Pete and Harry Morgan.

'It's the first time I've been escorted by a police officer,' Harry chuckled and at the same time winked at Ella.

'It could be worse – you could be on your skates with those youngsters,' Pete beamed at

Harry. Harry snorted and lent on his stick for support.

'My pins have a job holding me up even when hanging on to this.' He made an effort to raise his stick but found himself stumbling. Pete swiftly grabbed his arm.

'See, I can hardly keep my balance,' Harry quipped. Then turning to Craig. 'I think we've all been a little off balance with the rum things that's been happening here,' he added and shook his head in dismay. 'But thanks to you and young Roo you've got it all sorted.' With laboured movement, Harry turned to Pete. 'I take it you'll deal with them young devils properly.'

Pete nodded and placed his hand on Harry's shoulder. 'Don't worry, they will be dealt with.'

'I hope it's not a slap on the wrist and sending them off home and told to behave themselves. That won't do,' Harry added.

'Rest assured. What they have committed is serious, very serious. I can tell you they've been charged with various offences.' Pete looked stern. 'It's thanks to Craig and Roo we are where we are.'

Harry nodded, 'Local gems.'

'Let's not dwell on all of that for now. It's a time to support and admire these skaters and be reminded that there is far more good out there than bad,' Craig said. As he spoke, Roo and Taylor, holding hands, skated past at a pace. A loud cry of cheering erupted as the crowd clapped and shouted words of encouragement as more of the skaters rolled past.

The End

Printed in Great Britain
by Amazon

46554966R00128

CW01653557

前言

《西遊記》是我國四大古典文學名著之一，也是老少咸宜、耳熟能詳的作品，這部小說發揮了小說的無限空間與無限的想像力，每每讓人握卷入迷而不忍釋手，不但在我國有大量讀者，即使在鄰近的日本，也有相當多的學者在研究「她」呢！

本書是集衆人之手，匯民間鄉里各種傳說，收羅彙編，在《西遊記》之外，所發展出來的另一種文學形式，如果您已熟知《西遊記》，再來閱讀本書，相信會爲您帶來另一種情趣；即使您尚未看過《西遊記》，那麼，您就更非看本書不可了，因爲「她」是一本絶妙神奇的「外傳」！

《西遊記》外傳

陳民牛
朱秋楓／編著

可筑書房
KeeJwu Bookstore

目錄

《西遊記》外傳

怨憤成《西遊》

明朝時，江北淮安有個狀元叫沈坤，他組織鄉兵，抗倭得勝，於是，《狀元兵》的名聲很大。朝廷得知後，覺得用鄉兵抗倭倒也是一個省力的辦法，於是降旨將沈坤升官，並嚴斥淮安府無能。

旨意一到，知府大人就恨起沈坤來了：要不是你逞能，管那麼多閒事，哪會有這些麻煩，這不是要了我的前程嗎！整天悶悶不樂，一個勁地發脾氣。有個在知府面前幫閒的窮酸秀才看出了他的心思，覺得正是巴結的好機會，就對知府說：「沈坤圖謀不軌，有造反之意。」知府想：我被沈坤整得還不夠啊，你還去惹他？隨即把臉一沈，喝一聲：「不得胡說。」那秀才挨了訓斥，不但沒有退去，反而上前一步，從懷裏掏出一張紙頭遞了上去：「小人不敢胡說。這是小人聽到的民謠，明明白白就是反詩。」知府接過紙條，只見上面寫著：

沈坤鬧，百姓笑，

狀元兵，合人心；
三年之期一來到，
殺豬宰羊上北京。

這民謠本是老百姓聽說沈坤升官後編起來的，意思是說等沈坤三年母喪期滿之日，大家相約一起送他起程上京赴任。這哪是什麼反詩？知府早就知道這麼回事，他看看站在旁邊嬉皮笑臉的秀才，你這不是戲弄我嗎？心中老大不快，隨手將紙條一丟，拂袖就要走。

秀才拾起紙片，一揖到地，攔住知府說：「請問大人，當今皇上姓啥，龍庭在哪？」知府還沒回過味來，他又接著說：「當今皇上姓朱，龍庭在北京，民謠裏說『殺朱宰羊上北京』不就是要造反坐龍庭嗎？『沈坤鬧，百姓笑』不就是說老百姓都擁護沈坤造反嗎？」

知府這下明白，秀才這是叫他栽陷。辦法倒是不錯，可這是要留千載罵名的呀！他腦筋一轉，想出個借刀殺人的主意來。他對秀才說：「你告沈坤謀反一事，本大人管不了，你可上京去，本知府派人相陪。」這句話裏，說他管不了是實，鬼就鬼在派人陪送秀才上京，實際上就是說：我派人領你上京城去告狀。

狀告到了監察御史面前。碰巧這位御史是剛剛升任的，幾個月來，辦了幾件事都不順手，新官上任的三把火一把也沒燒成，正窩著一肚子火哩！看看狀詞上說有人造反，那還了得，連忙奏明皇上。

自古以來，做皇帝的最忌諱別人造反篡權，嘉靖皇帝雖然說一心求仙，甚事不問，可「謀反」二字也是容不得的，隨即由太監代筆，批個「下獄」。錦衣衛到淮安，二話不說，扣上沈坤就走。那沈坤本是剛強之人，無緣無故地被逮下獄，受不了，幾天就得了重病。

消息傳到淮安，老百姓氣不過，抓住那個告狀的秀才，把嘴唇割掉作爲懲罰。後來吳承恩在《西遊記》裏把他寫成一個小妖怪，叫奔波兒霸，取他喜歡奔波而且霸道的意思，也是個沒嘴唇的。

沈坤受冤，吳承恩心裏難受啊！他們是多年的老朋友了，起兵抗倭的主意實骨子是他出的。他收拾收拾行裝，決心上京爲沈坤喊冤。

他把主意告訴了另一個老朋友——光福寺的智廣法師。法師不贊成，說他又犯書呆子氣了。法師說：「皇上聽人說造反，就像我們佛家被人罵禿驢一樣，這個冤，你喊不回頭。」那怎麼辦哩？法師出了個主意：「你不是準備寫書嗎？當今皇上一心拜佛求仙，你要是能寫出修道的書獻去，皇上一高興，或許你能救回沈狀元。」

這一說提醒了吳承恩。幾年前，他和沈坤合作寫書，才開了個頭：開天闢地、妖魔鬼怪……後來因爲倭寇騷擾，沒能寫下去。現在要把書寫完，並不費事，可那些都是罵皇上、發牢騷的，能行嗎？他把這話告訴了法師，法師點撥他說：「世上事，本無定例，你不妨移花接木，把你寫的和我們佛家玄奘法師西天取經的事合在一起吧，既省事，又是講佛的。」

「那不是不倫不類了嗎？」

法師笑了起來：「求仙證道，哪一件不是奇奇怪怪的？」說得吳承恩也會意地笑了。此後，他在法師的幫助下，寫起了《西遊記》，別看他東拉西扯，一會兒取經，一會兒鬼怪的，可就是受人歡迎，留芳千古哩！

可惜，吳承恩書未寫成，沈坤已經死在獄中了。

沈坤死後，吳承恩悲憤之餘，把《西遊記》又重寫了一遍，乾脆把皇上都寫成昏君，把求道的都寫成無道之人，只少個沒指名道姓地罵嘉靖皇帝。又把猴行者改寫爲孫行者，以紀念沈坤，只不過爲了不讓官家看出來，將「沈」字換成了「孫」字。又因爲皇上姓朱，太祖朱元璋是和尚出身，就寫了一個提不上手的和尚豬八戒。當時書是從唐僧取經寫起的，孫行者的故事還不多，讀著好像覺得不過癮，聽人說海州猴子的傳說多，他又跑到海州去蹲了一段時間，回來後增加了鬧天宮一段，這才覺得出了一口悶氣。

蔡鐵鷹／搜集整理

三別葉夫人

據說，吳承恩到七十一歲的時候，才開始寫《西遊記》。在這以前，他作過許多詩，寫過不少文章，筆頭子很有功夫。《西遊記》這樣大部頭的書，他老早就在心裏打譜了，只因爲頭緒還沒有完全理清，加上生活不太寬裕，要做些散事糊口，所以遲遲落下不筆來。

隆慶年間，吳承恩有了點積蓄，生活安順一些了，便定下心來揣摩《西遊記》。這天夜晚，吳承恩躺在床上，思量著怎樣才能把《西遊記》寫得帶勁一點，厚實一點，有趣一點，動人一點。要做到這幾「點」，不容易呀！他想得很苦，身子骨翻過來，轉過去，轉過去，翻過來，就跟烙大餅似地翻個不斷，轉個沒完。老伴見他翻轉著身子不安生，勸他：「快睡吧，快睡吧。」可他只當沒聽見，還是輾轉反側，想來想去。

吳承恩想呵，想呵，直想得頭皮子發脹，耳朵裏發響，心口窩發悶，總覺得原先打譜的一些套套稀鬆平常，不夠實在。想到半夜子時，他忽然叫一聲：「有了！」隨手掀開被子，起了身，下了床。老伴見吳承恩驚驚乍乍的樣子，以爲他又跟往常一樣發了詩興，便也連忙起身下床，想泡壺茶給老頭子提提神，好讓他寫詩。

吳承恩並沒有動筆。只見他從箱子裏拿出兩件換身衣服和幾小塊散碎銀子，連同筆、墨、紙、硯，打了個小包袱拎在手裏，又從牆上取下雨傘，往胳肢窩一夾，對老伴說：

「夫人！今番我要出一趟遠門，少則數月半載，多則年把兩年，事情辦妥就回，望夫人保重身體，不要牽掛。」

說罷就走。

老伴急了！趁吳承恩沒有在意，「唰」一下把雨傘奪了過。吳承恩一打楞兒，手中的小包袱也挨老伴拉住了。

吳承恩的老伴姓葉，出身於書香人家，識文解字，十分賢慧。她跟吳承恩成親以後，既沒生男，也沒生女，曾經勸說吳承恩娶「小」立子，支撐門戶，吳承恩怎麼也不答應。這麼一來，她待吳承恩又敬重，又親熱，寧願自個不吃不喝，也要照顧好身旁唯一的親人。幾十年光景，夫妻二人你扶我幫，同心相伴，越到老年情意越深。眼下裏，葉夫人聽吳承恩說這趟遠門要年把兩年才能回來，哪裏捨得讓他走呵！

吳承恩見老伴不讓他走，也急了，連說：「夫人，夫人，後腿扯不得，後腿扯不得！」

葉夫人問：「你要上哪去？」

吳承恩說：「海州雲台山。」

「呵？」葉夫人嚇了一跳。怎麼啦？原來她聽人講過，海州雲台山離吳承恩的家鄉有好幾百里路，坐落在波浪滔滔的大海裏，山很深，林很密，有狼蟲，有虎豹，一般人皆不敢去。葉夫人心想：老頭子迷了心竅啦，怎麼半夜三更爬起來要上雲台山呢？就說：

「算了，那地方又遠又凶險，不去也罷。」

吳承恩搖搖頭說：「不去不好辦！」

「什麼大事不好辦呢？」

吳承恩說：「我打譜要寫的《西遊記》，架子搭好了，就是有些眞情實景摸不著底兒。比如，書裏要寫山，寫海，寫奇花，寫異草，寫飛禽走獸之類的生靈，不到山上、海裏去見識見識，怎好動手寫書呢？剛才想到了這步棋，沒說的，非走不可！」

葉夫人聽吳承恩這麼一講，覺得有道理，又見他走的決心很大，感到留不住了，只好應允，說：「等等再走，我給你弄點乾糧帶著。」

吳承恩笑笑說：「好！」

葉夫人趕緊放下雨傘，洗手和麵，吳承恩也放下包袱，到灶房裏幫著燒鍋。老倆口忙操一陣子，弄好了十多斤乾糧。吳承恩把香噴噴的烙餅用幾張乾荷葉包起來，裝在布口袋裏；

又找出一條舊汗巾，搓成繩子，一頭拴著小包袱，一頭繫著乾糧袋，朝肩上一挎，拿過雨傘，對老伴說：

「夫人保重，我走啦！」

說罷就走。

不料想，葉夫人一把拉住他的手，二話沒說，只是掉淚。老伴一哭，吳承恩心裏，頭也酸滋辣味的，很不好受，忙說：「夫人，不要難過，我儘量早回就是了。」說著，抬腿就往門外跨。哪知葉夫人拉著他硬是不肯撒手，說：「在家待著，別走啦！」

怎麼辦了乾糧又不讓走呵？原來，葉夫人的心裏發了怵。發了什麼怵呢？一是想到吳承恩的歲數六十好幾，快往七十上爬了，不像年輕那會兒能夠經得起風吹雨打；二是想到吳承恩有股子迷勁，寫起東西來，飯也忘了吃，覺也不想睡，在跟前還能勸說勸說，照料照料，出門在外可就沒人關心了。後首又想到頂重要的一條，就是：吳承恩的筆頭帶鈎子，以前作詩寫文章，時常拐著要彎兒諷喻世態，爲這惹出過不少麻煩，只落得多次趕考不得中，兩袖清風白了頭。葉夫人心裏想，禍從口出，災自筆來，難得家裏有了積蓄，安安穩穩過個晚年算了，還拼老命寫什麼書呀！七想八想，打定了主意。吳承恩一要走，她就哭；一要走，她就哭。

吳承恩急了，把脚一跺說：

「夫人！你讀過書，也知理，怎麼今天這麼樣的不懂事！」

葉夫人抹了把淚，說：「時光催人老，可知白髮飄？」

吳承恩把腰一挺：「人老骨頭硬，大器爭晚成！」

葉夫人搖了下頭，說：「山遠路迢迢，飢寒誰照料？」

吳承恩把手一伸：「生就兩隻手，自會作應酬。」

葉夫人嘆了口氣，說：「筆底生禍端，不如討個安。」

吳承恩把眼一睜：「為人立天地，豈能沒出息！」

老倆口你言來，我語去，一個往東，一個奔西，越說越岔。不管吳承恩怎說怎講，葉夫人還是「瞎子揹鮎魚，高低不撒手」！吳承恩急得頭上冒汗，心裏著火，覺得很為難：硬走吧，會傷了老夫老妻的和氣；不走吧，寫書的打算就要落空。怎麼辦呢？他想了想，說：「好吧，謹遵夫人之命，不走啦！」說著，將那小包袱、乾糧袋和雨傘統統放下來。

這時候，約莫有四更多天，外面霧濛濛的，「唏唏啦啦」下著小雨。吳承恩打了個呵欠，自言自語說：「離天亮還早，睡覺睡覺，不走啦。」一邊說，一邊解衣上床。工夫不大，便打起呼嚕睡著了。

葉夫人經過拉拉扯扯一番折騰，感到精疲力盡，睏得不行，見吳承恩呼呼大睡，也就吹燈上床，一會兒睡著啦。

第二天清早，葉夫人一覺醒來，伸了伸腿兒，呃？腳頭涼颼颼的，沒人。她慌了，趕緊爬起來看看，屋子裏連個人影也沒有。再一瞧，小包袱不見了，乾糧袋不見了，雨傘也不見了，只見書桌當中平擺著一張四四方方的白紙，上頭壓著筆筒。葉夫人連忙下床，把筆筒拿到一邊，看那白紙上，寫著好幾行字，墨跡溼漉漉的還沒乾呢。頭一行是題目，五個字：「送我入門來❶。」

葉夫人曉得吳承恩的筆下愛兜圈子，一看「送我入門來」，便知道這是一句以「入」爲「出」的反話，說是「入門來」，實爲「出門去」。不用說，老頭子玩花樣走了！

再往下看，寫的是：

玄鬢垂雲，忽然而雪，不知何處潛來？吟嘯臨風，未許壯心灰。嚴霜積雪俱經過，
試探梅花開未開？安排事付與天公管領，我肯❷安排！
狗有三升糠分，馬有三分龍性，況丈夫哉？富貴無心，只恐轉相催❸。雖貧杜甫還
詩伯❹，縱老廉頗是將才。漫❺說些痴話，賺他兒女輩，亂驚猜。

了不得！這是一首不服老、抖壯志的絕妙好詞。葉夫人接連看了好幾遍，眞是越看越想看，越看越愛看，不由得心領神會，脫口念出兩句讚詩：

老馬抖威志千里，
羞煞房內愚夫人！

這當口，忽聽窗外一聲歡叫：

「夫人保重，待我去也！」

葉夫人奔到窗前，朝外一看，只見吳承恩肩上挎著小包袱和乾糧袋，手裏打著傘，在那濛濛春雨之中，騰雲駕霧似地朝著雲台山方向去了。

姜　威／搜集整理

❶這首詞，見《吳承恩詩文集》。
❷肯：能。

❸這兩句的意思是：我無心於富貴，只擔心時光催人衰老。

❹詩伯：詩壇首領。伯，同霸。

❺漫：隨便，信口。

文筆峰

在高公島南部，有個美麗的小山灣。這兒三面靑山，錦繡如畫，好像擺在書案上的畫屏；山灣裏的平地上，直立著一塊大靑石，活像一支毛筆，人們叫它文筆峰。文筆峰北邊，有塊大山崖，石階一層壓一層，活像一摞厚厚的書，人們叫它萬卷書。萬卷書旁邊，還有一塊大靑石，兩個駝峰中間似乎可以擱筆，人們叫它筆架石。老輩人說，這些都是吳承恩的遺物。怎麼吳承恩的畫屏、毛筆、筆架和書會變成石頭呢？原來有個故事。

相傳吳承恩上雲台山的三元宮裏，花了三年工夫寫成了《西遊記》，接著，又寫成另一部神怪小說《禹鼎志》。這一天，他備了幾樣酒菜，帶著筆硯、書案和這兩部書稿，來到水簾洞，要在這兒將兩部書再潤色一番。

吳承恩十分喜歡水簾洞，夏天常到這裏寫作。洞內既幽靜又淸涼。洞壁泉水細流，晶瑩耀眼，好像珍珠簾子一般。洞中有口小井，井水又涼又甜，吳承恩寫作疲勞了，就用它洗把臉，抖抖精神。今天，因爲兩部作品都已寫成，如同卸下千斤重擔，渾身舒暢極了，一邊呷著酒，一邊考慮著怎樣修改。

這時，有個老猴精帶著一群小猴，跑到水簾洞前，猴子們一個個跳樹攀枝，採花摘果；抛石子，扔果殼；砌寶塔，刨沙窩；趕蜻蜓，追飛蛾；捉虱子，搔腦勺；挨的挨，磨的磨；壓的壓，扯的扯，玩得好不歡樂！吳承恩越看越高興，大腿一拍，連聲叫好，提起筆來，唰唰唰，把衆猴嬉耍的情景，活靈活現地寫進了《西遊記》。

吳承恩在洞裏美滋滋地喝一陣酒，改一會稿，不知不覺酩酊大醉，躺在案上睡著了。

這時，在外面玩耍的幾個小猴，看見喝酒的老頭趴在案上不動了，就好奇地跳進洞裏，輕輕地抬起吳承恩的手臂，把兩部書稿都偷出來交給老猴子看。老猴子打開《西遊記》一看，哈哈大笑，衆猴子都圍上來爭著看。老猴講：「太好了，這老頭把咱大王說成是美猴王、齊天大聖，衆妖魔都怕他，連王母娘娘都辨他不得，咱們臉上多有光彩呵！」小猴一聽高興得又蹦又跳直翻跟頭。老猴叫大家別鬧，再看看這部《禹鼎志》。衆猴子一齊湊過來一看，原來也是一本神話故事。老猴子講：「不行！我們要讓天下人都知道咱美猴王，要讓這老頭的《西遊記》獨傳天下，我看不如把《禹鼎志》給扔掉！」有個小猴子把手一擺說：「扔了他不會重寫嗎？乾脆，連他的筆硯一起偷出來扔掉！」衆猴齊聲說這個主意好！

衆猴又躡手躡脚走進水簾洞，剛要彎腰下手，忽聽吳承恩一聲大叫，衆猴嚇得一齊逃出

洞外。過了一會，聽聽洞裏沒有動靜，回來細看，原來吳承恩醉得人事不省，剛才是說夢話呢。這一下，衆猴樂了，一個個跳的跳，叫的叫，搶的搶，奪的奪，擁的擁，拖的拖，有的抱書稿，有的抓硯台，有的扛毛筆，有的拿筆架，有的搶畫屏，有的奪酒菜，一陣風似地席捲而去。還有幾個淘氣的小猴，爭著翻看《西遊記》，喜得指指點點，抓耳撓腮。直到老猴催叫，他們才把《西遊記》端端正正擺在案上，笑嘻嘻逃走了。

爲了使吳承恩永遠找不到他的筆硯、書稿，老猴精帶著群猴跑啊，跑啊，一氣翻越了四十九個山頭，來到高公島的大海邊。老猴一聲令下，衆猴把手裏的東西往山下一拋。只聽呼啦啦一聲響，畫屏落在海灘上，化作一座「錦鏽山」；毛筆插在山灣裏，化作一座「文筆峰」；筆架滾在山溝裏，化作一塊「筆架石」；《禹鼎志》擱在半山腰，化作巨石「萬卷書」。從此，《禹鼎記》變成了石頭，只有個書樣子了，誰也沒看過，就失傳了。吳承恩的硯台呢？只因拿硯台的小猴貪玩偷懶，剛出水簾洞不遠，就把它扔在花果山腰「八戒石」旁，變成了一塊「仙硯石」了。

還有人講，經常來高公島摸摸文筆峰，可以使你才思敏捷，聰明多智呢。

薛鴻迎／搜集整理

硯台村

花果山東面有個老窯，如今人都叫它連雲港。連雲港西邊不遠，有個陶庵，它的南面有座丫髻山，像一個站著的少女，峰頂上還有兩個羊角石柱，像古時孩童頭上的「抓髻」，這裏鄉親都叫它丫髻山。在這丫髻山下有條五龍溝，溝旁有塊幾庹❶長的大磐石，長方形，光潔似玉，用手摸摸光溜溜，像是磨墨用的硯池。硯池的一頭，還有一個水槽，槽裏的水是供磨墨用的。

人們傳說，這就是吳承恩寫《西遊記》時用過的大石硯台。如果說起這石硯台的來歷，還有一個有趣的故事呢！

那年春天，吳承恩寫《西遊記》，當他寫到孫悟空要去東海龍宮借兵器時，忽然心血來潮，想去看看東海。於是，吳承恩在一天清晨，就帶著兩個書童，男書童挑著吃用，女書童（丫環）背著筆硯，三人一起下了花果山，就順著雲台山根一溜向東海走去。

黃昏，吳承恩來到溝庵，看見這裏的山海美景，一下就被迷住了。南山，樹木參天，溝旁山坡野花撲鼻香，五龍溝流水嘩嘩響，萬丈崖飛瀑像打雷；向北一望，好傢伙，萬頃海浪無邊，海鷗戲舊舟，漁號聲連連。

吳承恩見此情景，不斷拍手叫好。當他看見海灘上聳立著一塊沖天石柱，忙問鄉親，村民告訴他，那沖天石柱叫定潮針。吳承恩聽了很受啓發，便叫書童快借鄉親茅屋住下，當夜就備筆疾書，不顧一天跋涉辛勞，雞叫三遍仍不停地寫著。寫著寫著，忽然發現墨水沒有了，抬頭一看，案邊的丫環已伏案睡著了，可她磨起了血泡的手指還握著墨塊。吳承恩看見她熟睡的樣子，怪心疼的，忙脫下自己長衫蓋在她身上。這時，天已亮了，吳承恩想再去看看海灘沖天石柱，便擱筆向海邊走去。

丫環醒來，太陽已升竹竿高了。她看看身上蓋的是先生的長衫，自己手裏還拿著墨塊，再看看案桌上的硯台，哎呀，不但墨池起鍋巴，連水也沒有了，心裏很難過，後悔打盹耽誤先生用墨，忙抱著長衫，找吳承恩去了。

丫環走過五龍溝時，看見一個石匠老人在打石頭。丫環是個機靈、聰明的姑娘，看見長方大白石，黑眼珠一轉，心想：要是老爹爹肯幫個忙，給先生打個大大的石硯台，那該多好！只要我們磨一會兒墨，保管先生寫幾天，不耽誤先生用墨，《西遊記》就會很快地寫出來。她想到這裏，心裏覺得甜滋滋的，就不問三七二十一，跑到老人面前，「撲通」一聲跪下。

石匠老人一楞，忙扶起丫環，說：「孩子，有什麼爲難，快說吧！」

丫環說：「老爺爺，我家吳承恩大人天天趕寫《西遊記》，他白天不是上山畫啊，就是下海寫啦，還要和鄉親們啦呱，到了晚上，拿筆寫文章一直不休息，我們兩個書童可忙啦，就是不停地倒水磨墨，常常耽誤先生使用，可把我們急壞啦，老爺爺請您幫忙給打個大大的石硯台，那該多好啊！」

丫環說得高興就比手劃脚，石匠老人也給說樂了。當他看見丫環手指上的血泡時，心裏疼得直打顫顫。

石匠老人覺得丫環姑娘說得有道理，沈思一下說：「姑娘放心吧，打硯台的事我包下，你告訴承恩先生，兩天後，請他來看大石硯台。」

丫環聽了，高興地喊聲：「老爺爺眞好！」就離開老人去找吳承恩。

丫環一直跑到海灘上，找到吳承恩，把打石硯台的事告訴他。吳承恩聽了，高興得哈哈大笑，說：「這裏的人眞好，眞是人好水甜，人傑地靈啊！」

兩天後，石匠老人帶著吳承恩去看石硯台，到了五龍溝上坡，看見一塊長方形白色磐石，老人告訴吳承恩：「先生，這是你的石硯台。」

吳承恩一看，果然是個大石硯台！有五庹長，兩庹寬，半人高，硯台面有水槽，還有光溜溜的磨墨池，剛要叫好，老人說：「先生，不要小看這石塊，它是白骨魚石，那眞是光潔如玉，磨墨可光滑啦；那水槽也不一般，槽裏的水永遠用不完，水槽下面有個泉水石臼，臼底通五龍溝，你舀一瓢後，不一會兒，水槽的水又滿了，請先生試試。」

吳承恩高興地用水瓢舀了一瓢，不一會兒，果然水槽又滿了。吳承恩拉著石匠老人說：「老爺爺，這叫我承恩如何感謝您老人家呢！」

老人說：「不用謝了，鄉親們都說你寫書可辛苦啦，爲看定潮崖，脚被蠣殼劃破了；爲看萬丈崖，鞋壞了不能走，就用葛藤綁起來；夜裏寫書不休息……唉，這些鄉親們都懂，他們過一會兒都要來看你。」

石匠老人的話一住嘴，果然從五龍溝走來一群鄉親，吳承恩高興地迎上去。鄉親們是給吳承恩送土特產來的，有的送上一包雲霧茶，有的送上兩包葛藤粉，還有人送了一籃活蹦亂跳的魚蝦。

鄉親們的關懷，使吳承恩感動得熱淚盈眶。石匠老人對吳承恩說：「有幾個鄉親上山砍茅草去了，我們要在這大石硯台上搭個棚，叫你在這裏寫書，風雨打不著，太陽曬不著。」吳承恩不停地向老人和鄉親作揖道謝。

傳說，吳承恩就是用這個大石硯台，寫完《西遊記》的。石硯台風霜斑駁，墨池被磨得很深，可見當年吳承恩著書的辛苦了。這裏原來村名叫亂石頭，鄉親爲了懷念吳承恩，改爲硯台村。

又傳說，吳承恩離開陶庵那年，正好海州地區發大水，那時墟溝南面黃九埝還未堵好，怕丫環行走不便，就把丫環留給陶庵鄉親。丫環思念先生成病，還天天爬到南山頂上眺望。年年望，月月望，後來化爲山峰。人們爲了懷念這位俊秀、聰明的姑娘，就叫南山爲丫髻山。

江希露／搜集整理

❶成人兩臂左右平伸時兩手之間的距離，約五尺。

話說傲來國

《西遊記》第一回，寫到孫悟空的「國籍」，說是在東勝神洲傲來國。怎麼不叫這，不叫那，要叫傲來國呢？這裏有個七彎八拐的傳說。

起初，吳承恩想把孫悟空安排在高麗國，然後讓美猴王嫌那高麗國地盤小，翻不下筋斗，就跑到中原大邦落了戶，這才遇見唐僧。他把這麼個想法告訴一位老朋友，老朋友搖搖頭說：「不好不好。高麗國和咱們國家只隔一條江，是鄰邦，處得不錯。你讓孫悟空嫌棄人家，人家看了你的書，能高興嗎？」

吳承恩覺得老朋友說的有道理，就讓孫悟空土生土長，根紮中原，起了個國名叫「大漢國」。那位老朋友得知消息，急忙找到吳承恩，又搖搖頭說：「不好不好。怎麼能叫『大漢國』呢？你寫的是神話故事，地名也罷，國名也罷，宜虛不宜實，最好讓人感覺到有點神奇味兒。『大漢國』這名字實而不虛，正而不奇，還是改一改爲好！」

聽完老朋友這番話，吳承恩想想，也對。他揣摩了好幾天，便把「大漢國」改名「猴兒國」。哪知這麼一改，竟惹出了一場風波！怎麼回事呢？

原來，吳承恩寫東西有個習慣：每逢寫出點什麼，總要讀上幾遍，試一試拗不拗口，好不好聽。這天，吳承恩想好了「猴兒國」的名字，落筆寫了下來，鬍子一捋，拉長音調讀道：

「猴兒……國，猴兒……，猴……」

正讀著，忽聽「哐噹」一聲，房門被人踢開了！吳承恩抬頭瞧瞧，是個賣肉的。這人姓侯，名叫侯二，做生意很不規矩。有一回，吳承恩買他二斤肉，他欺負文人，一傢伙扣了五兩！事後吳承恩的老伴發覺肉少了，要去找侯二補齊，吳承恩沒容許，說往後不買他的肉就是了，何必去找麻煩呢！從此不再光顧侯二的肉攤。怎麼侯二又突然凶撲撲地闖進門來了？吳承恩覺得奇怪，笑著說：「兄弟，請坐。」「不坐！」「兄弟，請用茶。」「不渴！」吳承恩還是笑著，問道：「兄弟，光臨寒舍，有何貴幹哪？」侯二把眼一瞪說：「我問你，爲啥在屋子裏罵我？」吳承恩莫名其妙，說道：「沒有罵你呀！」

「沒罵？」侯二「哼」了聲說：「你罵我是龜，還接二連三一個勁罵，當我是聾子聽不見哪！」

吳承恩一聽這話，才明白是怎麼回事。那會兒淮安人口音偏侉，國家的「國」字讀「龜」，不讀「郭」。侯二路過吳承恩家門口，把「猴兒國」聽走味了：「侯二……龜，侯二龜……」

嗯，罵我是烏龜？侯二占過吳承恩的便宜，心裏有鬼，認定吳承恩是在罵他。他越聽越難受，越聽越來火，想給吳承恩點顏色看看，就踢門進屋，找岔子吵鬧。

吳承恩再三解釋：是「猴兒國」，不是「侯二龜」；是書裏的國名，不是故意罵人。侯二拽住吳承恩的袖子，嚷叫說：「胡扯胡扯，世上哪有什麼猴兒國？分明是你買肉沒占到便宜，躲在家裏罵我！」侯二硬是要把吳承恩拉到街上講「理」。吳承恩氣得鬍子直抖，幸虧那位老朋友來到他家，好說歹說，才把侯二打發出去。

這場風波，攪得吳承恩哭笑不得，決定把「猴兒園」給抹掉了。換個什麼國名好呢？他和老朋友嘀咕來，嘀咕去，設想了幾十個國名，不是覺得不中聽，就是感到不神奇；有的呢，又怕引起不三不四的人誤會，招惹麻煩，總是不滿意。老朋友說：「算啦！頭昏腦脹的，出去散散心，回來再想吧！」吳承恩說：「好！」就和老朋友走出家門。

二人一頭走，一頭閒聊，不知不覺走到郊外，這時侯正值陽春三月，村莊裏桃花紅，楊柳綠，田地裏麥苗青，菜花黃，天空中黃鶯飛，喜鵲唱，眞是滿眼春花。吳承恩心裏本來有悶氣，一看景色迷人，悶也不悶了，氣也不氣了，覺得渾身舒暢，詩興大發，隨口吟了兩句：「人間春色好，第一是田莊！」吳承恩正要把這兩句詩念給老朋友聽，忽然間，農田裏傳來農民打號子的聲音：

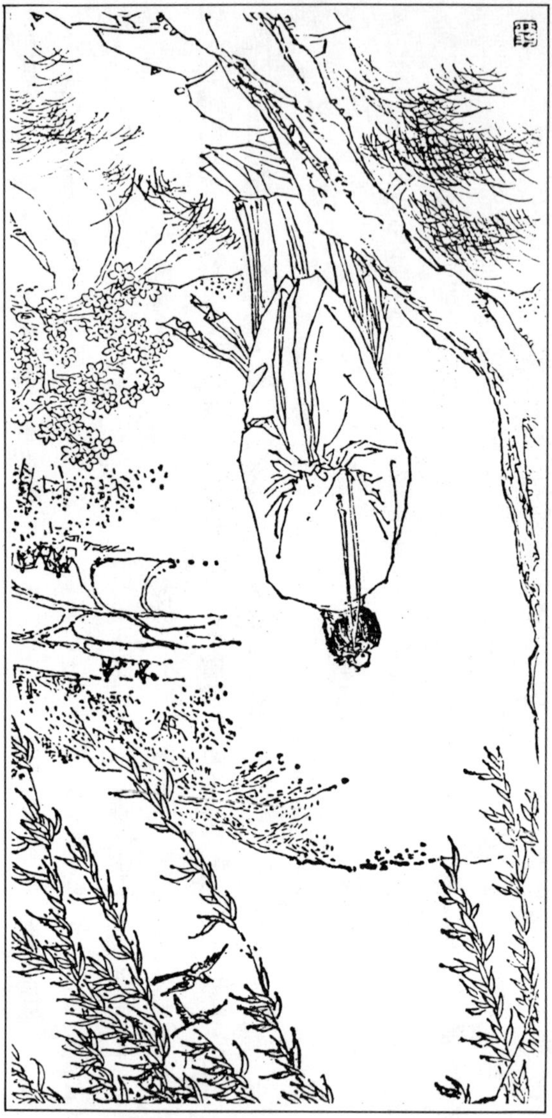

「噢……嘞！噢……嘞！」

號子聲嘹亮，悠揚，聽來十分悅耳。吳承恩心裏一動：呃！「噢嘞」，「噢嘞」，這不是滿好的國名嗎？他趕緊把想法告訴老朋友，老朋友眼睛一亮，連連點頭說：「好，好，這個名字很好！一是出人意料之外，占個『奇』字；二是琅琅上口，占個『順』字；三是不沾名，不掛姓，誰都沒有理由找上門來胡鬧！」

這樣，吳承恩就把孫悟空的「國籍」敲定了。落筆以後，覺得「噢嘞」二字筆劃太多，寫起來費事，又考慮到孫悟空天不怕、地不怕性情的形成，不會在溫順之邦，於是將「噢嘞」改爲「傲來」，音調相似，意味不同，從此有了「傲來國」。

姜　威／搜集整理

花果山和水簾洞

吳承恩離開家鄉淮安，連天帶夜趕到海州。他請一位老漁民幫忙乘船過海，上了雲台山。雲台山方圓三百多里，前有前雲台，中有中雲台，後有後雲台，大大小小的山頭總共三百六十個。經老漁民指點，吳承恩順著中雲台的一條山路往上走。他一頭爬山，一頭留心山景，起先只是看到馬尾松、葛藤根什麼的；可彎子一拐，了不得！只見山裏頭到處都是果木樹，樹上那些花呀，有紅的，有黃的，有紫的，有白的，五顏六色，鮮豔奪目，飄散出濃濃的香味兒。這時候，忽見果樹林子裏搖搖晃晃出現一個人影，仔細一看，原來是個挑水的小和尚。

吳承恩上前問道：「小師父，這滿山的果樹，是誰栽的呀？」

小和尚朝吳承恩望望，答道：「說來話長呵！聽俺師父說，二十多年前，有一天夜間，山中闖進來千把個黑瘦的漢子，一打聽，才曉得他們是山東一帶的窮苦百姓，因爲受不了財主的盤剝和貪官的欺壓，就舞刀弄槍拼起命來了，一拼拼得家破人亡，剩下千把人從海上脫身，躲到這裏。不久，官兵突然進山，圍困了六六三十六天，廝殺了八八六十四回，漢子們寡不敵衆，皆被打死了。官兵放上一把火，燒光了這裏的山林！如今的滿山花果，是死去的漢子們留下來的。他們吃野果，棄下許許多多果核子，後來生了根，開了花。二十多年的工夫，這裏變成花果山啦。」

花果山的不凡來歷，引起吳承恩的興趣，他向小和尚道了謝，又往山上走。一走走進翠竹林，忽然發現林子盡頭露出一個很大的洞口。他趕緊奔到洞前，只見洞門兩丈多高，上邊窄，下邊寬，像個「人」字。奇妙的是，洞門口倒掛著幾十股細細的流水，如同一串串珠玉穿成的簾子；水簾被太陽一照，就像綴著無數顆寶石，一閃一閃地放著光彩。吳承恩正看著，從洞邊走來一個砍柴的樵夫。這樵夫熱情口快，見洞前站著遊人，便指指點點說：

「這洞叫水簾洞，傳說很早很早以前，有個石猴精帶著一群小猴子在山澗裏洗澡，洗著洗著，一個猴子忽然說：『咦，這山澗裏的水是從哪兒裏來的？俺們去找找源頭吧！』衆猴說：『好！』就蹦蹦跳跳順著山澗往前找，找到這兒，見洞口流水不斷，以爲源頭就在洞裏，齊聲喊：『進去看看，進去看看！』可是光喊不敢進，怕裏面有妖怪。在這節骨眼上，只聽石猴精大叫一聲：『閃開！』縱身一跳，跳進洞中。過了一會兒，石猴精在裏面喊：『弟兄們，這裏可好玩啦，都快進來呀！』衆猴聽到石猴精打招呼，不怕了，一個個跳了進去。後來，石猴精就住在這洞裏，當起猴王來了。」

吳承恩很感興地問：「眞有石猴精嗎？」

「說有又沒有，說沒有又有。」樵夫說著，把吳承恩領到離水簾洞不遠的一個地方。這裏的山岩奇形怪狀，內中有兩塊岩石又高又大，中間夾著一塊小石頭，笆斗似的，滾圓溜光，上面有三個字，叫「媧遺石」。

樵夫指著媧遺石說：「相傳這是女媧娘娘煉的石頭，補天沒用完，朝下一扔，啪！正好掉在這兩塊山岩的夾當裏。過了十萬八千年，從石肚子裏蹦出一個猴子來，就是衆人傳說的石猴精！」

吳承恩越聽越覺得有趣，很想看看石猴精的住處，便轉身走進了水簾洞。洞裏很寬敞，約莫有四五間房子那樣大，洞壁上扯扯連連攀著許多藤蔓，石縫中長出不少花草。片片白雲飄進水簾洞，一些好看的山鳥在白雲間飛來飛去，唱著動聽的歌兒。置身水簾洞，神思入奇境，吳承恩興奮得不得了，心裏想：此處甚是美妙，怪不得石猴精要在這塊兒落戶哩。

後來，吳承恩就把孫悟空的家，從原先安排的平常地方搬到花果山水簾洞了。

姜　威／搜集整理

大鬧天宮的由來

大鬧天宮是《西遊記》裏最精彩的章節，最初刻印的《西遊記》並沒有這個情節，這個熱鬧非凡的場面是後來才加上去的。提起這倒有個動人的故事哩！

傳說吳承恩只有一個獨生女兒。老伴去世後，他無心料理家務，便把一點微薄的家產都交給了過繼兒子。自己躲到「射陽簃」裏專心致志地寫書去了。待他女兒快出嫁時，他的《西遊記》初稿已經完成。

有一天，女兒對他說：「爹爹，您僅有我這一個親骨肉，家產全給了哥哥。難道女兒出嫁，就空手跑到人家去不成？」吳承恩安慰女兒說：「我早替妳準備好了，足夠妳一輩子用的。」女兒一聽，滿心歡喜，也就不再追問了。

女兒的婚期越來越近了。她看父親一點動靜也沒有，放心不下，又問父親。吳承恩才從床底下拖出一只木箱子，揭開箱子指著一部書稿，說：「這是我寫的一部《西遊記》，給妳做嫁妝，就憑這部書，足夠妳享用一輩子的了。」

轉眼，女兒的婚期到了。在準備發嫁妝的時候，過繼的哥哥突然發現一只從未見過的鎖著的箱子，他估計一定是過繼老子私下替妹妹準備的幾套上等衣服、珍貴首飾，覺得要打開箱子看看才放心。於是，他偷偷找到鑰匙，暗中打開箱子一看，原來是老頭子寫的書稿——無價之寶。他隨即不聲不響地把書稿取走，仍舊鎖好箱子。於是，一只空箱子隨嫁妝一起抬到婆婆家去了。

一晃幾個月過去了。有一天，女婿急匆匆地從外邊回來，一進門就責問妻子：「妳說岳父寫了部《西遊記》書稿給妳作嫁妝，怎麼現在外邊書攤上已有這部書賣了？莫非是岳父騙了妳？」女兒一聽十分驚疑，楞了半天，才說：「啊！不會的，我親眼看見這部書稿鎖進書箱的，書攤上賣的可能是別人寫的。」「不！」女婿肯定地說：「《西遊記》今天上書攤，買的人很多。我特地看看作者，署名『吳承恩』三個字，一字不錯。」

女兒將信將疑地說：「哪能有這樣的怪事，書稿還鎖在我箱子裏，攤上就賣了？讓我打開箱子來看看。」說著，夫妻倆就一起抬出箱子，打開鎖揭開箱蓋一看，「啊」地一聲驚呆了，原來是一只空箱子。她二話沒說，轉身就跑回家去，見到父親吳承恩就放聲大哭起來。吳承恩聽女兒一講，把眉頭一皺，連忙說：「啊？空箱！妳莫哭。一哭就無法挽救了。」他停了一下子繼續說：「書稿肯定是被妳哥哥拿去偷印了。好在底稿還在我手中，尚能重新修改整理，如果一吵鬧出去，再讓妳哥哥知道就難辦了。妳先回去告訴妳丈夫，只當沒有這回事，不要聲張。我自有道理。」女兒只好回家等候消息。

第二天，吳承恩藉故外出，瞞著兒子，找個安靜的地方，重新修改整理他的著作《西遊記》。

一日兩，兩日三，一晃兩個月過去了。吳承恩整理好書稿，便背著包袱來到女兒家，把重新修改整理好的書稿當面交給女兒說：「叫妳丈夫馬上拿去刻印吧，印好後，再印一份廣告，上面寫：要看《西遊記》，必須看有孫悟空大鬧天宮的《西遊記》。」這「大鬧天宮」的情節，就是吳承恩爲女兒特地寫進去的，也是全書最動人的一部分。

不久，有孫悟空大鬧天宮的《西遊記》新書刻印出來了。廣告一出，大家都爭著來買有大鬧天宮的《西遊記》。從此，先前沒有大鬧天宮的那本《西遊記》，無人過問，再也賣不出去了。

陳民牛／搜集整理

取經與唐太宗

唐代貞觀年間，長安有位算命先生，叫諸葛玄方。他在街上開了一爿算命測字店，門前寫了一副對聯：

上測天上仙界安危
下算地下凡人禍福

橫批是：「無所不知」。

一日，天上管雨水的金岳老龍下凡，來長安街上遊玩，見到這副對聯十分生氣，心想這個凡人也太狂妄了，竟敢誇此大口，決心要治他一治。

金岳老龍化作一個農夫，走進店去，要玄方替他算一算命。玄方問他生年生月生日和時辰八字。金岳老龍說：「我不是算人命，見你招牌上寫著上知天文，下知地理，無所不知，無所不曉，我們種田人最關心的是雨水，俗話說風調雨順，五穀豐登，請你算一算，明天長安能下多少雨水？」

玄方先生掐指一算，說：「天上玉皇有旨，命龍王給都城降三斗六升雨水。」

金岳老龍一聽楞住了，玉帝給我的聖旨正是這個數目呀，他怎麼會知道的？金岳老龍又問：「你再給我算算，這些雨水城外下多少？城內下多少？」

玄方先生又掐指一算，說：「七分城外，三分城內。」

金岳老龍一聽發呆了，這是怎麼一回事，怎麼天上的事情他都知道？金岳老龍很不服氣，心想這下雨多少是玉帝規定的，可是在什麼地方下多少，這是我的權力，本當是應該城外下七分，城內下三分，現在我偏偏倒過來，改爲城外三分，城內七分，出出他的醜。想定了，他又問玄方：「先生，你不會算錯吧？」

玄方先生說：「千眞萬確，不差分毫，若差一分，你就來砸我的招牌。」

金岳老龍伸出手去，與玄方一擊手掌：「好，一言爲定。」他以爲這是穩贏的。

這一回，由於金岳老龍把下雨的比例作了個顚倒，城外三分，城內七分，這樣城內大雨傾盆，造成洪水暴發，城牆沖垮，百姓淹死無數；而城外下的是小雨，造成田地缺水，禾苗枯乾，人畜乾死無數，這一嚴重情況，早有各地土地神、灶司爺秉告了玉帝，玉帝聞訊大怒，給金岳老龍定了死罪，並命唐朝宰相魏徵處斬。

金岳老龍聽到玉帝要斬他，嚇得魂飛天外，急忙向唐朝皇帝李世民求救，說玉帝有旨，明日午時三刻，你的宰相魏徵奉旨要來斬我了，望你救我一救。李世民說這個好辦，他是我的臣子，到明天午時三刻，我管住他，不讓他出門，他就斬不成你了。挨過午時三刻，你的死罪也免了，不就好了嘛。

金岳老龍說此計甚好，我永不忘您的救命之恩，今後我一定保祐大唐天下風調雨順，五穀豐登，國泰民安。

第二天午時未到，李世民就把魏徵叫住，要他陪著下棋。下著，下著，見魏徵伏在棋盤上睡著了。他想，魏徵近日來日理萬機，甚爲辛苦，他一定是疲勞了，就讓他好好歇會兒吧。於是就在橫盤邊上坐著。

忽然，李世民見魏徵頭冒青煙，汗流浹背。這時正是三伏天氣，李世民體卹下臣，就拿起扇子替魏徵打扇，扇了三扇，魏徵醒過來了，見皇上在替他打扇，連忙跪下說：「臣該死，讓萬歲等久了。」

李世民一看午時三刻已過，就說：「魏愛卿，你太辛苦了，快回家歇去吧，隔日我們再下棋。」

到了晚上，李世民在龍床上睡得正香，忽然，窗口伸進一個血淋淋的龍頭來。李世民嚇得渾身顫抖，正想叫人，卻見那龍頭破口大罵：「李世民，你言而無信！你不配做皇帝，我與你死不罷休！」

李世民被罵得莫名其妙，但聽聲音像是金岳老龍，定神一看，果然是金岳老龍的頭：「啊呀！你怎麼被人砍下了頭顱？是誰砍的？」

金岳老龍一聽更生氣了！「你還假惺惺地來問我，我叫你管住魏徵，你當面答應，轉背不但沒管住他，而且在他追殺我的時候，你還助他龍風三陣，不然我怎麼會被他追上，砍下頭顱，成了無頭冤鬼！俗話說債有主，冤有頭，我今日找你算賬來了。」

李世民還是莫名其妙，他想：我什麼時候助魏徵三陣龍風了……

原來他與魏徵下棋時，一到午時三刻，魏徵在睡夢中去追殺金岳老龍去了。一個追，一個逃，魏徵正追得滿頭大汗，追不上金岳老龍，李世民見魏徵冒汗，認為他熱了，就替他打扇，這就給魏徵助了三陣龍風，追上了金岳老龍，砍下了龍頭。

李世民一聽這樣，連忙解釋說：「我實在不知道他在夢中追殺你，我以為只要將他管住就行了。常言道：不知者無罪，你既已被斬，我可命高僧超度，使你亡靈早日升天。」

金岳老龍心想頭也被砍了，也只好如此了。於是說：「可我是天上的神龍，不比一般凡人，做個水陸道場就行了！你需要派一德性高尚的高僧，到西方佛國去取來眞經，方能超度我的亡靈歸天。」

李世民說：「這有何難，我大唐國中有的是和尚道士，我下道聖旨，召來幾名德性高尚的和尚，叫他們赴西天佛國去取經就是了！」

後來，李世民選了一個高僧玄奘，擔此重任。這就是唐僧取經的由來。

宏　聲／搜集整理

看相者

看相的在《西遊記》上出現過一次，但他的本領特大，不像我國其他古典小說，把看相的寫成走江湖、賣狗皮膏藥。吳承恩爲啥對看相的，有忒好的感情呢？這裏也有個傳說。

淮海東邊有個李家莊，在明嘉靖年間出了個狀元，叫李春芳，官越來越大，直到宰相。這人比吳承恩小七歲，跟吳承恩也熟。他怎麼當上狀元呢？據說是嘉靖在面試舉子時，以國號「嘉靖」爲題，要他們做詩。這個李春芳把「嘉靖」兩字拆成「士、口、一、〓、加、立、主、月」八個單字，成詩曰：

士本朝廷一丈夫，
口稱萬歲與三呼。
一橫直貫乾坤大，
兩豎橫飛社稷扶；

加職加官加爵祿，
立綱立紀立宏圖；
主公問我名和姓，
月明當空照五湖。

嘉靖看了詩，欣喜異常，欽點狀元。李春芳一下抖發了，本來這人就不正，這下更忘乎所以了。常言說，「一人得道，雞犬升天」，凡李家的人，不管有能無能，都沾了李春芳的光做上了官。大家對這現象不滿，吳承恩也不滿。

有年，吳承恩在一個集上，看到一個老者擺了個看相的攤子，上聯：能卜天空陰晴事；下聯：難斷人間是非情。橫批：不怕的請來。

衆人擠擠擁擁，鬧鬧哄哄的，但是沒有一個去看相。吳承恩見此聯語不凡，心中暗暗納罕，遂佇足觀看，好大一會兒沒有一個人問津，那老者也不急躁，仍舊手拈鬍鬚，微笑地看著衆人。

吳承恩想呀想，猛然悟到：這先生對聯掛得特別，所以沒人看相。看相的人們只是問問吉凶，問官問財，誰敢來判斷人間是非，惹那個麻煩呢？

想到這裏，吳承恩暗自高興，這老頭倒是個「額頭上放扁擔——頭挑人物」，待我辦了事，好好與他聊上一聊。於是，吳承恩便急急忙忙去辦事，待事辦完，跑到街頭來找，人已不知去向了。

吳承恩不免惆悵四望，站在那裏發楞。這時，一個老頭走過來，說：「先生，你在尋找啥？」

吳承恩說：「那看相先生呢？」

「走啦。」

「爲啥走得這樣早呢？」

「嗨，人家不是眞看相的。」

「那做啥呢？」

老頭四顧無人，說：「他呀，是當朝御史李春芳的叔父。李春芳做了京官後，一門李全做了官，獨有他拒絕了，說我不做那坑害人的官，留在家中自食其力。有時候，出門擺個看相攤子，講是看相，實是出官府的洋相，大罵做官的貪贓枉法，顚倒黑白。所以他說能知天上陰晴，難判人間是非。是個奇人啊！」

吳承恩聽了，點點頭：「是個奇人！」

「他說了倒不礙事，因爲官府礙著他姪兒面，對他不敢怎樣。可是對那些在旁聽他講的人，就不客氣了，一概抓起來。所以就沒人請他看相了。」

吳承恩聽了這番話語，就徒步追到李家莊訪他，哪知這老頭根本沒有回來。

吳承恩一連訪了數次，可就是見不到這老者。之後，耳縫裡颳來風聲，說李春芳得知叔父所爲，勃然大怒，手諭地方官員照抓不誤。但是老頭子不知去向了。

吳承恩越發對他欽佩。心裏老是轉翻著這個「相貌稀奇，儀容端莊」的老頭。此時，嘉靖昏庸，社會黑暗，地方官吏胡作非爲，人民處在水深火熱之中。他想：如果有這樣一個李老頭能一品當朝，倒能救救嘉靖，可是嘉靖哪裏會認得他呢？因此，也就沒救了。想到這些，吳承恩寫《西遊記》時，就寫了看相的袁守誠，也是唐朝京官的叔父。涇河老龍雖然不善，但最後還是設法救它。結果是救不了，老龍還被魏徵斬了。吳承恩這樣寫，算是表達對李的叔父一點敬意，也暗暗地敲了嘉靖一棒：再如此下去，當心被斬龍的人斬了。

李子全／講述
黎邦農／搜集整理

將猴入書

傳說吳承恩的父親是吃八方飯、五湖四海都到過的生意人。他走東闖西，聽到好多稀奇古怪的故事，回來就一個一個地講給吳承恩聽。

承恩最愛聽故事了，父親講了一個他還要一個，以致父親常常講到深夜，他也全神貫注地聽到深夜。

承恩稍大些，便跟著父親南來北往，見識了不少人，聽到不少故事，他記性特別好，過目不忘，充耳能誦，一閒下來便生龍活現地侃侃而講，吸引著好多人。

有一次，父親見承恩故事講得特別拿人，便勸他說：「兒呀，你跑了不少地方，也聽了不少故事，將來能不能記下來，傳給大家看看？也省得你天天講個沒完沒了的。」

承恩一想，父親說得有理，便照父親的話做了，把自己聽到的故事，統統地記下來，這樣陸陸續續記了上千個故事，可惜沒有一根紅線把這些故事串聯起來。正在爲難之時，他聽到了陳玄奘去印度取經的故事；又傳聞楚州城裏有兩個婦女生了怪胎：一個生下個尖嘴猴腮的猴子，一個生下個嘴長耳大的豬兒。吳承恩茅塞頓開，高興得跳了起來，說：「有了，有了。」於是他決定以取經爲線索，以猴豬爲人物，把手頭的故事串起來。但猴豬家在哪兒，有什麼本事？他心裏還沒有個準兒，於是到處雲遊。一玩玩到東海邊上，來到一座深山裏邊。這座山好嘞！山青水秀，雲霧繚繞，忽見一隻猴子在前面一蹦一跳的，好玩得很，不知不覺地跟著猴子進了山洞。

不知走了多少時候，走了多少路程，前面來了個白髮蒼蒼的老頭兒，走路飄飄然的。吳承恩仔細一看，曉得自己遇上仙人了，趕緊上前跪下就拜。

老頭問：「你是什麼人？」

吳承恩答道：「楚州吳承恩。」

「你來有什麼事？」

吳承恩把寫書的根根節節都敘說了一遍。

那老頭說：「好，你跟我來。」

吳承恩在老人帶領下走進一個洞口，洞邊停著一隻沒底的船，吳承恩一看，心裏害怕了：「這無底船不把人淹死了嗎？」老頭跨上一步說：「來啊！」承恩閉上眼睛，往船上一站，耳邊只聽得嘩啦嘩啦的水響，也不知船行了多少路，承恩不敢睜開眼，過了一會兒，水聲沒了，只聽得老人說，「到了，上岸吧！」

承恩上了岸，一看可樂壞了，這塊地方好嘞！活像水晶宮殿似的，亮晶晶的，明晃晃的，仙桃擺滿桌，筆墨放在桌上。山洞裏有數不清的猴子，見承恩來了，都很親熱，一個個圍著他轉，那老人對猴子說：「你們好生服侍這位書生。」說著，老頭不見了，睜眼一看，原來是個夢。於是，吳承恩便以這山這洞爲孫猴子的家，分別取名爲「花果山」和「水簾洞」。孫猴子的家找到了，吳承恩進入了寫作，寫著寫著，他又寫不下去了。因爲他光爲孫猴子找到了家，但孫猴子究竟是什麼樣子，又有什麼本事，他心中還是空空的，沒有個譜兒。這可怎麼辦呢？

正好時近春節，吳承恩索性擱下筆，回到故鄉——楚州（淮安）歡度春節了。除夕晚上，他和鄰居老人一邊守歲，一邊談天，輪流講故事。他先講了幾個，老人聽得入了迷。老人知道承恩喜歡故事，也給他講了淮安渭河的水神無支祁興風作浪，阻撓大禹治水，被大禹擒獲，鎮於淮陰龜山脚下的神話故事。吳承恩越聽越高興，連聲催促老人繼續講下去。

那老人呼嚕嚕地吸了兩口水菸，清下嗓子，又講了起來：

很古很古的時候，中原地區有個稱王稱霸、無惡不作的水怪叫無支祁。他依仗權勢，興風作浪，肆無忌憚地殘害百姓。他心血來潮，只要吹口氣，就遍地洪水，淹沒莊稼，沖毀房屋，使百姓流離失所。大禹恨透了無支祁，爲除此害，他首先請來童律、烏本田出戰，但因無支祁本領太大，童律、烏本田制服不了他。原來無支祁非常狡猾、凶猛，他的形貌像猿猴，高額頭，塌鼻樑，灰白色的腦袋殼，青銅色的身軀，一口雪白鋒利的牙齒，兩隻金黃賊亮的眼睛。膀子伸出來，足有百尺長，力氣特別大，能敵九條蛟龍。平時他出沒水中，十分敏捷，一會兒在東，一會兒到西，很不容易擒獲。後來，大禹請來掌管時間的天神庚辰，無支祁見到庚辰渾身活靈靈的，不寒而慄，想潛水逃竄，只聽「鏗」的一聲，早被庚辰手中的大戟擊中，受傷就擒了。大禹下令把無支祁的膀頸用繩索鎖住，鼻子穿上一串金鈴，鎮壓在淮水下游的龜山之下，叫他千年萬載再也不能橫行霸道，四處作惡了。

吳承恩聽後，高興得跳了起來拍手叫好，他心裏豁然開朗：「無支祁能飛行太空，力敵九龍；孫猴子爲什麼不能拿來天河定底的神珍鐵柱、一個筋斗十萬八千里呢？無支祁火眼金睛，口吐水漲，善於變化；孫猴子爲什麼不能呼風喚雨，七十二變呢？……」

孫猴子的本事、形象在吳承恩的腦海裏逐漸形成了。吳承恩欣喜若狂地連夜奔到射陽簃裏，磨濃墨，蘸飽筆，揮筆大寫起來。樹葉落了，樹葉青了，他整整花了三年時間，終於寫出了膾炙人口的《西遊記》。

陳民牛／搜集整理

孫侯與孫猴

吳承恩在長興縣做縣丞時，結識了一個名醫叫孫厚。這人古怪得很，他的醫寓貼了一副對聯：

醫病不醫命
救人先救心

吳承恩初聞時，心想，這人口氣太大，恐怕也是個「吹牛皮不犯死罪」的角色，也就未把他放在心上。

一日，知縣老母得病，幾個醫生越醫越不行，眼看就要上黃泉路了。這時，孫厚來了。他切了脈，開了藥，竟把老太太醫好了。知縣大喜，當即封了百兩銀子謝禮，孫厚不收，但又不離開。知縣以爲他嫌少，又加了百兩，孫厚還是不收。兩眼盯著知縣夫人身邊的一個丫環。知縣也乖巧，就說：「孫醫生，是否看中了賤內身邊的丫環？」

孫厚點點頭。知縣說：「好說，好說。」

當即贈了一身衣服，把丫環打扮打扮，派吳承恩送她去孫家。人們都哂笑這個老不正經的醫生。

哪知吳承恩帶了丫環一進孫府，孫厚就對一個老大娘說：「大娘，妳的『藥』來了，妳快領她回去作妳兒媳吧！」

原來，這個鄉下老大娘得病三年，日不思食，夜不安眠，身體乾枯，吃藥無效，兒子就把她帶到孫家求醫。孫厚通過望聞問切，知道大娘家窮，思慮獨子婚事，而得了這個病，於是說：「大娘，妳是『憂慮傷脾』，不能安睡，一時無藥，等兩天吧！」

現在大娘見孫厚把知縣家的丫環賞給她作兒媳，眉開眼笑，千恩萬謝，領了丫環回家，讓她和兒成了親。老大娘一高興，也就睡得安穩啦，病眞的好了。

這是吳承恩意料不到的事，他打心眼裏敬佩孫厚，因此兩人遂成莫逆，無話不談了。漸漸地，吳承恩知道孫厚的身世。原來，孫厚是個秀才，天資聰明，讀書認眞，但是不會巴結權貴，賄賂考官，屢試不第。四十歲發誓不考了。人們問他爲啥不考？他笑笑說：「我們姓孫的，有孫山醫國，讓我孫厚醫人啦！孫山醫國，可以封侯；我孫厚醫人，也可封侯。哈哈。」

人們聽了，也一陣哄笑，遂把他稱爲「孫侯」。他一心鑽讀《內經》、《素問》、《本草》，醫道大進，遠近聞名。

一天，孫、吳兩人在一起閒聊。吳承恩說：「碰上絕症，你怎麼辦？」

孫厚說：「我一面開藥，一面勸病家準備後事。」

「開啥藥？」

「烏金丸。」

「啥烏金丸？」

「就是用百草霜、醋、童尿，拌糊爲丸。百草霜，鍋灰也。這藥百病無礙，無病吃了也不礙。」

吳承恩聽了，笑笑說：「眞有你的，唬人的本事還眞大咧。」

孫厚一本正經說：「我說眞話，人家忌諱，但又不能害人，只好唬人啦。沒法子，這也是被逼的。說起來，有個笑話，你們那位知縣的老母八十四歲啦，常言說，『七十三，八十四，閻王不請，自己去』。感了風寒臥床，當然越醫越糟。仗著兒子作官，把我接到縣衙，實在煩人。到第三天，還不放我回去。我就說：老太太的病轉爲『臨老不走』症，需烏金丸，讓我回去拿吧！」

「知縣就讓衙役跟我回去拿。一時無藥，衙役在家坐等，我就讓藥倌刮鍋灰現製，找不到小孩尿，藥倌倒機靈，就到後園接了點馬尿，拌糊成丸。想不到衙役拿回，老太太吃了，竟好了。知縣很高興，就設宴感謝，把我和藥倌都請去。年輕人三杯下肚，嘴就不鎖了，說：『知縣大人，你甭謝，那藥是馬……馬……』我趕忙打斷他的話，說：『那藥是馬兜鈴。』知縣接著問道：『馬兜鈴是何味，主治何症？』醫官接過話，念道：『馬兜鈴味苦無毒，定喘消痰大有功；通氣最能是上品，補虛寧咳又寬中！』知縣聽了，大喜，又敬了我師徒一盅。哈哈。」

吳承恩聽了，也哈哈大笑，連說：「有意思，有意思。」

吳承恩一直忘不了這個故事。後來，他寫《西遊記》寫到孫悟空在朱紫國為國王治病，高興地說：「老朋友的事用上了，讓孫侯成為孫悟空吧！」於是揮筆，一口氣寫下去，使那段文字妙趣橫生，人情味十足。

駱雲齊／講述
黎邦農／搜集整理

三說寫八戒

豬八戒這個角色，早先在民間流傳的唐僧取經的故事裏，連個影子也沒有。吳承恩寫《西遊記》的時候，起初也沒有想到是否把老豬加進去。後來他爲啥要寫豬八戒呢？有幾個說法蠻有趣，給大夥講講。

第一個說法：有人逼他寫。

吳承恩有個表姪，住在淮安鄉下，擅長種西瓜，大家叫他「西瓜狀元」。有一天，表姪像個紅臉關公，闖到吳承恩家裏，怒氣沖沖地說：「表叔，幫我寫！幫我寫！」吳承恩奇怪了：你冒冒失失要我幫你寫，寫什麼呀？就問情由。表姪說一氣，罵一氣，連說帶罵講了老大會兒，吳承恩才知底細。

原來是這麼回事：表姪種的西瓜，個大，味甜，籽少，紅瓤，在四鄉八鎮出了名，人人都想買，不料因此得罪了一個人。

哪個呢？這人姓朱名八，是個又懶又饞的二流子。朱八見「西瓜狀元」的瓜好，想吃，可腰裏又沒有錢，就今天偷一個，明天偷一個，天天都來偷。有一次被「西瓜狀元」逮到了，「西瓜狀元」當場訓了朱八一頓，訓過之後，好心地勸朱八往後不要再偷，臨走還送了朱八兩個大西瓜。哪知朱八西瓜吃下肚，沒兩天又犯老毛病，一偷偷了半口袋。「西瓜狀元」逮住他，氣憤不過，照他肋上狠狠踢了一腳。

這一腳可踢出仇來了！不知朱八怎麼搗鼓的，一會兒把十幾頭豬趕到「西瓜狀元」的瓜地裏。豬見西瓜還能老實嗎？「呱嗒，呱嗒」，連吃加拱，把兩畝好好的西瓜給糟蹋了一半多。「西瓜狀元」正在瓜棚裏睏晌覺呢，聽見響聲出來一看，差點沒氣死！他趕緊託人看著瓜地，跑來找表叔幫他寫狀紙，告朱八。

吳承恩對表姪說：「幫你寫可以，不過，打官司非同兒戲，我不能光聽一面之詞，得查證查證再說。」「西瓜狀元」知道吳承恩一向按葫蘆摳籽兒，不做玄事，也就沒說別的，只求表叔早點查證，快點寫。

當天下午，吳承恩出了淮安城，來到表姪的西瓜地裏。他一看，瓜藤子亂七八糟，滿地都是西瓜皮、西瓜瓤和豬蹄印子。吳承恩點點頭，沒吱聲，走出瓜地，繞著田裏察看。他忽然發現一樣東西，拾起來瞧瞧，原來是隻死螻蛄。螻蛄身上纏著好多道細麻線，麻線解開來，有五尺多長，一頭拴在螻蛄的腰上。

吳承恩覺得蹊蹺，忙問表姪：「你看這是什麼玩意兒？」

「西瓜狀元」瞅了瞅死螻蛄，說：「這是偷雞賊在螻蛄的肚子裏戳進一根鐵釘，扔到雞跟前，雞一吞，一嚥，線一抖，一拽，鐵釘卡在雞嗓子裏出不來，偷雞賊就人不知、鬼不覺地把雞偷到手了！」

吳承恩點點頭，沒吱聲。他離開西瓜地，朝村子裏走，來到朱八的住處。進門一看，只見院子裏擠著許多人，正圍著一個黑臉漢子，指指戳戳罵個不停。

有的罵：「你朱八太缺德啦，把俺家的豬趕出去，糟蹋人家『西瓜狀元』的好西瓜！」有的罵：「你朱八太孬啦，俺家裏幾隻下蛋的老母雞，都讓你偷來了！」罵的全是朱八好吃懶做、偷偷摸摸的醜事。有幾個娘兒們從朱八的屋裏抱出幾隻雞，雞嘴裏都有一根細痲線。

吳承恩點點頭，還是沒吱聲。臨走，他找到幾個證人，在一塊合計合計，沒費多大事兒，就把狀紙寫好了。

第二天清早，「西瓜狀元」來找吳承恩，拿到了狀紙，非常高興，直奔縣衙，去告朱八。哪知一頓早飯工夫，朱八突然竄到吳承恩家裏，凶神惡煞地說：「吳先生，聽說你幫人寫狀紙告我？」吳承恩說：「不錯。」朱八眼一瞪：「姓吳的！我與你往日無冤，近日無仇，憑什麼亂揷槓子搗我的蛋？這事你看著辦吧！想『文了』還是想『武了』？」「『文了』怎說？」「撕掉狀紙，各走各路。」「『武了』怎講？」「白的進去，紅的出來！」

吳承恩笑笑，說：「朱老弟！依我看，這事一不用『文了』，二不用『武了』，好辦得很。」朱八忙問：「怎麼辦？」吳承恩把指頭一叉：「八個字。」「哪八個字？」「投案自首，改邪歸正！」

朱八一聽這話，「嗖」拔出一把匕首，野貓似地逼進吳承恩，說：「把狀紙拿出來！」吳承恩說聲：「可笑！」「那你快把狀紙撕掉！」吳承恩說聲：「可恥！」「再犟，要你的老命！」吳承恩說聲：「可惡！」

朱八急了，舉起匕首，劈胸就扎，只聽「嘩啦」、「噹啷」，吳承恩紋絲沒動，朱八倒被恰在此刻趕到的公差鎖了起來，朱八竄蹦想跑，公差把鎖鏈一抖，喝聲：「走！」把他帶往縣衙去了。

爲這事，吳承恩考慮好幾天，朱八這人老在他心裏轉。思來想去，覺得朱八只有戒懶戒饞戒偷摸，經些磨鍊才能變成好人，又覺得世人應以朱八爲戒，不可做醜事。二五一湊，十分激動，就在《西遊記》裏寫出一個「豬八戒」來！

第二個說法：有人逗他寫

吳承恩在雲台山上寫書的時候，常到東山頭轉轉，看看，算是休息。後來他在東山頭轉夠了，看膩了，就往西山頭轉。

有一天正轉著，迎面走來一個打獵的老人。老獵人見到吳承恩，說：「先生，上山看景哪？」吳承恩順口回答說：「正是，正是。」老獵人「嗤」一笑說：「不會看，滿山轉；要看景，找人領。」一聽這話，吳承恩忙作揖施禮，請老獵人領路導遊。老獵人並不推辭，領著吳承恩，不往東，不奔西，不朝南，不向北，一溜往下面的山窪裏走去。

吳承恩想：山窪裏盡是些石頭塊、水塘子，有什麼「景」可看呵？正想著，老獵人忽然說：「到啦。」吳承恩急忙停下脚步，老獵人說：「先生，轉過身來，順我手指的方向，朝上頭仔細看！」

吳承恩依照老人的吩咐，轉身一看，果然看到了奇景：在一座說高不高、說矮又不矮的嶺子尖上，頂著一塊好大好大的石頭，這塊大石頭的樣子活像一個大豬頭，嘴巴撅著，眼睛瞇著，大耳朵耷拉著，好像在睏覺。

老獵人告訴吳承恩，那石頭有個名字，叫「豬頭石」，只有站在這兒看，才像豬頭的模樣，

別處看不像。

吳承恩連聲讚嘆說：「奇景！奇景！」老獵人又是「嗤」一笑說：「光看不聽，等於白跑。」一聽這話，吳承恩忙又作揖施禮，請老獵人講講豬頭石的傳說。老獵人也不推辭，清了清嗓子，馬上開講了：

相傳這山上有七十二個洞，洞洞有妖精，內中一個洞裏頭，是頭野豬精。這個野豬精相貌醜陋，又懶又饞，各洞妖精都瞧不起它，免不了受欺侮。十回八回以後，野豬精受不了啦，耳朵一搧，嘴巴一呱嗒，有了主意，練本事，揍它們！狠心一下，還眞的來了勁頭。

野豬精砍砍剁剁動手做了個九齒釘耙，跑到僻靜地方，練，練，練！練了八八六十四天，覺得本事可以了，就去罵陣。一罵，各洞妖精來氣了，統統都竄了出來，圍住野豬精，要把它逮住吃掉。野豬精也不含糊，舞動釘耙和衆妖對打。只見它左一耙，右一耙，前一耙，後一耙，打死了好幾個小妖。但終究寡不敵衆，打著打著，野豬精覺得身子軟了，骨架散了，再打下去想活命也就晚了，這才殺開一條血路，朝山下逃跑。衆妖跟在後面緊迫，還一齊喊：「抓住野豬精！抓住野豬精！」

野豬精眼看跑不掉了，正在危急關頭，正巧有個石猴精從外面回山，聽到喊聲，抬頭一看，見許多妖精追趕一個黑傻大個，心想：這不是明擺著欺負人嗎？便跳上去舉棒就打。石猴精沒費多大勁，把衆妖精打得死的死，傷的傷，剩下幾個逃命去了。野豬精得救後，感激不盡，就跟石猴精拜上把兄弟，一口一個「猴哥」，叫得蜜甜。

自從有了石猴精坐鎮，山上十分平安。哪知日子一長，野豬精又犯了又懶又饞的老毛病，睡了吃，吃了睡，吃飽睡足以後，就跑到一個天池裏去洗澡。這個天池，本是仙女洗澡的地方，野豬精以往站也不敢站，看也不敢看，怕犯天條受處罰。這會兒依仗本領高強的「猴哥」撐腰，他膽子大了，想洗就來洗，想玩就來玩，氣得衆仙女紛紛避開他，跑到王母娘娘跟前去告狀。

王母娘娘十分生氣，就派東海龍王三太子前來捉拿野豬精。

龍王三太子駕著雲頭，到天池上空朝下一看，只見野豬精挺著個大肚皮，躺在天池裏打呼嚕。三太子不由來了火，跳下雲頭，大喝一聲：「醜八怪，招打！」「啪！」就是一鞭子，正好打在野豬精的肚皮上。野豬精一嚇，醒了，見是龍王三太子打他，也來了火，「呼」竄出天池，抄起九齒釘耙和龍王三太子對打起來。

這一仗，從晌午打到傍晚，打得野豬精精疲力盡，渾身發熱，就跑到嶺子尖上睡覺乘涼。不想一覺睡下去，再也沒有睡醒，後來就變成了「豬頭石」啦！

老獵人講的故事，吳承恩覺得挺有趣。心裏一高興，就把野豬精變化變化，改裝改裝，寫到《西遊記》裏了。

還有個說法：不得不寫。

《西遊記》寫到第十七回，「孫行者大鬧黑風山，觀世音收伏熊羆怪」，吳承恩突然覺得寫不下去了。吳承恩想來想去，頭都想疼了，也沒找出個道道來。

當晚，吳承恩把毛筆朝筆帽子裏一套，蓋上硯台，決意熄燈睡覺，鬆鬆腦子改日再想。豈不知「心中有事入夢難」，熬了兩三個時辰，好不容易才算睡著。

剛入夢，忽聽有人在門外大叫一聲：「吳老頭！」

吳承恩一楞，心想：衆人都叫我「吳先生」，是誰這麼衝，叫我「吳老頭」？又一想：這樣叫也好，倒是顯得不外氣哩，連忙起床去開門。門剛開，不料「撲」一聲，從門外蹦進來一隻猴子。

吳承恩一看，呵，原來是孫悟空！忙問：「大聖，找我作甚？」

孫悟空說：「你讓俺鬧天宮，俺鬧了，你派俺保唐僧，俺保了，可你，也該體諒體諒俺老孫的難處呵！」

吳承恩忙說：「大聖，你有什麼難處？」

孫悟空說：「據你講，俺師父這回到西天取經，路上要遭九九八十一難。俺老孫縱有三頭六臂，也保不了師父的險哪！就這事，你看著辦吧！」說完，一個筋斗翻出門去。

孫悟空走了不多會兒，門外又有人叫：「施主吳公！」身影一晃，人進來了。吳承恩一看，原來是唐僧，忙問：「聖僧，找我作甚？」唐僧並不答話，閉著眼睛念念有詞：「徒弟少了，一個不好；徒弟少了，一個不好……」顛來倒去念了好多遍。念完，轉身走了。

師徒兩人你來我去，吳承恩聽出了門道：噢，怪不得寫不下去，原來是一師一徒筆頭轉不開，如果添個角色，這比孫悟空包拼包打不是好寫多了嗎？想到這裏，滿心高興。那麼添個什麼角色呢？吳承恩不覺犯了難。

正在這時，忽聽外頭又有人帶著哭腔在叫：「吳先生，吳先生！」吳承恩連忙走到門外，一看，原來是一頭大豬。說來奇怪，那豬見到吳承恩，「撲通」，跪倒，又作揖，又磕頭，連說：「先生救命，我要出家！我要出家！」

吳承恩聽了好笑，便問：「豬呵，什麼叫出家，你懂嗎？『出家』就是當和尚。你是一頭豬，怎能當和尚呢？」那豬把頭一歪，說：「猴子能當，我也能當。」

「喲！」吳承恩心想：這豬倒是不笨哩，連我寫《西遊記》的事它也曉得了。就說：「豬呵，人家猴子有本事，能保唐僧去取經，你呢？」

「我也有本事！」那豬說著，「呼」地站起來，肩膀一扛，扛倒了一棵蟠龍松，嘴巴一拱，拱翻了一塊臥虎石，在吳承恩面前露了兩手。那豬正得意時，忽然山坡上亮起了燈籠火把，好多山民拿著棍棒，提著繩索，一頭跑一頭喊：「哧溜」一下子，一頭竄進吳承恩的書房。

吳承恩叫聲：「不好！」一驚嚇，醒了，原來是場夢！

吳承恩醒來後，想想夢中的情形，原來這野豬是爲了逃避山民的追捕才要出家的，便說了聲：「有意思！」急忙提筆寫第十八回：「觀音院唐僧脫難，高老莊大聖除魔」。

書裏添了個豬八戒，既熱鬧，又有情趣，寫起來得心應手，不感到筆頭發澀了。

此地有人講「八戒夢中來」，指的就是上面這麼個說法。究竟是眞是假，不過傳說罷了，無須考證。

姜　威／搜集整理

南瓜進貢

南瓜是極普通的食物，而吳承恩在《西遊記》裏卻把它寫成貢品。這是爲啥呢？

據說吳承恩在二十多歲到四十多歲的這二十年間，經常發水災的淮安卻小旱三次。大旱五次，餓死了不少人。吳承恩三十歲那年，大旱旱得嚇人，土地龜裂，顆粒不收，十個人中就有七個餓死，有一些村子竟一人不剩。次年清明，好心的吳承恩覺得這些餓死的人，斷根絕代，無人祭祀，就買了點紙錢，步出城，走一段路，散一些紙錢。他越走越遠，不覺中午已過，他手中的紙錢也散完了。他又渴又餓，想到附近村莊去弄點水喝，弄點東西塾塾肚子。可是一進村子，卻是萬戶蕭疏，人毛不見，都餓死啦。

吳承恩就這樣走著，在日沈樹梢頭時，來到一個村莊。這個村子竟是樹木葱綠，水清花紅，人聲喧嚷。吳承恩心裏一怔，就來到村東最熱鬧的一家，看到許多人帶了綢緞金銀，雞魚蛋麵，來看一對老夫妻。他們說：「大伯大嬸，多虧您們的南瓜，我才沒有餓死，這點東西感謝您救命之恩，請收下吧！」

老兩口子連連擺手，說：「你們只要記住種南瓜就行了，禮物一概不收。」說罷，舀了綠豆南瓜湯分遞給來人。來人們還要送東西，老倆口臉一板，說：「我有南瓜度荒年，焉用金銀裝門面。甭再囉唆了。」

人們無法，只好收下禮物，嘖嘖稱讚了幾句。

原來，這老兩口子無兒無女，平時多種瓜果，尤其是南瓜，每年都收藏了一屋，遇到荒春，便拿出賑濟，不知救了多少條性命。

吳承恩也吃了一碗南瓜綠豆湯，對「爲善不求報」的老兩口子異常佩服。回城後，常常向朋友說起這事。

不久，兩個老人相繼去世了，送葬的人成千上萬，吳承恩也去送了。看到那場面，吳承恩心想：世人最富有的是「爲善不求報」的人。

後來，吳承恩寫《西遊記》，還是忘不了這件事，就特意寫了一章唐僧到烏雞國，正逢烏雞國乾旱，老百姓逃的逃，死的死，連國王和王后也餓翻在床上，於是叫孫悟空回東土，向唐王要了千擔南瓜去救災。

寫好後，吳承恩很高興，就拿著書稿到文殊院，給他的好友——濟善長老看。並說：「這是我對種南瓜的老兩口子表示的一點敬意。」

濟善看後，皺著眉頭說：「這哪是對南瓜老兩口子的敬意？你寫的是『王救王』嘛！」

吳承恩脹紅了臉，說：「這，這……」

濟善不客氣地說：「你應該寫『窮人救窮，窮人救國王』嘛。」

吳承恩聽了，點點頭說：「長老，你講的對。只是很對不起，我不知他倆的姓名啊！」

「這不礙事，你就寫個好像，大差不差就得了。」

吳承恩聽了，大喜，說：「高，高，長老說得對，我就給他倆起名叫相公相婆。」

濟善長老雙手合掌，念了聲：「阿彌陀佛！」

於是，經過幾天思考，就把《西遊記》這一段改成現在的樣子。

黎邦農／搜集整理

玄奘出世

相傳唐朝的時候，雲台大村東小寨有個陳員外。陳員外老倆口半輩子只生一個兒子，名子春，字光蕊。陳子春才三歲，父親就去世了。母親把全部希望寄託在他的身上，五歲上，就給他請來一個教書先生。那陳子春天資聰明，念起書來十分用功，九歲他就能吟詩作賦；十七歲他就成了有名的天才。

這年，陳子春二十歲。母親看孩子到了成家立業的歲數，就託媒人給陳子春說媳婦。媒人給陳子春說了東家的美姐，陳子春說不要；媒人又給陳子春說了西家的巧妹，陳子春又說不要。

雲台山最香的花是海仙花，雲台山最美的姑娘是殷溫嬌。陳子春一心想娶溫嬌，他走路想著溫嬌，吃飯念著溫嬌，睡覺也夢著溫嬌。

殷溫嬌的家就住在大村北邊的小村，父親是唐朝的宰相殷開山。殷開山老倆口年過半百，只有這麼個寶貝女兒。殷溫嬌長得實在俊秀，鳥兒看見她不飛，魚兒看見她不游，花兒看見她不香，月兒看見她不亮。

殷溫嬌不僅模樣長得標致，而且能寫詩會畫畫，還彈得一手好琴，寫得一手好字。殷開山老倆口對殷溫嬌如掌上明珠，一心想招個倒插門的女婿。這女婿一要好模樣，二要狀元郎。所以，殷溫嬌長到一十八歲，還沒個婆家。

陳子春的母親見兒子看上了殷家小姐，就託媒人到小村提親。論起陳子春的人品才貌，不要說雲台十八村，就是在整個海州，也是打燈籠沒處找的後生。殷開山犯難了：不答應吧，怕以後挑不出這樣的好女婿；答應吧，又擔心他考不中狀元。最後，他就來了個既不答應也不推辭的辦法，對媒人說：「陳家兒郎品貌好，考中狀元娶溫嬌。」

陳子春母親聽說這話，就在背地裏勸兒子道：「考生上千人，狀元取一名，兒啊，你難道就能考中？」陳子春說：「世上無難事，只怕有心人。」母親又說：「天下好女千名，難道非娶溫嬌不行？兒啊，不要誤了終身。」陳子春說：「任石爛海枯，非溫嬌不娶！」母親見兒子這樣執迷，焦得飯也吃不香，愁得覺也睡不好，三焦兩愁，就病倒了。

陳子春見母親病倒了，便到處請郎中給母親看病。眼看考期就要到了，母親的病還不見好，陳子春心裏又焦又急。

聽人說鯉魚湯能治好母親的病，他就上街買了一條金色大鯉魚。當他要殺魚時，鯉魚直流眼淚，陳子春感到很奇怪，就問鯉魚：「鯉魚鯉魚，流淚何故？鯉魚鯉魚，鄉居何處？」鯉魚答道：「陳家相公聽仔細，我是龍王三太子。只因貪玩出龍宮，失足掉進魚網裏。」陳子春說：「鯉魚鯉魚，放你可以，我母有病，如何醫治？」鯉魚又答道：「陳家相公請放心，揭下三片大魚鱗。熬成一碗魚鱗湯，包你母親得健康。」說完，鯉魚就一動不動地躺在籃子裏。陳子春揭下三片大魚鱗後，就把鯉魚放回大海。

陳子春母親喝下了魚鱗湯，病果然好了。於是，陳子春就放心地去京城趕考。也是陳子春時來運轉，一考就中了個頭名狀元。皇上很看重他，叫他去做海州的州官。陳子春謝罷皇恩，又去拜殷宰相。殷開山見他中了狀元，就把女兒許配給了他。

陳子春回到雲台大村，很快就和殷溫嬌成了親。從此，他和母親就不在大村住了，一起搬到了小村宰相府。過了不久，陳子春就準備帶著殷溫嬌去海州上任。

那時候，雲台山在海中，去海州還得坐船。陳子春和殷溫嬌乘坐一條大船向海州而來。不一會，他們就來到了海州的蒼梧渡口。

就在他們剛要離船上岸的當兒，突然從西北方向飄過來一片黑雲，那黑雲上站著一個青面獠牙的妖怪。你道這是什麼妖怪？原來是海州蜘蛛山蜘蛛洞裏的蜘蛛精。蜘蛛精正要返回妖洞，忽見船上下來一個如花似玉的女子，頓起不良之心，就撥轉雲頭，向蜘蛛洞而去。

也是陳子春命不該絕，他剛剛沈到海底，就遇上了東海龍王的巡海夜叉。巡海夜叉叫來一隻大海龜，把他馱進了龍宮。

龍王三太子聞訊趕來，一看，原來是陳子春，便對東海龍王說：「父王，這是我的救命恩人。」東海龍王聽說，忙叫手下人解開陳子春身上的蛛絲。烏龜頂來了一柄七星劍，割啊割，劍鋒鈍了，蛛絲卻紋風未動。螃蟹又扛來了兩把宣花斧，砍啊砍，斧刃壞了，蛛絲還是紋風不動。

龍王三太子上前說道：「要想蛛絲解得開，還得請我大姐來。」

龍王說：「那就快去把你大姐叫來。」

龍王三太子就來到大姐居住的水晶宮，對大龍女說：「父王叫妳快進宮，救我恩人陳子春。」

大龍女拿起神剪刀趕到龍宮，對東海龍王說：「父王父王聽端詳，女兒心事有一樁。只要父王答應我，我就救他狀元郎。」

龍王說：「女兒有事只管講，爲父給妳作主張。」

大龍女說：「那年學藝瀛洲上，師母曾經對我講，雲台有個狀元郎，與我龍女配成雙。」

龍王說：「既然師母有話，爲父豈能打壩？」

大龍女見龍王答應，她就揮動神剪，陳子春身上的蛛絲一根根迎刃而解。

陳子春身上的蛛絲雖然被解開，可他還是昏迷不醒。三太子又上前對龍王說：「要想恩人魂靈回，還得請我二姐來。」龍王說：「那就快去把你二姐叫來。」三太子來到二姐住的珊瑚館，對二龍女說：「父王叫妳快進來，救我恩人陳子春。」二龍女帶上回春丹奔到龍宮，對東海龍王說：「父王父王聽我講，女兒有事心中藏，只要父王答應我，我就救他魂還陽。」龍王說：「女兒有事只管講，爲父給妳作主張。」二龍女說：「那年學藝神洲上，師母曾經對我講，雲台有個陳子春，與我雙雙配成婚。」龍王說：「既然師母有話，爲父豈能打壩？」二龍女見龍王答應，就取出神丹讓陳子春服下。

陳子春魂兒回來了，可他還不能說話。三太子又上前對龍王說：「要想恩人嘴能開，還得請我三妹來。」龍王說：「就快去把你三妹叫來。」三太子來到三妹住的珍珠樓，對三龍女說：「父王叫妳快進宮，救我恩人陳子春。」三龍女帶上解啞散跑到龍宮，對東海龍王說：「父王父王聽我言，女兒有事在心間。只要父王答應我，我就救他陳狀元。」龍王說：「女兒有事只管講，爲父給妳作主張。」三龍女說道：「那年學藝蓬萊島，師母給我當月老，雲台狀元陳子春，與我結成百年好。」龍王說：「既然師母有話，爲父豈能打壩？」三龍女見父王答應，就把解啞散給陳子春服下。

再說殷溫嬌被蜘蛛精搶進蜘蛛洞以後，那妖怪就逼著她跟它成親，殷溫嬌死也不從。蜘蛛精雖然碰了幾次鼻子，還是不死心，三天兩頭一趟，纏著殷溫嬌要拜天地，殷溫嬌總是又哭又鬧。可是有一天，殷溫嬌突然不哭了，也不鬧了。她對妖怪說：「除非你順我一條心意，不然，我就碰死在這洞裏。」蜘蛛精連連說道：「只要妳依從我，不要說一條，一百條也行。」殷溫嬌說：「按照海州風俗，丈夫死三年才能改嫁。」那妖怪一聽說三年，無可奈何地說：「三年就依妳三年。」蜘蛛精哪裏知道，這是殷溫嬌的緩兵之計，爲的是保全已懷的身孕。

轉眼間，一年過去了。這天，殷溫嬌只覺得肚子陣陣疼痛，不一會，她就生下了一個男孩。殷溫嬌眞是又喜又憂。喜的是，陳家有了後代；憂的是，怕蜘蛛精知道了會糟蹋這孩子。

那蜘蛛洞外是一個深谷，海水一直漫到洞口。殷溫嬌把孩子放在床板上，用繩子紮好。趁蜘蛛精還沒有回洞，把床板推出了洞門，哪知洞門外有一個漩渦，只見那床板在水上突溜溜亂轉。殷溫嬌急得禱告蒼天，蒼天不答；殷溫嬌又禱告大海，大海也不應；殷溫嬌只好禱告山神，山神說話了：「溫嬌溫嬌莫悲傷，山神給妳作主張。」殷溫嬌看得淸淸楚楚，先前合著的山峰突然裂開了，從裏邊走出一個白髮蒼蒼的老人。只見那老人把手中的拐杖向水上拋去，頓時，那床板就跟著拐杖離開了洞口。

再說那陳子春，打從到龍王宮以後，雖然有天仙般的三個龍女作伴，但心頭總還是掛念著溫嬌，時常悶悶不樂。

這一天，陳子春又在宮裏唉聲嘆氣，三龍女過來勸道：「相公不要煩惱，待奴家前往海州打聽。」陳子春說：「妳大姐去了七七四十九天，回來說沒有消息；妳二姐又去了七七四十九天，還是說沒有下落；妳就是再去七七四十九天，恐怕也是白跑一趟。」三龍女說：「相公保重，奴家去了。」只聽三龍女念起避水咒，頓時出了東海，駕起彩雲向海州而去。

三龍女來到海州，她先去問城隍，城隍老爺說不知道；她又去問土地，土地老爺說不清楚；她只好去問山神，山神爺爺告訴她說：「蜘蛛山上蜘蛛洞，蜘蛛洞裏鎖佳人。溫嬌懷胎生一男，小神送他離洞門。公主快尋漂流兒，救了孩子再搬兵。」三龍女一聽，不敢怠慢，她謝過山神，就撥轉雲頭回到東海上空。

三龍女望啊望，但見茫茫煙海，不見孩兒蹤影。三龍女聽啊聽，但聞陣陣波濤聲，不聞孩兒啼哭聲。三龍女走啊走，尋遍了雲台九十九個海灣，繞過了雲台九十九個山峰，也未尋到漂流兒。這一天，三龍女又來到一個地方，忽然，她看見海灣裏鳥兒結隊成群，於是，她就按落雲頭。那群鳥兒見三龍女到來，呼啦一下全飛走了。三龍女仔細一看。果然，木板上睡著一個嬰孩，和山神爺爺說的一模一樣。她趕緊把孩子抱起，念起避水咒返回龍宮。

陳子春聽說殷溫嬌有了下落，又看見了自己的孩子，反而更加悲傷起來，那眼淚撲簌簌地落個不止。三龍女上前勸道：「相公不要悲傷，趕快前去救人要緊。」於是，陳子春就和三龍女一起趕往龍宮。

東海龍王得知詳情，連忙叫來三個太子，點起蝦兵蟹將，殺奔蜘蛛山蜘蛛洞。

那蜘蛛精正在洞裏睡覺，忽被一片喊殺聲驚醒，連忙跑到洞外，爬在半空，一看勢頭不妙，趕緊向妖洞逃去。這時，龍王大太子忽地變成一條火龍騰空而起，將蜘蛛精當頭截住。只見龍王大太子口吐神火，那團團烈焰直向蜘蛛精噴去。那妖怪「哎喲」一聲，從空中掉了下來。

蜘蛛精被除掉了，殷溫嬌被救出來了，陳子春一家又團圓了。於是，陳子春就告別了東海龍王和龍王的三個太子，帶著殷溫嬌和三個龍女返回雲台小村。

後來，陳子春在海州做了不少年的州官，爲當地老百姓辦了不少好事。死後，他就葬在雲台大村。陳子春和殷溫嬌生的孩子，他就是以後去西天取經的唐僧玄奘。陳子春和三個龍女生的三個男孩，長大後都在雲台山水簾洞出了家。修心得道成了神仙。玉皇大帝還封唐僧的三個弟弟爲天官、地官、水官，號稱「三元」。

明朝萬曆年間，人們在水簾洞西上方蓋了一座廟。那廟裏正中供的是陳子春，兩邊是殷溫嬌和三個龍女。殷溫嬌懷裏抱著小時候的唐僧，三個龍女懷裏抱著小時候的三元大帝，這正是陳子春一家團圓的像。所以，人們就稱它「團圓宮」。同時，人們又在團圓宮前蓋了一座廟，廟裏供奉著唐僧的三個弟弟——三元大帝的神像。所以，人們就稱它爲「三元宮」。

一直到今天，人們來到雲台山，還可以看到三元宮和團圓宮的遺址。如果你到大村和小村去，不僅可以找到「陳子春遺冢」和「宰相府遺址」，人們還會給你講陳子春一家團圓、玄奘出世的故事。

丁義珍／搜集整理

玄奘辯學

玄奘爲了求賢訪能，走遍了整個印度。他對大乘經教義，提出了許多獨到見解。因此，摩揭陀國（今印度比哈爾邦南部）那爛陀寺（在比哈爾邦巴臘貢地方）的主持成賢法師，便叫他主持佛教講席。因他博學多才，對大乘經有著不少創新解釋，名揚四海，不少高僧慕名不遠千里來請教。這引起了一些和尙的嫉妒，認爲佛教源於天竺，卻叫一個唐人主持佛學講席，這是天大的荒唐。

這天，玄奘正在誦經，一個小和尙慌慌張張進來稟報：「師父，不好了，有人在寺門上掛了牌子。」玄奘隨小和尙出來一看，已圍了不少僧人。他朝牌子看去，原來是一個婆羅門教徒寫了四十條經義，並揚言如果有人能破得一條，他情願把頭砍下來。玄奘看罷，未予理睬，轉身便回寺裏去了。轉眼三天過去了，圍觀的僧人越來越多，竟沒有一個人能破解得出。

這天，玄奘外出回來，剛走到寺院門口，衆僧人忙讓開了一條路說：「玄奘大師來了，只有他能破解得出。」

玄奘笑著搖了搖頭。那婆羅門教徒這天一直等在這裏，他把牌子掛在那爛陀寺門口，就是對著玄奘來的。見玄奘竟一直不睬，就以爲他破不了，越發放肆起來：「玄奘，你在那爛陀寺主持佛學講席，能破經義中的一條嗎？」玄奘仍不答話，只顧朝寺裏走。婆羅門教徒越發猖狂起來，竟一把抓住玄奘的袈裟說：「想溜嗎？你破不了我的經義，請讓出佛學講席的位置來。」幾個婆羅門教徒也跟著喊了起來。玄奘說：「眼下我事多，沒時間跟你辯論。」說罷又要走。婆羅門教徒說：「怎麼，你害怕了！那你就乖乖讓位，滾回你的中原去。」

玄奘終於被惹怒了。他看著那婆羅門教徒，說：「你乃出家之人，怎能出言不遜。我不和你辯論，是可憐你。眞是個糊塗僧人。」那婆羅門教徒聽了不但不悔悟，反而咬牙切齒地說：「好大的口氣！你只破得其中一條，我便當著衆僧的面，把頭砍下來。」

玄奘義正詞嚴地說：「此四十條，我逐條破給你，若有一條說不對，甘把頭顱掛在那爛陀寺的門前。」

衆僧人驚得目瞪口呆。此四十條經義，不要說沒有準備，就是有準備，也很難解得沒有破綻，不禁都爲玄奘捏了一把汗。那婆羅門教徒得意地說：「一言爲定，絕不許反悔！」

玄奘說：「你的屍首如何料理？請早做安排，免得曝屍曠野。」

婆羅門教徒冷笑著說：「少說大話，你速速破來！」

玄奘走上台階，不慌不忙地對那四十條經義逐一批駁，直駁得那婆羅門教徒張口結舌，目瞪口呆。衆僧人止不住爲玄奘的博學和雄辯喝彩。

那婆羅門教徒臉色蒼白，爲了履行諾言，不得不抽出劍來，立刻準備自刎。說時遲，那時快，玄奘上前一步，一把按住鋼刃說：「幾句玩笑話，竟也當了眞嗎！我對你敢於辯論的自信精神和勇氣是很佩服的。辯則明，沒有辯論，我們佛教便無生氣了。願我們成爲親密的教友，能經常一起探求佛法。」

婆羅門教徒聽了，非常感動，誠心實意地拜玄奘爲師。

焦炳崑／搜集整理

靈岩寺護松

一天，唐僧路過靈岩寺。

孫悟空化緣去了。突然，一陣狂風捲來，飛沙走石，天昏地暗，弄得唐僧暈頭轉向，只見山塢塢，一片黑霧，辨不清東南西北。

唐僧急得無法，只得對著寺旁一株松樹說：「松樹呀松樹，請你指點我們去西天佛國之路吧！你若有靈，可將樹枝向西伸！」

「呼嚕，呼嚕！」這根木松樹竟搖晃起來，拼命倒向一邊。

唐僧驚異萬分。此時孫悟空剛好化緣回來，見有妖霧，本想尋找妖魔算賬，奈因唐僧一再規勸，催促大家快快按照松樹所指的方向前行，只得作罷。

豈知唐僧他們一走，這妖魔竟祭起妖法，對著松樹噴出魔火，使松樹燒了起來。

冬去春來，其他樹木已開始發芽生長，只有這松樹卻奄奄一息，即將枯死。

正值此時，唐僧師徒從西天取回眞經，原路回到了靈岩寺，見這株松樹竟渾身上下一片

枯焦，樹葉黃蒼蒼的。唐僧慈悲大發，就對天禱告說：「天呀天，我祝願松樹四季長青，千年不爛。」話音剛落，就傳來隆隆雷聲，接著，大雨滂沱。啊喲喲，只見樹葉一簇簇如針一樣，由黃變綠，樹活了！

從此，松樹沒有張張樹葉，只有一簇簇的松針，樹身上還留著焦褐色的樹皮，樹幹上滲出來的樹汁，成爲松脂。若將松樹砍掉，丟進水底，它眞的千年不爛不朽呢。

不過，那妖魔自不量力，爲了再次刁難唐僧師徒，竟呼呼地颳起幾股旋風。孫悟空一嗅便嗅出妖氣來，他眨了眨眼，躍上前去，奮起金箍棒，只聽得「噌」的一聲，妖魔被打死在地，現出了原形，原來是一隻大頭螞蟻精。

這大頭螞蟻精的屍體，經風吹雨淋，變成了一群小白蟻。這小白蟻至今還專門與松樹作對，老是在蛀松樹哩！

諸葛珮／搜集整理

黃鱔之變

一天，唐僧師徒四人越過火焰山，來到一條小河邊。

唐僧累了，就在河邊停歇下來。因爲雙脚被火焰山的餘熱燙得難受，就在河邊水裏洗洗脚。哪知用手擦了幾下，竟搔下了幾塊脚底皮來。剛巧，這時游來幾條泥鰍在水中覓食，一眼看見水中沈落一些脚底皮，它們就爭著吞食起來。

說也奇怪，吃了唐僧脚皮的泥鰍，個個肚皮都一下子脹得圓鼓鼓的，變成一個個圓咕嚨咚的東西。遲來了一步的幾條泥鰍，看了也目瞪口呆。

這些泥鰍馬上將這一奇事報告了水族之王——海龍王。海龍王一聽很覺奇怪，立即派出蝦兵蟹將去查看。經過調查，知道是吃到了唐僧高僧的脚底皮。

這是一個千載難逢的好機會。海龍王也聽說過誰要是能吃了唐僧肉，就可以長生不老。因此，他怒不可遏，立即傳令蝦兵蟹將去將那些吃了不死藥的泥鰍擒來問罪。

這些變了種的泥鰍，肚皮一大，行動不便，逃得更慢，只好使盡平生之力，往河邊的泥裏鑽。鑽呀鑽，頭鑽成三角扁形，可尾巴卻被追來的蟹將咬住。蝦兵蟹將拼命地將它們往外拖。一拖兩拖，將它們的身子拖得很長，而且一個個都被嚇破了膽。從此，它們就棲身在湖泊池塘邊，鑽個泥洞，躲在裏面。它們白天不敢出洞，只有到晚上才偷偷地出外覓食。

據說，這些泥鰍吃了唐僧的脚底皮，有了仙氣，雖不能長生不老，可壽命卻長了不少。而且死了，哪怕是炎熱的夏天，既不腐爛也不發臭。人們看看這些變了種的泥鰍，顏色大都是黃的；形似蛇而不咬人，心是善的，所以就叫它「黃鱔」。

不過海龍王還不甘心，竟發誓說：「好呀，你長壽，你死了不爛、不臭；但如你死在我的地域，我就要叫你爛，叫你臭！」

信不信由你，直至今日，黃鱔如果死在水裏，那就眞的會發臭發爛哩！

章翠娥／口述
諸葛珮／搜集整理

大蒜、韭菜、葱

唐僧師徒四人一路而行，越來越近天竺國，他滿心歡喜，精神倍增。這天傍晚，路過一個集鎮。八戒滿以爲要住宿吃飯了，不料唐僧仍叫繼續趕路。八戒急煞，忙道：「師父，徒弟早餓壞了，趕路也得塡飽肚子再走呀！」

唐僧用馬鞭一指，道：「徒弟莫慌，進了前面山腰再說吧！」

八戒不耐煩地嚷道：「師父，你難道忘記逢山有妖，遇水有怪嗎？」

唐僧笑道：「已近佛國，不會再有妖怪了。」

悟空跳上雲端，用火眼金睛四處一望，道：「此山腰住的都是信佛的善人、齋僧的居士，儘管放心吧！」

於是師徒四人，繼續前進，進入山腰，轉過幾個山灣，早就露出一所莊園來。唐僧感到離佛國近，恐徒弟們失禮，親自進去化齋。一位老者迎了出來。老者生得慈眉善目，童顏鶴髮。他與唐僧攀談之後，知道他們是東土大唐國高僧，忙請師徒們進屋，安頓好行李馬匹，便陪伴用茶。不到一刻工夫，忽聞陣陣清香撲鼻，家人端上五大碗炒麵，一大盆煎豆腐。八戒早饞涎欲滴，一聞味道鮮美，就囫圇吞棗，把五碗炒麵吞下肚去，還連喊添麵添麵。家人又端來五大碗湯麵，都被八戒吞吃了，還連聲稱讚好香好香。

唐僧細瞧碗內，見炒麵的拌料，綠綠的，扁扁的；湯麵上還放著一小撮青葱葱空心短段兒；煎豆腐的佐料，顏色也是又綠又扁，只是比上兩種肥點粗點，吃起來色、香、味三者俱佳。

他們在西遊路上，從未嚐過這種好吃的東西，唐僧不禁問道：「請問居士，這樣好吃的菜產在何地？」

老者答道：「敝莊已近佛國，家家都茹長齋，不吃五葷。此菜只有我處獨有。」

唐僧喜道：「這三種菜，定有很多好處？」

老者一本正經地介紹：「湯麵上放的一撮是葱，種在地上或盆罐內，異香爽口，能除腥通竅，葱上結的葱罩，便是它的後代。炒麵用的是韭菜，清香美味，能補血強神，秋後花開結子，可以種植在地裏。煎豆腐的是大蒜，有除穢、祛病、護身等功能，根子結的是蒜頭，可以入藥。」

唐僧聽後不覺嘆道：「可惜我東土大唐卻缺少這三種佳品。」

老者熱情地道：「如高僧不嫌棄，老漢願即奉贈。」說罷取出三樣種子來。唐僧大喜，大禮相謝。就把葱罩種擺在僧帽子；韭菜種放在袖籠裏；大蒜種藏在襪筒中。第二天，千恩萬謝，辭別了老者繼續西行。

唐僧西天取經回來，把這三種佳菜帶到東土大唐，因爲葱罩種放在帽子，所以有異香；韭菜種擺在袖籠裏，所以有清香；大蒜種藏在襪筒裏，所以是濁香。

董永祺／搜集整理

烏龜裂背

烏龜的背甲為什麼分裂成十三塊？據說這與唐僧去西天取經有關。當年唐僧帶著徒兒孫悟空、豬八戒、沙和尚，歷盡千年萬苦，從西天取得眞經五千零四十八卷。在回來的路上，師徒好不高興。

一日，當他們來到通天河西岸，正愁無法渡河，忽聽一陣喊聲：「唐聖僧，快到這裏來呀！」

唐僧師徒聽了，都覺得驚奇，忙抬頭向四處探望。可是既不見人跡，又不見舟船，卻見一個很大的白癩頭黿在岸邊探頭叫喊：「老師父，我在此已經等候幾年了，快來吧，我馱你們過河去。」

悟空一看，喜出望外，原來，它就是當年馱渡的老黿。悟空把喜訊告訴了師父和師弟，大家都很高興，連忙一齊向河邊走去。

悟空先到，便對老黿說道：「老黿，你若有接渡之誠意，就上岸來吧！」

老黿果然緩緩地爬上了河岸，伏在地上，像座小山。唐僧一行四人，連馬五口，一齊上了黿背，老黿蹬開四脚，游水如行平地，穩穩當當地直向東岸而去。

快到岸邊時，天色將晚，老黿突然想起一事，向唐僧道：「當年我託師父向如來佛祖問問我的年壽，不知是否問個明白？」

唐僧專心取經，忘了代問年壽之事，聽老黿問及，支支吾吾，不知如何回答。老黿心中已經明白，十分生氣，便將身子一搖，竟欲沈下去。

悟空用金箍棒輕輕地點了幾下，老黿的背硬，絲毫沒有感覺。一霎時，唐僧師徒連馬帶經，都已浸在水中了。

這一下把悟空惹火了，揮起金箍棒，朝老黿背上「叭叭叭」敲了起來。

老黿痛得連喊：「師父饒命！師父饒命！」

唐僧連忙喝住悟空：「徒兒，休得無禮！」

悟空圓瞪雙眼，說：「你再敢往下沈，我便結果了你的性命！」

老黿哪敢再反抗，只好重新浮上水面，嘴裏不斷哼著：「喔唷！喔唷！」繼續乖乖地將唐僧師徒安全渡上東岸。

因為悟空的金箍棒在這老黿硬背上前前後後一連敲了十三下，所以這隻癩頭黿背殼，就

分裂爲十三塊。從此以後，這隻老黿的子孫後代，背上都有了同樣的裂紋。

這隻老黿不但硬背殼被孫悟空的金箍棒打得碎裂，同時，它的肉也都變成烏青色了，從此人們便稱它爲「烏龜」。

後來唐僧在京師立慶功碑，忽然念及當年老黿馱渡通天河時，因自己的健忘而遭到悟空毆打，心裏很過意不去，便向如來請求，增添老黿壽齡。因此，烏龜雖受過傷，背殼有了裂痕，渾身一片烏青，但它的壽命卻特別長了。

沈標榮／口述
諸葛珮／搜集整理

敲不出《回生經》

在四川燈影峽南峰頂頂上，有四塊天生的大石頭，活像孫悟空、豬八戒、唐三藏、沙和尚。按照它各自的形狀，有人給編了一首順口溜：

孫悟空開路瞭望，
豬八戒牽馬過山，
唐三藏岸然端坐，
沙和尚經囊上肩。

說起這幾塊神奇的石頭，還有一段神奇的傳說哩。

那是唐朝的時候，唐僧騎著白龍馬，帶著徒弟孫悟空、豬八戒、沙和尚到西天取經，走到西陵峽，碰到大江攔了路。唐僧叫孫悟空去找過河船。

孫悟空一個筋斗翻到半天，往下看了好久，沒有一隻船。他落下雲頭，看見一個砍柴的，問他爲什麼沒有過河船。

砍柴的說：「從前有船，自從來了個豬婆龍❶，呼雲喚雨，興風作浪，害了許多人命，駕船的都嚇跑了。」

孫悟空一聽豬婆龍作惡，便想叫豬八戒去把它引出來除掉。他跑回來對豬八戒說：「河邊有一株大紅桔，你快去把大紅桔摘來給師父充飢。」

豬八戒正餓得慌，滿口答應，跑到河邊，眞的有株大紅桔。他摘了一堆，放在肚兜裏，又揀一個大的往嘴裏送。這時，非魚非龍的豬婆龍爬上岸來，說豬八戒偷吃了它的仙果，張口吐出一條白涎，將豬八戒緊緊纏住。

孫悟空在雲裏頭看見豬婆龍捉了八戒，便臨空一棒打來。豬婆龍趕忙縮回腦殼，滾下水去一看，原來是保唐僧取經的孫大聖，嚇出一身汗來。它想：這猴頭很厲害，鬥不贏他，何不做個好人，托他師徒過江，請唐僧在西天佛爺面前說個情，讓我早些脫殼成仙。於是，它又漂出水面，拱了拱前爪說：「不知是孫大聖，小鼉有眼無珠，有罪有罪！這裏沒有船，我願托師父過河。」

孫悟空用金箍棒挑斷白涎，救了豬八戒。豬八戒掄起釘耙要打豬婆龍。孫悟空攔住八戒，叫他快請師父來過河。

豬婆龍把唐僧師徒托過了河，唐僧要謝它。它說：「師父不要謝，小鼉修道千年，不能成仙，請師父向佛爺說個情，比謝我還好些。」

唐僧答應豬婆龍的請求，帶著徒弟走了。

山迴路轉，雲馳星移，過了很久很久，唐僧取經回來。豬婆龍歡歡喜喜迎出水面，託他們過河，游到河心，問起所託之事，可唐僧忘了向佛爺說。豬婆龍一氣，沈到水下，把師徒和經書都甩到河裏去了。

孫悟空、豬八戒、沙和尚慌忙救起唐僧，打撈經書，鋪在一個大山坡上翻曬——以後人們便把這地方叫做「曬經坪」了。

豬婆龍見他們撈起經書，又爬出水來口吐狂風，要把經書吹散。孫悟空隨手撿起一塊小石頭，拋到豬婆龍面前，變成一塊大石牌，擋住了狂風。豬婆龍又騰空而起，來打孫悟空。孫悟空不想和它糾纏，一邊叫豬八戒、沙和尚快收經書，一邊拔下四根毫毛，吹口氣，甩到山頂，變成了四個化身，引開了豬婆龍。

後來就變成四塊活像孫悟空、豬八戒、唐三藏、沙和尚的大石頭。

唐僧師徒回到京城，把經書一清理，不多不少，恰巧少了一部《起死回生經》。唐僧斷定是豬婆龍吃了，忙叫孫悟空把它捉來，用金箍棒敲打，要它吐出《起死回生經》。豬婆龍硬是不肯吐出來。所以，以後的和尚在念經的時候，都要敲打豬婆龍，要它吐出《起死回生經》。這就是和尚敲木魚的來歷。

來層林／搜集整理

❶豬婆龍：鼉的俗稱。

拱諸洋

著名的官廳水庫大壩這段河道，當地老年人稱爲諸洋河口。相傳早在唐朝之前，流經涿鹿、懷來的桑乾河、洋河這一帶，全被諸洋河海水浸占著。後來因爲豬八戒把諸洋河拱開一個決口，才出現現在的懷（來）、涿（鹿）盆地。

說的是唐僧師徒四人到西天求得眞經，辭別如來佛祖，一路上興致勃勃，曉行夜宿，好不快活。不覺寒冬已過，春暖花開。一日晌午，師徒四人又回到諸洋河西岸。唐僧一望這無邊無沿、白浪滔天的諸洋河，頓時又愁上眉頭。說道：「徒弟啊，咱前番來時，輕裝快馬這河尚且不得過，多虧神龜馱渡，才過得此河；今番回來，人擔馬馱，盡是重載，更休想輕易過去，你等看如何是好？」

唐僧話音未落，只見諸洋河水猛的掀起滔天巨浪。巨浪過後，那神龜突然又出現在岸邊，向三藏頻頻點頭說道：「師父莫愁，俺神龜已在此恭候多時了。」

唐僧一見，情不自禁地說：「善哉，善哉！前番已打攪神龜不淺，這回又勞你相助，叫貧僧何以報答？」說著話，唐僧師徒四人，急忙牽馬挑擔，一併上了龜背。神龜四肢輕擺，好似一隻小船，穩穩悠悠地向東岸渡去。

神龜游到諸洋河中心，回頭問唐僧：「師父，這次見到如來佛祖，可曾問到我何時成仙得道之事？」唐僧見問，突然想起這這事，由於當時匆忙，竟把這事忘了。這當兒想起，眞是悔恨交集，只好慚愧地說：「哎呀，實不相瞞，因時間倉卒，貧僧竟把你所託之事忘了……」神龜一聽，頓時怒從心起，猛地將身子一抖，「嘩啦」一下，將唐僧師徒四人連人帶馬全翻到河裏，自己一游而去。

唐僧被悟空、八戒等救上岸來，頓足大哭道：「徒弟啊，咱師徒四人，一路上受盡千辛萬苦，好容易才取得眞經，原指望能從此普渡衆生，不料卻把經卷全部葬送在這汪洋大海，這便如何是好？」

悟空、沙僧不善於水性，只急得抓耳撓腮，唯有八戒善於水性，這時卻不吭一聲。原來八戒想起一路上受盡悟空嘲弄耍笑，這時有意將悟空的軍。悟空呢，也早已看透了八戒的心思，暗自思忖道：此時若叫這呆子去打撈經卷，肯定要故意爲難。調兵不如激將，我且激他一激，且看他如何。主意拿定，悟空愁眉苦臉地對唐僧說道：「師父啊，俺老孫和沙僧都不識水性，剩下個豬八戒更是呆頭呆腦，只會貪嘴，啥也幹不了。依俺之見，倒不如咱們乾脆散伙算啦……」

悟空話沒說完，早把個八戒氣得騰的跳將起來，「呼哧呼哧」喘著粗氣罵道：「潑猴，你一路上還說俺老豬哩，想不到今日你也說這喪氣話。你說俺幹不了，咱們就打個賭，看俺老豬能不能把經卷打撈上來？」

悟空心裏暗笑，嘴裏卻故作驚訝地說：「眞的？賢弟若眞能把經卷打撈上來，俺老孫請你開戒動葷，飽吃一頓山珍海味！」

八戒一聽，饞得口水直流：「潑猴，咱一言爲定，到時候弄不到山珍海味再算帳。」八戒說罷興沖沖地分開水正要下河，忽然想起自己這樣下去，豈不等於大海裏撈針，一個人尋覓到何時？罷，罷，潑猴笑俺老豬笨，這回也動動俺這笨腦筋。他摸著後腦勺往四外一瞅，只見這諸洋河東南角上，兩座高山挾著一個山峽，這山峽又被一座土丘擋住。八戒一看，頓時生出了一個主意，不由自言自語地說：俺老豬要是把這座土丘豁開，把諸洋河水排乾，水落經出，豈不省事？主意想妥，八戒扛起九齒釘耙，甩開大步，搖搖擺擺的直向土丘奔去。

八戒趕到這土丘前，舉起九齒釘耙，使出吃奶的力氣，猛的一耙，只聽「撲哧」一聲，釘耙陷在泥裏，竟拔也拔不出，豁也豁不開。原來這土丘乃是由千年的污泥淤積而成，軟中帶硬。八戒想起和悟空打賭之事，心裏一急，一時逗得性起，索性把釘耙一撂，頭一低，竟用他那又長又硬的豬鼻子拱了起來。拱啊拱的，最後當眞拱開一個口子，只聽山崩地裂般地一聲響，諸洋河水順著口子奔湧而下，決口越拉越大，越拉越深。奔騰咆哮的河水猶如天河決口，一泄千里。把個八戒樂得張著大嘴，汗也顧不得擦，趕忙又把九齒釘耙攔在豁口上。就這樣，不到半天時間，便把諸洋河水全給泄乾了，經卷也露了出來。

八戒見悟空過來，得意地甩著大耳朵道：「潑猴，請老豬吃山珍海味，這話可得算數呀！」悟空一把擰住八戒的大耳朵，呵呵笑著說：「算數，算數！呆子，你看滿海底這麼多鮮貨，還不夠你受用？」八戒低頭一看，可不，只見滿河的魚跳蝦蹦，龜逃蟹爬，才猛的省悟過來，知道又上了潑猴的當。

當下兄弟三人，把經卷搬到岸上，又一本本攤開曬乾，最後又著實飽吃了一頓山珍海味，師徒四人這才又重新牽馬挑擔，啓程上路。

從那以後，便出現了現在的懷（來）、涿（鹿）盆地。後來人們陸續遷居到這一帶，男耕女織，人煙越來越多。現在附近的好多土台子，人們稱爲曬經台，據說這就是唐僧師徒當年曾經曬過經書的地方。

吳桂珍／講述
梅迎春／搜集整理

眞經漂東土

日本的佛教從何時傳入，據說這也與唐僧取經有關。故事是這樣的：

唐僧師徒四人在渡通天河時，馱載他們過河的老鼂，中途得知唐僧未曾替它問得年壽之事，便故意下沈，使一部分眞經浸溼。好在大家搶救及時，將眞經打撈上岸，但其中有一個經包，卻被河水捲走，氽得無蹤無影。

這個經包，隨著河水流呀流，一直流入金沙江；流呀流，一直流入長江；流呀流，一直流入大海。眞是條條河流歸大海，它幾經轉折，竟流到日本的一個小海島邊，擱淺在海灘上。

小島上居住著一個打漁的老漢。老漢這幾天晚上經常發現海灘邊上金光閃閃，明亮奪目，白天魚兒也打得特別多。老漢心中犯疑，他想，這海灘上有什麼寶貝？想去看看，又怕碰上水怪，一到白天，金光又不見了。

這天晚上，老漢喝了一碗酒壯了壯膽，撐起小船，朝那閃閃發光的海灘駛去。搖呀搖，搖呀搖，搖到灘頭一看，見是一個黃布包裹，隨著海浪一上一下地在閃光。老漢操起竹篙，打撈起來，一看是一部書。他雖認不出這是什麼，但總感到事非尋常，便特地趕到京裏，當面獻給國王。日本國王召集天下賢人，才認出那是唐朝高僧從西天佛國取回的眞經。這就是最早流入日本的一部佛經。

直到以後鑒眞和尙東渡，許多佛經才又陸續傳入日本，而最早的一部，則是從通天河流入日本的。

諸葛珮／搜集整理

醉臥玉峰山

相傳，齊天大聖孫悟空偷喝了王母娘娘蟠桃會上的仙酒後，覺得仙酒味美醇厚，清香撲鼻，便打算帶些回去給花果山的猴子們嘗嘗。於是，他把仙酒一杯一杯，一罎一罎，全都倒入乾坤袋內，往肩上一扛，一個筋斗，朝東海濱飄然而去。

因爲這蟠桃仙酒乃三千年開花，三千年結果，三千年釀造而成的，味道雖好，後勁卻大得嚇人。所以，這時的孫悟空已醉醺醺不能自持。他片刻便到了東海邊，醉眼朦朧，只見滔滔海水簇擁著一座秀麗的山頭，以爲老家花果山到了，就喜悠悠地按落雲頭。到地面一看，才知鬧了個誤會，這是江蘇的崑山。孫悟空想離去，可誰知正好酒性發作，他只覺得四肢乏力，頭暈眼花，搖搖晃晃，站立不穩，「啪」地倒下，一下便呼呼地睡著了。

孫悟空是個一刻也閒不住的「猢猻精」，即使睡著了，也不停地伸腿蹬足。他有十萬八千斤力氣，脚一蹬，把平展展的長山梁蹬了個大豁口，所以這崑山後來又稱爲馬鞍山。孫悟空手一抓，把身邊的乾坤袋也抓開了一條裂縫，裏面裝的仙酒直往外流。待他一覺醒來，袋內

仙酒已流掉大半。這流出的仙酒滲透力特別強，立刻就滲到了山石骨子裏，轉眼，灰褐色的小砂礫山，變成了亮晶晶、白花花的玉石山。從此，這座小山就有了「玉峰山」的美稱。直到今天，凡到崑山遊覽的旅客，總要去玉峰山玩，並以能撿到一些潔白晶瑩、玲瓏剔透的玉石爲快呢！

華　船／搜集整理

盜鹽磚

古時候，海水是不鹹的。

傳說，孫悟空保唐僧去西天取經，兩次打跑白骨精，唐僧說他誤傷兩條人命，不容分說，將他攆回了花果山水簾洞。衆猴兒見悟空回來，高興得跳跳蹦蹦，連忙擺酒席替悟空洗塵。悟空一口一杯，喝得十分痛快，可是，伸筷夾口菜一吃，皺起眉頭問：「這菜，怎麼沒滋沒味？」衆猴兒七嘴八舌地說：「如今沒鹽吃了，所以炒菜燒湯都沒味。」有幾個猴兒還直著脖子來到悟空身邊說：「大聖你看，沒有鹽吃，我們都得了這病，脖子不痛不癢就發粗了。」悟空心想：怪事！現在怎麼沒鹽呢？待我把當方土地神找來問問。悟空一念咒語，喚來了土地神，這才知道鹽被玉皇大帝收煉去了。

鹽，只有人間才有。玉帝聽說它是很好的調味品，但不知眞假。一天，他遊山看景，來到了東海邊的九九咯啦山。當方的山神、土地沒宴招待。吃飯時，玉帝覺得這菜肴鮮鹹合口，比天上的龍肝鳳膽還有味。就問：「這菜放了哪些佐料？」山神、土地告訴他，除了葱蒜生薑，還放了些鹽。玉帝忙叫拿來給他看看。山神、土地拿了些鹽粒兒來。玉帝一看，一顆顆晶瑩雪亮，用舌尖舔舔，又鮮又鹹，挺開胃口的，心裏就打起了主意。

玉帝回到天宮之後，就命太陽神將地上的鹽烤煉成兩塊鹽磚。一塊送給西天佛祖如來，一塊自己留著。從此，人間就吃不到鹽了。

衆猴兒聽了，一個個氣得眼睛通紅，紛紛要跟悟空打上天宮，奪回鹽磚。悟空說：「這點小事，哪用你們跟著？」說畢，他提著金箍棒，一個筋斗，翻到空中，騰雲駕霧，向靈霄寶殿飛去了。玉帝見悟空滿臉怒氣，心中一驚。悟空手提金箍棒問：「你爲何將人間的食鹽收煉到天上？」玉帝說：「天上人間，都歸我管，把食鹽收煉到天上，關你甚事？」悟空見玉帝態度蠻橫，一股無名火直沖上來，恨不得一棒將他打翻在地。但想到鹽磚還不知下落，只得捺下急性，暗中思量。

正在這時，忽見一個官兒端著盤子從前廳走過。盤子裏放著一塊四角方方，色似漢玉的東西，閃閃發光。悟空估計定是鹽磚，心中大喜，就使個分身法，把假身留在那裏同玉帝周旋，眞身卻變作一隻蒼蠅，跟著那個官兒。那個官兒將盤子端到廚房，就站在鍋邊看廚師炒菜。每炒一菜，就用小刀在那雪白的方塊上刮點兒屑子放進鍋裏。炒好菜後，還嘗嘗鹹淡如何。這一切，悟空看得清清楚楚，乘他們不注意時，拔根毫毛，變作一塊假鹽磚，將眞鹽磚換了下來。

悟空得了鹽磚，立即離開靈霄寶殿。他想：這回定要讓天下的百姓們都能吃到鹽。他把金箍棒變作一把刀子，在天上一邊駕雲慢慢兜圈子，一邊用刀子在鹽磚上刮。鹽屑子像雪花一樣從天上飄落下來。

再說那個廚師還在炒菜。他在假鹽磚上刮了許多屑子放進菜裏，仍然一點鹹味都沒有。管鹽磚的見此情景，慌忙向玉帝報告。玉帝一聽，知道壞事了，向悟空的假身大聲喝道：「你這猴頭好大膽！怎麼把我的鹽磚偷換去了？」悟空知道事情已經暴露，收了假身，在空中答道：「鹽磚原是你從人間收煉來的，俺如今仍把它歸還給人間！」說著就駕起雲頭，向花果山方向去了。玉帝急忙傳令，叫托塔天王父子和二郎真君帶領天兵天將，速速將鹽磚追回，不得有誤！

這時，悟空已到了東海上空。他回頭一看，天兵天將已到身後，心中暗想：剩下的這半截鹽磚，恐怕是來不及撒了。他們人多勢衆，與其被他們再搶回去，何不扔到大海裏，叫他們竹籃打水——一場空？托塔天王追來叫道：「悟空，快把鹽磚交來，免得我們動手！」悟空說：「玉帝將人間食鹽弄到天庭，供自己享受，這實在太不公道了！我現在要把它扔進東海裏，讓海水變鹹，誰要鹽，誰就舀，又省事又公平合理！」說著，就舉起鹽磚，向海裏扔去。天兵天將慌忙阻攔說：「扔不得！扔不得！」一邊說，一邊來奪。說時遲，那時快，只聽「撲通」一聲，鹽磚落進了海裏。托塔天王急令哪吒下水去撈，哪裡還有鹽磚的影子？原來這東西一沾水就化掉了。哪吒沒有撈到鹽磚，只得跳出海面覆命。大家聞到他身上都散發著鹹味，知道鹽磚已經化在海裏。悟空見此情景，哈哈大笑，一個筋斗走了。

從那以後，海水一漲潮，就在海灘上留下鹹水，經太陽一曬，就出現了一片白白的鹽粒兒。百姓們把鹽粒收起來，送到各地，大家都有鹽吃了。

單士前、華　泉／搜集整理

智賺芭蕉扇

唐僧師徒四人往西天取經。這一天，他們走著，走著，忽然感到天氣炎熱難忍，豬八戒甩著兩隻大耳朵直叫：「熱死了！」唐僧也熱得汗流浹背，氣喘吁吁。他問八戒：「現在已是仲秋季節，因何還有這等炎熱？」

豬八戒想了想說：「師父，我們上當了！」

唐僧詫異地問：「上了什麼人的當了？」

豬八戒說：「那個短命的猢猻，東走西闖，一定是走錯路了，把我們領到太陽裏面去了……」

說話時，孫悟空從半空中下來，說：「師父，大事不好，前面有八百里路火焰山擋住了去路，人要靠近此山，就會化成煙塵。」

唐僧一聽，聽得全身顫抖：「這如何是好？」

孫悟空忙說：「師父勿必驚慌，徒兒已經探聽明白，那前面有芭蕉洞，芭蕉洞內有位鐵扇公主，她有一把芭蕉扇，只要用這把芭蕉搧一搧，火焰山的火就會立即熄滅。那鐵扇公主是牛魔王的妻子，牛魔王我認識，我去把扇子借來，保護師父過山。」

唐僧一聽十分高興，可是豬八戒在旁不斷發出冷笑。孫悟空問他爲什麼冷笑。

豬八戒說：「你這猴頭，眞是聰明一世，糊塗一時，前次你與紅孩兒交戰，戰他不贏，請觀音菩薩將他收去。那紅孩兒是鐵扇公主的獨養兒子，你害他們母子不能團聚，那鐵扇公主恨之入骨，正要與你算帳，你這一去，正好是羊落虎口，不但借不到芭蕉扇，而且性命都難保。」

唐僧一聽這話慌了：「大徒兒，你看如何是好？」

孫悟空被豬八戒一提醒，覺得這倒是一個難題，但他憑著自己的本領，自信地說：「她若不借扇，我叫她嘗嘗我這通天棍的厲害。」

豬八戒一聽又是一陣冷笑，說：「你的通天棍果然厲害，可是人家鐵扇公主的芭蕉扇比你更厲害，她要拿芭蕉扇朝你一搧，你就像秋風掃落葉，飄到九霄雲外，連回來的路也找不到了！」

豬八戒見大師兄被他一軍將住了，在旁搖頭晃腦，十分得意。

唐僧心裏著急，見豬八戒這個樣子，就問：「八戒，你有什麼好的辦法？」

豬八戒當即說：「師父，辦法我有，就怕你們不肯依我的辦法去做。」

「就依你的辦法，你快快說來。」

「據我所知，這火焰山乃是當年猴頭大鬧天宮時，捅了太白金星的煉丹爐，掉下來的火磚變化而成，要是借不到鐵扇公主的芭蕉扇是萬萬不能過去的。所以，依我說還是散伙，你師父回轉大唐國，猴頭回轉花果山，沙鍬回轉流沙河，我老豬回轉高老莊。」

唐僧一聽生氣了：「你這逆徒，凡心未退，自從西行以來，一再思念還俗，不肯盡心保師取經，幾次煽動散伙，爲師要念咒懲罰你了。」

唐僧合起雙手，就準備念，嚇得八戒急忙下跪求饒：「師父饒命，師父饒命，徒兒絕不再說散伙的話了。」

於是唐僧就命他趕緊想辦法過火焰山。

豬八戒被唐僧催促，就脫口說：「師父，依我說，這芭蕉扇用借、搶都不行，只有一法——騙。」

孫悟空問他如何騙去？豬八戒卻搖頭答不上來。可孫悟空受到他的啓發，心裏一轉：「有了！」就在豬八戒的耳邊如此這般地說了一番，說得豬八戒哈哈大笑，連聲說好計好計。

於是孫悟空就命沙僧保護師父，說：「我與八戒取芭蕉扇去也！」

原來鐵扇公主每餐飯後都有喝茶的習慣。孫悟空變作一隻小蟲飛進了芭蕉洞，待鐵扇公主吃好飯，小妖捧茶上來時，孫悟空就變作一根茶葉梗子，落在杯中。鐵扇公主喝茶時，不留神把這茶葉梗子喝了下去。

孫悟空鑽進鐵扇公主肚子裏，用頭頂、足蹬、拳打，一時痛得鐵扇公主滿地打滾，哇哇直叫，嚇得衆小妖手足無措。

這時，有人來敲洞門，小妖開門一看，門外站著一個牛不像牛、豬不像豬的怪物，小妖責問：「你是何處妖怪，竟敢來闖芭蕉洞府？」

原來這妖物是豬八戒變化的，因爲他法道不大，變得不全，所以是牛不牛豬不豬的。八戒見機關被識破，靈機一動，忙說：「你們不認識我嗎？難怪，難怪！我在這洞府住的時候，你們還沒有出生呢，我乃是牛魔王的叔公。方才在宮中忽然心血來潮，掐指一算，我的姪孫媳婦身患急病，所以急急趕來，特爲她治病。」

小妖們一聽這個來頭，連忙引入洞內。

豬八戒見鐵扇公主痛得不省人事，正在地上打滾，上前叫了聲姪孫媳婦，煞有介事地看了看鐵扇公主的病情，對小妖們說：「你家公主生的是熱蒸傷寒，我這裏有清涼退熱丹一粒，吞下去肚痛即可止住。」

小妖們拿丹丸給鐵扇公主呑下，果然肚痛止住了。但渾身仍舊火燙——這是孫悟空在她肚子裏噴火。

豬八戒又說：「我姪孫媳婦的身子像火燒一樣，這不是一般的火，是太上老君煉丹的眞火，需要拿你家公主的芭蕉扇，搧上三扇燒才能退盡。」

那小妖取來一把芭蕉扇交與八戒，豬八戒拿到芭蕉扇，欣喜若狂，掰開鐵扇公主的嘴巴，對著嘴說：「行了行了，猴頭快走吧。」

孫悟空一下從鐵扇公主嘴中跳出來，二人拿著芭蕉扇就離開芭蕉洞府，搧滅烈火，過了火焰山。

宏　聲／搜集整理

跌入豬身

傳說天上的神仙和咱凡人一樣，也與年年過生日祝壽。王母娘娘是三月初三過生日，每年三月初三，天上的大小神仙都到王母娘娘宮中來給她祝壽。每次，她都在瑤池裏擺下酒宴，盛情款待諸位神仙。

衆神之中，要數天蓬水神酒量最大。他特別愛喝王母娘娘宮裏的醇香桂酒，因爲平時很難得到這種好酒，所以，他喝起來就沒完沒夠，不醉不散。

有一次，他來到王母娘娘宮中，拜完壽就坐下來喝酒。他左一杯，右一盞，一直喝到頭重脚輕，分不清東南西北，才暈頭轉向地離開宴席準備回去。因他喝酒太多，出了瑤池便摸錯了方向，糊裡糊塗地闖進了廣寒宮。

天庭裏有三十三座天宮，七十二重寶殿，座座天宮富麗堂皇，重重寶殿金碧輝煌。各宮各殿裏都住著大帝天王，神兵天將。唯獨廣寒宮不同，裏面住的全是仙女。這些天仙一個比一個長得俊，一位比一位長得美。特別是嫦娥天仙更加出衆，天蓬水神見了她特別喜歡。他一來到廣寒宮，就嬉皮笑臉地纏著她聊天。

俗話說：「酒喝多了誤事。」他在廣寒宮裏耽擱的時間太長，誤了時辰，被糾察靈官捉住，押上了靈霄寶殿。玉皇大帝龍顏大怒，以違犯天規的罪名，把他貶下凡間，讓他到東海的一個荒島上去受苦。天蓬水神後悔已晚，只得駕起黑雲出了南天門，離開天庭向東海飄去。

從南天門到東海有十萬八千里路程。天蓬水神邊哭邊走，不知不覺地來到徐州上空。此時，正遇上孫猴子在花果山上降生，「轟」的一聲巨響，山崩石裂，把他嚇慌了神，一失腳，化作一團黑球從雲端滾下，正好栽到一頭在白龍山腳下曬太陽的老母豬肚子裏，變成了一頭小豬崽。

這頭老母豬已經懷胎，正躺在山坡上「呼嚕呼嚕」地睡大覺，冷不防被天上掉下來的黑球砸得嗷嗷直叫，疼得它在石頭上亂滾亂翻，連小豬落地都不知道。老母豬在山石上滾出了一個石坑，陷進了坑底，化成一眼清泉；這窩小豬全都拋在石坑外面，除了天蓬水神變成的小豬崽活著跑走了，其他豬崽全都在坑邊變成了黑色的石頭塊。老遠瞅著，好像是一窩小豬正聚在母豬身邊爭著吃奶。這就是「母豬泉」的由來。

這母豬泉不但形成像豬，周圍的黑石頭也像一群小豬。從泉眼裏冒出來的泉水，是五個小珠連成一串，「嘟嚕，嘟嚕」地向外冒。無論旱天澇天，泉水總是平著地面。後來有位朝廷大官路過這裏，又給它起了一個名字，把它叫成了「五珠泉」。直到如今，這個泉的叫法不一：本村百姓叫它「五珠泉」；方圓百里的群衆，還叫它「母豬泉」。

天蓬水神變成的這頭小豬崽，生下來十分潑辣，見風就長，能走能跑，四下裏找食吃。沒滿月，它就走南闖北，不管是樹上長的，水裏生的，盡揀好的吃。滿月那天，它跑到茅村，被小張家村的一位老漢捉住，帶回家裏圈養起來。

這頭小豬食量大，性子野。老漢給它準備一天的吃食，它一頓就吃盡了，吃完之後又「哼，哼，哼」地叫著要食。漸漸地它長得又高又大，吃的就更多了，沒有吃的就往外跑。老漢用石頭壘的豬圈管不住它，它只要用鼻子一拱，石頭牆就倒了。

後來，它經常出去蹓躂蹓躂。從徐州到利國，沿途有十八個清水泉。天旱的時候，它上「澇泉」去洗澡；天澇了，它去「葦泉」打滾玩。除了生養它的「母豬泉」，各泉都有它的豬蹄印。每到一處，都把清泉糟蹋得不成樣子。

它還喜歡爬山找食吃。上了山就把山上的花草樹木啃光吃盡，吃完了又把山上的紅土拱到河裏，使周圍所有的山嶺都成了光山禿嶺，所有的溝河都被填平。從此，這一帶山上光禿禿，流水無正路，這都是它造的孽。

這頭豬走到哪禍害到哪，時間越長，禍害越大。老漢看了心裏非常難受。他想來想去，最後用鐵鏈子把豬拴在家裏，這才把它治住。據說，徐州農村過去餵豬不用豬圈，只用一根鐵鏈子拴著餵就行了。這種方法就是從那時候傳下來的。

這頭豬被老漢拴在家中院子裏，性情逐漸溫馴起來，變成了一頭貪吃貪睡的大懶豬了。它整天吃飽了睡，睡醒了吃，養得肥頭大耳，渾身溜圓。老漢看了心裏非常高興。到了年底，老漢想痛痛快快地過個大肥年，從茅村請來了兩個殺豬匠，準備殺豬過年。

每天，這頭大肥豬睡醒了，總是瞪著兩眼盼老漢來給它餵食。這天，它看到老漢走路的架勢不對，手裏也沒有食盆，只是提著一根粗繩子，嚇了一跳，便警覺起來。等殺豬匠走過，它嗅著那味道，才知道大禍臨頭，便靜斷鐵鏈子，在院子裏亂躲亂閃。三個人忙了半天，也沒抓到一根豬毛。老漢又從外面找了兩個伙計來幫忙。大肥豬看情況不妙，「蹬」一下跳出了院牆，逃到季山，闖進山頂上的和尚廟。

天蓬水神下凡以後，玉皇大帝知道他走錯了路，投錯了胎，已變成一頭大肥豬，便派太白金星下凡來點化它成人。太白金星領旨下凡，在徐州西北的季山頂上點石成廟，坐等肥豬進廟取經。

大肥豬闖進廟裏，見到方丈就躺在地上連連磕頭。方丈知道天機不可錯過，便把雙手一合，念了一聲：「阿彌陀佛！」然後喝道：「大難臨頭上山來，消災除難入佛門。」

大肥豬聽了，連連點頭。

「佛門大戒嚴，善惡如水火，從善法無邊，萬惡全解脫！」

大肥豬聽了，又連連點頭。

方丈把它領進後殿，命它參究禪宗修行，求得「明心見性」，以便早日成得人形。

第一年，大肥豬在後殿學念經，漸漸修成了人形；第二年，他早早晚晚背佛經，懂得了佛法，有了神通；到了第三年，他已經知道自己是天蓬水神轉世，覺得根底不淺，心裏已經滿足，就不再專心念經了。他在後殿念了三年經，吃了三年齋，心裏老覺得不自在，便背著方丈施弄法術，從外面弄來酒菜開了戒。他還妄自尊大，自稱「大老豬」，整天想著下山去尋個快活。

方丈原是太白金星的化身。第一年，他見犯了天規的天蓬水神有悔改之意，便讓他脫掉豬身，成了人形；第二年，本想早日幫他脫下凡胎，修成正果，盡快返回天庭，不料他破壞了佛門清規，一時難成正果；第三年，便打發他下山去另謀生路。

一天，方丈對大老豬說：「你入廟三年，現已期滿，下山另投名師去吧！」

這話正中大老豬心懷，便高高興興地點頭，答應了。他收拾好行裝，方丈把他送出廟門。臨分手時，方丈又對他說：「我還有兩句話，你要牢牢記在心上：第一，從今以後，不管走

到哪裏，不要說你是季山廟裏出家的和尙；第二，不管到何年何日，不許重提你的出生地點。」

大老豬一想早日下山去吃香喝辣玩個夠，別說兩句話，再多他也同意。最後，他跪在方丈面前說道：「徒兒全都聽明白了。如果說出去，就叫大伙割我的耳朵，切了我的舌頭下酒吃。」

師徒分離，方丈爲何要提出這兩條呢？他心裏有數：大老豬下季山，一時不會走上正道，必然會惹是生非，掀起風波來。到那時，人家找到季山廟裏可不好應付；要是外地人知道他的老家在這裏，那不是給咱們臉上抹黑嗎？

別看大老豬咋咋唬唬，丟三拉四的混了一輩子，可他確實沒有忘記方丈最後對他說的那兩句話，所以世上很少有人知道他是季山廟裏出家的和尙，更不知道他是在徐州城北「母豬泉」出生的。

姚克明／搜集整理

八戒與高小姐

豬八戒在高老莊做了三年女婿，他和高小姐的這段姻緣詳情細節怎樣呢？民間講的頭頭是道，比《西遊記》裏寫的還有意思。

說那高小姐高翠蘭容貌俊秀，性情溫柔，不單針線活兒做得好，還能作詩畫畫，是個心靈手巧的才女。高太公把大姐香蘭、二姐玉蘭都嫁出去了，唯獨留下翠蘭小姐，愛如掌上明珠，打譜給她招個才貌雙全的過門女婿。

豬八戒早見過高小姐。聽說高太公要給高小姐招女婿，他心裏想：應當趁早上門求親，或許好事能成。又一想：自個的臉面不大好看，肚子裏也沒啥才學，怎辦呢？苦惱了好多天，忽然想出個主意來。

這天，豬八戒刮掉臉上的黑毛，抹了滿臉白粉，穿上綾羅衣衫，戴上錦繡帽子，瞅瞅像個白面書生了，便拿起一把摺扇，一步三搖，來到了高老莊。他一見高太公，躬身施禮，假充斯文，說：「太公在上，小生有禮了。」

高太公上了年紀，眼睛有點昏花，恍惚間看到豬八戒彬彬有禮，頓生幾分喜歡；又見豬八戒白生生的臉面，穿戴挺闊氣，身架也滿有派頭，更添了幾分歡喜，於是和顏悅色地問道：「你是哪家公子？前來敝宅作甚？」

豬八戒說他姓羊，獨子，二十二歲，尚未娶妻，家裏本是書香門第，不料年前遭了火災，房舍家財被大火燒個精光，二老爹媽不幸葬身火中，可憐自己孤身一人，走投無路，特來拜見太公，願做門下小婿。

說著說著就跪下「咕咚，咕咚」給高太公磕了三個響頭。

這麼一講一磕頭，高太公深受感動，心想：這人無根無絆，實意誠心，招他為婿，倒也合適；但不知才學怎樣，得考上一考。

說來也巧，高太公不考這，不考那，單單要豬八戒背一段《詩經》，正好與老豬事先準備的一點「才學」對上了號頭。豬八戒搖頭晃腦背誦道：「關關雎鳩，在河之洲，窈窕淑女，君子好逑。」

高太公滿心高興，又想女兒一向孝順，不會有話，就當場把親事定下來了。

成親這天，高家紅燭高照，鼓樂喧天，賓客盈門，好不熱鬧。晌午時分，一聲「拜天地」，只見兩個伴娘把高小姐攙到堂前，就是不見新郎到場！

豬八戒哪去啦？原來，他見自己耍的花招成功，得意洋洋，忘乎所以，每天喝醉了就睡覺。這會兒，豬八戒醉成一攤泥，正在床上做著美夢。

新郎不到場，怎好拜天地？衆人等得發躁，不免議論紛紛。高太公急了，忙派人去叫豬八戒。不多會兒，只聽大聲傳呼：「新郎羊公子到——」

諸親好友齊朝豬八戒觀看，不看還好，一看哪，嗑！只見豬八戒挺著個大肚子，炭黑臉掛著汗，水瓢嘴直呱嗒，晃晃蕩蕩、迷迷糊糊地走了過來。衆人見新郎這般模樣，先是捂著嘴「嗤嗤」發笑，接著交頭接耳，嘁嘁喳喳，都說高太公老糊塗了，不該把好閨女許配給這麼個醜八怪。

高小姐聽了衆人嘀咕，不由吃了一驚。想看看新郎吧，頭上蒙著喜布，怎好意思自個掀開呢？不看看吧，心裏老不踏實。想來想去，想去想來，忽然「哎喲」一聲，癱倒在地。

高家傭人一見高小姐出了事，趕緊向高太公稟報。哪曉得，高太公在書房裏頭也癱倒了！怎麼啦？原來，他剛才發覺豬八戒相貌醜陋，舉止粗俗，自知受騙上了當，氣惱之下，昏了過去。

這麼一來，高家可就亂套了！衆人吆吆喝喝，有的喊：「快救救高小姐呀！」有的叫：「快救救高太公呵！」豬八戒聽到喊叫，打了個愣怔，揉揉眼，酒醒了。他瞅見高小姐躺在地上，連忙竄到跟前，伸手就要拉扯。不料高小姐就像春燕似的，騰地躍起身來，奔向高太公的書房。

高小姐有心計呀，她是故意癱倒的，想用裝病的辦法暫避一時。聽到衆人吆喝「快救救高太公」，高小姐顧不得多想什麼了，飛身奔進書房，撲到高太公的床前，連聲問道：「爹呀，爹呀，你怎麼啦？你怎麼啦？」

高太公悔恨說：「沒想到呵，爹爹竟給妳選了個醜八怪。唉，我挨騙了。」

一聽這話，高小姐反倒舒開緊鎖的眉頭，說：「爹呀，爹呀，不礙事。常言道：『不拜堂不成親。』我與那人沒有拜堂，算不上什麼。事不宜遲，快將那騙人精趕走吧！」

話音剛落，忽聽「嘭」的一聲，豬八戒闖進門來。高太公和高小姐嚇了一跳，以爲這傢伙要行凶，哪知豬八戒雙膝跪下，舉起巴掌，朝著自個的嘴臉左右開弓「啪啪啪啪」打個不停。

高太公覺得奇怪，問道：「這是爲何？」

豬八戒哭腔哭調說：「太公呃，我錯嘍，不該哄騙你老人家。實說了吧，我姓豬，不姓羊，家裏也不是啥書香門第，我來求親以前，把墨臉塗成白臉，冒充白面書生，爲的是討你老人家喜歡。好太公呃，你罵我也行，打我也行，我眞的是孤身一人哪，只求你留我作女婿，從今往後我一定老老實實的，再也不敢撒謊啦。」說完，又噼哩啪啦自打嘴巴。

高太公見豬八戒認錯的樣子滿誠懇，就有點心軟了，轉臉望望高小姐，意思是說：妳看怎辦哪？

高小姐朝豬八戒打量一番，想了想，便貼著老父親的耳朵，滿面含羞地講了自己的心意。高太公微微一笑，說聲「好」，回頭問豬八戒：「你會幹活嗎？」

豬八戒聽高太公問這話，陡然來了神氣，連忙說：「會呀！會呀！」

「那好，」高太公說，「我家東邊有百畝旱田，乾裂難耕，如果你能在三天之內把它刨完，我就認你爲婿。」「這話當眞？」「絕無戲言。」

「好好好，這就去刨！」豬八戒說著，「砰」地衝出門外。他向高家傭人要來一把九齒釘耙，奔到高太公指點的農田裡，好傢伙，你看他拼命啦！前一耙，後一耙，左一耙，右一耙，只見釘耙上下翻飛，如同雄鷹展翅；泥土開花捲浪，好似大海揚波。不到半天工夫，嘿，百畝旱田全都刨了個底朝天！

眞是「一勤遮百醜」呵！豬八戒的壯舉，贏得衆人讚不絕口。高太公樂呵呵的，覺得有了面子。高小姐呢，心意就在一個「勤」字兒，覺得嫁給勤勞的壯漢滿光彩，便同豬八戒拜堂成了親。

豬八戒當了新郎，好不自在！開頭個把月，他忙裏忙外，幹得挺歡。可是過不多久，懶毛病又犯了，整天吃了睡，睡了吃，啥活都不想幹。高小姐以爲他累過頭了，就說：「這樣吧，暫時不要幹活，我教你寫字。」

「好呵好呵！」豬八戒高興得亂蹦。

小姐先教豬八戒寫字。可是豬八戒寫呀，寫呀，橫七豎八，彎彎扭扭，就是寫不好。結果，他憋出了滿頭大汗，「啪！」把筆一甩，嚷嚷說：「太難了，太難了！不寫了，不寫了。」

豬八戒老是寫不好字，高小姐說：「算了吧，我教你畫畫。」

「好呵好呵！」豬八戒又是很高興。

頭一天，高小姐畫了個圓圈圈，說：「這是十五的月亮，你照著畫吧。」豬八戒畫呵，畫呵，畫了七七四十九個，沒一個是圓的！

第二天，高小姐畫了個方塊塊，說：「這是一片農田，你照著畫吧。」豬八戒畫呵，畫呵，畫了八八六十四塊，沒一塊是方的！

第三天，高小姐只畫了一豎，說：「這是一根擎樑柱，你照著畫吧。」豬八戒畫呵，畫呵，畫了九九八十一根，沒一根是直的。

冬去春來，又教了一年多，豬八戒還是笨手笨脚，畫啥都不像。

眼看豬八戒教不成材，高小姐十分焦急，早早晚晚少不得數落一番。一回數落，兩回數落，十回八回，豬八戒火了，大叫大嚷地說：「我老豬生來就笨，有啥法子？不學啦，不學啦，啥也不學啦！」

不學就不學吧，你還去幹活呵。哪知豬八戒自暴自棄，越來越懶，一天到晚吃吃睡睡，不想動彈。高小姐好心好意勸他幹活，練練身手，他不但不睬，反而砸這個，摔那個，時常發酒瘋。為這，高小姐傷透了心，整天哭呵，哭呵，直哭得天旋地又轉，淚水流成河。高太公見這情形，乾著急也沒法子整治豬八戒，只好搖頭嘆氣，自認倒楣。

恰好這時候，唐僧取經路過高老莊。正像《西遊記》裏寫的，孫悟空施展本領，把豬八戒給降住了。高小姐聽說豬八戒要跟唐僧去西天取經，不禁轉憂為喜。

畢竟是三年相伴呵，分別之前，高小姐操持針線，做了一身青布衣衫和一雙厚底雲鞋，雙手捧給豬八戒，隨口作了四句詩，念道：

豬郎取經奔西天，
攀山越嶺莫畏難，
但願此去開心竅，
增才長智報喜還！

高小姐這麼有情有義，把個老豬感動得淚水直淌。臨走，豬八戒一步三回頭，望著高小姐戀戀不捨。後來在取經路上，豬八戒動不動就嚷嚷：要回高老莊，去見高小姐。那是因爲高小姐待他不錯，難忘呵！

高從善等／口述
姜　威／搜集整理

截斷釘齒耙

據說，南天門外有棵松樹，八千年前已長得十來丈高，九個人手拉手圍不著。一天，太上老君順手折了個樹枝，魯班拿它做了把鋤菜園的釘齒耙。當時官拜天河水神的朱精漢（豬八戒未入沙門前的名字），沒有稱心的武器，見這個釘齒耙亮閃閃明晃晃的，就握在手裏舞將起來。舞了幾下，得心應手，也不經魯班同意，就背起來走了。

這個釘齒耙十分厲害：十一根鐵釘尖如利爪，一丈八尺八寸長，一伸能伸出十萬八千里以外，一舞舞得天昏地暗鬼神驚！

卻說孫悟空跟隨唐僧去西天取經，路過高老莊時，正好碰上高太公的家人去請法師，要捉拿高太公的妖怪女婿。孫悟空得知後，自告奮勇上門除妖。高太公聽家人通報說，有人願除妖怪，就出來笑臉相迎。讓到屋裏坐定後，高太公說道：「三年前來了一個漢子，自稱姓朱，家住福陵山上，我就招他做了女婿。那人剛來時倒也謹慎，誰知後來卻變成了個長嘴巴、大耳朵的呆子；又會擺弄風雲，鬧得我一家不得安生。他還把我女兒關在後宅院裏，成天不叫出來，現在也不知是死是活。」孫悟空聽罷，氣得怒目圓睜：「待俺老孫去會會他。」說罷，提起金箍棒就去捉拿妖怪。

孫悟空用金箍棒搗開了後院大門，只見妖怪正躺在院裏睡覺，就揮棒朝妖怪打去。那妖怪也怪機靈，見勢不妙，連忙躲過，掄起釘齒耙打將起來。你道妖怪是誰？他就是天河水神朱精漢。那他怎又到高老莊做了女婿呢？原來朱精漢貪酒誤事，被貶到福陵山下。誰知他投錯胎，成了豬的模樣，改姓叫做豬精漢，來到了高家莊。打聽到高太公要招女婿，就搖身一變，成了精明漢子，巧言花語騙住了太公，做了女婿。

再說孫悟空和豬精漢鬥了幾十回合，不分勝負。孫悟空暗想：這傢伙也會幾下子哩，待俺老孫用智擒他。就賣了破綻，打跟斗跑了。豬精漢見孫悟空跑了，拿起釘齒耙就摟。孫悟空一個跟斗能跑十萬八千里，那豬精漢的釘齒耙一伸也能摟十萬八千里。孫悟空一看就要被摟著，心中不由得暗暗吃驚。好在豬精漢正要往回摟，忽然聞得一陣酒香，就忘了這事，順著香氣找酒喝去了。

孫悟空見豬精漢走了，心想：只有把那釘耙毀壞，才能勝他。就回到屋裏，把高太公的女兒喊出來，讓高太公領走後，孫悟空變得跟那女子一模一樣，躺在床上等豬精漢。

不多時，豬精漢醉醺醺地回來。進屋一頭扎在床上，怕著悟空說道：「娘子快起來給我

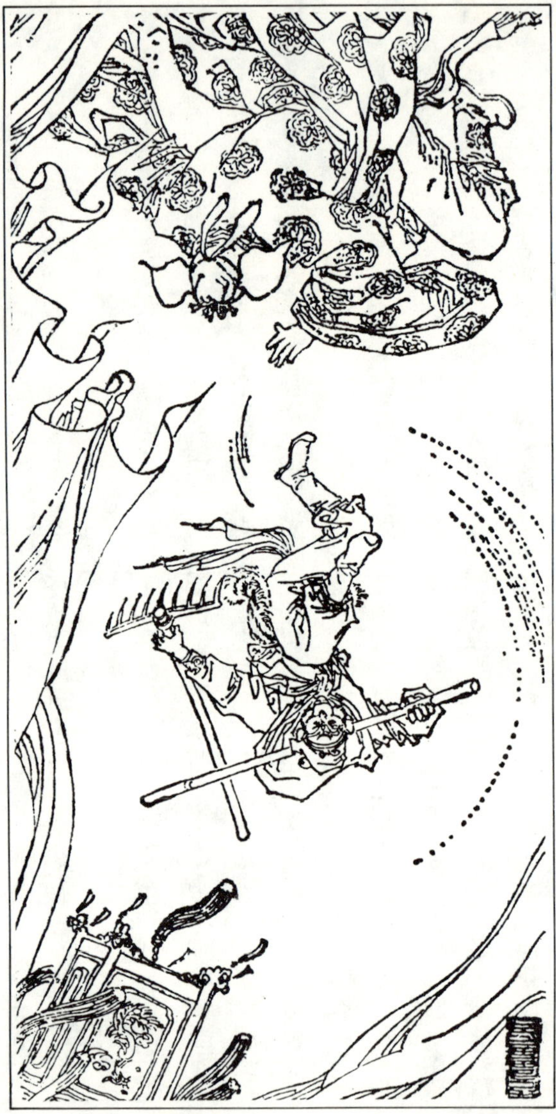

倒茶！」孫悟空裝出不情願的樣子，給他倒了杯茶。喝完茶，豬精漢酒醉矇矓，忽然想起一件事，說：「那個毛猴來了沒有？」悟空便裝出帶哭的樣子說：「你一天在外也不管我，叫我怎過呢？父母隔牆丟磚扔瓦的砸我，他們又請來個鬧過天宮的齊天大聖，說要捉拿你呢！最好你教會我使你那釘齒耙，咱夫妻兩人也好共同對他們。」豬精漢說：「那你就拿著練吧。」

悟空掂起釘齒耙說：「唉，太長、太重了，要是再短點才得勁哩。」豬精漢不耐煩地說：「那你就截點短吧。」孫悟空聽罷，心中暗喜，一下子截了一大半，又取下了兩根鐵齒。豬精漢見了，跳下床吼道：「叫你截點短，你怎截了一大半？」說著，舉拳朝悟空打來。

孫悟空一手拿著釘齒耙，一手從耳朵裏取出金箍棒，顯了原形，大聲說道：「好你個妖怪，我是你孫悟空爺爺！」豬精漢一抬頭，見面前站的是孫悟空，自己手中已沒了武器，便嚇得兩條腿一軟，癱倒在地。孫悟空拔根汗毛，吹口氣變成繩，捆著豬精漢見師父去了。

豬精漢見了唐僧，連連磕頭求饒，表示願改惡從善，摩頂受戒。唐僧就收他做了徒弟，取法名為豬八戒。豬八戒的釘齒耙被截掉一大半、十一齒變成九齒後，再也敵不過孫悟空了，所以他惱恨在心。據說現在豬見猴子又恨又害怕，就是這個緣故。

馮天佑／搜集整理

燠館涼台

在南雁蕩山的仙姑洞北面，有一個叫順溪的小集鎮。從這裏順著峽谷向北走，不到五里，便到渡颸橋。過橋，一塊巨大的岩石擋住去路，轉個彎兒，繞過大石，就看到另外有兩塊大岩石，一塊筆直立著，一塊像鷹嘴一樣伸過來，成爲一個兩頭通透的洞，而在鷹嘴岩下又有一個小洞。不要以爲這個洞沒啥好看，當你在鷹嘴岩下坐下來，才覺得怪哩！

夏天，你來到這裏，走得直冒汗，只要在鷹嘴岩下一坐，乖乖，一股冷氣從岩下小洞裏冒出來，覺得涼絲絲的，只要一會兒，所有汗珠兒都跑了，滿身涼快。冬天，這個洞卻是熱騰騰，暖烘烘，叫你周身舒展，捨不得離開哩。因爲這個洞生得怪，那些咬筆頭的文人，便給它起了個古裡古怪的名字，叫「燠館涼台」。這裏還流傳著一個故事——

當年孫大聖偷了王母的仙桃，逃出天宮，急急忙忙回水簾洞。當他路過南雁蕩山，降下雲頭，來到觀山亭向南一望，前面一帶岩峰拔地而起，中開一關，十分雄偉，關內站著一位石將軍。石將軍已接到上天捉拿大聖的命令，把雲關把守得嚴嚴實實，連個蒼蠅蚊子飛過也要檢查。孫大聖衣兜裏還留著十幾只仙桃，心裏明白是檢查不得的。他來到關前，抓抓腮，拿出個仙桃，雙手捧到石將軍面前說：「將軍，這仙桃得來不易，敬獻將軍一只。」石將軍顯得很喜歡，接過仙桃，客客氣氣請大聖過關。大聖剛進入關內，冷不防石將軍出奇兵用一根捆仙索把他五花大綁綁起來，押送天宮。

玉帝大怒，傳旨把大聖的弼馬溫官職革去。大聖大笑：「我才不要這個瘟官呢。」玉帝喝道：「沒這樣便宜，罰你到南雁蕩山下看管三百個水碓，每個水碓每天要搗白米三千斤，三百個水碓合九十萬斤，供給天下僧人每天的吃食。」即刻令石將軍押解大聖到南雁蕩山下。

南雁蕩山下沿溪兩旁的三百個水碓，日夜不停，輪子伊呀伊呀地叫，搗臼蹦隆蹦隆地響，珍珠一樣的穀子，舂出玉粒一樣的白米。大聖看看聽聽滿新鮮，滿有趣。但不多幾天，就覺得那聲音太單調，那顏色太乏味了。他向東山一望，觀音洞像個獅子大張口，獅子口裏一溜房子，畫棟雕樑，好像是掛在那裏，很像天宮的瓊樓玉宇，夜晚燈火一亮，分外好看。大聖抓抓腮，想：我何不偷上觀音洞散散心呢？

大聖來到觀音洞，只見許多和尚正在做晚課，個個閉目低眉合掌，呆頭呆腦，拖長聲音念阿彌陀佛。大聖東瞧瞧，西瞧瞧，一眼看到觀音大士手裏拿的玉淨瓶，怪可愛的，便一躍上了蓮座，偷了玉淨瓶就溜了。

玉帝知道觀音大士失落玉淨瓶，還是大聖玩的把戲，眞是火上加油，氣得頓脚，便令石將軍把大聖押到鷹嘴岩下的石洞中，看管起來。冬天用三百六十把大扇搧，夏天用三百六十個火盤烤，叫他吃吃苦頭。

哪裏知道玉帝只知天時，不懂地理。天上的節序和人間恰好相反，天上冬天地上熱，地上夏日天上冷。石將軍雖知地理，因爲奉的是玉旨，不敢違抗，也就照辦了。冬天烤火盤、夏天搧大扇，大聖在洞裏不但沒有吃苦，還過得十分舒服。

許多年後，大聖回水簾洞去了。只有那「煥館涼台」，一直留傳至今。

徐祥地、蕭耘春／搜集整理

神鐘仙鼓

百年一度瑤池宴，千年一度蟠桃會。

天上的蟠桃會呵，是仙界的大慶典。這一天，東南西北，天上地下，人間冥界，江河海洋，幾乎所有的神仙都受到了玉帝的詔請，各帶神異珍寶趕往凌霄宮，以便當衆獻寶，各顯神通。

在各界被詔請的神佛大仙裏，可缺一個大名鼎鼎的人物孫悟空。這猴頭早年鬧了天庭，攪得天上雲亂星散，弄得玉帝也不敢去坐凌霄宮，只得讓他自稱爲「齊天大聖」，並連哄帶騙賜封了個「弼馬溫」。這次蟠桃會上詔請的，非佛即神，非神也是仙，孫悟空性屬「妖類」，怎能躋身於神佛群中！

孫悟空聞知要開蟠桃會，心想：俺老孫是堂堂「齊天大聖」，又是御封的「弼馬溫」，玉帝老哥是不會不相邀的。誰知左等右等，就是不見「請柬」，打聽了一下，方知各路神仙菩薩都已獲詔請，他差點氣炸了肺，心想：呸！看來那凌霄殿又得俺老孫去砸啦，那醜帝王的幾簇長鬍子又得俺老孫去拔啦！於是，孫悟空從耳中取出金箍棒，念咒變大，掄在手裏，幾個猴跳，直往凌霄宮去找玉帝。

孫悟空急步走著，眼看快到南天門了，忽見迎面哼哼哈哈過來一個道裝老頭，老頭肩荷肩擔，肩擔上一頭掛著大鼓，一頭是只大鐘。孫悟空素來好管閒事，見老頭挺陌生，就主動相問，方知來者是賴太上老君這老頭推荐，剛從凡界道士晉入仙班的張天師。

張天師聽了孫悟空的介紹，不由肅然起敬地說道：「哎呀呀，原來是孫大聖，久聞大名，幸會幸會！」

孫悟空也學會了幾分客套，忙應酬了幾句，隨即問道：「張天師這麼急匆匆挑著鐘和鼓，是往哪裏去哇？」

張天師告訴孫悟空，他是得到詔請上天宮赴蟠桃會的，隨後又問孫悟空：「大聖，你也是去赴蟠桃會的吧？」

孫悟空點頭嗯了一聲，然後說：「看來玉帝老哥太忙，連俺老孫的請柬也給忘啦！」

張天師見孫悟空沒受詔請，頓時感到自個兒高他一等，於是把挑著的鐘鼓換轉個肩，大聲說道：「哎喲喲，沒有玉帝的詔請，哪有資格赴如此隆重的蟠桃盛會！」

孫悟空道：「難道俺老孫還沒資格？」

剛被太上老君荐入仙班的張天師十分得意地說：「能赴蟠桃宴的，都是堂堂的正路神仙菩薩，你算什麼？」

「俺是齊天大聖！」

「呵哈，那是自吹自封的。」

「俺是玉帝御封的弼馬溫！」

「嘿嘿，管馬的臭頭兒，算什麼神，哪路仙？還不是跟人間的牧童差不離！」

孫悟空一聽，氣得眼睛裏幾乎冒出火星，他一把揪住張天師的衣襟，大喝道：「老混蛋，狗妖道，你講什麼？」

張天師被揪得上氣接不著下氣，一邊用手狠力去扳孫悟空的手，一邊連聲說：「嗯嗯，大聖快鬆手，快鬆手，兄弟說的可是實話，弼馬溫就是馬夫頭，比凡界的牧童強不了多少吶！」

孫悟空聽如此一說，惱得哇哇直嚷，手一推，把張天師摔出三丈遠。張天師仰天躺倒在雲頭，老久爬不起來，那扁擔和挑著的神鐘仙鼓，被摔得飛下了雲頭。

孫悟空摔開張天師，跺脚大嚷：「呸，好個玉帝臭老兒，敢欺侮俺老孫，老孫今朝不搗爛凌霄宮，不拔光你的鬍子毛，難消俺心頭之恨！」

說罷，孫悟空就取出金箍棒，捅進南天門，直闖凌霄殿，又在天宮大鬧了起來。

不說孫悟空重新又大鬧天宮，且說那被孫悟空摔得連扁擔一並飛開去的神鐘和仙鼓，那條大扁擔晃晃蕩蕩，落到浙江麗水和縉雲交界的一個山溝裏，山溝被一掀一震，成了一道沒峰的平頂山巒，這山巒就叫「扁擔山」·，那對鐘鼓呢？飄呀落的，嘩啦啦掉落在麗水曳嶺區崇義鄉西北一側，成了兩座相並相對的大岩峰，仙鼓落在東邊，就叫「東岩」，老輩人也稱「鼓岩」。神鐘落在西邊，就稱「西岩」。東岩和西岩，合稱「東西岩」，也有人叫它爲「鐘鼓岩」。「東西岩」如今已是浙南有名的風景區哩！

袁春根、唐宗龍／搜集整理

大聖觀海

猴子望海，又叫猴子望太平，是黃山美景之一。

傳說在很古的時候，孫悟空由石猴煉成活猴，便把他的原身石頭扔在黃山獅子峰北的一座平頂山峰上，它蹲著，像是在吃桃，腳底下還有幾個石子，像是堆著的桃子。後來，猴子站了起來，這才變成現在的樣子，因爲山底下就是太平縣，所以又叫猴子望太平。

相傳在很久之前，松谷庵邊上來了兄弟倆，哥哥叫大海，弟弟叫小海。他倆原住在水邊上，一場大水，淹了家園，淹死父母，弟兄倆便逃荒到這裏。一見這片土地雜草叢生，無人居住，大海便對小海說：

「小海啊，我倆這樣像撐船似的到處飄，也不是個辦法，我看這裏山景好，土也不孬，不如就在這裏落脚。」

小海點點頭，說：「哥，你說得對。」

於是，弟兄倆停下挑子，圈個棚住下來。日出而作，日沒而息。兄弟倆砍荆棘，揀石頭做田裏……汗水淌了一條河，血泡破了無數個。連那山坡上跳躍的小猴子也被感動，有時也下來幫兄弟倆拔草揀石頭。十年下來，開了許多田，種上稻子，一望無邊，微風一吹，碧波蕩漾，可喜人咧。

豐收了，有了米穀。兄弟倆想到無糧的苦愁，就經常拿出米糧救濟窮人和鰥寡孤幼；並且用米釀了甜酒，有人路過這裏，就請進屋裏，喝杯酒解除疲累，吃飽肚子再趕路。

四面八方的人得到兄弟倆許多好處，都稱讚不止。常言說，說話的無心，聽話的有意。一天，大財主臧員外的管家在酒店聽人稱讚大海兄弟，回去就向臧員外稟告。貪心的臧員外立即帶著管家、爪牙騎馬而來。他們放馬跑了一圈，被綠油油的稻海饞得口水流有三尺長，臧員外頓起黑心，命管家把兄弟倆叫到馬前，黑虎著臉說：「哪裏來的野民，種了我這麼多地，竟敢不交租子？」

大海說：「啓稟員外，這兒過去是荒地，是我們一鍬一鋤開的。員外，你莫非看錯了。」

小海說：「我們開荒也不是一年二年，怎麼地做熟了，就有人來認？」

臧員外怒道：「渾蛋！什麼你開的？常言說，普天之下，莫非王土，這地是皇上封給我的。」

老實的大海，一時不知所措。

聰明的小海，頂上去說：「員外，既然是皇上封的，必定有封書，請你把皇封拿給我們看看。」

臧員外原以爲這兩個泥巴腿年輕人，一嚇唬不就沒招了嗎，誰知小海來了這一手。只見他臉由白變紅，由紅變紫，老鼠眼四處亂轉溜，猛地，他看到臧家墳地上的大葉楊樹，把枝葉伸到稻田上空，在稻禾上留下一片樹蔭，他頭一點，歹計上心，只聽他嘿嘿冷笑說：「你這狡猾的傢伙，皇封你沒資格看。爲了使你心服，我叫你看——喏，那是我臧家墳地不假吧，那枝條都伸到田裏，這叫樹——替——主——認——地！」

誠實的大海說：「員外，請息怒，租子我們交吧！」

勇敢的小海說：「哥，慢著。樹又不是人，怎麼能算數呢？那我家門前的大槐樹，樹蔭也蓋上稻田，比他那片還大咧，又怎說呢？」

臧員外大怒：「大膽的野民，給我捆起來，送縣衙問罪。」立時上來幾個如狼似虎的爪牙，就把手無寸鐵的小海捆綁起來，拉到一邊。

大海一見，慌了，說：「員外，我們交租就是了，你放了我弟弟吧！」

臧員外說：「好吧，管家的你算算吧！」

管家拿出算盤，劈哩嘩啦地撥了一陣說：「老爺，一畝一石米，百畝百石糧，十年交千石，外加前九年的利息，就是三千三百三十三石！」

大海一聽嚇得癱到地上。臧員外指著他凶狠地說：「告訴你，十天內，租、息全交上。要不，殺了小海，還要抓你坐牢。」

說罷，騎上馬，帶著爪牙，架著小海，揚長而去。

大海看著臧員外抓走弟弟，放聲大哭，邊哭邊訴說：「哪裏來這麼多米交租子，怎麼才能救弟弟呢？」他擔心這個心毒手狠的臧員外會把弟弟殺害。他越哭越傷心，越傷心越哭，他把太陽哭落山了，他把星星哭出來了。哭得淚珠兒變成血珠兒，哭呀哭呀，竟哭昏過去了。

朦朧中，突然一隻猴兒向他走來說：「大海哥，石猴身邊石子下都是金子，快去取吧！」

大海說：「人家遇到危難這麼傷心，你還來尋開心！」

「誰來尋開心？人家來幫助你，你還狗咬呂洞賓——不認好人心！不去算啦！」

大海忙說：「對不起，猴老弟。」一把未拽住，竟跌了一跤。他猛然驚醒，爬起來，揉著眼，此時旭日初升，滿山滴翠。遠處山坡上，一個猴兒正朝石猴那裏走，還不斷回頭向他招手。他心想，猴兒絕不會像臧員外那樣歹毒，也來捉弄我。唉，「死馬當活馬醫」，爲了救弟弟，也只有這一條路啦。他爬起來，攀山上去，越走越有勁。那猴兒走到石猴面前停下來，用手在石子下面一扒，霎時，土裏黃燦燦的東西在閃光。大海走到跟前拾起一塊來看，「天哪，眞是金子呀！可以交租救弟弟啦！」

再一看，那猴兒已不知去向，大海就拜倒石猴下面，然後用土把剩下的金子蓋起來。

這天，臧員外吃罷早飯，坐在客廳裏，架起二郎腿，用掃帚苗剔牙齒，眼眯成一條線，正爲他不費吹灰之力，就要得到一百畝好地而得意。猛地，管家走了進來，稟告說：「大海，來交租！」

「放他進來。」

臧員外看見大海喜顛顛的樣子，十分奇怪：「你用銀子交租？」

「金子。」

「金子？」

「是金子。小的絕不敢在老爺面前撒謊。」大海說罷，掏出一塊金塊。

管家接過金塊一看，眼睜得像雞蛋，嘴咧得像瓢，又遞給臧員外。臧員外也快活得沒法說，他讓管家一算，不多不少，剛好夠上交租息。

臧員外看著黃燦燦的金子，忽然說：「大海，你這個跟泥巴打交道的人，在這山野裏是撿不到金子的。這金子非偷即搶，你要老實地說。」

大海是個老實巴交的人，連忙說：

「員外，小人雖窮，還行得正，坐得直。你不能這樣血口噴人，只要你放了我弟弟，我就說。」

臧員外一看有機可乘，馬上變怒臉為笑臉說：「皇天在上，祖宗在地，我說話算數。要是你說了眞情，不放小海，那我就被亂石砸死！」

大海聽了臧員外的血誓，便把經過一五一十說了。臧員外便把小海放了。

小海出來，大海高興地說：「弟弟，我們快回去吧！」

出了臧員外的門，小海就向大海：「哥啊，你哪來的租來？」

大海就如實地講了情況。小海說：「哥啊，臧員外賊狼生了個狐狸——不是好種。你哪能這麼糊塗，把金子得來的情況告訴他？這可對不起好心的石猴。」

大海一聽，用拳擊著自己的腦袋，說：「唉，救弟心切，一時欠考慮。只是常言說，善有善報，惡有惡報，石猴也會原諒我們的。」

小海聽大海這麼說，嘆了口氣，說：「只好如此啦！」

說著，雙雙歸家了。

第二天，臧員外讓管家帶著钁子、痲袋，按大海講的路線，對直不打彎地來到「石猴玩石」的地方，在石桃那處，就用钁子刨，一钁子下去，便露出黃燦燦的金子。兩人高興得發瘋，死命地往麻袋裏裝。忽然，轟隆一聲巨響，地動山搖。石猴憤怒了，它站了起來。一刹那，塵煙滾滾，飛沙走石，把兩個貪心傢伙砸成肉餅。那飛沙走石還淹沒了臧員外的房屋田園。石猴怕飛石砸壞大海兄弟及其他鄰居的土地、房屋，就用眼向那邊看著。要說也怪，飛沙走石從上空過去了，那裏的田園房屋絲毫未受到損害。剛好那地場屬太平縣，也就變成猴子觀太平了。自那，石猴就再也未蹲下來，一直站著望咧！

說也奇，在有雲天，猴子看雲海，挺神；在無雲天，猴子就能望到那片莊稼，看到太平縣府——甘棠鎮，也挺神！

黎邦農／搜集整理

悟空取靈藥

中華九州大地，地名相同的很多，稱金沙河的有十八處，稱西湖的有三十六處，稱薑山的有七十二處。相傳，這「十八金沙，三十六西湖，七十二薑山」都與唐僧西天取經有關，你道奇是不奇，怪是不怪？

一、十八金沙

相傳唐僧取經路過安安國的時候，突然患了一種下肢出血症：每天夜晚一覺醒來，便發現下肢膝彎裏出血。白天時候，出血點的傷口雖然凝結好了，但第二天清早，又會發現新的出血點。這樣一連幾天，把唐僧這個壯胖子拖得三分像人，七分像鬼，求醫服藥，都無濟於事。弄得孫悟空、豬八戒、沙和尚三個徒弟束手無策，眼看往西天取經的時日就要耽誤了。

孫悟空沒法，只好一個筋斗回到東土大唐，請通曉醫道的黎山老藥師去給唐僧看病。黎山藥師隨孫悟空到安安國給唐僧一診視，搖搖頭說：「大聖，你師父這病不是受風寒瘟溼、鞍馬勞累之故，而是遇到了世上最惡毒的吸血鬼螞蟥精了。吃藥不頂用，你只有把螞蟥精除了，這病才會好。」

這一說，使三個徒弟頓時開了竅。原來唐僧有個習慣，每晚安歇前，一定要用清水洗足，叫做「日必除塵」，那螞蟥精可能就是趁師父每晚洗足時，鑽進他的小腿的。

「請問老藥師，那螞蟥精是什麼模樣？住在什麼地方？我可前去捉拿。」孫悟空拱拱雙手，眞心誠意地懇求說。

老藥師沈思半晌道：「那螞蟥精有口無目，全憑血腥味接近生人，吸血如命。這妖精神通廣大，能變成針尖一般細的小蟲，鑽入生人毛孔，待生人睡熟後，他便吸血飽肚。據貧道所知，這妖精便住在我大唐國的金沙河金沙潭裏。」

不知是孫悟空性急的緣故，還是粗心大意，他未問清金沙河坐落的地點，便送別黎山藥師，匆匆去找螞蟥精算帳。

孫悟空站在雲頭上朝九州大地四面一看，只見一條條大江小河的河邊上，都有一片片金黃色的沙灘，而且沙灘邊的岩石上，都刻著「金沙河」三個大字。他左右前後一數，共有十八條金沙河。這許多條金沙河究竟哪一條是藏匿螞蟥精的地方呢？他落下雲頭一連問了好幾處，當地的老鄉都說，螞蟥是有的，但不曾見過精怪。孫悟空碰了幾次鼻子之後，便又去請教黎山老藥師。老藥師告訴他說：「我們的談話已經被螞蟥精聽到了，他事先在十八條河灘上都撒滿了黃沙，刻上了河名，而自己卻躲到別的地方去了。你回去告訴師父，叫他以後改用熱湯洗足，這樣螞蟥精就變不成小蟲，鑽不進小腿了！」

孫悟空拜別黎山老藥師，一個筋斗，回到唐僧的病榻邊，把沒有捉到螞蟥精的原因說了一遍；又關照師父以後要用熱湯洗足，以免再給螞蟥精以可乘之機。

唐僧聽了，頻頻點頭，並緩緩言道：「悟空，出家人慈悲爲懷。那螞蟥精以後不來作孽，也就罷了，不要再去難爲他！」

孫悟空知道師父最怕得罪妖怪，因此只好點頭應諾。由於他一時疏忽，使得狡猾的螞蟥精施了一個脫身之計。自從那時起，九州大地，便有了十八條金沙河。

二、三十六西湖

用熱湯洗足之後，唐僧的下肢出血症果然好了。但因失血過多，加上螞蟥精吸血時留下的毒液作祟，唐僧依然臥床不起，不能騎馬趕路，這可把徒兒們急壞了。三人商量後，決定再派孫悟空去請教那黎山老藥師。黎山老藥師聽了悟空的話後，皺起眉頭說：「如此說來，你師父的脾胃已被毒液所浸，如果毒液入心，便有生命危險。爲救你師父性命，你必須於三日之內，尋到解除毒性的靈藥。」

悟空一聽有解救之藥，心中暗喜，忙問道：「請問藥師，那靈藥生於何山？長於何處？叫何藥名？」

黎山老藥師搔搔頭皮，面露難色說：「不瞞大聖，貧道雖然熟認百草，但這解螞蟥毒的靈藥卻不曾見過，只是前年聽黎山老母說，普天下只有千年綠毛龜知道採靈藥的地方。」

「哦，千年綠毛龜！他住在什麼地方？我去問問他便是。」

「這龜大哥喜歡清靜，就住在西湖岸邊的老柳樹下……」

不知是孫悟空性急的緣故，還是粗心大意，他未問清西湖岸邊老柳樹的坐落地點，便拜別黎山老藥師，匆匆去找千年綠毛龜打聽採摘靈藥的地方。

孫悟空在雲頭上朝九州大地四面一看，只見一個個湖泊的岸邊，都有一棵棵高大的柳樹，而且每個湖的湖面上，都有搖船女在唱讚美西湖的歌。他左右前後一數，共有三十六個西湖。這麼多西湖，究竟哪一個西湖是千年綠毛龜的洞府呢？

孫悟空又只好回身去找黎山老藥師問個清楚。剛進他的藥堂，便見一個滿頭披綠毛的老翁向他站起身來。未等悟空動問，在旁的黎山老藥師便先開了口：「大聖，我知道你性急要壞事，你走後，我便把龜大哥請來了，他會告訴你採靈丹妙藥的地方的。」

悟空見眼前的老者就是千年綠毛龜，不禁肅然起敬，一面作揖，一面將急於救師父性命的事說了一遍。那綠毛龜長相雖然難看，但心地卻很善良，頻頻點頭道：「大聖，那螞蟥精暗中傷人，是我水族敗類，我也曾與他結下三百年冤仇。解其妖毒不難，只要你照此訣語去做就行。」說罷，從懷裏掏出一紙訣語，交給悟空。悟空接過一看，見上面寫道：

雷音山上甘露長，
自結靈藥如佛掌。
百叢裏面採一枝，
人間功德可無量。

再看那訣語下面，還有幾行採藥的規矩。悟空看得明白，心中有數，便告辭老藥師和龜大哥，匆匆趕路採藥去了。

螞蟥精沒有難倒孫悟空，但三十六個綠柳環抱的湖泊，從那時起，便都叫作西湖了。

三、七十二葷山

孫悟空一個筋斗，翻上十八層雲天，急急向西天最高峰雷音山飛去。經過半個時辰的遁行，穿過無數險峰白雲，終於來到極樂境界的雷音山巔。定神看去，見雷音峰雷音岩的南坡，有一片金黃色的沙土，那沙土之上，長著一叢似竹非竹、似蘭非蘭的仙草，並且開著黃色的長舌花，芳香撲鼻。悟空低頭一數，那仙草共有一百叢，與訣語上說的正好相符。他知道西方佛界不可冒失，便輕輕叫了一聲：「神聖寶地，可有佛在？」

話音剛落，便見岩壁後面，轉出一位長眉大耳的怪和尚來。那怪和尚似乎認得悟空，未等悟空說明原委，便開口言道：「哦，大聖，佛祖已知唐僧染病，也曉得你要來此採藥，故而命我在此等候。此靈藥可發汗利溼，生津解毒，人間無有，不可擅失天機。」說罷，撩起袖子，拔起一棵仙草來。悟空細細一看，只見那仙草根部，結著手掌大的一塊肉果，有枝有椏，很像一隻大佛掌，正同訣語上說的一模一樣。

那怪和尚將枝葉摘去，拂去沙土，然後將肉果交給悟空道：「每日三次，每次三片，三日之後，你師父必定康復如常。」

悟空接過靈藥，藏在懷內，拜別怪和尚，急急回到安安國驛站。那時，唐僧的病已很重，豬八戒和沙和尚，早已經急得手足無措。他們見悟空取回靈藥，驚喜不已，馬上動手給師父煎服。說來奇怪，三片靈藥服下，唐僧便手足發汗，神智也清了許多；再服下兩劑，那積聚在體內的毒液竟全隨汗水排出體外；三天共服二十七片之後，唐僧的病果然全好了。師徒三人欣喜若狂，準備重新上路。臨行前，唐僧整理香擔衣包，發現尚有一小塊帶有芽頭的靈藥留在箱底，便對悟空說：「悟空，這靈藥確是靈驗，多餘下來的這個根芽，可能還會長枝結實，你把它栽到我大唐的靈山上去吧！」

悟空覺得師父言之有理，連連說：「好，好。師父稍等，我去去就回。」說罷，接過那個根芽，直往東土大唐的崑崙山巔飛去。在崑崙山的南坡上，他揀了一塊暖溼之地，栽下根芽，然後返回安安國，繼續保護唐僧上西天取經。

靈藥的根芽栽在崑崙山上後，第二年就長枝抽葉，開花結實，而且長得十分茂盛。這樣春去秋來，不知度過了多少年代。當時普天之下，只有一個人知道崑崙山上有仙藥，這個人就是《白蛇傳》裏的白娘子。因爲白娘子在四川峨眉山修煉時，曾遨遊過崑崙山，採過百草，所以曉得仙藥生長的地方。但那時她不敢隨便採摘，因爲上界神仙已經派鶴鹿仙童在那裏看守了。

到那年端午節許仙被白蛇眞身嚇死之後，白娘子才不得不上崑崙山動武採藥。雖然當時仙翁老頭同意白娘子採藥，但她終究有點心慌意亂，採藥時，連枝帶根，連土帶葉，一股腦兒往懷裏塞。當白娘子盜得仙草回蘇州時，法海和尚又在三山五岳到處升起煙霧，使得白娘子一時迷了方向。因此，在從崑崙山到蘇州的途中，白娘子懷裏的靈藥，有許多根芽和枝葉散落在九州大地上。回到蘇州家中時，只剩下中間的一塊肉掌了。仙藥一到，許仙的病自然也就好了。

那散落在九州大地上的許多根芽枝葉，都落地生根，開花結實了。這仙藥不僅好入藥，而且可當菜，老百姓都紛紛種植。據說當時有人看到，這種仙藥美食，是一位美女從天上撒下來的，所以取名叫「姜」，就是今天家家戶戶少不了「生薑」。由於生薑有散熱解毒、利溼提神的作用，所以成了白娘子救許仙的仙草。

又據說當年從白娘子懷裏掉下來的根芽枝葉，落在長江黃河間的七十二座土質鬆軟、氣候適度的山頭上，並且都長出了生薑，所以當地老百姓都叫它們爲薑山。這就是「七十二薑山」的由來。

禾　家／搜集整理

討勿如偷

唐僧和尚帶著二個徒弟取經到西天，如來佛祖很高興，拿出仙桃仙酒招待。酒宴上有一道菜，一瓣瓣像剝了皮的桔子，並有一股撲鼻的清香味。仙酒、仙桃、仙雞、仙鴨，孫悟空吃得多了，一點勿稀奇；獨獨這種像一瓣瓣桔子的東西，以前還無沒見著過，用嘴巴一嚼，吔，噴噴香，還有點辣火火，味道眞好哩！

如來佛祖看出唐僧師徒四個對這個菜感興趣，笑著說：「這菜你們沒有吃過吧？這是西天仙果，不但好吃，還能防病，名字叫大蒜！」豬八戒連忙接上去說：「是呀是呀，這麼好的仙果，我們今朝吃過就沒得吃了，大家多吃點，多吃點！」

這辰光，孫悟空就想了，介好的東西，都由你佛祖獨自享用，太勿公平了！我得設法偷點回去發發種。孫悟空拿著筷子呆在那裏，烏眼珠骨碌碌轉個勿停。如來一看，便曉得這個猢猻肚裏又在打主意，就說：「唔！佛門弟子，六根要清淨，邪念勿可有，邪心勿可動！西天聖物，可看的你們看點去，可吃的吃點去，眞想要的話，討點去也是可以的。」

「哼！這有啥稀奇！」孫悟空三勿相信的脾氣又上來了，「討勿如偷，我就來個偷吧！」主意雖已打定，但心裏畢竟有點慌，因爲他知道如來佛法無邊，一勿小心就會被他捉牢，因此必須小心從事。

孫悟空一天到晚搔頭皮、抓屁股，還是想勿出好法子。轉眼到了回轉的日子，唐僧、八戒、沙僧都在忙著收拾行李了，孫悟空還在呆呆地想。豬八戒看到孫悟空一副靈魂出竅的樣子，走到他背後，對著他的屁股踢了一脚。孫悟空一下子好像開了竅，突然仰天大笑起來：「八戒，你個呆豬！今天饒了你，回去再算帳！」說罷，顧自溜到南山坡菜園裏去了。

臨走辰光，師徒四人去向如來佛祖告別。

如來問：「悟空，你有沒有了拿了我西天的聖物？」

「沒有，沒有！你佛祖講過，想要什麼東西，可以討嘛，我何必偷呢！」說完，轉向唐僧，「師父，快點走吧！」

「慢來！」如來一笑，「你個短命猢猻，騙得了別人騙不了我！來來來，把帽子拿掉看看！」

兩個大蒜頭從帽子裏滾了出來。

「把虎皮裙解開看看！」

腰骨上縛著一串蒜頭。

「還有沒有了？」

「佛祖，眞個沒有了！」悟空一面回答，一面忙向殿外走去。如來「呼」的一下，隨即把手伸到殿門口，扭住孫悟空耳朵。「你還不老實？」

說著，一把將孫悟空拉到身邊，半尺長的指甲往悟空耳朵裏就掏，掏掏一個，掏掏一個，兩隻耳朵裏掏出足有一鉢頭大蒜頭。

如來笑笑說：「你猢猻有多少花樣，會逃得過我的眼睛？想在我面前耍滑頭，你著實還要脫幾層皮嘞！」

「是，是！」孫悟空只好服貼了，「我老孫不過是同你老人家開開玩笑。想勿到你老人家如今還同當年一樣，佛法無邊……」

幾句好話一說，如來「哈哈哈哈」大笑起來，就不再追究，打發唐僧師徒四人上路回東土大唐。

走到半路，豬八戒不由嘆了一口氣：「佛祖也太小氣了，一個大蒜頭也勿給我們。往後，再也吃勿到這好味道的仙果了！」

孫悟空「撲哧」一笑，走到豬八戒身邊，脫掉褲子，把個屁股翹得半天高。豬八戒連連後退：「師兄，你這是什麼？」

話音未落，只見孫悟空一用勁，屁眼裏翻出個大蒜頭來。

豬八戒一見大蒜頭，高興得跳將起來：「嘿，人說如來一雙慧眼，無所勿見，到底給師兄瞞過了，還是師兄聰明！」

孫悟空就這樣把大蒜帶到了下界。這東西勿但好吃，還能治病，大家稱其爲「靈丹」。只是有一點勿大舒服，大蒜吃過後，嘴裏會有一股怪味，這是因爲孫悟空偷來時藏的地方勿好的緣故。

吳成良／講述

周迪清／搜集整理

熬過羅索國

唐僧上西天取經回來的路上，一定要經過羅索國。這年，羅索國剛剛巧發生過一場搶奪王位的混戰：老國王被一個有妖術的山大王殺死，宮裏的金銀珠寶、妃子宮女，全都落入山大王之手。山大王自立爲王之後，封他的軍師叔叔爲相爺，大肆殺戮舊臣，把個好端端的羅索國，攪得烏煙瘴氣。

這天，山大王聽說東土大唐的高僧從西天取經回來，心裏便盤算起來：「哼，人說我不信佛，好殺生，這回我偏擺個信佛的樣子，讓唐僧將眞經給我留下一半，我也可以造個藏經樓，把它供奉起來，表明我也是信佛好善的！」主意一定，便吩咐手下的武士說：「小子們，你們去把唐僧和他的三個徒弟抓來，就說在我羅索國王面前，要留下半擔眞經作爲買路錢！」

未等武士們應諾，站在國王背後的那個瘦個兒相爺急忙插嘴說：「大王，扣下半擔眞經作爲買路錢，爲臣十分同意。但那唐僧的三個徒兒不是等閒之輩，特別是那個孫悟空，法術通天，恐怕治他不了！」

國王聽了，頓時一呆，便問：「哦！那依你之見呢？」

相爺道：「強取不如巧奪。我們可以請他們進城來，然後提幾件難事難難他們。如果他們做不到，便可以扣下半擔眞經了！」

「提哪兒件難事呢？」

「這由爲臣安排，大王儘管放心好了！」那相爺在國王耳邊嘰嘰咕咕地說了一陣之後，便命令武士們道：「傳大王的旨意：將唐僧等帶到宮門前的石板地上，我有話吩咐。」

不一會，唐僧騎著白馬，沙和尙挑著經擔，由孫悟空和豬八戒前後保鏢，慢吞吞地來到宮門前的石板地上。剛立定脚根，便見王宮的門樓上鑽出一伙帶弓箭的武士來，並急急地站立兩旁。在一陣歡呼聲中，四個宮女扶著新國王出現在門樓上。

唐僧一見國王，忙跨下馬來，雙手合十，表示敬意。

那國王假惺惺地說：「東土高僧聽了，你等從西天取回眞經，孤王萬分敬佩。但孤王新近就位，立下一條法規，凡途經敝國之遠方商賈僧人，均需做得三件難事。如果三件難事有一件不能做到，就要扣下你半擔眞經，作爲買路錢！」

唐僧聽了，不覺心頭一驚，忙躬身道：「善哉善哉！天下難事千萬件，我出家人怎能件件做得，還是冀求大王，放我們過行吧！」

在旁的孫悟空早就聽得不耐煩了，便口出怨言道：「師父，跟這無賴國王嚕嗦也是白搭。什麼三件難事，分明是想要我們這擔眞經！哼，他不讓路，我就打碎他的王宮！」

這時，豬八戒也壯起膽來了，揚揚手中的九齒釘耙說：「對。師父莫怕，有我老豬在，看他能不讓我們過路！」

那相爺似乎聽到了孫悟空和豬八戒的嘀咕，壯著膽大聲地說：「你們別小看我們新大王的仙術！老實照我們的話辦吧！」

唐僧唯恐事情鬧大，連忙打躬作揖道：「是，是！我們一定尊重大王旨意。請問大王，不知是哪三件難事？」

那國王得意地笑了一陣後說：「這三件難事嘛，要說難，也不難。頭一件，你們師徒四個，要三天三夜不吃飯，不喝水，就給我坐在這石板地上，我派三百武士看住你們。」說完，便進宮去了。

一聽三天三夜不准吃飯喝水，那豬八戒和沙和尚，都一下子被嚇呆了。唐僧覺得餓上三天，雖然苦不堪言，但還是可以忍受。他怕孫悟空受不了這種窩囊氣，便輕聲地問道：「悟空，爲了平安返回大唐，你有這個耐性嗎？」

孫悟空知道師父善於逆來忍受，便也心平氣和地說：「聽師父的話，我也願意餓三天三夜。」

在三百武士的監視下，唐僧師徒四人，完全失去了自由。一天一夜過去了，大家的肚子已經餓得咕咕直響。正當難以忍受之際，忽然從孫悟空的手裏，「索索索」地擲出三串佛珠。豬八戒接過一聞，馬上覺察到一股食物的香味，便趁數佛珠之際，將一粒粒佛珠飛快地丟到嘴裏，一嚼，果然是一串好吃的東西。豬八戒使眼色給沙和尚，沙和尚也偷偷吃起佛珠來了。孫悟空使眼色給師父，唐僧也偷偷吃了起來。這樣，三天三夜熬過，四串佛珠吃光了，唐僧師徒四人，一個也沒有餓倒。

國王見第一件難事難不倒唐僧，便命軍師傳下第二件難事：要唐僧師徒四人三天三夜不得睡覺，只准席地而坐，不准東倒西臥。

這可是一件眞正的難事啊！那羅索國地方，白天炎熱，晚間寒冷；白天石板地上像火燒鐵板，晚上寒風一起，像一座凍城。爲了熬過難關，師徒四人硬著頭皮，一直從中午坐到黃昏。半夜一過，寒風刺骨，豬八戒冷得縮成一團，渾身抖索，嗚嗚直叫；沙和尚和唐僧也耐不住了。這時，只見孫悟空從經擔上解下一個葫蘆，悄悄地遞給唐僧和豬八戒、沙和尚，叫大家喝上兩口甘泉。三人喝了後，不僅覺得香氣撲鼻，而且渾身上下都暖和起來，連瞌睡鬼也趕跑了。這樣一連三天三夜，全靠孫悟空仙葫蘆裏的甘泉熬過了漫漫長夜。

那國王得知唐僧師徒四個眞的三天三夜沒有睡覺，感到又驚奇又害怕，心想：那孫悟空、豬八戒、沙和尚三個原是妖精，能熬過兩件難事，倒也不怪；只怪那凡人唐僧，怎能有此能耐。他百思不得其解，便問那軍師道：「兩件難事都難不倒他們，那第三件難事能眞的難倒他們嗎？」

軍師自以爲是地晃晃腦袋說：「大王，三天三夜不吃、不睡，我們已經將他們折磨得半死不活了，如果再下第三著妙棋，他們是一定會向大王討饒的，我們就能弄到半擔眞經了。」

國王聽了，便打起精神來說：「傳我的旨意：叫他們背三天三夜眞經，一刻也不能停，一字也不能錯！」

這第三件難事眞個把唐僧給嚇壞了，因爲他心裏明白，師徒四人剛剛取回眞經，還未曾熟讀，要將百卷眞經從頭至尾地背，而且一字也不能背錯，這是神仙也做不到的。便哭喪著臉對三個徒兒說：「看來這一回我們要被他難倒了。好徒兒，你們說怎麼辦呢？」

這時，經過六天六夜的凍餓，豬八戒和沙和尚已經有氣無力了，雙雙抱怨說：「師父，那羅索國王也太無理了，明明是刁難我們。受苦不如動武，平了他王宮衝出城去就是！」

孫悟空好像胸有成竹，笑笑說：「兩位師弟說得也是。先禮而後兵，如果那廝不講信用，我們再動武不遲！」

唐僧總是忍受在先，更怕徒兒們動武，便憂心忡忡地說：「悟空，兩件難事我們都忍受過來了，這第三件難事，怎麼對付好呢？」

悟空眨眨眼皮想了一會，輕聲地對大家說：「難是難，但我仍有辦法。」說罷，悄悄地在三人耳邊說了幾句。

背經卷的時刻到了。國王派了幾個懂經文的大臣來監聽，並且細細作了記錄。聽了三天三夜，記了三天三夜，那厚厚的記錄本裏，只是重複地記著一句經文：南無阿彌陀佛。原來唐僧師徒四人念的，就是這一句，其他什麼也沒有念，確實做到「從頭至尾地念，一句也沒有念錯，一刻也沒有停。」

監聽的大臣將監聽到的情況向國王報告後，國王以爲自己已經贏了，便趕到宮門前當場對唐僧道：「大唐和尚，你等四人雖然念了三天三夜，但只念一句，不是整卷經文。你們輸了，快把半擔眞經留下吧！」

未等國王說完，豬八戒和沙和尚便「啊」的一聲，提起釘耙、禪杖，準備動武。唐僧嚇得臉孔煞白，忙攔住八戒、沙僧說：「國王面前休得無理。」並轉身向國王合掌作揖，請求寬恕。

這時候，孫悟空可耐不住了。他「霍」的一下，竄到國王面前爭辯說：「大王，你說的三天三夜從頭至尾地背經文，我們都沒有間斷，也沒有背錯。如果你不相信的話，我可以拿出西天佛祖賜給我們的眞經作證明。」說罷，他扒開經箱，取出一卷名叫《南無佛》的眞經給國王看。國王接過一看，只見那卷眞經從頭至尾就是一句經文，即「南無阿彌陀佛」六個金光閃閃的梵文。國王見孫悟空說得有理，臉上露出懊喪的神色。那軍師忙擠到前邊，衝著孫悟空強詞奪理地說：「這《南無佛》的經文是你這妖猴化出來的，不要拿這假東西來騙人！」

這一下可把孫悟空的臉都氣紅了，他手捧經卷理直氣壯地說：「這經卷是佛祖用眞金寫的。眞金不怕火，你不信，可以當場燒一燒嘛！」

那國王以爲抓到了把柄，忙吩咐左右的武士說：「取火來，與我當場試一試！」

武士取來一個火把，試圖將經紙點燃，但燒了許久，非但那經文毫不變色，就連那經紙也不點沒有燒焦。國王和軍師見三件難事都難不倒唐僧師徒，心裏有些害怕，也知道眞經不可輕得，便無可奈何地將他們送出城門。

在離開羅索國的路上，唐僧、豬八戒、沙和尙都誇獎孫悟空機靈聰明，並問他那佛珠、甘泉是什麼東西？那《南無佛》眞經又是從什麼地方來的？孫悟空聽了，手舞足蹈地笑了一陣，才說出個中原由：

原來，孫悟空早料到羅索國的新國王要出來從中刁難，因此早早地在西天佛國採了一大袋蠶豆，串成四條大佛珠。那蠶豆最耐飢，吃上一小把，就能活兩三天，所以一串佛珠，就熬過了三天三夜。因爲那蠶豆的樣子很像一張張羅漢的臉孔，所以後來人都叫它「羅漢豆」。

那「甘泉」爲什麼能御寒呢？原來那寶葫裏的甘泉不是什麼仙水，而是用西天佛國裏的青稞釀成的甜酒。喝了甜酒，渾身發熱，這也是孫悟空事先準備好的。

《南無佛》眞經又是怎麼來的呢？原來孫悟空認字不多，寫梵文的本領更差，在聽西天佛祖講經時，他只能在經紙上記下「南無阿彌陀佛」六個字，因此一堂課下來，他只記了一本的「南無阿彌陀佛」。正好，這卷只有一句經文的眞經，這回在羅索國王面前派了大用場，順利地通過了第三道難關。

爲了頌揚孫悟空的機靈聰明和他記錄《南無佛》眞經的功勞，直到今天，人們還將蠶豆稱爲羅漢豆或者佛豆，將用青稞釀成的美酒稱爲佛酒，將「南無阿彌陀佛」一句經文作爲所有西天眞經的代名詞和佛家的口頭語。

周亦子／搜集整理

馬蹄跡與曬經松

在雲南省西北面巍峨的白馬山上，有一幢古老莊嚴的傳經寺，寺前懸崖上，有像馬蹄的痕跡俗稱「馬蹄跡」。在寺院周圍的百餘畝土地上，盡長著些矮矮的小松樹。這種小松樹有個特點：長不高，也長不大，最高只有人腰高，最大也不過團簟那麼大。當地老鄉都叫它「曬經松」。

說起「馬蹄跡」和「曬經松」，當地還流傳著一段《西遊記》的故事。

唐朝皇帝李世民派唐僧到天竺取經，來回都經過金沙江。在渡金沙江時，江水突然猛漲，無船無橋，幸有金魚成精，馱渡唐僧一行過岸。

唐僧上岸後，雙手合十，對金魚稱謝。金魚說：「不必謝，聽說西天佛祖無滅無生，能知過去未來。我在此間整整修行了一千三百餘年，雖然延壽，又能說人話，但只望脫殼變人。請師父到西天替我問問佛祖，我何時能脫殼變人？」

唐僧滿口答應說：「我一定問，一定問！」只聽一聲水響，金魚就不見了。

唐僧高興地唱道：「志堅心誠不懼死，金魚馱渡過天河。」師徒們邊唱邊走，又不知走了多少路程，爬過多少山坡，涉過多少江河，經過多少艱難險阻，才到了西天。唐僧到了西天後，拜見了佛祖如來，取得經書三十五部，五千零四十八卷。來回四十七個春秋，行程十萬八千里。

在回來的路上，再過金沙江時，又請金魚馱渡。當金魚把唐僧一行馱渡到江中時，便問起當年託唐僧代問佛祖的事。

金魚說：「老師父，十七年前，我請你代問佛祖，我還有多少年壽才能脫殼變人。你可曾問過了？」

原來唐僧到西天後，一心只顧取經，哪有工夫去管魚精蝦怪之事，但又不好回答，沈吟了半天。金魚看出唐僧未曾代問，心裏極爲不滿，就將身子一晃，嘩啦啦一聲潛入江底，把唐僧一行連馬帶經，全落水中。幸虧白馬是龍，八戒、沙僧會水，又有孫悟空大顯神通，將唐僧扶駕上岸，但是經書已淹溼了。

待孫悟空使分水法，潛入江中追捕魚怪時，只撈起一個死魚頭，這就是後來僧人念經時，邊念邊敲的那個「木魚」，每念一個字，就要敲它一下，以示對它溼經的懲罰。

經溼了怎麼辦呢？師徒一行整裝來到猛崗河與零川江（今龍川江）分水嶺的山峰上，把經書全部打開，鋪曬在松樹和崖石上。當山下村民們一傳十，十傳百，三五成群地上山探望時，唐僧一時早已遠走高飛了。只見崖石上有白馬蹄跡，松樹壓得平平的，有曬過經的痕跡。從此，這座山就叫白馬山，「曬經松」也就由此得名了。

後人爲了崇敬唐僧取經，於明崇禎十年，在白馬山建傳經寺。寺裏還塑有唐僧像，有鐵杖、鐵鞋、九齒釘耙。歷代遊人題詩在卷：

奇峰萬疊響嵯峨，
傳說高僧自此過。
遺跡石留飛白馬，
曬經松古伴青籬。

楊春茂／搜集整理

仙桃洞

天都峰，顧名思義是天上的都會，海拔一千八百一十米，爲黃山三大主峰中最險峻峭拔的一座奇妙的山峰。峰巔有「登峰造極」石刻。極目遠望，雲天相接，江河一線；俯瞰四周，萬峰拜倒脚下，有心曠神怡的無窮樂趣。鯽魚背險道，是攀登天都峰必經的咽喉之地。過了鯽魚背再穿過三個山洞就來到了峰頂，其中第一個山洞名叫仙桃洞。這個洞的頂部是三塊碩大無比、形如蟠桃的天成巧石堆壘而成；從石縫仙桃洞長出來的松樹，形同桃柄和桃葉。親臨觀賞的遊客，往往情不自禁地稱讚第一位替此景命名的人好眼力。

相傳這兒原是彩雲繚繞的天宮通往人間的一條便道，離王母娘娘的蟠桃園很近。有一年三月初三，王母娘娘舉辦蟠桃盛會，慶祝她的八十八萬八千八百八十大壽，各路神仙都趕來參加這「五八」壽宴，連看守蟠桃園的彩女雲童，也擅離崗位看熱鬧、享口福去了。一向放蕩不羈的齊天大聖孫悟空，深認蟠桃珍貴，陡生偷摘之心，要讓他的師父、師弟同享口福，便乘機潛入園中採摘。他被枝頭碩果纍纍、氣味甘芳的景色喜壞了，邊摘邊嘗，邊嘗邊摘，連數字也無心去記，用左手摘下夾在右胳膊窩裏，以右手摘的又藏到左胳膊下面，弄得遍地殘枝滿地桃。一貫貪嘴又自私的豬八戒，明知偷蟠桃是違犯天規的，但早已對這天庭絕妙佳果垂涎三尺了。他悄悄跟在大師兄的背後，坐收漁利。他早已想好，萬一被玉帝、王母發現，他就站出來「反戈一擊」。他趁孫悟空正在採摘之際，偷吃一飽，還扛起一串，又提起幾只，匆匆地翻院越牆，跑到這鯽魚背前休息。

不說王母的壽宴如何豐盛，也不說太白金星如何在清點人數時發現守蟠桃的彩女、雲童擅離職守，單說那孫悟空突然警覺到自己在園內不可久留，就稍經打點收拾，迅速駕起雲頭，來到師父面前。他把自己採摘來的仙桃，進獻給了師父和師弟。那唐三藏越吃越覺得鮮美可口，又能充飢，待吃完之後便追問孫悟空從哪裏弄來的。孫悟空不會說謊，就一五一十和盤托出。唐僧得知這是偷竊來的，連稱這是「不義之食」，除大聲訓斥外，又一下念起緊箍咒，把孫悟空痛得滿地打滾，幸虧沙和尚求情才饒了他。

唐僧命令孫悟空快去尋回豬八戒，大家一起上路，孫悟空找啊找啊，直找到鯽魚背前，發現他躺在一堆蟠桃邊睡大覺。孫悟空一看他那肚鼓腰圓的樣兒，什麼都明白了。於是先使出「釘物法」，把那堆蟠桃穩穩地釘在那裏，這才開口叫醒豬八戒。睡足了的豬八戒，打了幾聲呵欠後，故意裝出渴得喉嚨冒煙的樣子，假獻殷勤：「猴哥，我找你找得好苦呀，估摸著你是去採蟠桃了。我進園後怎麼也找你不到，只見遍地殘枝落果，就順便拾了幾個。心裏想著你們，我哪裏捨得吃喲。來、來、來，你我先嘗嘗吧。」當他使出力氣拿它不起來時，這才知道猴哥弄了鬼。

這仙桃擱在鯽魚背前面久了，就漸漸幻成石桃了。越過仙桃洞，步入登天都峰必經的第二個山洞時，有一石人站立門旁，人稱「仙人把洞門」。傳說這是玉帝、王母發現蟠桃被偷後，特地採取的防守措施。

曹同基／講述
周　吾／搜集整理

虎丘石桃

姑蘇虎丘歷史悠久，風景幽美，古蹟頗多，譽爲「吳中第一名勝」。虎丘試劍石對面道旁，有一塊形似桃子的石頭，那就是「石桃」。你知道它的來歷嗎？

相傳，當年齊天大聖孫悟空在崑崙山大鬧了王母娘娘的蟠桃會，一個筋斗翻出南天門，急急忙忙趕回花果山。他一邊騰雲駕霧，一邊還往嘴裏塞了一個仙桃，使勁嚼了起來。不一會兒他來到一個地方，這地方風景奇秀，市井繁華。孫悟空心想，這是什麼去處？於是降下雲頭，睜大火眼金睛一看，見有一城廓，城門上寫著「閶門」兩個大字，知是到了姑蘇城。因爲他早就聽諸神談起姑蘇風光，交口稱讚。當時，他心中很不服氣，心想我老孫的花果山天下第一，你姑蘇算老幾，我倒要見識見識。今日碰巧到了這裏，何不仔細觀看一下，比試比試？於是他在空中立定，細細地觀看起來。

姑蘇城外，湖泊羅列，白帆片片，隨波蕩漾；山巒橫臥，松柏森森，枝頭鳥啼。姑蘇城內，青樓重門，園林座座，寺塔遍地，鐘磬聲聲。只見那亭台樓閣，各具巧妙，或傍山而築，或依水而點：傍山築，氣勢不凡；依水點，玲瓏雅致。池石林泉，曲徑通幽；花木掩映，別有洞天。又見那遊人或三三兩兩倚平橋低欄，賞花觀魚；或三五成群穿行於假山洞壑之間，嬉笑玩耍。水榭迴廊，有才子佳人在琴棋書畫；山野茅廬，有霜染老翁在煮茗清淡。竹橋鎖處飄出絲絲酒香；禪寺靜處傳來陣陣蟬鳴。更見那虎丘塔山頂雄峙，重檐覆宇，翼角翬飛，氣勢磅礴。劍池水水深莫測，池邊雙崖壁立，陡峭奇險。遊人或臨池旁，談古論今；或登寶塔，遠眺佳景。整個姑蘇城內外，有如山水畫卷，說不盡的江南美，道不完的姑蘇秀。

孫悟空早看呆了，止不住大叫起來：「好景！好景……」一聲未盡，嘴裏那嚼剩的桃核噴了出來，正好落在虎丘山上。由於孫悟空本是隻神猴，那桃核受了他的仙氣，落地後也就慢慢長成了一隻大石桃。據說石桃本來還要長，因有一好事的人在石桃上刻上了「石桃」兩個大篆字，漏了仙氣，石桃就不長了。要不然，石桃會長得比虎丘山還高呢。

梁順華／搜集整理

泰安爲什麼神全

有句俗話說：「泰安的神全，濟南府的人全。」「濟南府的人全」，且不去說它；「泰安的神全」，可眞名不虛傳。泰安，從縣城裏到泰山頂，到底有多少廟？供著多少神？誰也說不清楚，反正從天神到地神，從水神到海神，什麼神都有。

泰安爲什麼神全？這還是當年大鬧天宮的齊天大聖孫悟空給請來的。有一回，他偷了觀音菩薩的淨瓶。這淨瓶是件寶貝，不論什麼神仙鬼怪，只要把它的名字喊三聲，它應三聲，就給裝進去了。孫悟空偷了淨瓶到五洲四海去遊玩，遇到神仙就將它往瓶裏裝，玩得好不痛快。後來觀音菩薩發現淨瓶丢了，掐指一算，知道是孫悟空偷去了，便一路追趕，一直追到泰安才追上。

這孫悟空原先不過想同神仙們開開玩笑，發現觀音菩薩追了上來，知道闖了大禍，便把淨瓶往地上一扔，一個筋斗就溜了。誰知他扔得重了點，淨瓶落地粉碎，原來裝在裏面的神仙紛紛站了起來。

觀音菩薩只顧收拾破瓶碴兒，再去煉她的寶貝，顧不上這些神仙。這些神仙看到泰安這地方有山有水，風景幽美，也不想再回到原籍，便各占地盤，在泰安落了戶。好在泰安這地方背靠泰山，有的是地方。

泰安城裏，特別是泰山上，三步一廟，五步一院，那些好玩的地方，都給這些神仙占了。從此泰安也就有了「神全」的名聲。

蕭寶萬等／講述
車錫倫／搜集整理

獼猴桃的來歷

獼猴桃原是一種野生植物的果實，其貌不揚，但有極高的營養價值，近年來已成為世界上的高檔水果。關於獼猴桃的來歷，在民間文學的海洋裏，有多種說法。今擇帶有普遍性的三說，分別介紹如下：

一、彈打嘯天犬

當年孫悟空被玉帝封為「弼馬溫」之後，心裏十分不快，為了清閒解悶，天天到蟠桃園裏去偷吃蟠桃。天上的蟠桃不僅鮮甜可口，而且是長生不老果。別看孫悟空性急好動，可他也是有小心眼兒的。他一面吃一面想：這蟠桃這般鮮甜，何不將桃核留它半袋，悄悄帶到老家花果山去栽種栽種，也好讓兒孫們嘗嘗仙果的味道。主意一定，便小心地將桃核收藏起來，不到三天，便積了滿滿的一袋。

第四天，王母娘娘在瑤池開蟠桃大會，孫悟空聽說沒有邀請他，氣得汗毛直豎。他靈機一動，冒充赤脚大仙，搶先闖入蟠桃大會，偷吃了許多瓊漿玉液、仙丹甘露，然後醉醺醺地離開瑤池，心想乘機趕回花果山，讓孩兒們也去偷吃些好東西。

誰知一出西天門，那通往玉清宮的白雲大道上，蹲著一隻渾身油光黑亮、雙耳直豎的神犬。孫悟空雖然有些酒醉，但還一眼認得出來，那巨犬不是普通坐騎，而是二郎神豢養的無敵神獸嘯天犬。這嘯天犬是玉帝命二郎神用來看守天門的，它有神奇的嗅覺，能嗅出偷盜天宮禁物和偷吃天上仙桃的神仙鬼怪；還能用鋒利的牙齒咬住偷竊犯的衣襟，拖回天庭。更可怕的是，它那叫聲似颶風入谷，海嘯沖天，故名「嘯天犬」。

孫悟空因為偷吃了天上禁果，難免有些心虛。他一見嘯天犬擋道，不由得倒吸了一口冷氣。為了避開神犬，悟空縱身一躍，竄到嘯天犬背後。他以為用此一招，即可脫身。誰知那嘯天犬更為機靈，輕輕騰空一跳，將孫悟空的褲管咬住。悟空欲將神犬甩開，便使勁翻了一個筋斗，但聽得「吱」的一聲，神犬雖然被甩脫了，但褲管已被撕去了一半。悟空回首看去，那嘯天犬仍然緊追不捨。

這時候的孫悟空，肚裏的熱酒已經變成冷汗。他知道從耳朵孔裏掏出金箍棒已經來不及了，而身邊又沒有其他武器。危急間，一摸肚兜，發現兜裏尚有半袋桃核。他靈機一動，便以桃核為武器，一面飛遁，一面回手向嘯天犬擲去。一連串的桃核，雨點般地落在嘯天犬的額角上。嘯天犬突然受擊，以爲是什麼鋼丸鐵彈，要抓也抓不住，要避又避不開，不禁害怕起來。心裏一怕，四條腿也就跑不快了，不一會，就遠遠地落在孫悟空的後面，要追也追不上了。

就這樣，孫悟空靠半袋蟠桃核打退了嘯天犬。那桃核飛出之後，再也收不回來了。飛出的桃核，落在千山萬壑間，長成了一棵棵的桃樹。但是由於天上人間水土氣候不同，大蟠桃樹變成小毛桃樹了。奇怪的是：即使個兒變小，但那鮮美可口的味兒，跟天上的蟠桃一模一樣，可稱得上是「人間仙果」。

二、猴王撒尿

在往西天取經的路上，孫悟空爲除滅白骨精，接連三次打死白骨精的化身，這引起了唐僧的猜疑。又由於豬八戒的花言巧語，唐僧一氣之下，竟將孫悟空趕回花果山。

孫悟空回到花果山一看，不由得大吃一驚。原來那嘯天犬的主人二郎神懷恨在心，竟派天兵天將，將花果山燒得樹焦草枯，洞坍岩倒。幸好衆孩兒們躲在洞穴深處，才免被全部燒死。爲了重建花果山，孫悟空帶領衆孩兒移花栽草，插柳種梅，還在山南向陽坡上，種了幾千棵桃樹。

當花草果木成活之後，這猴王心裏非常高興，經常親自去巡視看守。有一天，孫悟空出洞巡視時，發現一大群孩兒們在地上、河邊撒尿，把個鳥語花香的花果山弄得臭氣沖天。悟空心想，這太不雅觀了，拉尿拉屎，應該有個規矩才好。於是他召集全山孩兒們發布命令道：「我花果山乃爲乾淨快樂之地，不許隨地便溺。現南坡上有三千六百棵桃樹，每棵桃樹根部，都有一個土坑。你們每認定一個土坑爲方便之處，每次拉尿拉屎之後，都撒上一把沙土，以免臭氣外溢，毒蟲滋生。」

這聖令一下，花果山的大小猴子，都老老實實地到桃樹坑裏去大小便了。孫悟空以身作則，也揀了一個桃樹坑作爲解手的地方，說來奇怪，經常由孫悟空撒尿的那棵桃樹，後來結出來的桃子竟與別處的不同，不僅個兒大，紅得早，而且格外香甜。據說，這是因爲孫悟空仙果吃得太多的緣故，所以由他的尿澆灌出來的桃子，也帶有仙氣，格外好吃。這種桃，就是後來流傳到各地的獮猴桃。

三、擒王識仙果

黃山地方，山水靈秀，草木豐茂，那高山溪谷間，猴群特別多。黃山猴多數屬獮猴一類，故人稱「黃山獮猴」。

相傳清朝乾隆年間，黃山南麓桃花峰南坡，發生過一件奇怪的事情。原來桃花峰下，有一片野生的桃樹，每年桃子紅熟的時候，棲息在峰巒間的一大群猴子，便下山來吃桃子。當年那地方人煙稀少，猴子偷吃野桃的事，並不引起人們注意，少數進出砍柴採藥的人，也不當一回事。

這年，成片的野桃長得特別多，個兒也比往年大。附近的幾戶山民聽說野桃可以釀酒，便結伙前去採摘。誰知到桃林近處一看，只見其中有一棵桃樹長得有些特別：樹幹並不高，桃子的個兒也並不大，但水靈靈的，紅得可愛。更奇怪的是，別的桃樹上，連青桃也被猴群摘光了，但這棵桃樹上，卻掛得滿滿的，那些調皮的猴子，誰都不敢靠近它。

山民們覺得有些蹊蹺，便小心翼翼地靠近那棵桃樹，準備採摘。誰知還未爬上樹幹，幾十隻猴子吱吱地尖叫著，咧牙舞爪，直向人群撲來。一個年長的山民知道不可強摘，便吩咐大家退了回來，並躲在柴蓬裏細細觀察。不一會，只見一隻頭皮脫頂、體形高大的老猴，從林中跳將出來，不慌不忙地爬上那棵桃樹，坐在枝椏上，攀過桃枝，慢吞吞地嘗起那又紅又脆的桃子來。其他猴子，或跳躍在四周樹上，或來回奔跑於林間，好像在保衛那老猴子。

看到這一切，山民們的心裏都明白了：原來那隻老猴子就是猴王，那棵最好的桃樹上的桃子，是專門供猴王享用的。當時有種說法，認爲猴王的腦髓是世界上最珍貴的補品。幾個膽大的山民，便動起捕捉猴王的腦筋來。第二天，他們在猴群經常竄越的岩崖間，布了一張由機關控制的大網，並隨帶鳥槍土銃，埋伏在桃園附近。當猴王帶領猴群下山來吃桃時，他們鳴槍放銃。一聽槍聲，那猴王吱吱直叫，好像在指揮部下退兵。當猴群基本上山後，它才向岩崖跳去，一面還不時回頭觀看動靜，頗有點大將風度。正當猴王要跳過岩崖時，躲在岩縫隙的山民立即拉動機關，「啪」的一聲，猴王被網住了。山民們七手八脚地將它抬回村裏。

當天晚上，大批猴子將只有十來戶山民的村莊團團圍住，有的拋石子，有的擲瓦片，鬧得全村一刻也不得安寧。正當山民們在屋裏商量對策的時候，突然來了一位陌生的老頭。那老頭身穿土黃色長袍，手提青藤拐杖，顫巍巍地對山民們說：「老朽是這百里黃山的當方土地，爲了這猴王的事，今晚不得不奉勸你們幾句。我勸你們馬上放掉這隻猴王。不然，村裏將遭大難，因爲這猴王是有來歷的。」

「什麼來歷？」村民們驚訝地問。

土地老頭坐下來說：「當年孫悟空大鬧天宮，與天兵天將戰了三天三夜。孫悟空有些累了，便按落雲頭，到黃山頂上歇息。誰知黃山山溝裏的蛤蟆精偏跟大聖作對，不讓他在黃山歇足。孫悟空沒法，只好拔下一根毫毛，呼地一吹，變成一員猴將，命他去同蛤蟆精打鬥，自己依然躺在天都峰上睡覺。可是一覺醒來，蛤蟆精被趕跑了，但那根毫毛卻忘記收了回去。

從那時起，由孫悟空的毫毛變成的這員猴將，就一直留在黃山，剛才你們捕到的這隻猴王，就是當年孫悟空忘了收回的那員猴將的子孫。如果你們不信的話，可以仔細看看這猴王的腦袋上，不是還留著一條緊箍圈的印記嗎？」

聽了土地老頭的話，山民們個個都驚呆了，仔細一看，那猴王的腦袋上，果然有一條緊箍圈的印記。爲了求得全村的平安，便當夜將猴王放回深山。

土地老頭還告訴山民，那棵奇怪的桃樹上結出的桃子叫獼猴桃，是世代猴王所享有的。你們想嘗嘗那桃子的味道的話，不可強摘，只要剪那枝條去嫁接，便可收穫同樣美味的果實。

山民們依照土地老頭的話剪枝嫁接，果然如願以償。直到今天，嫁接過的獼猴桃，不僅個兒要比一般的野生獼猴桃大，而且甜美異常。

禾　家／搜集整理

如來滴汗育石猴

吳承恩寫到《西遊記》裏的孫悟空，是從東海花果山頂一塊仙石中爆出來的；至於石猴是怎樣變的，他還沒有交代。這裏有一段傳說。

當初，太陽佛與如來佛爭大小。太陽佛認爲自己光照大地，主宰世界萬物，凡界統歸他管轄，沒有把如來佛放在眼裏。如來佛認爲天庭地宮由他所管，神仙、百姓任他調遣，也沒有把太陽佛放在眼裏。雙方賭了氣。

太陽佛不服如來佛，他要將凡間大曬三年，看如來佛怎樣安頓黎民生計。

太陽佛想到做到，凡間眞的曬了三年，草木枯乾、牲畜死亡、岩石熔化，都成了火球啦，連如來佛的額頭也被曬出一滴汗珠來。

如來佛服輸了。

說來也巧，如來佛這滴汗珠滴在女媧遺下的山石上，經過年長月久，日曬雨淋，慢慢地孕育了一個仙胎。

忽一日風化出來，便是一隻石猴，能禮拜天地，能直立行走，這就是孫悟空。因爲孫悟空原來是如來佛的一點汗，所以孫悟空逃不出如來佛的掌心，一切都得聽從如來佛的調遣。

陳林翠／講述

周臣朱／搜集整理

觀音牙齒孕悟空

《西遊記》裏說，孫悟空原是東海花果山上的一隻石猴變的。石猴爲什麼有這麼大的本領呢？這與觀音菩薩有關。

三千六百多年前，有一天，王母娘娘做生日，邀請上界三十六天神、凡界七十二洞仙以及四海龍王到崑崙山瑤池仙台參加蟠桃盛會。在蟠桃會上，觀音菩薩一時高興，多喝了幾杯酒。那酒是天上的甘露釀成的，十分香甜。

酒筵散後，觀音菩薩與東海龍王一起步出瑤池。東海龍王見觀音滿面紅光，興致忒高，便又邀請她到東海一走，順便看看他的龍宮寶藏。觀音菩薩答應了，便與東海王一起駕著祥雲，緩緩向東海飄去。到花果山上空時，觀音菩薩感到有些口渴，便與東海龍王一起，降落在花果山的岩崖上。那花果山的當方土地見觀音與龍王駕到，忙從果園裏摘來一籃桃子，獻給他們。觀音見桃子鮮紅可愛，便隨手拿起一個，輕輕咬了一口，一嚼，覺得味道十分鮮美，便又咬了一口。誰知這一口咬得過快，「咯」的一聲，那堅硬的桃核，竟折斷了觀音的半顆牙齒。觀音見東海龍王及當方土地都在身邊，不好意思聲張，便將口中的桃肉連同那半顆牙齒，悄悄地往身後一吐。只聽得「骨碌」一聲，那半顆牙齒竟滾到石頭縫隙去了。

這半顆嵌在石頭縫隙的牙齒，一是由於自身有靈氣，二是由於受日月精華之孕育，終於慢慢地變成一個大石卵。石卵一旦爆裂，便蹦出個孫悟空來了。

由於孫悟空是觀音菩薩的半顆牙齒變的，所以有金剛不敗之體。在大鬧大宮時，任憑天兵天將刀斧砍、爐火煉，都沒有傷著他一根毫毛；即使後來如來佛將他壓在五行山下，也沒有將他壓扁，道理就在這裏。

周亦子／搜集整理

孫悟空的親爹娘

浙江紹興人有句俗話：

「虎生虎來貓生貓，韭菜生不出靈芝草。」

*

石頭裏爆出來的孫悟空，也是有爹有娘的。

東勝神州傲來國花果山上有塊頑石，年長月久，吸取了天地正氣，收受了日月精華，變得晶瑩玲瓏，叫人喜歡。因爲它在高山之巔，孤峰頂端，勿要講看勿到人的脚印，就是野獸也上不去，老鷹也飛勿過。

有一日，如來佛從西竺國往東土去，駕起祥雲經過花果山，慧眼望見這塊石頭，光潔如玉，隱隱閃光，一時心裏歡喜，就降落雲端，在頑石上盤膝打了個瞌睡。

哪曉得九對羅漢、八大金剛、五百阿羅、三千揭諦見如來佛祖在此打坐，也都趕來在他身邊聽候差遣。如來佛見驚動了這許多人，就駕起祥雲回雷音寺去了。誰曉得，如來佛打個瞌睡一息息辰光，凡間已過去了許多年。

這塊頑石因爲受過如來佛體覆罩，溫熱勿散，本來一塊冷冰冰的石頭，焐成熱烘烘的仙石，花果山頂上，從此就有一股瑞氣，陣陣往南海飄去。

南海普陀紫竹林裏蓮台上打坐的觀音菩薩，也聞到瑞氣，覺得奇怪，便駕起一朵祥雲來到花果山。她降落到仙石上，拔了根頭髮吹吹氣，變成一支針，在自己食指上輕輕刺出三點鮮血，滴到石頭上，嘴裏念聲「善哉，善哉」，又駕雲回洛伽山去了。

這塊仙石，先受如來佛元氣罩體，後受觀音鮮血滋潤，陰陽結合，形成聖胎，五體具備。後來功行圓滿，山裂石破，滾出一個石卵來，迎風化成石猴。

這石猴雙眼金光灼灼，直沖斗牛。天兵神將裏的千里眼、順風耳，忙上靈霄寶殿奏知玉皇大帝，趕快除掉石猴。虧得玉帝寬宏大量，沒有把石猴當妖怪殺掉。

石猴一出世就神通廣大，簡直把玉帝老頭都勿放在眼裏。後來大鬧天宮，打敗了各路天兵天將，鬧得靈霄寶殿勿得安寧，玉皇大帝只得請如來佛出手。

孫悟空勿曉得如來佛是親爹，也乒乒乓乓跟他鬥起來。孫悟空本事再大，到底勿是他親爹的對手，十萬八千里一個筋斗翻勿出如來佛的手掌心。如來捨勿得殺，就把它鎮在五行山下，讓它吃了五百年苦頭。後來唐僧取經路過，才被放了出來，隨他西天取經，斬妖殺魔，立功成了正果。

觀音大士是親娘，越發愛護孫悟空。孫悟空西天路上碰到千災百難，都是她親自出馬，幫孫悟空降妖伏魔的。

應梅堂、董永祺／搜集整理

老猴披衣

話說孫悟空隨唐僧去西天取經以後，他的老家花果山水簾洞中的成千上萬猴頭，就誰也管不了誰，吵吵嚷嚷地鬧開了！它們有的跑到黃山，有的跑到泰山，有的跑到峨眉山，有的跑到華頂山，也有的跑到雁蕩山。

據傳，跑到雁蕩山的一隻猴頭，住在淨名寺附近。這淨名寺，背靠一個很別致的岩洞。這岩洞的頂縫隙，伏著一尾青色的石龍，成年累月噴吐著碧水。這支碧水灑下來，化爲銀白色的水簾，遮住洞口。叮叮咚咚，其聲如琴弦撥動；閃閃爍爍，其狀似明珠飛舞。多麼迷人的仙境呵！這猴頭想起了老家花果山的水簾洞，就把這裏也稱作「水簾洞」。從此以後，它日日夜夜在這裏蹦躂攀緣、遊戲玩耍，日子過得可快活啦！

當時，淨名寺住著兩個和尚：一個老和尚，一個小和尚。這老和尚對待小和尚十分苛刻，他要小和尚白天砍柴燒飯，晚上通宵達旦地代他敲木魚、念經。一不稱心，還要對小和尚毒罵、鞭打。

這猴頭可機靈呢！它把這一切都看在眼裏，記在心頭。它可憐小和尚，討厭老和尚。它經常偷偷地幫助小和尚撿枯枝當柴，也很想尋機會跟老和尚開個玩笑。

剛巧有一回，天台山的弘光禪師要來淨名寺督經。老和尚因好久未念經文了，只怕禪師面查時會出紕漏，於是趕忙「臨時抱佛脚」，連夜敲起木魚，念起經來。誰知因爲懶惰成性，貪睡成癮，老和尚的木魚槌，越敲越輕，最後竟然發不出一點聲音來。小和尚見老和尚發出了鼾聲，也就放大膽子打起瞌睡來了。

猴頭看到這般模樣，覺得好笑，便踮起脚尖，走到老和尚的背後，慢慢地脫下他的袈裟，飛一般地跑出淨名寺。

天亮了，老和尚驚醒過來。他發現自己身上的袈裟不見了，以爲禪師已經到來，見他貪睡失禮，剝去了他的袈裟，不禁嚇得渾身哆嗦，冷汗直冒，趕忙跳起來，四處去尋禪師。誰知跑遍了整個寺院，也不見禪師影子。後來走到寺院大門口，卻見一隻猴頭，正披著他的袈裟，在向他擠眉弄眼哩！他又氣又惱，忙叫小和尚與他同去抓那猴頭。

那猴頭見老和尚出來追他，便靈活地從這個山頭，跳到那個山頭。老和尚身體長得肥胖，哪裏追趕得上，直累得腰酸腿痳，氣喘如牛，跌了好幾個跟斗。

後來，猴頭站著不走了。老和尚一見，拼著老命，蹬蹬蹬地撲了過去，一把抓住猴頭身上的那件袈裟。誰知道，剛一抓走，那猴頭和袈裟卻忽然都變作了一塊岩石。原來那猴頭往日跟孫悟空學會了一些法術，以岩石作替身，而自己的眞身，卻早已遁走了。

老和尚左剝右剝，剝不下石猴身上的石袈裟，又恐等會兒禪師來到責怪他失職，不覺更加心慌，便號啕大哭起來，直哭得昏死過去。

至今，從淨名寺東望，能見到一岩頗似披著袈裟的猴頭，人們就叫它爲「老猴披衣」。

楊曉明／整理

豬八戒前傳

哭泉往東十里，深山中有一個村子，叫相窪。村子的西北方有一去處，山陡石險，樹雜溝深，朝夕之時常見雲霧繚繞，據傳這叫雲洞溝。《西遊記》中唐僧的二徒弟豬八戒，曾在這個洞府獨霸一方，當過魔王。後來豬八戒保師父西天取經，一路上協助孫悟空擒妖捉怪，雖說因爲好吃貪睡，頗多失誤，卻也屢立大功。這裏要講的故事，乃是八戒「出山」之前的一段傳說。

八戒居住的「雲洞溝」，《西遊記》上稱之爲「黑風洞」，而今天人稱之爲「銀洞溝」。因爲豬八戒在這裏當過魔王，那洞中肯定少不了金銀財寶。關於這洞，還有一段生動的傳奇。若論仔細還得從「料石坡」、「高老莊」這兩個村子的村名說起。

話說豬八戒被謫降人間，從廟山梁按落雲頭，一眼相中了「雲洞溝」這塊仙地奇境。他決心斬惡除暴，扶危濟貧，替天行道。他運用「遠交近攻」的計謀，東殺西討，南征北戰。經過無數次的驚險搏鬥，先後把那些害人的「金身大王」(金錢豹精)、「林中大盜」(老虎精)、

「穿山大仙」（蟒蛇精）、「千年狐仙」等八路洞府妖怪都統統斬殺或驅逐出境，從此這裏成了八戒的天下。他除了巡山鎮妖，閒來無事就揮起九齒釘耙，走出洞府，幫他治下的百姓幹活種莊稼。他經常袒胸露乳，擺動大耳朵，張著大嘴，噴著滿口白沫，與老百姓高談闊論、說古道今。老百姓非但不覺著他醜，反而對他樸實的作風、多變的神通、高強的武藝、直爽的性格分外敬重。他成了百姓的好朋友。

八戒也時常有失於檢點的地方。有一次，他幫東方的一位孤寡老太太幹活，非常賣力，揮汗如雨，不到中午，肚裏咕咕直叫。八戒一溜煙跑回老太太家裏，一頭扎進廚房，拿起碗在鍋裏盛起還未煮熟的飯就往肚裏送。一鍋飯吃完了，還餓得慌，見屋裏堆著土豆，抓起就吃，一邊吃，邊一邊誇「好脆好甜」。吃飽了，又跑到河灘喝足了涼水，然後很愜意地在河邊的一棵核桃樹下躺下，響起了雷鳴般的鼾聲。一覺棵來，他感到陣陣肚疼，直想發嘔。肚子越疼越厲害，八戒好不難受。他坐臥不寧，索性雙手捧起大肚子亂顛亂跑。他跑上一條山梁，終於忍不住了，頓時上吐下瀉。他吃東西狼吞虎嚥，囫圇吞棗，到肚裏來不及消化，吐瀉出來的東西滿山坡亂淌亂滾，大的像拳頭，小的像核桃、棗，簡直是鋪山蓋野。事後，他照常替老太太幹活，還呵呵大笑自己的貪吃出醜。後來，這裏滿坡都是怪模怪樣不成形狀的料石，於是留下了「料石坡」這個村名。料石坡村位於哭泉東南七里的山坡下。如今這裏已成了美麗富饒的山鄉了。

再說這一天，八戒巡視他北方的治下，進了三岔地界，來到高老莊。高老莊百姓載歌載舞，以高員外為首的山民拿出最好的食品盛情款待八戒。八戒更是喜氣洋洋，連聲說：「感謝衆位父老的盛情，老豬慚愧，慚愧……」八戒正與民同樂、歌舞昇平，忽然他發現舞隊中高員外的獨生女兒——高小姐長得異常美貌，且歌喉圓潤嘹亮好聽，愛慕之心油然而生。八戒說話做事直來直去，不摻半點假，就當面向高員外求親。高員外夫婦一來愁年高無人照應，二來敬重八戒的為人，就滿口答應了。誰知高小姐嫌八戒的長相醜陋，有失文雅，可是父母答應了，又十分為難。還算八戒粗中有細，看出了高小姐的難言之隱，他呵呵地笑著說：「小姐，我八戒人雖醜，心地卻好，做事也不懶。而且我整整容貌，修修邊幅，也蠻可觀哩。」過了幾天，八戒來了，果然不錯。雖說還是個粗大的黑漢子，卻也收拾得樸實可愛，文氣了許多，確實有一派落落大方的瀟灑風度。不久，八戒與高小姐拜堂成親，結為夫婦，十分恩愛。

後來，八戒為協助唐僧完成西天取經的大業，毅然離家，跋險山，渡惡水，作萬里之行。一路上與悟空、沙僧斬妖捉怪，捨生忘死，終於成了正果，被如來佛封為淨壇使者。

董文賓／搜集整理

陳十四除黑豬精

據傳，浙江縉雲南鄉有一戶小財主，有個兒子叫有德，結婚沒幾日，便要出外做生意。夫妻倆本是表兄妹，從小青梅竹馬，恩恩愛愛。現在有德要出門，妻子的心裏眞個難受。拔下一枝金釵折成兩段，分一段給丈夫，讓他帶在身邊作表記。

有德在路上走吃力了，便在一座石塔下歇歇氣，拿出妻子的半截金釵，看了又看，吻了又吻。恰巧黑豬精住在這座石塔洞裏，把有德的一舉一動都看了個清清楚楚。它「呼」地一變，化成一個青年後生，折了段黃金柴枝，叫聲「變」，就變成了半截金釵，與有德手裏的那段一模一樣。它也裝著出門做生意的樣子，與有德東拉西扯。有德是個老實人，把家裏的情況講了個一清二楚。黑豬精用半截黃金柴偷換來半截眞金釵，與有德分了手。

日子過去了三個月，有德在外做生意很勿順利，便索性關了店門，結了帳，回轉家裏與妻子一起過日子。

這天當有德趕到自家房門前時，已是半夜了。有德「篤篤篤」地敲門，口口聲聲喊：「娘子開門，娘子開門！」娘子睡在床上，矇矇矓矓聽到丈夫聲音，摸摸身邊，丈夫好端端地躺著，推了好一會兒，才把他推醒。原來這是黑豬精變的。黑豬精醒來後，聽到門外的叫喊聲，就想出個主意來，對娘子講：「三更半夜來敲門，一定是鬼。」娘子一聽是鬼，嚇落了魂。有德在門外喊了又喊，敲了又敲，卻不見動靜，沒辦法，只好跑到爹娘那邊去敲門。

有德娘以爲是兒子與媳婦吵了架，慌忙起床開門，傻楞楞地問：「兒呀，半夜三更還來叫我們，吵架了？」有德說：「我出外幾個月，生意做勿好，現時才回家，沒吵架。」爹娘一聽，覺得勿對頭，忙說：「你勿是三個月前就回家了，怎講是現時才回來？」有德娘拿了燈，把個兒子從上到下，從前到後，仔仔細細地看了看。不錯，正是兒子呀！又去叫媳婦開門，把床上的那個有德仔仔細細看了一遍，也勿錯呀，確確實實是兒子。老夫妻倆你看看我，我看看你。眞是糊塗人碰上糊塗事了。

老頭子開口問：「你說你是我的兒子，我且問你，你外公叫啥名字？住在哪兒？今年高齡多少？」

有德回答得一點勿錯。

老頭子又問：「你的第一位先生是誰？教你讀什麼書？」

有德回答得滿爽口。

有德爹正想開口問問黑豬精，不料黑豬精連忙擺手說：「爹爹，你別問東問西了。娘子最清楚，我們當日分別時，娘子送我半截金釵作表記，現在一看就分明。」有德一聽，忙從口袋裏拿出半截金釵。老夫妻倆接過一看，卻是一段黃金柴。

黑豬精緊緊抱住娘子：「你們看看，黃金柴當金釵，一定是黑豬精變的大妖怪。」這一招，可真把大家蒙住了。老夫妻倆不由分說，將有德推出屋外，趕緊關上大門。

有德坐在村口，一直哭到天濛濛亮。正哭得迷迷糊糊的時候，來了個四十多歲年紀，背揷雌雄寶劍，生一雙柳葉眉，長一張瓜子臉的端莊女人，她就是陳十四❶。

有德慌忙跪下，口口聲聲哀求：「娘娘大慈大悲，快快救救我啊！」接著，忙把娘子受妖精迷害之事說了一遍。

陳十四一聽，沈思道：「哦，一定又是那黑豬精在作祟了！」

「什麼黑豬精？」有德驚訝地問。

陳十四說：「當年唐僧上西天取經路上，黑豬精被孫悟空關在石牢裏，但豬八戒起了同情心，偷偷把它放了。這黑豬精惡習不改，直到如今，還在人世間欺蒙、誘姦良家婦女。今日我非懲治這個妖精不可。」

有德連忙揩乾眼淚，領陳十四走回家門。

這時，睡在床上的黑豬精知道不好了，連忙變成一隻田雞，東跳西竄，最後見到水缸的蓋子開著，慌忙跳進去。陳十四娘娘不慌不忙地走過去，突然伸手一把將它抓了出來，只一劍就結果了它的性命。

這時，有德的老婆躺在床上「哼唷、哼唷」地大喊起來。原來她肚子痛，要生孩子了。陳十四娘娘嘴裏不說，心裏明白，就守候在有德妻子跟前。不一會兒，有德妻子果然做產了，只見她生下來的不是人，卻是一隻隻小豬。每生下一隻，陳十四就給它一劍。直到有德老婆生了第十三隻時，陳十四娘娘才收住寶劍，嘆口氣說：「唉，就留你這一條畜生吧，免得絕了種。不過，只許你在深山野林裏過日子，再不准進入百姓家裏作惡。」

從此以後，世界上再也沒有黑豬精作祟了，只有野豬在深山野林裏活動。

潘奶兒／講述
丁雲法／搜集整理

❶陳十四：即陳十四娘娘，傳說中的神，浙南閩北許多鄉間有廟供奉。

「西遊迷」考「西遊迷」

明朝萬曆年間，《西遊記》一書已經在社會上廣爲流傳了，不僅一般村夫市民愛看，連在朝爲官的所謂京官士大夫，也都十分愛看。

這年秋天，正好遇上大比之年。在京師負責主考的考官姓米，名祐禧。由於他有「熟讀《西遊記》」的美名，因此一些好事者將他的大名來一個「倒讀」，成了名符其實的「西遊迷」。事有巧合，在當年爭奪「三鼎甲」的名單中，也有兩個被稱爲「西遊迷」的考生，一個叫周秉善，一個叫吳邦奇。考試結果，周、吳二人均列在該科貢生的前茅，待主考官推薦並由皇帝殿試之後，很可能一個中狀元，一個中榜眼。

在殿試的前一天晚上，主考官爲了最後試一試這兩位考生的才學，便暗暗將他倆召進官邸，並別出心裁地出了兩道與《西遊記》有關的題目。第一道題叫「《西遊記》嵌十」，他要求兩位考生以「嵌十字」的格式，用十句「七言」來概括《西遊記》全書，所用詞匯都不得雷同與重複。

姓周的考生沈思一會，便順口唸道：

唐太宗一統天下。
二將軍宮門驅鬼。
唐三藏西天取經。
斬老龍四海歸心。
五行山悟空得救。
收猿心六賊無蹤。
盤絲洞七情迷本。
濯垢泉八戒忘形。
九九數完魔滅盡。
十分功德載經歸。

主考官見周秉善用「嵌十字」不僅自然熟練，而且言簡意明，心中甚是高興。忙說：「好，好，周賢契熟稔《西遊》，果然名不虛傳……」

未等主考官讚嘆完，只聽得那吳邦奇也琅琅地念將起來：

靈霄殿一聲令下。
二郎神智擒妖猴。
屍魔三對唐三藏。
四聖落凡試禪心。
悟空大鬧五莊觀。
六欲未淨豬老弟。
七經在心沙和尚。
八卦爐中煉眞身。
九齒釘耙扎犀牛。
十惡不赦白龜精。

一聽吳邦奇的「嵌十字」順口溜，主考官更是欣喜萬分，特別是最後「十惡不赦白龜精」一句，把取經回來路上老白龜沈河淹經之事，說得十分眞切與妥貼。

主考官對周、吳二人誇獎了一番之後，便亮出第二道題目：他要兩位考生說一說《西遊記》裏誰的力氣最大。這道題看來不難，但其中卻有某種奧妙。

周秉善搶先說：「大人，依學生看來，《西遊記》裏要數孫悟空的力氣最大，因爲他使的『如意金箍棒』有一萬三千五百斤重。這樣重的兵器他運用自如，在《西遊記》裏，沒有第二個人了。」

「不。」吳邦奇馬上反駁說：「孫悟空雖然能使一萬三千五百斤重的金箍棒，但他的力氣遠沒有如來佛大；因爲孫悟空在如來佛的手掌心，猶如鴻毛一片，如來佛一翻掌，這猴王連同它那條重過萬斤的金箍棒，全被壓在五行山下了。可見，《西遊記》裏力氣最大的，還是如來佛！」

如此一說，那姓周的考生便啞口無言了。主考這時才點點頭說：「兩位賢契說的都在理。周賢契重『實』，吳賢契重『理』，比較起來，還是吳賢契才高一籌。」說罷，便將兩套金陵世德堂「新刻出像官板大字」《西遊記》，分別送給他們，表示對他倆才學的賞識；並根據兩位考生的眞才實學，向皇上作了推荐。發榜之日，果見吳邦奇中了狀元，周秉善中了榜眼。

從此之後，「西遊迷」考「西遊迷」，便成了民間佳話。

周亦子／搜集整理

可筑書房
KeeJwu Bookstore

★傳奇文學之旅　書目

01 蘇東坡的故事　歐少游編　一三〇元

千古風流人物的典範，蘇東坡是我國文壇上最負盛名的偉大文學家，關於他的傳奇性故事，實在多如三月春花，燦爛無比，本書是喜歡蘇東坡的入門書。

02 少林寺傳奇　歐少游編　一三〇元

「少林寺」在中國的武壇上，享譽數百年了，然而關於「少林寺」在小說中所見的已幾近走火入魔，荒謬不堪；所以我們對少林寺的眞面目，可是說停留在一知半解中，本書根據史實與鄉野傳聞，揉和了知性與感性，可讀性獲極高的評價。

03 王羲之傳奇 歐少游編 一二〇元

中國書聖——王羲之的故事，在本書中有極其出神入化的描述，除了讓您了解這位書法大家的生平之餘，還有故事性相當濃厚的傳奇軼聞……

04 絲路之旅傳奇 歐少游編 一五〇元

永遠是中國最迷濛的夢，「絲路」一直是每一個中國人的嚮往，隨著喜多郎的音樂發表以來，「絲路之旅」的脚步是近了，然而這裡面有許多好美好美的故事，您怎能不去探勝呢？

05 孫中山軼事 石靜宜編 一二〇元

06 孫中山傳奇 石靜宜編 一二〇元

將中國五千年帝王專制劃下一個句點的世界性偉大人物——孫中山先生，也是每個中國人的民主之父——國父。其一生中的坎坷奔波，自有其不能抹煞的史實面，然而本書卻以簡短生動的小品，將孫中山先生的生平用傳奇文學的饒奇有味的方式表達出來，千萬不要錯過！

07 紅塵俠女傳奇 邱小盈編 一二〇元

08 風塵奇女傳奇 邱小盈編 一二〇元

自古俠女出風塵，江湖兒女在草莽豪傑與紈袴官家弟子之間的恩怨情仇，是最能吸引人們關懷注視的眼神，來自古典的戲劇、小說、詩詞，幾乎都離不開這份素材，是永恒性的傳奇文學……

09 八仙傳奇 歐陽晶宜編 一三〇元

10 八仙的故事 歐陽晶宜編 一三〇元

民間傳說中的「八仙」大多是片面性的蛛絲馬跡，而且絕大多數也只是繞著其中之一的「呂洞賓」打轉，然而此系列卻費了相當大的心力去網羅所有可能的傳說，在民間文學的地位上，有重要的突破，在閱讀的領域也是一趟愉快的旅程……

11 帝王傳奇錄〈處世篇〉 蕭逸文編 一二〇元

12 帝王傳奇錄〈風雲篇〉 蕭逸文編 一二〇元

13 帝王傳奇錄〈風流篇〉 蕭逸文編 一二〇元

這是一部中國帝王的傳奇錄，全書共分三輯，詳述歷史與野史所能搜集的帝王故事，是一部價值成分相當高的傳奇史，不可諱言的這和您在閱讀歷史課本不同，由此書您可以輕鬆的獲得歷史軼事、掌故，並由這部作品中學習到爲人處世、領導統御的眞髓！

14 蘇東坡逸事 秦靜萍編 一五〇元

繼「蘇東坡的故事」之後，又以另一個角度，另一種筆觸來描繪人們心中永不褪色的——蘇東坡。

15 朱元璋傳奇 林淑芬編 一五〇元

朱元璋是中國歷史上第一個平民皇帝，因爲他是庶民出身，所以生平的傳奇，直追到他的童年時代，是一部趣味性相當濃郁的作品，千萬不宜錯失！

16 敦煌傳奇 葉歡編 一二〇元

由「敦煌壁畫」中,我們可以窺見繪畫藝術的奧妙堂殿，由電影的「敦煌」中，我們可以踏入傳奇之旅的行程；敦煌這個美麗的名字，將永遠烙印在每一個中國人的心中……

17 李白傳 李朋敍編 一五〇元

一代「詩仙」的精彩故事，作者以長篇小說的寫法看來更具傳神，擁抱著中國文士的飄逸灑脫與憂國憂民之情！是部令人百看低迴不已的名作，也是一部令人激賞的感動之作！

18 紀曉嵐傳奇　野叟編　一五〇元

歷代文壇上最風趣、最睿智的奇才，人們都還津津樂道他與乾隆皇帝的各種機智應對！本書搜集紀氏在坊間的各種傳說，而以文學探究的心爲其脈絡，是一部極具價值的好作品。

19 龍的傳說　司馬悟明編　一二〇元

「龍」一向是中華民族的圖騰形象，是爲華夏一族從古以來的敬奉。本書以輕鬆的筆觸掀開一個美麗的傳說故事，讓您輕鬆怡然的開卷……

20 大相國寺傳奇　野叟編　一三〇元

大相國寺這個名字對喜歡閱讀武俠小說的朋友來說，都不是一個陌生的字眼。然而，在史實上開封的大相國寺却是一個集中國古代的悲劇、喜劇、鬧劇等重大歷史事件於一身之地……它的魅力永遠存在於人心。

21 蘇東坡傳奇 蘇凡編 一三〇元

大江東去浪淘盡，千古風流人物！

蘇東坡是個親切的人物，也是大衆最愛的文學奇才，他身上的傳奇故事也像一個寶礦挖掘不完，隔了一陣子就又有新發現，永遠是那麼生動、那麼傳神、那麼的光彩奪目。

22 唐伯虎傳奇 梁燕編 一三〇元

聽說唐伯虎的畫，都是活的，有一次他在一個客棧中就是以一幅猛虎的畫，嚇退了一群盜賊。唐伯虎在《四傑傳》也是一個名不虛傳的人物，然而他眞的有奇妙的神來之筆嗎？答案即在本書之中。

23 梁山泊傳奇 董易人編 一五〇元

《水滸傳》是我國文學作品中最叫人回味無窮的好書，它最引人入勝的地方，就是梁山泊的一〇八條好漢，個個特立獨行，作者賦予他們身上的合理誇張，讓他們躍然於字裡行間，每每叫人拍案叫絕！本書中的故事與《水滸傳》有異曲同工之妙，您不宜錯過！

24 北京傳奇錄 沈　香編 一五〇元

在交織着〈龍的子嗣〉之美夢與現實的疆域之中，北京永遠是個熱烈的舞台，閃爍着遙遠迷人的光輝……本書擁有相當豐富的材料，娓娓道出——順治、康熙、雍正、乾隆、劉墉、曹雪芹以及慈禧太后等人的傳奇故事。

25 一代宗師傳奇 董易人編 一五〇元

五千年來的神州，這片大好河山孕育了許多傑出人物。一代宗師傳奇，描繪出許多趣味、生動、感人的故事，你可以當成小說閱讀；然而，從另外一個角度而言，這是一部不折不扣的歷史名人成功故事，幸運的是故事化的筆觸，讓人讀來輕鬆愉快！

26 中國武林傳奇 張　樹編 一五〇元

滙集我國武林道上的各類武俠傳聞，俠客、俠女之軼事，是一部能滿足我們崇尚武藝、敬仰俠義行爲的傑作。如您耳熟能詳的江南八俠呂四娘……馬永貞、霍元甲，還有大刀王五……等人的武俠傳奇！

27 中國貨幣傳奇 張惠信 一五〇元

本書作者目前仍在銀行做事，而却在公務之餘仍然猛向〝錢〞看，以研究學問、追求眞理的精神，從古代貝殼作爲交易貨幣之始，到琳琅滿目的銀錢誕生故事，揭開幾千年來中國人〝在錢堆裡打滾〞的有趣面紗，是一部錢的歷史，也是一部鈔票的精彩故事……